Tears of the Dead

* * *

The Chronicles of Fu Xi Book II

Brian L. Braden

For Jenny, thank you for your love and patience.

Table of Contents

ACKNOWLEDGMENTS

Edited by Grace Bryan Butler.

Also, thanks to John Colarusso for his book *Nart Sagas From the Caucasus*, which partially inspired this story.

Prologue: The Lion and the Snake

"In Hur-ar it was said, the Narim were the gods of the poor, Ba'al god of the rich. But the only true god in Hur-ar was gold." - Conversations with the Uros.

The Chronicle of Fu Xi

***

Before the Cataclysm.

Head held high, chest puffed with pride, the Lion of Hur-ar marched to glory. The crimson glow silhouetting the mountains announced dawn's imminent arrival, ushering in his ascendency as one of Hur-ar's most powerful men. He only need ensure nothing went wrong during this morning's routine ceremony.

He gazed up at the Black Fortress only a few yards ahead, its darkness untouched by the rose-colored rays chasing the stars from the sky. Bal-eeb, Captain of the Wall, sidestepped to the Cliff Road's edge and inspected the procession as it passed. The ceremonial guard marched by two abreast, sandaled feet crunching the gravel in unison. Eyes locked forward, their misty breath floated on the chilly autumn air. Highly polished bronze chest plates clinked softly against chainmail and provided an eerie music to accompany the trade delegation.

Behind the warriors, six muscled slaves, nude and sweating in the morning chill, struggled under the gilded litter's weight. They bore lounging Norrufi, Supreme Royal Trader and second cousin to the King. Rolls of perfumed fat spilled from underneath an ornate blanket, jiggling in rhythm with the jostling litter. His threadbare beard hung under a perpetually dour expression and did nothing to conceal the eunuch's many chins.

Bal-eeb nodded in deference as the litter passed by, trying not to wrinkle his nose in disgust.

He smells like a woman. Suitable, I suppose, for someone who traded his balls for power.

Men possessing such power and wealth could not be trusted with an heir to challenge the King. Nevertheless, the Supreme Royal Trader held significant influence in court and Bal-eeb suffered the fat fool's insolence. He needed Norrufi's well-placed whispers if he were to depose the Captain of the Palace Guard. The man reclining on the golden litter assured Bal-eeb this morning's duties played no small part in advancing this goal.

In many ways Norrufi's opposite, Bal-eeb stood half a head taller than most men, in the prime of youth and well-muscled. Powerful, wealthy, and brutally ambitious, the city idolized the man they called the Lion of Hur-ar.

The warriors crested the cliff overlooking the city just as dawn's first rays crept over the mountain beyond the Black Gate. They split into two ranks of five and formed a wide opening for Norrufi's litter and the wagons.

"Look sharp, lions of Hur!" Bal-eeb barked.

A simple assignment, yes, but there could be no mistakes this morning.

Three massive ox-drawn wagons, almost too wide to negotiate the narrow Cliff Road, rumbled close behind Norrufi's litter. Goods from Hur-ar's vast trading empire, iron tools and bags stuffed with grain, packed each cart to the breaking point. With mouths foaming and eyes wide in agony, the oxen struggled up the mountain. A small army of slaves, scribes, and functionaries from the royal houses and trading guild, trudged in the caravan's dusty wake. Each man played a small part; from carrying the Supreme Trader's piss pot to interpreting the clay tablets left by the Narim.

Deep in thought, Bal-eeb stroked his curly, coal-black beard. His mind raced beyond this morning's proceedings, to plans and plots laid months, even years, earlier. His mother once instructed him, *Make fear and gold your friends and Ba'al will grant all the desires of your heart.* Like his mother, he knew what he wanted and did what was necessary to take it. Events put in motion by his role in this morning's trading ceremony, might eventually place him on the Throne of Gold, as King of Hur-ar. Today, he also took an important step in slipping from beneath his mother's long shadow.

Ashtoreth...common folk only spoke her name as a curse symbolizing seduction and betrayal. In court it dripped from noble lips, gushing with false reverence and adoration, knowing her spies lurked everywhere. Most in the city simply called her "The Snake".

She confided to Bal-eeb her fondness for the title.

Ashtoreth insinuated herself into the House of the Second Prince of Hur-ar as a lowly Sammujad consort, accompanied by her bastard son on the edge of manhood. She quickly bewitched the prince and, in only a few months, cunningly eliminated her rivals one-by-one to claim the role of First Wife. Ashtoreth and her son banished or slew the children of the deposed First Wife, leaving Bal-eeb to inherit the prince's fortune. After the prince's mysterious death, Ashtoreth reigned as the Court's most ruthless and feared noble.

In spite of her reputation for cruelty, Ashtoreth's beauty and sexual prowess fueled a fierce competition among Hurar's nobles to share her bed. Some say she was Ba'al's own concubine, summoned from hell by a rogue temple priest. If hell was a Sammujad village razed to the ground by Scythian raiders, then Bal-eeb would agree. He knew what truly motivated his mother, death and hunger.

Now only Hecktar, First Prince and Captain of the Palace Guard, stood between Ashtoreth's son and the throne. Ashtoreth arranged every step of his career, including his posting as Captain of the Wall. Bal-eeb vowed to supplant Hecktar by his own hand, without The Snake's gold or influence. The Lion carefully laid his own plans, which didn't include The Snake.

The King grew weary of holing up in the city, waiting for traders to bring the world's wealth to his doorstep. Unchallenged on the vast steppe, the Scythians grew more powerful and arrogant with each spring. The filthy horsemen demanded greater tribute to permit caravans to pass unmolested to Hur-ar. Only the mystique of the Narim and their Black Fortress kept the raiders at bay. However, this state of affairs was about to change.

Three successive Hur kings built a magnificent army, one possessing bows and horses every bit as powerful as Scythia's. The Hur legions would strike swiftly on winter's eve as the horsemen settled in their winter camps. They would torch the horsemen's winter food stocks, driving the haughty barbarians to starvation. With spring, the well fed and rested Hur army need only clean up the mess. With their western flank secure, the Hur armies would sweep from the edge of the northern Icelands, to the Great Sea, to the mountainous southwest. Booty and slaves would flood into the city. Then they would turn south, where the eastern shore of the Great Sea met the mighty Adyghe Mountains. These were the lands of the Thrax, who held the treacherous southern passes. Beyond the Thrax lay Havilah, where traders spoke of abundant gold, summoned from the ground not by Narim, but by men. Havilah, the ultimate prize, could not be seized without first liquidating the Scythian horde.

As the procession began to take their appointed places, he peered over his shoulder at the city far below. Torches twinkled across rooftops and in the streets. Bal-eeb thought of Hecktar asleep in the palace, blissfully unaware a delegation stood before the Black Gates this morning.

A thousand pardons, Norrufi would shrug to Hecktar before the sun set this day. *I'm sure all the required notifications were made. If the Captain of the Palace Guard cannot carry out his required duties, then the Captain of the Wall is obligated to escort the King's trade delegation.*

"Bureaucrats!" Bal-eeb chuckled. "Deadlier than assassins."

He studied the city far below, from the city wall to the base of Cliff Road, a thousand feet immediately below him.

So few of these soft city dwellers have ever ventured beyond the wall.

Bal-eeb secretly ventured far and wide to lay his plans, plots neither his mother, the Commander or the King knew of.

Bal-eeb knew Scythia stretched farther west than anyone in Hur-ar imagined, even the King. The horsemen could summon tens of thousands of kinsmen and roll over Hur's legions. If they ever lost their superstitious fear of the Black Fortress, they could take Hur-ar itself.

But only Bal-eeb knew the horsemen's weakness. Now *his* influence, *his* gold, *his* schemes would ensure his appointment as the campaign's second-in-command, next only to the Commander himself. The Lion, not the Snake, would eliminate Hecktar and seize the throne on his own terms.

The Captain of the Wall gazed into the darkness beyond the city, beyond the steppe.

The Great Sea and its endless marshes...that is the key to defeating Scythia.

7

Bal-eeb turned and climbed the short distance remaining to the top. There, he took his place and prepared for the trading ceremony.

The slaves deposited the Norrufi's litter softly on the crushed stone before the Black Gate. The wagons rolled between the columns of warriors and halted behind the litter. The entourage split into two halves; free men behind the warriors' right flank, slaves behind the left. The delegation crowded forward on the narrow ledge, avoiding the drop off by several paces.

With the help of his body slave, Norrufi sat up with a huff. Doughy fat spilled over his golden girdle as he adjusted his waist wrap and straightened his tall, conical cap. Despite the cool morning, sweat trickled down his bare chest. It took all of Bal-eeb's guile to mask his disgust.

Breathing heavily, Noruffi waddled up to the massive iron bell, suspended from a heavy kupar frame and secured to the gate with iron spikes. Offerings left by the city's poor; withering bundles of prairie flowers, clay jars of honey, and candles littered the black stained gravel before the Black Gate.

Noruffi took his place next to the bell's rope and peered into the crowd with narrow, pig-like eyes as if looking for someone. A tall, painfully thin man, with an axe-like face pushed through the line of warriors. Bal-eeb bowed slightly as Shellbaz, High Priest of Ba'al, passed by. A bejeweled golden jar in his bony clutches, he stank of sour wine. Beardless, like all of his order, the priest's black kaffiya and open chested robes fluttered behind him. To Bal-eeb, he resembled an emaciated crow.

The Order of Ba'al despised the Narim, constantly seeking to turn the city against the Masters of the Black Fortress. Only the Hur-po's love of the yellow metal spared the mysterious immortals the Black Dragon's wrath. However, during the last king's reign the Priests managed to inject themselves into trading ceremony.

Bal-eeb didn't believe in Ba'al, though his mother did. Bal-eeb believed only in power, gold and himself. However, that didn't stop him from courting the influential High Priest's favor, going so far as mandating his warriors wear the Black Dragon amulet.

Wearing a look of disgust, Shellbaz kicked several of the offerings aside and, in doing so, almost fell over. Steadying himself, he took his place beside the bell, opposite Noruffi. He held the jar high over his head and, with a slurred voice, shouted to the crowd, "Let the power of the god of this world, master of earthly princes and mortal thrones, sanctify these proceedings!"

He tipped the jar and let the crimson fluid pour onto the gravel. Shellbaz's hung-over, bloodshot eyes came alive, a hungry, sexual, grin flashing at the sight of blood. Norrufi stepped back to avoid being splattered. The priest tucked the empty jar back into his robes and nodded to Noruffi. From another fold he produced a bottle of wine and staggered back into the crowd.

Sludgy and full of clots, the blood seeped away from the gate. The Supreme Royal Trader covered his mouth and tried not to gag.

With the exception of the intercession of the priests, the trading ceremony remained unchanged since the Narim sealed themselves behind the Black Gate generations ago. The Supreme Royal Trader would ring the iron bell, and a few moments later, a brass bell answered from within. The outer gate would open, and the teamsters would wheel the wagons into a central holding area. After that, the Supreme Royal Trader rang the outer bell again, and the outer gates closed. A groan would rise beyond the wall as the inner gates opened. The delegation always listened intently as someone, or something, unloaded the wagons. After several minutes, the groan returned and the inner bell rang again. In short order, the outer gates reopened and the goods would be replaced with gold ore and clay tablets bearing magical markings. The markings held the Narim's wishes for the next trade delegation and could only be interpreted by guild scribes.

Norrufi grasped the gray, fraying rope and swung the bell, beginning the ceremony in earnest. Under Norrufi's soft, pudgy hands, it issued a single, dull clunk.

A child could ring the bell louder, Bal-eeb thought, but knew it didn't matter. The Narim always heard.

As he waited for the answer to the call for trade, Bal-eeb's mind drifted to a woman with olive skin and almond eyes uncannily like his mother's. She possessed ambition every bit as naked and ruthless as Ashtoreth's. He could not say he loved this woman, though he'd never loved a woman. She did hold a certain raw allure the pampered creatures in court lacked. This woman held a more important allure than her body. She held the key to defeating the Scythians.

An unexpected western breeze caressed his face. He could almost feel the Great Sea's sultry air and her lithe, sun washed body pressed against his in the tall marsh grass.

Patience, my little Marsh Snake. I will return soon enough.

The breeze shifted again, dry and cold, snapping him back to the moment.

Something is wrong.

The inner bell did not answer. The outer gates remained closed.

Norrufi wiped the sweat from his brow and smiled weakly. "Perhaps the Narim are still asleep." He snatched the rope and yanked with all his considerable bulk. The bell clanged twice, slightly louder this time.

But the inner bell remained silent. The sun shone fully over the mountains. By now the carts should have been in the holding area between the gates.

The Supreme Trader laughed nervously as the warriors began to fidget. The delegates looked at one another, sensing the situation beginning to deteriorate.

No! This can't be happening.

Bal-eeb marched up to the bell.

"Your Excellency, perhaps you are correct, and the Narim slumber. May I assist you?"

The fat man wiped the sweat from his face. "Well...ah,..."

Bal-eeb didn't wait for a response. He grasped the rope with both fists and pulled with all his might. The kupar mounts creaked, and the bell rang so loudly everyone on the cliff covered their ears. It echoed for several seconds off the surrounding mountains before silence returned to the cliff.

The Captain of the Wall and the Supreme Royal Trader stood side-by-side, as the brass bell remained mute.

The Narim never fail to answer a call to trade. Never.

The Hur-po would have been less shocked if the sun had failed to rise.

Bal-eeb stepped back and glared up at the Black Gate towering above. The inner bell remained stubbornly mute. A knot formed in his gut as Bal-eeb sensed his plans slipping away.

Singular laughter arose behind the delegation's pale faces. Everyone turned to look at Shellbaz, who stood with his back to the delegation. He held a bottle of wine in one hand, his penis in the other and pissed over the side of the cliff, laughing gleefully as his urine rained down over the City of Gold.

1. The Black Sea

The sea comes first. - Lo Proverb

The Chronicle of Fu Xi

***

Setenay, Ood-i, and Sarah were dead by only a few hours, but Okta quietly hummed. He meant no disrespect. The water, no matter how cold and black, filled his spirit with hope. He didn't need the sounds of nature to give his voice, his *halah*, life, as the raft drifted south upon swift water. Home, his beloved Great Sea, awaited him. He yearned for her warm and turquoise glimmer. Sethagasi, the sea goddess, would swallow this Black River, now swollen from horizon to horizon, purify its poison, and make everything right again.

The swirling current swept the tiny raft between grass-covered islands that, only days ago, were prairie hilltops. Okta strained against the rudder, crafted from split driftwood tied around a long, crooked pole. The current toyed with the raft, demanding all Okta's skill to prevent them from slamming against the crumbling islands.

Alone, Okta focused on the immediate danger while the others grieved. Ghalen sobbed, face buried in hands, as Levidi tried to comfort him. Ezra and the Scythian woman huddled in the raft's center, staring in shock across the watery expanse. Ba-lok, sullen and detached, slumped cross-legged at the front of the raft. The Uros stood alone, staring ahead.

A voyage of the desolate.

Okta grieved, too, but right now he needed to bring the raft under control, and he couldn't do it alone.

"Uros," he called.

Aizarg didn't respond.

"Uros!" he called again, glancing nervously at the jagged ice chunks drifting by.

We will rip out our bottom on a hidden promontory or be crushed by ice.

Okta cleared his throat and spoke loudly, "If there are still Lo men on this raft who care about the land of the living, I would greatly appreciate some help. Or must I hand the Scythian wench a pole?"

Levidi left Ghalen's side and took the rudder, as Okta made his way to the front. He gently touched Aizarg's shoulder. The Uros snapped out of his trance and looked upon Okta with red-rimmed eyes. Aizarg's desolate expression took Okta aback.

Today, the Uros lost his Isp and a daughter. Okta suddenly knew his place, his task.

"We are all in pain," Okta spoke slowly, but firmly. "I built this raft, but you are its master. The sea comes first. Bring us home, Uros." He emphasized the last word.

Aizarg focused on Okta and then looked around as if seeing everything anew.

"The sea comes first," Aizarg whispered.

Okta nodded with relief.

"Do we have enough poles?"

"Three. That will be enough to push off when required, though the water is too deep for anything else. We have a sail, but no mast," Okta replied.

Aizarg examined the raft.

Good, he's thinking about getting home.

"Place the men on the raft's corners," Aizarg commanded. "Do you think the raft will remain sound if we remove two beams for a mast?"

Okta warily eyed the gauntlet of small islands ahead, white water forming around their bases. The raft would shatter if they struck any of them at full speed.

"She's strong. Two beams from her gut will not weaken her significantly," Okta lied. He had hastily constructed the raft from two levels of scavenged logs, some barely straight or thick enough for the task, all tied together with strips of shredded deerskin clothing. Removing two logs from the center would significantly weaken it, but without a sail death surely awaited.

"So be it. Fashion a mast. Use one of the poles as a cross piece. Rig...," Aizarg paused for a moment, "...rig Setenay's sail upon it. That will give us some control. I pray the current will not be so swift when we reach the Great Sea."

Aizarg knelt down. "Loosen the bindings and I will slide them out."

Okta turned to Ghalen. "Get up!" he shouted. "That is what Setenay would say now if she were here. Get up, grab a pole!"

Ghalen wiped his tears and stood. He grabbed a pole off the deck and took his place at the forward port corner.

"Ba-lok, take the starboard corner," Okta commanded. Ba-lok glared at him for only a moment, and then took his place with the second pole.

"Ezra, time is against us boy, are you ready to begin your education as a Lo man?" Okta instructed the man-boy what needed to be done, impressed how quickly Ezra put his fear and mourning aside.

Okta loosened the straps binding the top-center logs just enough to allow some play. With some effort, Aizarg and Ezra jiggled and slid the middle log out. Water sloshed up and filled the long gap as Okta re-tightened the bindings.

Aizarg held the thick stick vertically and shook his head. "It's too short by itself. We need another."

"Levidi, hard left!" Ghalen shouted with pole poised to push off a looming hilltop. Levidi grunted against the rudder.

"Everyone brace!" Okta shouted and shoved Ezra to the deck. The raft shuddered as it gouged a slash in the hillside. Logs shifted uncomfortably under Okta's feet. Ba-lok leapt over Ezra and joined Ghalen, whose pole bent to the breaking point. Together, they struggled to dislodge the raft from the grassy island. The craft slowly turned, broke loose and once again hurtled downstream.

Okta inspected the raft. The logs were slightly skewed, but intact. He surveyed the waters ahead of them. Tiny islands dotted the surface as far south as he could see. Ba-lok resumed his post just in time to push away another chunk of ice.

We won't last much longer.

Okta turned to Aizarg. "The southerly wind blows hard. A full sail will do much to slow us down. We must risk another log."

Aizarg shook his head. "The center of the raft will have too much play. One more strike like that and it will shatter."

"Raise me a sail, Uros, and I guarantee we won't hit another island."

For a few quiet moments Aizarg gazed at the darkening southern sky.

"Do it."

They quickly pulled another log. Okta tightened the straps the best he could. With each step the deck beams gave slightly under his weight, reminding Okta of their desperate gamble.

They tied the two logs together.

"Use the remaining pole as a crosspiece to mount the sail," Okta said.

Aizarg lodged the new mast firmly in the gap, which helped tighten the deck logs, and secured it with the last of their leather strips.

Okta nervously watched the perilously close islands and ice floes.

It's only a matter of time.

Aizarg tied off the last strip of spare deerskin. "We have no more. Nothing remains for rigging or to secure the crosspiece to the mast."

Okta looked around, thinking of what they could use. His gaze fell on the Scythian woman and her long-sleeve cherkesska and deerskin trousers.

She shot him a distrustful stare and pulled her legs tighter against her chest.

"Ghalen," Okta said with a wry smile. "Give me your pole. I have a job for you."

***

Bloody scratches crisscrossed Ghalen's face and arms. Sana and Ghalen glared out over the water, neither looking at one another.

Okta beamed as the taut, billowed sail greatly diminished their forward speed. Levidi had more time to turn the ungainly craft, and Ghalen and Ba-lok could easily push off from the islands.

Sana knelt on port side, grasping a strap that used to be part of her trousers. It now secured the sail's bottom corner. She wrapped her free arm around her midriff, trying to shield her almost naked body from sight. Ezra knelt on the starboard side, holding the other strap and occasionally stealing glances at Sana. Together, they responded to Levidi's simple commands of "Pull left!" or "Pull right!"

Tattered remains of Sana's once proud cherkesska barely covered her breasts, the rest now sail rigging. Her long trousers reduced to a loin cloth, where she tucked the four small daggers Setenay let her keep. As Setenay predicted, not once did the Scythian woman raise her weapons against them; at least the bladed ones.

The woman is too furious to be afraid anymore, Okta thought. Ghalen tried to reason with her, but she had none of it and fought Ghalen like a lioness. Okta would be lying to himself if he didn't admit he found it amusing. Even Levidi let out a snicker. Sana only relented when Aizarg threatened to throw her overboard and promised her enough clothing to satisfy minimum a-g'an modesty.

Okta grudgingly acknowledged the Scythian girl's beauty. A wild mane of black hair framed deep brown eyes full of fire. Flawless olive skin and sculpted limbs, now liberated from dreadful a-g'an garb, were not unpleasing to behold. She reminded Okta somewhat of Ba-lok's wife, Kus-ge, only taller.

Beautiful, yes, but too wild to make a proper Lo woman. Why Setenay let her live mystified Okta.

A burst of warm air gusted across the deck, bringing a familiar smell and drawing Okta's attention. Smiles suddenly lit the men's faces, as they looked at one another knowingly.

"We approach the sea!" he said, the song in his heart kindled anew.

The hills slowly vanished, replaced by tree tops poking above the water, reduced to bush-like clumps bent in the current. Flotsam and ice chunks collected in tattered branches still clad in autumn colors. Okta's heart began to sink.

"This is what is left of the marshes," Aizarg said.

"I cannot see the marsh grass," Ba-lok said. "The water is too deep."

"The current is abating. I can feel it in the rudder," Levidi called from the back.

Okta looked south where the trees ceased in a line running east and west. The Black River swirled and blended with clearer, natural-looking water. Instead of the warm and sparkling Great Sea, an expanding expanse of flat, dark water mirrored the boiling clouds. He fell to his knees and plunged his hand into the water. One moment the current flowed warm against his skin, the next icy cold.

The raft slowed and began to flounder, even reverse in the face of the wind.

"The Black River and Great Sea do battle. We are unable to proceed; unable to go back from whence we came. We are between worlds," Aizarg said.

"The Black River is winning!" Okta lowered his head into his hands and moaned. "This foulness leaching from the g'an violates our blessed mother. The god of the Narim devours the sea."

Aizarg put his hand on Okta's shoulder and squeezed it hard. "I, too, fear this new, strange sea...this Black Sea. But do not lose faith. This new god did not bring us this far to abandon us now. Our people are out there, waiting for us. Wherever they are, that is our home."

Okta sobbed and grasped Aizarg's hand, unable to speak thoughts as dark as the Black Sea.

What if we can't find our home?

"I don't recognize this place," Ba-lok said. "We could be anywhere along the coast. Should we turn east or west once we clear the trees?"

Aizarg lifted Okta to his feet. "You know the ways of the sea better than any of us."

Okta tried to clear his thoughts. He glanced at Ezra, who stared out over the unbroken sea. Okta suddenly remembered his terror when setting out across the g'an only days ago and knew this boy must be every bit as frightened.

I am Lo. He is not. He needs a raft under his feet and under his spirit. I must be his raft.

Okta absently patted his waist pouch even though he knew it contained no more mud weed. He took a cleansing breath and studied the tree tops where a marsh once flourished.

"See how the trees are thick on either side of us? We are in a stream bed. We've been tracking southwest since we set sail. My best guess is we're somewhere east of Ba-lok's arun-ki." Okta looked to the young sco-lo-ti for confirmation.

Ba-lok nodded.

"Most of our nation lies west of my arun-ki," Okta continued. "We should follow the treetops west along the old shoreline until we encounter an arun-ki, Ba-lok's or another. If we turn east, we run a chance of missing all of them." He nodded, as if reassuring himself. "Yes, I council west. The current has lessened and the wind is in our favor."

"Our homes will be underwater," Ghalen quietly voiced their unspoken fears.

Something about that statement angered Okta. "Our homes are our boats."

Ghalen nodded. "True, Sco-lo-ti."

"Aizarg, do you hear that?" Ezra said, lifting his ear toward the thick trees to their immediate west.

Okta craned to listen. "I hear it, too. Voices."

"Not just voices," Aizarg said. "Shouting."

2. The Fall of Hur-ar, Part I

The most dangerous of mortals are those filled with ambition, but who lack compassion. Their hunger is never sated, their evil, always self-justified. Pride blinds them to the truth, even as their illusions crumble around them.

These men come closest to being gods.

The Chronicle of Fu Xi

***

The Captain of the Gate couldn't hear himself think.

Bal-eeb leaned over Hur-ar's mighty parapets and spit a thick wad of mucus into the mob pressed against the gates. The scene reminded him of cattle packed in the market stockades at auction; a mass of stinking, panicked animals sensing their imminent slaughter. He wanted to do more than spit on them, desiring nothing less than filling each and every one of them with arrows to quiet their screams. Their cries joined the mournful chorus rising from all the city's quarters.

People are sheep. Herded and slaughtered, that's all they're good for. Underneath his smooth, confident exterior he hated all humanity...except for his men, of course.

He merely despised them.

"A waste of good arrows," he murmured to himself.

"Sir?" his lieutenant asked.

"Reinforce the northern side of the gate. If these animals get out of hand, I want no less than twenty archers ready from both directions."

"Yes sir." The lieutenant nodded, and set about his task.

"Eight days," Bal-eeb murmured once his underling hurried beyond earshot. One ill omen after another befell the City of Gold in the eight days since that fateful morning at the Black Gate. Each subsequent disaster foiled his plans and thwarted his ravenous ambition.

Moments after that sunrise, when the Narim failed to answer the call to trade, the beasts answered another call. As if summoned by an unheard command, the city's feral dogs slinked from the shadows and released a chorus of howls so mournful people covered their ears. At that moment the oxen of the fields bolted their harnesses, and cattle crashed through their market pens and thundered down the Avenue of Merchants. In the noble houses, even in the King's palace, pampered cats hissed and leapt for the nearest windows. The worst came when the sewers disgorged a filthy, brown river of rats.

The animals stampeded toward the city gate, with the largest beasts, cattle and oxen, in the lead. They trampled anything in their path, leaving crushed bodies in their wake.

Even warriors fled before the living tide. The stampede rushed out of the city before Bal-eeb's watch officer could issue orders to seal the gates. The mass stampeded south across the Kupar Bridge and vanished. The few animals trapped within the city fell into a frenzy, attacking anyone who came near. Dozens of horses, including all those remaining in the army's stables, fell under warriors' arrows.

The farmers had no beasts of burden, the army no horses, and the city no meat. By sunset, the King summoned the priest and nobles. Prayers were offered and sacrifices made. Before the incense could rise below the enormous statue of the Black Dragon, the tremors began.

Over the next two days, a multitude of small earthquakes assaulted Hur-ar. While only powerful enough to break pottery and crack whitewashed plaster walls, they served to further unnerve an already frightened populace. The quakes also drove many foreign traders from the city, swearing under their breath the City of Gold was cursed. As a symbol of his goodwill and to ensure their quick return, the King sent armed escorts to accompanying the trader caravans to the edge of Hur territory. Bad turned to worse as the escorts quickly returned with reports of a rising Hur River.

A flat and sandy floodplain surrounded the wide, but shallow river. High, dry bluffs flanked both sides of the floodplain. In many places the bluffs were low enough for caravans to descend, ford the river, and ascend the other bank. Even at the height of summer, when the Hur River ran cold and swift from the distant Icelands, one could easily wade across. The great Kupar Bridge, the Narim's gargantuan handiwork, stretched from bluff to bluff, high above the flat river.

Four days after the incident at the Black Gate, the Hur River ran deep and fast halfway up the bluffs. In several places it spilled over into the stumps and fields on the west and east banks. The Hur River grew as if trying to become worthy of the bridge that lorded over it. The bridge still stood high and strong against the current, but now was truly a necessity. As the river rose, the ill omens continued.

On the morning of the seventh day, the Royal Supreme Trader led another delegation up Cliff Road in hopes the Narim would resume trading. This time the King's own bodyguard, led by Hecktar, accompanied the wagons. Bal-eeb and his troops were left behind, a devastating blow to his honor.

An astonishing thing occurred that morning. The Black Gate opened as shouts of joy went up from the delegation. The wagons rolled between the gates, and the outer gate closed. The brass bell rang out, and the gate opened again. Their elation died as the delegation discovered the wagons untouched and fully loaded. Three Narim stood next to the wagons, white hair gleaming in the morning sun just as the legends said.

And Hecktar, that fool, simply let them walk away! Just thinking about it made him simmer in renewed rage.

The three Narim strolled through the city to the gates. Worse yet, Bal-eeb's former lieutenant simply watched the Narim as they walked out the gate and vanished to the west. He didn't even wake Bal-eeb to report the event. Bal-eeb beheaded him on the spot. The Black Gates closed again, and the Narim remaining inside still refused to trade.

Bal-eeb would have stopped them and forced them to answer for what they had done. Narim or not, they interfered with his plans, his ambition. Just as Hur-ar endured setbacks, so had he.

The day before the Narim strolled out of the city, one of his soldiers, a trouble maker named Gilga, was killed escorting a slaver and whore to the city barracks. Bal-eeb intended the pleasure slave, a rare wench with silver hair, as a personal gift for the Commander; a bribe to stay in his good graces. His warrior slain and his bribe stolen right under the nose of the city garrison, Bal-eeb's standing amongst the Captains of Hur plummeted again.

His mother's rebuke this morning still rung in his ears. "Must I sleep with the Commander, too? Even I cannot wield enough influence to compensate for your failures!"

Like the thickening clouds to the south, Bal-eeb's foul mood grew darker. He slammed his fist down on the parapet.

His sentries shuffled farther away without looking too obvious.

The final blow came last night, when the Commander summoned his captains, and informed them the campaign against the Scythians was on indefinite hold. Instead of grinding the nomads of the steppe under their heels, the legion fought to keep the city under control. The army would dip into its invasion stores to survive the winter.

Leaving the garrison barracks last night, he thought it couldn't get any worse. This morning, it did.

At dawn a terrible fireball cleaved the sky in two. Now thin clouds veiled the heavens. Sheets of falling stars streaked out of the southern sky in broad daylight. The city roiled in full-fledge panic. Inside, thousands pressed to escape the cursed city. Outside, throngs of field slaves and stump farmers pressed to get inside, fleeing the rising Hur River. Dozens on both sides were being crushed to death, but he didn't care.

The market descended into chaos. What was left in the fields could not be harvested. The Commander deployed the city guard to the last man; half the garrison manned the walls while the other half barely kept order in the streets. Bal-eeb knew by next week the market would be bare and the granaries empty. Then the real riots would begin.

He wasn't concerned about starving. The army would always be the priority for food, the King and nobles wisely saw to that. He wasn't even concerned about the looming riots. The Commander made it clear, if things got out of hand they would slaughter slaves and civilians until things were back under control.

Deep inside the city, the priests of Ba'al prayed under the statue of the Black Dragon, beseeching the dark god to bring back the animals, tame the river, and quiet the earth. After the fireball appeared, huge crowds gathered outside the temple and waited for the priests to emerge.

Bal-eeb only wanted to silence the screams.

On the city-side of the wall, a small detachment of soldiers armed with whips and spears cut a bloody channel through the mob. They bore the red waist wraps of the Royal Guard.

Hecktar's men. Bal-eeb ordered several warriors off the wall to open a channel through the crowd. As the Royal Guard approached, Bal-eeb recognized the man at the head of the column.

Cuts and bruises covered the small, well groomed son of the First Prince.

"Bal-eeb...," Hecktar panted, trying to catch his breath. "The city has gone mad. We almost didn't make it here. Water... please."

"You'll get water after you do you duty. What news do you bring?" Bal-eeb sneered.

Hecktar's expression hardened at Bal-eeb's offense. "It is the Narim. Shellbaz...the High Priest...emerged from the temple. He said the Narim are the cause of our ill fortune. They have offended Ba'al and have cursed us. That is why they are leaving the city. Shellbaz says we must march on the Black Fortress and burn the rest of them out."

Bal-eeb didn't care what the priests said, as long as it helped get everyone off the streets.

"What does the King say?"

"We cannot reach the King. The mob cut us off from the palace."

Bal-eeb laughed. "The King is isolated and defenseless, and the Captain of the Royal Guard stands here, on *my* wall?"

Hecktar reached for his hilt. "The Commander summoned me, or I would be at the palace. I, unlike some captains, trust my lieutenants. The King is safe and I come bearing a message from the Commander himself."

"Ah, I see." Bal-eeb nodded. "A message. So tell me, *messenger boy*, what does the Commander require of me?"

Hecktar's grip tightened. Bal-eeb grinned, pleased he could so easily rattle his rival.

Hecktar spoke slowly, words seething. "The Commander demands each captain send twenty men to ensure any gold or food found in the Black Fortress is secured for the crown. Otherwise, we are not to interfere with the mob."

Bal-eeb grinned. *Even deranged sheep can be useful. It's about time we cleaned out the Narim. If the men of Havilah can find their own gold, so can the Hur-po.*

Bal-eeb quickly issued orders to his lieutenant. "Summon twenty men, ten off the north and south walls, and follow this *messenger*." He absolutely delighted in speaking that word. If his men were present at the sacking of the Black Fortress, he would share in the glory and booty. He knew that fact must chaff Hecktar to no end.

In a few minutes Bal-eeb watched Hecktar's squad, bolstered with the new swords and whips, cut a fresh path through the mob and vanish into the city's belly.

Bal-eeb felt better. He hoped a substantial number of the rioters would perish in the attack on the Black Fortress.

The fewer mouths to feed, the better.

A cry went out from the lookout on the parapet tower. "Dust cloud to the southwest! A caravan approaches from across the river!"

Bal-eeb shielded his eyes and peered to the southwest. An enormous cloud of yellow dust turned the entire western horizon tan. It all looked surreal under the shooting stars streaking across the noon sky.

His blood ran cold. "That's no caravan. Only an army can create a dust cloud like that."

And only the Scythians can summon an army.

"Sound the siege horn!" Bal-eeb shouted.

***

Noah knew no ordinary army created the dust cloud Bal-eeb saw from his vantage far below.

He stood on the walkway atop the Black Wall overlooking the vast Hur Valley. Shem and Japheth manned the wheels, ready to open the outer and inner gates at their father's command. The women waited deep inside the Ark.

Noah intently studied the western ridge, the long line of high hills separating the Hur Valley from the steppe. What he saw made his ancient heart beat faster. An inky sea dotted with hundreds of tiny islands covered what was once an endless, rolling prairie. The western ridge acted as a tenuous dam, protecting the thin strip of dry land remaining between the ridge and the bloated Hur River. The Kupar Bridge clung like a thread, straining to hold the two banks together.

Noah shivered as the dust cloud approached the bridge's western ramp. Awed by his God's power, alternating waves of gratitude and guilt washed over him.

This is only the beginning.

He lifted his eyes to the heavens swarming with shooting stars. "I have tried to walk in Your ways," Noah whispered. "I've struggled my whole life to find favor in Your eyes, but why us, Oh Lord? Is the world truly so wicked, to deserve this?"

"I have prayed that prayer every day since the Lord touched you," a voice startled him from behind.

He turned to see Emzara staring beyond the wall. "I prayed to Him when you and our sons raised the Kupar Bridge. You built it without question. And I served. And I waited; even though I saw in that bridge a terrible purpose.

"I prayed to Him when you built the Black Gate and we walled ourselves into exile. I served and I waited, even as our cold prison rose around us.

"I prayed until my knees bled when you built the Ark. Each time the Lord was silent. I served. I waited. I prayed, but He saved his revelations for your ears. For me, He is mute."

Noah reached out to tenderly stroke her cheek. "The Lord speaks to us all in His own way. Do not fear, wife. He has promised us safe passage."

She pulled away, unexpected anger flared in her grey eyes reflecting the shooting stars above. "I am not afraid! Have you listened to God's voice so long, my husband, you are deaf to all else, including your own wife?" She marched to the wall's edge and jabbed her finger at the city below. "Listen! Do you not hear it?"

He paused and listened. There, just above the wind, rose the faint cries of the terrified throngs far below.

"I hear them," he said flatly, unable to look her in the eyes.

"I am sad because I know there is still *goodness* down there!" She began to tremble. "There are children and babies in Hur-ar..." she swept an exasperated hand across the horizon, "...and beyond who are blameless. Their only transgression was being born into a fallen world. I can hear them crying! Tell me husband, does God?"

Noah lowered his head to his chest.

"Look at me!" she shouted.

"What if it were us? What if those were our babies about to die?" She placed her hands over her ears and began to cry. "I cannot reconcile the love I feel for my God and the suffering about to befall the innocent. Oh, curse my long life, I will hear their screams to the end of my days!"

Noah didn't know how to answer her. In all their long life together, she had never once raised her voice to him until now.

"I..." Noah choked back the emotion.

Emzara's eyes softened in pity. "Do not be cross with me, Noah. I will not curse God, but I am angry with Him. I must be angry with Him, because you will not."

Emzara drew near and lightly touched Noah's broad chest, "I am afraid, but I will serve. I will wait. I will trust." Her fingers found their way under his bearded chin. She lifted his head until their teary eyes met. "I will love."

The wind whipped her graying hair and made the crow's feet around her eyes more vivid. For the first time in many years Noah saw his wife as she was.

Emotions so long suppressed by the weight of tireless duty threatened to break through. He breathed deeply, vigorously rubbing and considering his hands.

He hesitated, stumbling to find his words, not his God's. "I wore callouses upon my flesh from building His Ark. I never stopped to consider those you carried upon you heart as you built our family."

"Do not apologize for following the word of God." She looked over his shoulder at the Ark. "We are about to exchange one set of walls for another. One cold, dark place for another. But, together we will wait. We will serve. We will trust and know the sun awaits us at the end of our journey."

Emzara smiled up at her husband, and in her half-moon eyes he saw the maiden he loved all those years ago when the world was young and the Garden lived fresh in his people's hearts and minds.

Emzara took him arm-in-arm and led him down off the parapet, but not before she took one more glance over her shoulder at the hell unleashed beyond the Black Wall.

"Did Aizarg tell you his wife's name?" she whispered.

"Atamoda. Why do you ask?"

"It will make it easier to pray for her."

3. Heaven's Onslaught

The realm of angels lies along the boundary of light and mist, of dreams and death, of twilight and dawn. Their power is the whisper planted within the soul. The earthly plane is a mystery they can influence, but never fully comprehend...except for the Nephilim.

More than divine messengers, the Ten Guardians of Creation transcend spirit and flesh; creatures of two worlds and neither. Mother told me she drifted into our world like a snowflake from Heaven, settling gently upon the earthly plane the Nephilim called the Water. The Nephilim were never created to remain one with the Water, but destined by Grace to transform again into spiritual beings, once their early tasks were complete.

Like snowflakes, they melted into the Water and lost their way.

The Chronicle of Fu Xi

***

The world turned her emerald face to the east and pulled a milky veil over her gaping wound. The spirit felt the earth shudder under Heaven's onslaught. The beautiful blue jewel suffered for her children's sins.

Her macabre duties did not command her presence here, but this hellish womb gave birth to the Cataclysm.

It begins here. I must bear witness to this, even if I am only spirit.

The Angel of Death plunged into the maelstrom, flitting and twisting downward in the form that pleased her most - a golden, wingless spirit dragon. She passed through the loam of existence as a mote of dust transcends light and shadow.

But Nuwa's memories carried substance, physical power almost too heavy for her spirit to bear. She knew what the black clouds should look like, what the sea should smell like, what thunder should sound like. She also knew what truly transpired in the human heart, and that knowledge carried a high price. The afterglow of a thousand earthly lives carried staggering emotional power; memories so raw they filled her with intense longing.

More than anything else, she wanted to see her sons again, especially Fu Xi, and hold him once more.

No sunlight penetrated the enormous mushroom cloud's boiling cauldron. From its hellish belly, it spawned countless storms that piled one on top of another, until they flattened into anvils against the vault of the sky, casting shadows over the emerald ocean. The storms fed off of one another and began to swell outward in all directions. By nightfall the entire southern ocean would be covered, and then the storms would march against three of the seven continents. In a matter of days they would engulf the world.

Even through the storm clouds, Nuwa sensed the turbulent ocean below. It tumbled in over itself as it rushed to cover the scar in the earth's crust. She broke out of the clouds only a few hundred feet above the hole in the ocean. Though she could not smell it, she knew the air reeked of sulfur and fire.

Swaths of exposed magma at the bottom of what was once miles-deep ocean, painted the storm's underbelly a ruddy orange. The bedrock instantly melted to lava where a heavenly body the size of a mountain hurtled from the void and slammed into the ocean. The impact vaporized countless billions of tons of seawater, which quickly formed storms, now spreading across the blue sphere. As the ocean raced back over raw lava, more vapor erupted into the sky to engorge the malignant storms.

She skimmed inches over the boiling lava, pursued by a wall of water two miles high roaring toward the center of the crater. Cool water smothered superheated rock and released megatons of energy in a continuous wave of explosions, rumbling for thousands of miles.

The Golden Dragon plunged into the lava without so much as a ripple in the fire rock. She wanted the searing heat to burn away the memories. Instead, she felt nothing, and emerged into the shimmering hell at the crater's center. She coiled up like a snake as titanic walls of water converged from all sides and collided; sealing for eternity all evidence of where heaven and earth touched for a brief, terrible instant.

The Golden Dragon rode the explosion of steam high into the heavens, until she emerged from the cauldron and hovered at the edge of cold, silent space. Curtains of boiling white slowly concealed earth's gentle blue curve as tens of thousands of lightning bolts illuminated the clouds from within.

She peered beyond the expanding line of clouds, to where the ocean still basked under the sun. There, a shock wave rippled through the deep water at almost the speed of sound. Fated to circle the globe several times before it died, the mega-tsunami would scour the world's coasts clean of all hints of mankind. This was only a taste of the destruction to come.

Fu Xi dwells down there, condemned to suffer for my sins.

Heaviness tugged at her, sapping her strength. Much work remained before she could lay down her burdens.

Nuwa sank back below the clouds and raced ahead of the rising tidal wave as the illusion of her dragon form melted away. She willed herself north, beyond the ocean and the continents, toward the top of the world. There, she would break the seals on damnation's pit and unleash a new scourge.

4. The Fall of Hur-ar Part II

Haughty, foolish Hur-po! You stack your bricks a few feet higher above the dusty ground than other peoples, and think yourselves gods. — Scythian Proverb

The Chronicle of Fu Xi

***

Only a few farmers remained west of the Hur River working the hardscrabble soil amongst the stumps and irrigation ditches. These diehard few took their chances against the strange omens. The stink and confinement of the city held no sanctuary for them. They chose to fight the enemy they knew and understood...hunger. Winter loomed, and grain remained to be gleaned among the stumps. They kept their eyes downcast on their work, afraid to look up at the shooting stars. Whatever doom the gods had in store, these peasants chose to meet it with full bellies.

They paused swinging their scythes as the earth began to tremble. At first they thought the deep, bass rumble only another earthquake. The stump farmers and their slaves shielded their eyes and gazed over the western ridgeline, the gateway to the steppe. That's when they saw the dust cloud building in the late morning sun.

They knew this sound, though never with this intensity. It was the thunder of hooves, the dust stirred by a horde.

"Scythians"! They screamed and dropped their tools, fleeing to the bridge.

Unknown to them, the Scythians tribes also fled, but to the west and without their horses, trying to outrun the icy waters invading the steppe.

***

For the first time since the ancient days when the Narim walked among them, the great bronze horn rang out from the southern watch tower, signaling enemies approached. A hush settled over the refugees outside the gate and the mob within.

"Thank Ba'al almighty, something has shut these people up!" Bal-eeb shouted as he drew his sword. He turned and addressed the masses inside packed against the gate and extending down the central avenue.

"The Scythian horde rides this way!" he shouted, so all could hear him. "Go back to your homes. If you stay, you die. Rest assured, if you clog my avenue, I will kill you myself."

Amidst screams the throng quickly disbanded, scattering into the city's bowels.

Bal-eeb felt much better, like he could breathe again. He motioned for his lieutenant as he made his way down the parapets toward the southern tower. He pointed the length of the wall. "I want every available archer deployed. Bring up the barrels of oil and tinder. Reinforce the gate as well. Send word to the Commander. I'm sure he heard the horn, and I don't want him showing up here without knowing what's going on. " He stopped and turned, raising his finger to the lieutenant to accentuate his point. "And send a runner to recall those troops I sent with that boy lover, Hecktar. I need every sword and spear on the wall."

He looked out over the broad plain in front of the city, toward the twin towers of the Kupar Bridge and suddenly had an idea.

"Sneak a squad of twenty of my finest archers out the hidden door in the south wall. Give them a triple portion of arrows, and tell them to run as fast as they can to the Kupar Bridge."

The lieutenant frowned and shook his head. "What good are twenty men against that many horsemen?"

"The river is flooded. The bridge is the only way to cross. Twenty good archers can turn the bridge into a bloodbath."

"And when they run out of arrows?" The lieutenant raised an eyebrow.

"Draw swords and fight to the death."

"As you command." The lieutenant bowed and then turned to leave. He stopped and turned around. "And what of the people trapped outside the wall?" The lieutenant pointed to the hundreds of people pounding at the gates.

"If we're lucky, they'll absorb of few Scythian arrows," Bal-eeb scoffed.

***

Captain Bal-eeb stood among a line of archers along the wall and watched the dust cloud grow. He'd fought the horsemen enough times to know the tell-tale signs of a mounted force, though he never thought they'd mount an attack on the city itself.

"They approach the Kupar Bridge. It must be the entire Scythian nation," a young archer said in astonishment. "Why do they attack? Surely they know they cannot breach the wall?"

"Who knows what goes through the heads of those filthy animals," Bal-eeb said, and motioned to the sky. "Perhaps they've seen the omens as a sign we are weak. They will feel our arrows and think differently."

Bal-eeb felt much better. This was something he understood. The heavens may be falling, but battle against a flesh and blood enemy was real. Here he would earn his glory. While Hecktar played about with the mob, Bal-eeb would save the city. His only regret was he wished he had a larger force deployed at the bridge.

With the river so flooded, Bal-eeb felt confident the archers could slow the horde long enough for the Commander to reinforce the wall.

The stump farmers began to arrive, exhausted and screaming of the doom approaching from the west.

"Captain!" his lieutenant pointed to the growing cloud. "The dust turns black and moves against the wind."

Bal-eeb saw it, too, though he couldn't understand what his eyes told him.

***

The east and west approaches to the Kupar Bridge were almost underwater by the time the archers arrived, exhausted and out of breath. Only narrow strips of dry land about fifty feet wide provided access to the mighty bridge. The swift, black river was almost over the cliffs, which were beginning to crumble into the current.

The young squad leader gave them a quick moment to guzzle some water before he deployed them. He positioned ten archers far enough down the bridge to kill anyone approaching the western ramp. The next ten were placed in a line adjacent to the eastern guard shack.

Giant sheets of ice raced downstream and occasionally slammed into the bridge's pillars. The bridge shuddered, but didn't yield. With each impact the archers nervously looked about. The river, the falling stars, the Scythians... it was overwhelming, but the young warriors didn't falter. They had little loyalty to the captain, but they loved their squad leader and knew their city counted on them. Here they would make their stand.

They didn't have to wait long.

The men in the first line wiped the sweat streaming from under their helmets, the approaching thunder of hooves hurting their ears. They discerned enormous shapes emerging from the dust beyond the bridge.

The Kupar Bridge stood for over a century, patiently waiting for its purpose to be fulfilled. Now, that time had come as the first invaders reached the eastern ramp.

With a deafening buzz, a black mass of flying insects erupted from above the dust. Shocked, the archers watched as the living cloud ebbed around the bridge's cables and towers above them, pausing only for a moment before descending.

Millions of flies, bees and hornets attacked the men, ruthlessly biting and stinging every exposed inch of flesh. The first line of men fled screaming, swatting at the air and covering their faces. Insects filled their noses and mouths and crawled into every nook and cranny of their armor. To the last man they jumped into the water to their death.

The second line of archers dropped their bows and fled across the fields. The insects did not pursue, but ascended into the sky toward the city. They were quickly followed by an enormous, screeching flock of birds of every feather. The birds and insects were not long gone when the first hoof set foot on the bridge.

A pair of woolly rhinoceroses, both massive bulls, galloped across the bridge. They slammed through the empty guard shacks on both ends, shattering them into tiny splinters, and continued at a full gallop toward the city.

The elephants followed several minutes later, flanked by hundreds of other animals bunched into a thick mass, cramming onto the bridge. Antelope, horses, deer, bison, sheep, bears, wolves, lions, pigs, foxes...the creatures of the marsh, steppe, and mountain filed across the Kupar Bridge. The din of their hooves carried all the way to the city gate.

Cables tightened, boards creaked, supports groaned. From below, the river began to rise at a visible pace. Ice slammed relentlessly into the structure, sending shockwaves throughout the bridge. Still, it withstood the assault from below and the tremendous weight from above.

The weight began to abate as the larger animals cleared the eastern ramp. The scampering creatures crossed last. The final pair, two fat beavers, scurried across just as the rushing water washed away the western access.

Ice, driftwood, logs and flotsam steadily built up against the bridge supports, adding their weight to the flood's already crushing force.

The beavers touched dry land and waddled up the eastern bank just as the access washed away. Now isolated and surrounded by rapidly rising water approaching the level of the road, the tops of the bridge's support towers trembled. Suddenly, a sharp crack, quickly followed by a peeling, tearing noise filled the air. The span began a slow, sickening counter-clockwise lurch, like a boat trying to turn about in a narrow channel. Cables snapped and fell limp into the water.

As if knowing its purpose fulfilled, the mighty Kupar Bridge surrendered to the flood. With a series of wet snapping pops, it aligned with the current for a moment, before the mighty twin support towers fell inward on top of one another. With a crash the span snapped in two. The structure disintegrated into a pall of dust swirling over the river.

The herd pressed towards Hur-ar.

***

The mob at the gates turned toward the thunder and saw the bridge collapse. A sickening silence followed.

The warriors rubbed their eyes and blinked in disbelief. A foundation of their lives, something as solid and permanent as the mountains themselves, suddenly vanished.

"The bridge," the lieutenant whispered. "It has fallen."

"The two towers have fallen!" another warrior screamed.

A wail went up from the mob, "The towers have fallen! The bridge is gone! The bridge is gone!"

Freeman and slave, man and women, pressed against the gates with renewed energy. Those in the front were crushed by the weight of those behind. Arms and hands stretched upward in supplication, begging for entry. Dead bodies began to pile up against the gates, which became step stools for those trying to climb up.

Those at the rear of the mob heard the deep bass concussions of approaching hooves and slowly turned.

"Riders!" the lookout on the north tower shouted. Across the plain, well ahead of the main dust cloud, two smaller dust trails approached at a full gallop.

Scouts?

Bal-eeb discerned two large shapes, but they didn't run like horses. They trundled, mighty shoulders lurching up and forward like unstoppable boulders rolling down a mountainside. As they drew nearer, it became obvious the two hulking beasts were riderless. At first he didn't recognize the monsters. Even as they drew closer his mind refused to acknowledge what his eyes told him.

"This cannot be," Bal-eeb whispered to himself.

Almost seven feet at the shoulder and seven thousand pounds, one woolly rhino galloped well ahead of the other. White foam spewed from its nostrils as its mighty heart approached the breaking point. An invisible force pushed it onward. It didn't know why it ran; only that it must.

The rest of the mob turned around to see what the sentries along the wall pointed at, but it was too late. The beast plowed into the mass of human flesh, swinging its thick head and tossing bodies high into the air. Bones cracked underneath its stocky legs as it cleared an opening all the way to the gate. The survivors parted and fled screaming in both directions along the length of the wall.

"Archers, FIRE!" Bal-eeb commanded. Hundreds of arrows rained down on the rhino. It turned and trotted off, dozens of shafts protruding from its thick hide.

A clear path to the gate awaited the second rhino, more massive than the first. It didn't slow, nor did it swing its head, or flinch as dozens of arrows found their mark. With full force, eight thousand pounds of flesh rammed head first into the wooden gate.

The gates convulsed and shuddered inward as a shock wave of dust flew up from the wall. The stone under Bal-eeb's feet quaked. The gates buckled but held as the rhino retreated. Stunned and bristling with arrows, it slowly staggered away.

The men began to back away from the parapets.

"These are devils!" one of the men shouted and bolted. He ran past Bal-eeb, who hooked him with his arm and ran him through with his sword.

"This is Scythian witchcraft, nothing more! Return to your posts." Bal-eeb shouted, and let the warrior's body fall to the stone.

The first rhino returned and slammed into the gate. The thick wood released a deeper, more alarming cracking sound.

Desperate to rally his men, Bal-eeb snatched the dead warriors bow. "Come, men! You've been doing nothing for the last week except belly aching about the lack of meat. Well, here's your meat!" He laughed and loosed an arrow into one of the beasts. His men found courage and resumed pelting the rhino with arrows.

After one more assault, which was nothing more than a bump, the smaller rhino stumbled to the side, blood pouring from a thousand punctures. Its eyes rolled into the back of its head, and it collapsed dead in the tall grass.

Just out of bowshot, the larger rhino huffed and pawed at the dirt. It panted heavily with wet, ragged snorts as it tried to catch its breath. Bloody flecks of foam shot from its nostrils and mouth. The rhino's beady eyes locked on the gate as it summoned the last of its strength.

Bal-eeb knew the gate wouldn't take another assault. "Hold your fire until it's in range, and then direct all your fire on the beast!" Bal-eeb's blood raced. He didn't understand what was happening, but it stirred his battle lust.

As if in response to Bal-eeb's challenge, the rhino charged. Like black rain, a cloud of arrows flew out to meet it.

Bal-eeb heard the arrows snapping off its trunk-like legs, only to be replaced by new shafts. Still, it thundered forward.

"Stop it!" he screamed. *It's going to hit.* Bal-eeb braced himself against the wall for the impact he knew would shatter the gate. The beast emerged from the rain of arrows and slammed into the gates.

The impact almost knocked Bal-eeb down. The rhino stumbled back, fell over and died amongst the bloody bodies of the field peasants.

"The gate holds!" someone shouted from behind the wall. A cry of victory went up amongst the men.

It will not hold for long if we don't reinforce it. Bal-eeb turned to give orders to brace the gate when he saw the elephants emerge from the dust cloud. Thousands of animals trundled down the road toward the gate.

There are not enough arrows in the world to stop this army.

Behind the soft rumble of hooves came a new sound, a sound beyond thunder, beyond the shaking of the earth in the worst of earthquakes. Bal-eeb peered out to the distant west.

Enormous waterfalls breeched the western ridge and spilled into the valley.

His men dropped their weapons and fled all along the wall. This time Bal-eeb didn't stop them.

There would be no victory today. There would be no glory. No bribe could turn back this enemy. This was the hand of an unseen god rising up against them. Hur-ar and her people were cursed.

He looked about and found himself alone, abandoned by warriors who neither owed him loyalty nor respect.

Bal-eeb took a deep breath and raised his bow toward the pair of approaching elephants.

Here I will fight. Here I will die.

In that last moment, Bal-eeb found the man he could have been. But it was too late, for both him and the city. Against the backdrop of the falling stars, the buzzing black cloud of insects descended on Bal-eeb. Screaming, he tore at his clothes and armor until he fell ingloriously from the wall.

Bal-eeb, Son of Ashtoreth and Captain of the Gate of Hur-ar, died. In the end, his blood was not made of gold, but flowed as red as any mortal's. It ran across the ground toward the wall, only to be soaked up by the dusty earth.

***

Overhead, the insects and birds flew over the wall and descended into the city, clearing the terrified mobs from the main streets and cutting a path from the city gates to the Cliff Road.

The elephants passed the bodies of the two rhinos and pressed their broad foreheads against the weakened gate. The gates bowed and split along the fractures inflicted by the rhinos and fell inward. Lions and wolves rushed by the elephants and raced far ahead into the city.

As the animals pressed into the city, people fled to the alleys and into the houses and shops. Some watched from windows as the procession moved swiftly down the main avenue and into the market.

The elephants crashed through the stalls and tents of the market place, plowing a straight path for the rest of the animals to follow. They paused briefly under the enormous statue of the Black Dragon. Both elephants pressed their heads against the base of the statue and sent it toppling into a thousand pieces against the market wall.

The first waves splashed against the city wall just as the last of the animals cleared the market. The water washed over the bodies in front of the gate and then poured into the city.

***

Shellbaz led the mob of thousands up the Cliff Road. The horde carried torches, bundles of sticks and jars of oil. Shellbaz carried a prophesy of death.

In the secret places of the temple, in visions fueled by blood and lust, Ba'al showed him the fate of the world. There would be no escape, but there could still be redemption.

The Narim have cursed the city and the world of men. The master's voice hissed through the flames as Shellbaz poured sacrificial blood into the fire. *The Narim must perish with the rest of the world. Do this and live forever in a place I have prepared for you. The Black Gate and the fortress within must burn!*

Shellbaz hurried ahead, his heavy black robes weighing him down and slowing him from his purpose. Wild eyed, he looked back at the mob and its meager escort of warriors.

"Hurry!" he shouted back at them. "We are almost there."

Just then screams went up from the crowd. Everyone turned to see the water flood into the city below, filling the maze of avenues and alleys. The western ridge was now a chain of waterfalls as the Hur Valley had joined the new sea. The will of the mob began to falter.

Shellbaz had to think fast. "We will be safe high on the cliff! The Narim know this. We must take their sanctuary for ourselves."

Cries of "Take the Black Fortress!" went up in response. Even the warriors seemed energized and began prodding the people forward.

The rabble hurried up the road again until fresh screams came from far to the rear of the column.

Shellbaz looked back, confused as to what transpired below.

The shrill cries grew louder and louder as people began leaping off the cliff to their deaths.

The warriors turned about trying to lower their spears through the crush of people. A brown blur leapt up and took one of them down.

A lion roared.

No!

Shellbaz snatched a torch, a bundle of sticks, and a jar of oil from the nearest man and fled up the road. The Black Gate loomed just ahead. The Black Dragon promised it would take very little to set it ablaze.

My reward awaits.

Behind him the crowd parted as lions and wolves ripped into human flesh. Those who did not leap were torn apart. The warriors could not wield their spears effectively among the masses and also fell under tooth and claw.

The Black Fortress filled Shellbaz's vision as oil sloshed over his robes and he tried to light the faggot of sticks. He dared a glance over his shoulder in time to see a burly black wolf hard on his heels.

A few more paces!

The wolf snapped at his robes, sending Shellbaz sprawling into the gravel. The torch and jar flew out ahead of him.

The wolf leapt over him, but didn't attack. It crouched uphill beyond the torch, which burned on its side next to the shattered clay jar. The wolf cocked its head to the side and considered the Priest of Ba'al, as if waiting for something. Shellbaz strained to reach the torch, but not before the stream of oil did. The oil erupted, sending flaming globs splattering onto his robe. Shellbaz leapt up, screaming and trying to extinguish the fire with his hands. It only served to hasten his transformation into a living torch.

The wolf stood as sentry between Shellbaz and the Black Gate, as the priest briefly stumbled in a dance of death before falling to the city below. He plummeted like a falling star, mimicking those streaking in the heavens above.

The enormous flock of birds circled the Black Gate.

The wolf, joined by others and the lions, assembled in two rows on either side of the Black Gate. Lions parted to the right and wolves to the left. Panting, they lay down and waited.

***

Far below, two lions remained as sentries at the base of the Cliff Road to discourage any humans unwise enough to seek refuge from the rising water. The elephants led the procession as they made their way up the Cliff Road.

The Hur-po crowded the roof tops and watched their city die. The icy water filled the streets and began to creep up the walls and over stoops. The city's thieves and underclass who dwelt in the sewers quickly drowned. Those who waded through the morass were pulled underwater by mysterious black claws, never to resurface. Poor and rich, slave and freeman, the people of Hur-ar were now truly equal.

The water reached the Cliff Road just as the two little beavers started up past the lions, which turned and followed.

***

The elephants reached the top of the cliff as the shooting stars began to wane in the heavens. The veil of clouds overhead thickened until the late afternoon sun vanished. The large bull elephant strode between the wolves and lions and pulled the bell with his trunk.

For the first time since the Black Fortress rose above the City of Gold, both the inner and outer gates opened at once.

The Ark waited.

5. The Longest Voyage

When the father of a Lo groom announced a betrothal, custom levied a unique dowry upon the father of the bride - one summer to construct a wedding barge.

The bride's entire arun-ki helped fashion this barge, the largest vessel crafted by the Lo. Scouting parties traveled far and wide to gather the strongest marsh oaks, so thick it often took days to chop down with their stone and bronze axes. These prized logs were carefully tethered and floated to the shore camp.

Of all the Lo watercraft, they said the wedding barge had to weather the roughest seas. The logs were coated with pitch, stacked two deep, and bound with only the thickest ropes, finest leathers, and choicest flax. The barges were sturdy enough to hold the entire wedding party, which might number up to fifty, for three days of feasting and celebration.

The ceremony commenced on the morning of the first day, with the wedding barge tethered to the groom's father's hut. The details of the wedding ceremony are chronicled elsewhere in these annals. At sunset, following three days of feasting and celebration, the husband and wife cast away the tethers of their childhood and sailed off alone on the longest of voyages.

The Chronicle of Fu Xi

***

Someone shouted from beyond a thick clump of trees a few hundred yards away.

"Levidi, take us over there...and carefully. I don't want to get snared in the trees."

In a few minutes, the men had swung the raft north around the thickest of the trees, with Ba-lok and Ghalen at the front pushing branches from their path. The shouting became clearer until it transformed into the distinct sound of someone cursing.

They rounded a corner and beheld two enormous, well-constructed rafts tangled deep in the trees, the current pushing them farther into foliage's embrace. Six burly, bearded men wrestled with the tree branches as a small, bald man shouted and cursed them.

Aizarg softly whistled through his teeth and shook his head. "The trees collect more than ice and flotsam. That is the last person I expected to ever see again," he said.

Okta squinted. "Those are wedding barges, but I feel confident those men are not part of a wedding procession."

One of the bearded men finally saw them and pointed. The small bald man turned around.

"Virag," Okta whispered.

"Greetings, men of the Lo!" Virag called out in a smooth, gracious voice. "Could you help a friend in these troubling times?"

Aizarg spoke softly to his men, "Weapons ready, but don't look hostile. I don't think he recognizes us. Move us around to the north side of the trees so the current keeps us from getting caught."

"What are you intentions?" Ba-lok asked.

Aizarg turned and winked. "Are you up for a game of raft-tipping?"

***

They hailed Virag from a distance and then secured their raft to a tree with a sail line. It stretched taunt but held. The current pulled them away from the clump of trees, while partially obscuring them from Virag's rafts.

Aizarg handed Levidi his staff. "Wave it over the water. We must make sure no demons lurk below."

Levidi did so, though there was no sign of the black creatures below the surface. "The only demon is on that wedding barge," Levidi huffed.

"Not including Virag, I count six, three on each raft," Ghalen said. "Their rafts are heavily loaded and lopsided. No wonder they lost control. They have no idea what they're doing."

"Those are Sammujad spearman. They outnumber you and wield sagar," Sana spoke up. "They will crush you."

Aizarg ignored her. "Call to them," he said to Okta.

"We are coming over to help! Stay put and don't move!" Okta shouted through the branches.

"Thank you, strangers!" Virag called back. "But leave your spears on your raft."

"He still doesn't recognize us. Let's go. Be wary of the current, mindful of the branches," Aizarg said and dropped his staff to the deck. In quick succession, he, Ghalen, and Levidi dove in and swam to Virag's rafts.

Aizarg found the water cold but not numbing, the current strong but manageable.

Levidi came up first, next to Virag's raft and held up his hand. "A hand up, friend?"

A warrior dressed in shaggy winter garb reached down, but quickly found himself head over heels in the water. The warrior came up gasping and thrashing, weighed down by his wet furs and skins. "Help me! I cannot swim! Do not let the demons take me!"

Levidi grabbed him by the nape and towed the helpless warrior to the trees. The Sammujad clung for life among the branches like a stranded kitten.

Levidi re-submerged.

"It's an ambush!" Virag shouted. "Kill them!"

The remaining warriors on both rafts cocked their heavy spears, waiting for the Lo to resurface.

A hand shot out of the water and grabbed a warrior's ankle. Soon, two wide-eyed, shivering warriors clung to the trees.

Virag scurried from side-to-side, jumped from raft-to-raft, pointing to bubbles and swirls. "They are here! Jab there!" he shouted, but could not coax the four remaining warriors any closer to the water.

Ghalen came up for air a dozen yards from the rafts. The nearest warrior hurled his sagar, but not before Ghalen submerged again. The spear splashed harmlessly into the water and then drifted away.

Virag and his men turned around to face Aizarg and Levidi standing on their raft, arms crossed

"Surrender your rafts. They are ours now. Do so, and you will live." Aizarg commanded.

"Ha!" Virag stepped back and signaled his men forward. "Kill them."

Aizarg leapt backwards to the most laden corner. The rapid weight shift forced the nearest of the four warriors to stumble forward. With expert timing, Levidi lunged and nudged him overboard. Ghalen quickly snatched the sputtering warrior and placed him in the tree with the rest.

Levidi and Aizarg again faced Virag and his remaining men, this time rocking the raft by jumping up and down. Off balance and with sagar extended, the Sammujad stumbled and bumped into each other.

One desperately lunged at Aizarg. The Uros easily sidestepped, grabbed the spear shaft, and pulled the warrior forward into the water.

"Slow down, Uros!" Ghalen laughed from the water. "You're throwing them in too fast for me."

Virag slapped the warrior nearest him. "They are only marsh men. Kill them!"

Pale and unsure, Virag's remaining warriors looked at each other uneasily. In a matter of minutes, the remaining three joined their compatriots clinging to the tree.

Surrounded, Virag crouched with knife extended toward Levidi and Aizarg.

"Perhaps we can come to an arrangement? I have much to trade."

"Surrender all you have, and I will let you and your men live."

"Then you condemn us to death."

"You are a desperate man," Aizarg said with speed and conviction. He stepped closer to Virag, but still remained wary of the slaver's knife. "Desperate men will pay any price. If the world is going to end, then my price is small."

Virag cocked his head and squinted. "Aizarg?

"Ha!" Virag relaxed and tucked the knife into his waist strap. He looked Aizarg up and down. "Why didn't you identify yourself? I am not your enemy, yet you attack us. This is an outrage. Get my men out of the tree and let us go at once. These rafts are mine by fair trade with your fellow sco-lo-ti, deals made long before this flood. They are rightfully mine."

"You rafts are now mine. Your goods are mine. Your lives are mine. Accept this or join your friends in the trees."

"I don't know how you survived the steppe, Aizarg, but I'm sure we can work something out."

Aizarg waived his finger. "No bartering. My price is final."

"My men and I will be dead in a day."

"Then so be it. That is not my concern."

Virag crossed his arms and slowly nodded, as if understanding the rules had changed. "A man of the Lo left my camp no more than five days ago. He reeked of mud and ranted about the end of the world. I was sure he was a fool bound for certain death. Now he returns smelling not of the sea, but of the steppe, ruthless and hard," Virag chuckled. "He returns *civilized*."

Virag's words stung. He thought of all the Lo forced to wear Virag's collar and of the torments Sarah suffered under this man. Part of him wanted Virag to make this easy, to fight and give him an excuse to put the little snake in the tree with the rest of his warriors.

"Your rafts." Aizarg remained firm.

Virag held out his hands, palms up, in supplication. "Mercy, sco-lo-ti. Or should I say, *Uros?* Strange that the Lo would have convened a war council, and I did not hear of it."

Ghalen pulled himself up onto the raft behind Aizarg. "Into the water with them! No good can come of this."

Virag ignored him and continued, voice low and smooth, "We are not Lo, but we have done you no harm, committed no crime. Where is the Lo custom of mercy, Aizarg? Did that die on the steppe, too?"

Aizarg opened his mouth to give the command to cast Virag into the water, but stopped. He considered the black, swirling water and then the faces of the shivering warriors in the tree. Branches sagged under the weight of what looked to Aizarg like a pitiful family of soaked, shivering bears.

What would Setenay council?

"Cast them into the water, Uros," Ghalen whispered. "He is a snake. Otherwise, treachery and death will be our reward. Isn't it because of the likes of him that the god of the Narim sends this curse?"

From darkness, mercy.

"Ghalen, get those Sammujad out of trees and onto the rafts. Show them how to properly redistribute the loads."

"Uros!" Ghalen clenched his teeth. "You cannot..."

"I can!" Aizarg snapped. "I am Uros."

"Aizarg, please, think about what you are about to do," Levidi said softly. "Ghalen is right, Virag is dangerous."

Virag's eyes darted from Aizarg to Ghalen to Levidi. The corner of his mouth lifted almost imperceptibly.

He senses us wavering. He thinks we're weak.

"Ghalen, Levidi...what do you council?"

"Throw them into the water, and let Psatina deal with them," Ghalen said.

Levidi nodded in agreement.

Words formed in Aizarg's mind, though he was not sure if they were his. He let them flow off his tongue unopposed, "The Goddess Psatina is gone, washed away with our beloved Great Sea. This new Black Sea has no gods, at least none that speak to me. We will not let the sea and its demons do our dirty work. Let what is decided by man, be administered by man. Levidi, take Virag's knife."

Levidi snatched the knife.

"Ghalen, if death is what you council, then slit the throats of these warriors. Levidi, if you feel death is justified, slice the slaver's throat now."

A wave of fear washed over the slaver's face. "Aizarg deals death like a Scythian warlord." Virag spit on the deck before Aizarg's feet.

Levidi looked at Ghalen with a pall of uncertainty and dropped the knife.

Ghalen stooped to pick it up. "I'll do it!"

Levidi gripped his wrist. "Please, don't. You'll regret it. This isn't like killing the Scythians. This is murder."

Ghalen hesitated and then cast the knife down. He spoke in a low, disgusted tone, "We will regret this. I know this to be truth." He shook his head. "We will pay a price for our mercy, a price of blood...and fire."

Virag's grin blossomed.

"Your heart knew better, and for that I am grateful." Aizarg sighed with relief. "Virag, you and your men are no longer Sammujad. Accept Lo ways and my rule or perish. Swear an oath on it. The world you knew is washing away. What you see before you is only the beginning. Live or die, the choice is yours."

Virag bent on one knee, bowed his head, and spread his arms. "I, Virag, give my fealty to Aizarg, Uros of the Lo." Virag looked up at Aizarg with a smile that did not reach his eyes.

Aizarg bent down and whispered in Virag's ear, "Do not confuse mercy for weakness. I do not trust you. If there is killing to be done, it will be done by my hand. Give me no reason."

***

Three rafts skirted west along the tree tops of a lost coast, sails fully unfurled, dancing between opposing currents and winds. The two stout wedding barges led the way, with Okta's tiny raft bringing up the rear. Aizarg equally divided the Sammujad warriors among the rafts, each having taken separate oaths. Ghalen held the tiller on the lead barge and calmly issued simple instructions to the two warriors flanking the sail. Levidi manned the center barge, also teaching the warriors the ways of the sea. Okta chose to stay on his own tiny raft with Ba-lok, shouting and cursing at the fumbling Sammujad.

Aizarg, Ezra, and Sana manned the lead barge, the two land dwellers clearly relieved to be aboard a more substantial vessel. Virag squatted in Sammujad fashion near Aizarg, who stared out over the water looking for signs of his people.

"Ood-i?" Virag asked.

Aizarg shook his head. For a moment a cloud pass over the slaver's face.

"I see you traded Ood-i's woman for another," Virag nodded to Sana. "I approve."

"She is a free woman and under my protection," Aizarg clenched his staff tighter, knowing he was going to have to live with the consequences of letting Virag live.

"Of course."

"The woman you sold to Ood-i lies buried beside him."

Both men returned their stares to the water in silence until Aizarg spoke again.

"Tell me, Virag, why does a trader of the steppe have a wedding barge, let alone two, that are fully equipped with ropes, sails, and rigging, all in Lo fashion and all in good condition?"

Virag shrugged without looking up at Aizarg. "I am a trader. Everything is for sale. Everything has its price."

That answer left Aizarg completely unsatisfied. "Who did you buy it from?"

"From the young sco-lo-ti's father," he jerked his thumb back towards the last raft.

Ba-lok's father? The former sco-lo-ti of the Minnow Clan was dead by almost a year. *I will have to question Ba-lok about this later.*

The dark clouds to the south loomed larger. Aizarg could not see the sun but knew it was close to setting. They would have to tie up on some trees soon and wait for morning.

Where are you, Atamoda?

"Uros...," Virag said. Aizarg turned to look at him.

"I liked you better with red hair." The slaver's cold laugh preceded them across the black water and into the rising darkness.

6. White Fire, Black Smoke

Each woman's soul carries a tiny shard reflecting some quality of Nuwa's spirit. I see my mother in the eyes of the pining maiden, in every hag chained to a past of regret, in every mother cradling her child. I search those glittering shards for clues to who Nuwa truly was. My heart tells me I will search until my immortal flesh is no more.

I, a god, have learned little about a woman's heart, but I know this. While a man must respect the tempest of a woman's scorn, he must fear the darkness of her regret the most. In a woman's heart are secrets so deep even the Emperor of Heaven must tread carefully, lest He lose His way.

The Chronicle of Fu Xi

***

Perched on the edge of the glacial cliff, the Angel of Death waited. Above her, falling stars etched glittering trails across the burning blue sky. Before her feet, a narrow waterfall, only a stone's throw across, cascaded into a perpetual, icy mist. Similar waterfalls, spaced dozens of miles apart, stretched thousands of miles along the edge of the glacier, feeding hundreds of rivers and streams pouring south across the tundra. Combined, they slowly drowned three continents.

To her right, a freshwater glacial ocean covered the top of the world. A tranquil blue mirror perfectly reflecting the falling stars, it stretched horizon to horizon, broken only by an occasional iceberg. Only when the water neared the waterfall, only inches from her feet, did it reveal its swift power. At glacier's rim only a thin membrane of ice a few feet thick protected the world below from the ocean. She felt the titanic pressure straining to explode forth. Only a nudge, a breath, would inundate the world.

Tsunamis generated by the great falling star scoured the world's coasts clean of mankind. Releasing the glacial ocean would now complete the divine genocide. The Spirit of Death knew she should feel something, but she didn't even feel the wind.

She cloaked herself in an ancient memory, an guise far different than Nuwa. She wore it the way a widow wears her wedding dress, a ghost of ancient passion, of love lost and dreams unfulfilled. White silken slippers hovered inches above the snow. Her white robe, emblazoned with the image of the golden dragon, hung as slack as her red hair.

She could not admit to herself why she waited. The deed should have already happened.

Fu Xi needs time to climb higher. I must allow the man with white hair to get his people farther to sea.

Now, however, eternity crushed impatiently on her.

He's not coming. His presence was the last thing she should desire, yet she did and hated herself for it.

Now history and bitter duty could wait no longer. She pointed at the waterfall as the Offering Blade materialized in her hand. Before she could deliver the cut, a dark shape flashed in the water next to her. And then another.

She lowered the blade as the demons approached like wind driven streaks. They crowded along the glacier rim, slithering over one another eager for release from epochs of imprisonment. They hummed in a filthy chorus.

Release us, oh Bringer of Death. Do as the Celestial Emperor promised!

Sometimes a smaller demon slipped through over the waterfall like a salmon over a boulder, to join the others already infesting the world.

Their prison weakens.

Deeper underwater, massive black shadows slipped to and fro like cloud shadows. The waterfalls were too small for these demons. They required the Angel of Death to release them.

Suddenly, the demons plunged into the depths, and the ocean fell silent again.

He is here. Anticipation and regret gripped her. *Why did I wait so long? What have I done?*

The man with hair spun from sunlight, skin as pale and flawless as the snow, and garb as black as midnight, materialized from the mist.

She knew she'd made a horrible mistake.

He assumed a relaxed pose opposite her across the waterfall, a vision of white fire and black smoke against the brilliant blue sky. A kindred spirit masquerading in human form, his high black boots hovered a hair's breathe above the glacier. Coal black trousers, long shirt, and cape hung limp, unruffled by the wind.

Why did he choose that form? But she already knew the answer. He cloaked himself in the form she loved best.

Blue eyes as cold and deep as the artic sky drank her in with a hint of lust. "You've been standing here for a quite some time. How long does it take to murder a world?"

"If you come here to stop me, you are more arrogant than even I could have imagined," she replied coldly.

"You know exactly how arrogant I am. I know how haughty you can be." His laugh flooded her with bittersweet memories of a thousand perfect spring days, casting an ancient magic on her heart, a charm she both longed for and feared. "And we both know I cannot stop you. Did you wait this long just to insult me?"

"Be gone."

"You don't want me to leave." His eyes danced playfully up and down her form. "I thought you would wear the memory of Nuwa. Yet, here you are as my beloved Gaia."

"It pleases me," she lied, crossed her arms and turned away.

"It pleases me, too. I would be more pleased if you were flesh. You wanted to see me here, didn't you?"

"I did not," she lied again. She wanted to ask him if his form was simple chance, but knew better. He did nothing by chance. Neither did she.

What have I done?

"Go," she said. "Your banter no longer charms my heart."

"Ahh, but you no longer have a heart, do you, love?" Like a snake sliding from a rotted log, his voice rolled through her mind with a silky smooth draw. Spirits can conceal little, even when imagining themselves as flesh. Truth shines through them like the sun through perfect crystal. She tried not to show how his words cut.

He, however, lied with perfection. She could only lie with perfection to herself.

"Why did you wait for me?" he pressed.

She lowered her head and wrapped her arms around her shoulders, shielding her will from his power like from a cold wind.

"You toy with me. Are you so cruel to think I haven't suffered?

"No," she whispered.

"Look at me," he begged with such tenderness it melted her resistance.

Hand outstretched, angelic face pleading as if begging her to save his life, his outline shimmered. The wind suddenly tousled his robes and hair. A shadow materialized behind him. With a soft crunch, his boots settled into the snow.

She tried not to show her astonishment. The power to transform spirit to flesh was a power reserved only for Him.

"I can give you a heart, Gaia. I may not have power in other domains, but I am master of this one. The only power left to Him here is destruction."

Another lie. She tried not to stare at the body she last touched long before she became Nuwa.

"Go," she repeated, with even less conviction as the demons slowly rose again from the depths. She gestured to the meandering black forms. "And take them with you!"

"Did you think them mine?" He sounded surprised. His laugh, born aloft on the wind, floated like a ray of light; airy and beautiful.

The man in black knelt next to the water and reached out. A few demons swam lazily back and forth like carp rising at the expectation of a thrown crumb. A small, childlike demon tentatively neared the surface and reached out, almost tenderly, with a gnarled claw. A thin sheet of black ice formed where it touched the surface, flat and perfectly mirrored.

"Are they not the Children of Chaos?" Genuinely shocked, she assumed these demons were his servants, wrestled from his control by the Celestial Emperor, to pick the flesh from the bones of the earth.

"The Children of Chaos are still chained in my domain, perhaps never to rise again. I have no power over these beasts, though I strongly desire it. If I commanded legions such as these, we would not be having this conversation. I would be master and not rebel."

"Save your lies."

"Lies?" He turned and transfixed her with an expression of such powerful melancholy, she found herself drawn into his eyes. "These are not my servants. They are born neither in Heaven or Hell. These are memories of mortal regret, the afterbirth of earthly grief given form. When confined to the human heart, they shred the human soul from within. When let loose upon the world, they devour the living and the dead."

He touched the disc of ice, and it flashed into flame. The demons fled once again into the deep.

He stood and faced her. "Tell your master He will fail. I cannot stop you, but I can pervert your purposes. Whatever He creates, I corrupt."

She wanted to reply, but knew he would only twist her words. She drank in his beauty out of the corner of her eye and remembered.

He pointed to the fireballs lazily arcing high above. "Behold His rage. He speaks of love, but I practice it. I love the world and He regrets it. It eats Him." His voice softened with tenderness. "Who is the evil one? Tell me!"

"I trust Him," she snapped.

For a long moment he considered her. His flesh made an even more effective cloak for his thoughts.

"Did he tell you *why* he wants to destroy it?" he finally asked.

"To set right your corruption. For love."

"Love?" He shook his head and stepped away from the ice cliff, eyes narrowed and tone sharp. "Do you find the lack of feeling comforting? Is it everything you wanted, everything you remembered? For what promise did you exchange your flesh? What prize so valuable you sacrificed the hot pleasures of the Water for a pale agape ghost?"

Nuwa wanted to feel rage, to lash out at the man in black with the Offering Blade. She could do neither.

"It is because of your sons you shed the flesh and cast your lot with Him." He casually lifted his nose like a wolf and sampled the air. "Fu Xi nears the Roof of The World, and here you stand, ready to unleash a tempest so powerful it could kill even him. If he dies, it is by your hand."

"No!"

"Did He promise to spare him?"

She lowered her eyes. "No," she whispered. "He only promised Fu Xi a chance."

"And what promise was given for your other son?"

He's turning the truth against me. Strike now and unleash the Scourge before his words turn my hand.

He raised an eyebrow at her silence. "I see. Once again you abandon your first born."

"You know that is a lie!"

"If it is a lie, why does it sting? Perhaps you still have a heart, if the truth can make it ache."

He returned his gaze to the tundra far below. "Turn your blade, Gaia. Come back to me. Let us finish what we started and transform this world into a paradise for both god and mortal. We will succeed where He failed."

She couldn't look at him, though she felt the unrelenting draw of his will. If she lingered, he would turn her heart. She could not, must not, let that happen.

"I am an instrument of His will. I've made my choice. Now go. You're wasting your time. I have work to do."

In a flash of smoke he vanished. The sunlight momentarily dimmed as if shrouded by dark lightning. Instantly, she sensed him behind her.

He touched her and spirit became flesh, beginning with her heart. Hot blood pounded into her body as frigid air poured into her lungs. She gasped as an eternity of memories burst forth. Once again, she became Gaia.

He grabbed her from behind, squeezing her wrists to the point of pain. He forced her hand, stiffly grasping the Offering Blade, toward the thin glacier wall. His lips hovered only inches from her neck, his warm breath gently caressing each hair follicle

"Then do it!" he whispered into her ear. "Let us do this together. Tell me, love, how much blood must I spill, for Him to offer me forgiveness? Is there enough blood in the entire world for me?"

His grip relaxed as his other arm encircled her waist.

"Can He give you this?" he whispered softly. The man in black pressed hard from behind and pulled her tightly against him.

She moaned at the sensation of his body pressing firm against her's through the thin, smooth silk robe.

"I have always loved you."

She hoped and feared to hear those words, lies she believed as truth. Lies she cherished and loathed with every fiber of her being.

She ran her fingers through his hair, turned, and kissed him. His tongue ran sweet and warm in her mouth. They embraced, and lifted by their passion, floated off the ice. With unyielding arms but tender hands, he hungrily sought her body's forbidden realms.

Her spirit filled every inch of this new, sensuous flesh. The wind pierced her robe with a thousand icy needles deliciously penetrating the nooks and crannies of their embrace. Heat, ice, and smooth silk simultaneously caressed flesh with overwhelming pleasure.

"Let the spirit and the flesh be one," he whispered.

The wind caught their robes and entwined the lovers in a twisted wreath of white silk and black satin. Their shadows darkened and wrestled across the virgin snow at the top of the world.

A line of wrathful clouds, pregnant with lightning, raced from the south and obscured the blue sky and falling stars. Demonic voyeurs slowly rose from the depths, drawn by forbidden passion. The water's surface crackled into a sheet of black ice.

Their robes merged and flapped like wings, but instead of lifting the lovers they sank, almost imperceptibly, to the snow. He reached up to strip away her robe just as her silken slipper touched the snow.

It melted through to her toes. Unlike the wind, it seeped against her flesh as dank and clammy as a grave.

Images of the stone garden in Nushen and the bodies of its dead flashed into her mind. Her eyes flew open.

"No!" She enveloped herself in a ball of fire as he flashed into a swirl of smoke. Flame and fume wrestled atop the glacier until all flesh and passion burned away.

The black ice shattered as demons fled to the deep once again.

Two spirits stood separated by the narrow stream, robes limp, feet not touching the ground. Offering Blade firmly clenched, she fully veiled herself in the image of Nuwa.

"You have chosen," he said and faded into the mist.

A single mortal tear, a tiny remnant of his dark gift, fell from her eye and dropped upon the Offering Blade. It slid down along the razor edge until it transformed into blood as red as the orichalcum metal.

The tear rolled off the tip and dropped into the water.

"It is done," she whispered.

A familiar voice rumbled on the wind from the approaching storm.

Keep your promise, and I will keep mine.

Nuwa transformed into the Golden Dragon and vanished.

The blood drop did not disperse and wash over the waterfall. Instead, it sank deeper into the ocean and grew, changing from crimson to black. The demons gathered into a twisting school of blackness and pursued it, drawn to its desolation and regret. They chased the bloody teardrop into the abyss until all sunlight vanished.

The tear grew into an enormous, sinister glob, larger than all the demons combined. Ruddy red eyes blinked to life, and armored plates clinked into existence down its long form until it became a monster of unimaginable power and size. The monster hurtled upward toward the surface, screeching demons trailing closely behind.

The beast suddenly turned and plunged into the ice wall encasing the sea. The ice wall exploded as the glacial ocean and countless demons cascaded thousands of feet to the tundra below.

In both directions the ice wall crumbled, and the ocean fell upon the land. The glacier itself, freed from the titanic weight, suddenly bobbed up hundreds of feet. A hidden ocean trapped below the ice, even larger than the vast surface ocean, blasted forth from its confinement near the bottom of the glacier.

Combined, they formed a wave of deathly cold water a mile high. As tsunamis wiped the world's coasts clean, the glacial juggernaut began to scour three continents from within.

Between the two, the rains began.

7. The Cold Forge

"The icy sea pushed south, the cold wind blew north. The world inhaled deeply, preparing for the long plunge into the abyss.

On that first night the God of the Narim showed me my fate, our fate. In a cold forge of water and ice a new people would be created."

- Conversations with the Uros

The Chronicle of Fu Xi

***

Levidi and Ghalen lashed the rafts together to form a platform and secured them to the treetops, unwilling to risk navigating the powerful current in the darkness without the stars. The lines tugged hard against the trees as the current strained to drag them out to sea. The expertly tied Lo knots held firm.

Night cloaked the world in darkness blacker than any Aizarg could remember, mirroring what he felt in his soul. He sensed the clouds thickening above them, pregnant with death.

The decks felt like ice. They found a sturdy Lo brazier among Virag's supplies and gathered plenty of dead limbs tangled in the tree tops.

Without regard to tribe, grudge or allegiance, they huddled in intimate closeness around the brazier. The wind whipped hard at the bronze pan, bending the flames and stripping embers away, casting them into the void.

Aizarg stood outside the circle, leaning on his staff and considering the motley assortment of lost souls gathered around the fire. He grasped for some idea what to do once the sun came up.

If it comes up...

Aizarg's thoughts raced, pondering the fate of those gathered around the brazier and his people lost somewhere beyond the darkness. Hope for Atamoda and his people burned like the brazier against the overwhelming darkness.

How will I find her without a shore or the stars to guide me?

Aizarg's gaze fell to Sana, hunched under a horsehide blanket and tense as the ropes securing the rafts to the trees. With the extra clothes they had scrounged from among Virag's supplies, and the Sammujad skins heaped on her shoulders, she looked every bit the a-g'an savage. The Sammujad henchmen eyed her from time to time, but made no move toward her.

Pity filled Aizarg's heart. He dearly wanted to hate the Scythian, but could not bring himself to do so.

She is truly alone. Her people are surely dead by now.

Virag sat closest to the fire, his perpetual grimace barely visible under a thick bearskin blanket. Ghalen sat opposite from Sana between Levidi and the six Sammujad, staring hard into the flames. Occasionally, Levidi tried to draw Ghalen into conversation, but Ghalen would have none of it.

Earlier, Levidi tried to do the same with Aizarg, but the Uros needed counsel not from a friend, but his Second.

Ba-lok, Second to the Uros, huddled alone in the cold shadows, his back to the party.

Darting outside in the firelight, Ezra followed Okta from raft to raft, helping him secure ropes and rigging. Okta doted over the rafts like they were children. It pleased Aizarg how Ezra threw himself into learning the ways of the sea, and Okta was obviously happy with his new apprentice.

Okta finds hope in purpose. Ezra is wise enough to recognize it.

Aizarg possessed a purpose, but he didn't know how to accomplish it.

He thought of Noah and the night they spent talking. He thought of Noah's Nameless God.

Open your heart. Speak in truth. Bow in humility. Do these things and He will listen, Noah had told him.

Aizarg took a deep breath and bowed his head. The voices of the Sammujad murmuring among themselves and Okta instructing Ezra barely penetrated the howling wind. Soon, Aizarg heard nothing and time seemed to stand still. The deck swayed gently under his feet. The staff seemed to warm in his hands.

Aizarg's eyes flew open as a thought sprung into his head. *It starts here.*

A pile of red embers glowed in the brazier, barely illuminating a circle of slumbering mounds, including Ezra and Okta.

Ba-lok still hunched in the shadows, staring into the distance.

I need my Second. "Ba-lok, throw some more sticks on the fire."

Ba-lok obeyed and the fire sprung back to life.

"Come here," Aizarg said. No one stirred as Ba-lok slowly shambled to Aizarg, shoulders stooped.

"Tell me about these wedding barges."

"I recognize them. We made them last summer, before Father went to heli-dar."

"Why does Virag buy wedding barges?"

Ba-lok shrugged. "Why does Virag do anything? He commissioned my father for two wedding barges. His price was generous, enough bronze to keep our village supplied for two seasons. Virag even supplied the axes without charge. My father kept his own council regarding his dealings with Virag."

"And Setenay had nothing to say? Wedding barges are not merely large rafts; they are sacred symbols of unity. I find it strange she would bless such a transaction."

"Father said a wedding barge is only sacred if used as a wedding barge. Grandmother remained silent as it was clearly a matter for men to decide, though I think she didn't approve."

Aizarg shook his head. "I do not regret your father's dealings. The feel of this sturdy deck below my feet is reassuring, you can be sure of that! It is only Virag's purposes that trouble me."

"Is that all, Uros? I grow weary," Ba-lok turned away.

With a firm grasp on Ba-lok's shoulder, Aizarg turned him around and pointed to the south. "What do you see?"

Ba-lok shrugged. "Darkness. Nothing."

Aizarg pointed to the group. "And now?"

"Ghalen, Levidi, Okta, and the Hur boy. I also see Sammujad scum and that Scythian bitch." Ba-lok spat out the last words with so much hate Aizarg recoiled.

Aizarg shuddered to think what Ba-lok suffered at the hands of the Scythians, knowing full well the horsemen's reputation for savagery to captives. But he needed to pull Ba-lok out of his simmering hate.

"Look again." Aizarg kept his voice calm and motioned back to the sleeping group.

Ba-lok yanked away from Aizarg's grip. "I see someone else's people. I see enemies! What do you see, Uros?"

"I see the köy-lo-hely," Aizarg whispered. "And out there, in the darkness, is death. Do you understand?"

"No."

He is broken. We are all broken; broken chain links of all shapes and sizes. What to do with them? Setenay and Sarah were our fire, our forge. Now our fire is dead.

"Where people drift in the darkness, we must be the light to gather them up. This is our charge. It must start here.

"I know you are in pain. All of us are in pain. Let it remind you to take your next breath, your next step."

"You left me!"

"No. You were taken. To believe anything else will only feed your anger until your soul is as dark as this night." Aizarg leaned in. "An Uros will fail without his Second. You were chosen for this task. Setenay knew it. I trusted her then, and I trust her now."

An impulse suddenly overtook Aizarg. He snatched Ba-lok's hand and thrust the staff into his palm. Ba-lok jerked away, but then his eyes grew wide at the realization that he felt no pain.

"You are Second. You were chosen. If I fall, you are Uros. Setenay knew, and so does the God of the Narim."

Ba-lok hefted the staff, which seemed to glow dimly, though Aizarg could not be sure it wasn't his eyes playing tricks on him.

"Help me forge this broken chain into a lifeline."

After a moment of hesitation Ba-lok handed Aizarg the staff and turned away.

Can I reach him when his grandmother could not?

Ba-lok stepped over the slumbering bodies, threw a few more sticks onto the brazier, and then settled in amongst them to sleep.

Aizarg lingered a little longer, staring into the void and wondering if the Nameless God watched over Atamoda and his boys, or even cared.

***

Daybreak arrived gray and dim under ever thickening clouds. Aizarg stood alongside of Okta on the makeshift raft as the wedding barges followed behind.

"Uros, the current strengthens from the north and the tree tops vanish. The old shore will disappear soon and the

Black Sea will stretch uninterrupted in all directions. The sails are taunt and fully tacked." Okta nodded to the south. "It will not be long before we will be pulled to the deep sea. Perhaps our people have already abandoned the coast for deeper water as well. I'm sure by now all our arun-ki are submerged."

"We will cling to the coast as long as we can. If the open sea is forced upon us, so be it, but I will not commit to deeper water until then."

"What is that?" Virag said from where he sat at the front of the raft. He pointed to an object caught in a nearby tree.

"Get us closer," Aizarg commanded Okta as he peered ahead. As they drew closer Aizarg's blood ran cold.

Under Okta's direction they maneuvered the rafts with full sail against a steadily strengthening current until they secured them to a tree top.

Aizarg hopped onto Ghalen's raft, which was closer. Ghalen reached out with a pole and snagged the boat.

"The stern is missing," Ghalen pointed to the ragged end of the two man fishing boat. "It's shredded."

Virag scoffed. "So what of it? I'm sure we will find many more caught in the trees."

"It wasn't shredded in the trees. It was torn off," Ghalen pointed to stains the inside of the craft. "Blood."

"Teeth marks," Aizarg said.

"Demons!" the warrior named Spako shouted from the farthest wedding barge. The giant Sammujad shrank to the center of their rafts while the Lo men leapt to the edges, gazing over the sea.

Water demons crept under the surface, swirling and slithering from beyond the trees and out to sea. They parted around the rafts, giving them a wide berth. They rejoined to form a long, greasy slick, a river of black within the Black Sea, meandering to a point south.

"There are hundreds, Aizarg. Thousands!" Levidi shook his head in dismay.

"Where are they going?" Ezra asked.

Aizarg followed the line until he spied an object on the horizon. At first, he could not make out what it was in the dim light. Then the shapes formed a coherent whole.

"Release the lines and lower the sails!" Aizarg shouted. "Man the tillers; we abandon the coast."

In the brightening gray dawn, they followed the stream of demons until they saw a flotilla and the black horde encircling it.

"The demons attack a gathering of anchored boats!" Okta shouted. "There must be over a hundred boats tied together."

"I can hear the people screaming! There are so many demons," Levidi shouted. "Can we stop them? Shall I wave the staff over the water, Uros?"

All eyes turned to Aizarg. After a pause, he spoke. "Do not wave it. Touch it to the water."

Levidi placed the tip of the staff in the water. To all their amazement, a glob of brilliant, white, liquid fire dripped from the red metal orb. It fell onto the water and spread away from the three rafts. A sheet of white flame danced on the surface, chasing the demons toward the floating island.

8. The Trail

Love burns brightest on the edge of oblivion. There, it is purged of the material life, leaving only the purest of essences ready to be bent to the will of the Emperor of Heaven.

Copper or iron, mortal or god, only the smithy knows how long the metal must lay in the coals. Alas, gods must be buried long and deep in the blazing embers, the bellows blowing long and hard, before divine metal glows even the dullest red.

I entered the forge several years before my fateful journey to Wu, when the Goddess Nuwa and I, unseen from the forest edge, watched a young orphan boy.

The Chronicle of Fu Xi

***

An ocean tossed from heaven.

The unending storm gushed against the cliff, trying to wash Fu Xi and his horse from the mountainside. Water consumed him, trying to fill his nostrils with each breath. Head bent low, with shoulder thrust into the howling gale, the demigod defied the torrent. His outstretched right hand felt along the rocky cliff while his left tightly grasped the horse's reins. Only the occasional nudge from behind or tug on the reins reassured Fu Xi that Heise still followed.

Ahead, the narrow path etched into the cliff revealed itself only a few feet at a time. Impenetrable shrouds of gray and black concealed towering mountains Fu Xi only sensed. He braved a glance down the precipice, unable to see the boiling river swallowing the valley far below. It announced its presence with a continuous, quaking crescendo shaking the mountain, as if conspiring with the storm to scrape him from the rocky wall.

But Fu Xi did not fear for himself. He didn't know how. Perhaps it was too late in his immortal life to learn. Instead, he concentrated on keeping his horse alive.

The saddlebags still bulged with grain and apples, but they wouldn't last forever. Grass this high was almost non-existent before the storms. Now, torrents and mudslides swept away or buried what little vegetation did grow.

If we remain on the roof of the world, starvation will eventually kill Heise.

Fu Xi glanced over his shoulder at the stallion he called Heise, which simply meant "black." He still didn't have a proper name for the beautiful animal. Only a shadow through the rain, Heise sagged under the crushing downpour. How the horse kept his footing on the treacherous goat path, Fu Xi did not know. His right shank scraped the cliff while saddlebags hung over the abyss to the left.

Food wasn't as much of a concern for the demigod. During his many quests he'd often gone days, even weeks without eating. He could function for days without a sip. While his body somehow adapted, Fu Xi's divinity didn't protect him from discomfort.

A cave, a ledge, any shelter I can find to build a fire and get Heise out of the elements. Then I can worry about foraging for food.

The only caves he'd found were thousands of small holes and ledges peppering the cliff-face, no more than handholds and nooks. Once nests for swifts, Fu Xi investigated them several times to see if any birds or eggs remained. The birds were gone, and the holes infested by hairy, vicious spiders, larger than Fu Xi's hand.

The demigod chuckled. *At least the spiders are dry.*

***

He stood alone in the garden of stone, beneath a sharp blue autumn sky, frost glittering like shattered glass at his feet. Head down, the boy silently cried between his father's freshly turned grave and his mother's overgrown plot.

"His name is Tiejiang, son of the deceased smithy," I said. "The Holy Mother arranged for him to live with his aunt."

"This is not acceptable," Mother said.

I frowned at the unexpected intervention of the Goddess in village affairs

"The child may have no father or mother, but my people have no blacksmith. He is the blacksmith's son."

"What do you intend, Mother?"

"I intend to send you on a quest."

"A quest? Am I to bring a smithy from the outreaches of Cin to Nushen? A stranger hasn't entered the purity of your abode in a thousand years." I searched my memory for the closest village with a blacksmith. It would be at least a two month journey.

"No, my child. Your quest shall be to Nushen itself. Go to Tiejiang and raise him until he is a man. Teach him the art of iron and bronze as you did to the Tall Men in ancient days. Until that time do not return to my mountain realm."

"You want me to dwell in Nushen, to live as one of them?"

"Dwell, yes; as one of them, no. His father's hut is now yours until Tiejiang is promised to a wife. On that day, you may return to my realm."

The Chronicle of Fu Xi

75

***

His trousers and shirt stuck to him like a second skin. Mud caked his legs and boots. He had put his oilskins to better use protecting the precious supplies on Heise's back.

Fu Xi looked up into the turbulent sky and let the cold rain spray his face and rush down his throat.

Finding water is not a concern.

He lowered his head and considered his horse with a mock scowl. "The things I do for you! You are more trouble than a woman."

Heise silently nuzzled his back, and Fu Xi stroked his snout in return, trying not to notice how little rock remained between Heise's hooves and the edge of the narrow path.

"Did they also teach you how to be a mountain goat in the stables of Wu? Perhaps your mother was a goat."

Fu Xi shook his head and gently tugged on the reins.

For many days they trod the spine of the world, occasionally straddling the very tops of the mountains. Denuded of glacial raiment, the peaks lay exposed, naked and jagged like dragon's teeth. Sometimes they found themselves blocked by granite walls, lightning exploding around them in a battle between earth and heaven. More than once impenetrable terrain forced Fu Xi to double back until he located a new path. Sometimes, these pathways dipped precariously in elevation to the tree line, just above the boiling, flooded valley. Each time they descended Fu Xi discovered the water higher than before. The mist never lightened enough for Fu Xi to glimpse the opposite side of the valley.

Will I come to land's end, unable to advance, unable to go back?

Carefully placing one foot in front of the other like a cat, Fu Xi picked his way down the path as it slowly descended. The roar from below steadily increased as the trail curved around the cliff face. Scrubby trees appeared out of the mist above and below them, misshapen sentinels clinging with gnarled roots to bare rock.

"If this trail does not ascend, we may have a slight problem," Fu Xi remarked. Heise could not turn around on this narrow path. If the trail wound all the way down to the water, the horse, and perhaps, even Fu Xi were doomed.

"Don't expect me to carry you!" Fu Xi huffed.

The trail steepened further and followed the cliff to the right, beyond his sight. He mentally drew a line through the mist from their present position to where he estimated the trail met the raging flood waters, still hidden from sight.

One hundred, perhaps two hundred yards before we encounter the torrent. His only hope, buoyed by the appearance of the trees, was the trail might widen below and at least afford them the opportunity to turn around.

Crack.

Fu Xi heard Heise's hoof slip before actually feeling the reins snap tight. The alarming heaviness of the sound, the surrender of the stallion's weight to the precipice, triggered the demigod's instincts. He spun about, and threw his back flat against the jagged rock, bracing his heels against the ledge. Time seemed to crawl as the horse's back haunches vanished over the cliff, Heise's head craning forward as his front legs paddled furiously for footing.

***

"Mother, this is perhaps the most unusual quest you've ever charged me with," I said playfully, truly intrigued. "Should I beg to ask the Goddess why?"

She didn't take her gaze off the boy. "A village without a forge, is a village without a heart. It will soon grow cold and die," she said. "I will instruct the Holy Mother to provide you anything you need. Should you ever require me, come to the edge of the forest at sunset."

"You banish me to Nushen for fifteen years so the village can have a blacksmith? I doubt this is your only reason."

"From the time mortals can walk, to the day they lie down to die, their existence is defined by the choices they make. Gods are only afforded two choices: rule or serve.

Now, go to him."

Elated with my task, I stepped from the shadows, eager to begin my exile with my new charge.

Mother touched my arm. "At no time shall you call him Son, nor shall he speak of you as Father. This is my command."

For fifteen years I lived in pleasant exile in Nushen, never once climbing the mountain to my mother's realm. I raised Tiejiang as a son, but never did either of us disobey Mother's command. Occasionally, he called me Lord Fu Xi, but more often addressed me as "Honored Teacher." I simply referred to him as "Honored Student."

The Chronicle of Fu Xi

***

In a blur, Fu Xi wrapped the reins several times around his right arm. Instinctively, he shot his full left arm into the nearest nest hole and braced for the shock of eight hundred pounds of horse slipping over the cliff.

The reins snapped and sliced into his arm. Heise's neck stretched, and the beast's eyes bulged in panic. The God of Names arched backward and slammed his shoulders against the rock. Biceps and neck muscles bunched into corded iron bands, sinews and tendons strained to the breaking point.

Rainwater poured unimpeded over Fu Xi's face and into his eyes, blurring his vision.

The horse's front legs hooked over the thin ledge as his back legs pedaled wildly against the cliff face with a loud mix of scraping and clopping.

The reins began to stretch. Fashioned from the finest leather in faraway Wu, they were strong but never designed to support a horse's full weight.

Fu Xi's left hand found a strong grip inside the nest hole, but with no room to back up, the ledge's narrowness prevented him from gaining further leverage. If he released his grip and tried to pull the horse down the trail, he'd lose his footing, and both of them would tumble over the precipice.

The reins cut deep into Fu Xi's right arm. Blood oozed from the gashes only to be washed away. His immortal flesh continuously healed itself, and to his horror, skin began to seal over the straps, enclosing the leather within his flesh. Every time the horse struggled, the reins tore and sliced from within, slowly sawing toward the bone.

Something brushed against his left hand. Course hair and segmented legs probed his arm, then another, and another. Fu Xi steeled himself for what would inevitably follow.

In rapid succession unseen spiders attacked the length of his left arm, fangs sinking deep like jagged icicles. He clenched his eyes even tighter as venom raced into his veins.

Fu Xi knew the spiders could not kill him, but that didn't make it hurt any less. His blood battled the venom, slowing its march to his heart. The pace of the bites began to slow, but not before his arm grew numb.

Fu Xi's legs started trembling.

The horse hung absurdly over the precipice like a cat. Heise's head craned forward, almost reaching Fu Xi's trembling knees. If Fu Xi had the presence of mind, he might have found it all amusing.

He spoke in short, halting sentences, trying to focus against the agony, "As much as I...understand your need for...a rest,...I must...insist...we resume our trek down the trail....I'm being stretched, sliced and eaten...at the same time."

Heise only stared at him with the same, terrified bulging eyes.

***

The autumn equinox found Tiejiang a young man and engaged to the beautiful daughter of a sonless farmer. By the ruddy light of an engorged moon I returned to Mother's Realm, my quest completed. I did not return until the following spring equinox, the day of my Honored Student's wedding.

After a night of feasting and strong wine, I desired quiet and solitude to put the events of the last fifteen years in perspective; though I did not wish to return to sterility of Tortoise Mountain.

Instead, jug of wine in hand, I wandered the lush fields at the edge of the forest. I did not find solitude, but instead the company of a former acolyte of Nuwa.

In a season of white smoke, she would have been favored by the goddess herself, of that I have no doubt. That fate passed her by, and the prior spring she removed her white robes and became eligible to take a husband. Every name of every acolyte of Nuwa stretching to the dawn of Nushen is etched in my mind. But, as if a spell dimmed my mind, hers is not. Gods do not forget, but for reasons I still cannot fathom, the young woman's name eludes me to this very day. Eyes deep and warm, cheekbones smooth and high with skin like the lightest of honey, her image is crystal in my inner eye.

Laughter drifted across moonlit pasture from the distant wedding celebration as she sought me out and offered her body. I took it. Buried deep in a hay stack's warm embrace, we gave each other a night of gentle pleasure.

I've loved countless mortal women before and since, but for a night the farm girl from Nushen made me forget I was a god. For a tiny sliver of night, I was not alone.

Perhaps her precious gift was instead a spell, and all spells come with a price. Maybe the memory of her name was that price, perhaps I will never truly know.

The Chronicle of Fu Xi

***

Fu Xi took as deep a breath as he could, sternum burning as ribs stretched to the bursting point. "I cannot...pull you up...by myself. You must...help me."

The horse didn't budge.

"I know you are...afraid," Fu Xi whispered. "But I cannot... let...you...die."

The horse eyes began to turn bloodshot under the strain. Both god and beast rapidly approached their breaking points.

Fu Xi knew if he failed they were both dead. The demigod willed his numb left arm to grip the rock, and pulled with all his strength with his right. The reins sank deeper until they met bone and could go no further. Agony like a thousand fires rippled through his core. Fu Xi screamed as the reins melded to his bone, adding his strength to the leather's.

Still, the horse didn't budge.

"Pull yourself up...damn you!" He shouted.

Heise stretched forward an inch. Fu Xi took up the slack, and the horse inched forward again. Now the horse's head pressed against Fu Xi's belly, gouts of hot breath caressing his abdomen.

He will not be able to turn! Panic gripped Fu Xi. The ledge was too narrow, the horse too big, and Fu Xi blocked the way.

He pulled again, though this time with diminished strength. Heise's front hoof slammed down on his foot, taking Fu Xi to new levels of pain.

Still, the demigod pulled.

"Damn you! You can't die...," Fu Xi heaved again. "...I haven't..." *Pull!* "...Even..." *Pull!* "...Properly..." "...Named..." *Pull!* "...You..." *Pull!* "...Yet!"

A back right hoof found level rock. The horse bolted upward and slid right, slamming Fu Xi against the cliff.

And that's where the horse halted, head down and shaking violently.

Fu Xi's trembling rivaled the horse's, his muscles shouting in relief.

Now, how am I going to get out of this?

Fu Xi knew the horse couldn't back up, so he'd have to slide down and ingloriously crawl from between the horse's legs. The reins, now fused with his arm, made this plan somewhat problematic.

He'd have to cut the reins and pull them from his flesh. To do that, he'd needed his left arm.

If the spiders still feasted on his arm, he couldn't feel it, the venom completely rendering the limb numb. He tugged, but his arm didn't budge. He pulled again with the same result.

It's swollen inside the hole.

Fu Xi took a deep breath and braced himself again. He slid down on one knee below the horse's belly, all the while pulling his left arm. He sensed, but could not feel, ragged stone scraping away skin, taking gouges of flesh with it.

His arm broke free with a gush of blood and pus-filled fluid.

Several flattened spiders, each the size of a small squirrel, flopped onto the ledge, hairy legs pulled tightly against their abdomen. Fu Xi hoped they had suffered and brushed them over the ledge.

He slid fully underneath the horse, left arm dangling, sleeve torn and bloody. Skin hung in tattered sheets. He extended the limb from under the horse and let the downpour wash it clean. Before his eyes, damaged skin fell away, and the flesh began to knit together and heal. The residual venom kept him from feeling too much pain. Part of him wished the spiders had bitten his right hand, too.

***

As we slept in each other's embrace, a chilly sunrise crept into our hiding place. Dawn's faint caress lightly probed the haystack, reminding us of our true places in the world and slowly picking away the spell's fragile weave.

Without opening her eyes, she smiled broadly and snuggled against me. I lightly brushed her thigh, marveling at her smooth, soft skin. My hand found its way to her stomach where I playfully traced circles around her belly button.

What would it be like to put a child there and know it was mine? What would it be like to wake up to this beautiful woman every morning, to know my children sleep in the next room, to see her age, and my sons grow?

My Honored Student would know all these joys. I knew across the village he lay next to his bride and likely had already planted a seed in her womb.

I rolled onto my back, relishing the prickly hay against my back and the satin of her thighs over my stomach. I pulled her onto me and let her rich black hair spill over my face. She stretched and smiled as my hands explored her hips, eager to love her again.

The Chronicle of Fu Xi

***

Locked in spasms of agony, Fu Xi could not unclench his fist from around the reins. As feeling began to return to his left hand, he tried to pry his right hand open. He winced and peeled the leather from his right index finger's skin. He shuddered as he beheld his open palm.

The reins emerged from a bruised mound in his palm. The mound, mottled and purplish, encircled his wrist, then wrapped around his arm like a vine until the reins reemerged just below his elbow. He tore away the remaining cotton material from his sleeve and fully exposed his right arm. Sharp, painful tingling rippled up and down his right arm in contrast to the dull throbbing ache engulfing his left arm. While one limb healed, the other fought to reject the infiltrating foreign body.

Fumbling, he gripped the reins just below his right palm. Shielded beneath the horse from most of the rain, his breath came in misty clouds and joined the steam rising off Heise's shivering flanks.

He reached up with his left arm and patted the horse's belly.

"If you piss on me, I'm going to throw you off the cliff myself."

Heise whinnied, his shivering slowly subsiding.

"Listen carefully. I am going to scream, old friend. Don't be frightened, do not run. It will be over quickly, and we will be on our way. Maybe there is a cave around the bend, and I can start a fire, and we can warm ourselves."

Fu Xi took a deep breath, wrapped the reins once around his left arm and steeled himself...

...then yanked.

Fu Xi's scream echoed off unseen canyon walls before being swallowed by the downpour. The agony burned deep into his bone, but the reins did not budge.

The leather is fused to my bone.

He would not be able to pull them straight out at the palm. That left only one choice.

Without hesitation and with the determination of a god, Fu Xi yanked the reins upward, ripping them from skin and tissue. The leather emerged from his arm with a wet, tearing sound. His stomach heaved at the unnatural, bone searing pain.

And then it ended.

His head pressed against cold rock, Fu Xi held the bloody reins like a perverse afterbirth. Heise craned his head underneath his belly and nudged Fu Xi as a mare might nudge of newborn foal. The demigod's breath came in big gulps as the pain subsided. The deep, ripping gash encircling his right arm began to stitch itself closed. He extended both arms over the ledge into the downpour and let the water wash away the remaining blood and tissue from his flesh and leather straps. In a matter of minutes only clean, unbroken flesh remained. The only remaining scars seared deep into Fu Xi's memory.

Gods do not forget.

Fu Xi crawled out from under the horse. He cradled the steed's head and gently stroked its nose.

"All is well, but watch your step, old friend. I don't think I can do that again."

The horse's trembling finally stopped.

Fu Xi tied the straps to the reins as best he could.

They will have to do until I can fashion new ones.

He grasped the reins below the knots and turned back down the trail.

Horse and god vanished into the rain.

***

Silhouetted against a fresh born blue sky, the sunlight finally found her. She opened her eyes and gazed down upon me. The lingering tenderness evaporated, replaced by reverence.

The spell broken, the woman saw the god, and the god saw the mortal.

She lowered her eyes and crossed her arms over her breasts. "It is my sincerest wish I have pleased you, great Lord Fu Xi."

To sleep with a god came with divine blessing. Now I had a duty to fulfill. I touched her belly lightly and repeated the blessing I'd uttered countless other mornings across the land of Cin.

"You have pleased me, and in return, your womb is blessed by the Goddess Nuwa herself. You will marry well. Your husband will cherish you, and you shall bear him many children, many boys. Daughter of Nuwa, you will never know loneliness, even unto the end of your days."

Joyful tears filled her eyes. "Thank you, Lord Fu Xi! Thank you!"

I snatched her back down to me, my lips eagerly seeking hers. I wasn't ready for the magic to end. The god could wait; I needed a few more moments as a man.

"Great Lord Fu Xi, are you going to roll around all morning in the hay with my cousin, or are you going to come out here and eat?" A voice called from beyond the hay.

I pushed her up. "You are Tiejiang's cousin?"

She nodded innocently, lips pursed trying to suppress a smile. "First cousins, Lord Fu Xi."

I sighed and sank back into the hay. All in Nushen were related in some manner, but I tried not to bed those closely related to Tiejiang or Nuwa's current husband.

I gently slapped her on the thigh. "Get up. Get dressed. Go home."

She cloaked herself in the cotton robe she wore to last night's wedding and slid out of the haystack. Elated, she ran home filled with the divine blessing and glowing after a night with a god.

From beyond the haystack I detected the scent of fresh bread and rice. With a growling belly, I slipped on the ceremonial robes I wore the last night.

The rooster crowed, announcing another dawn in my endless life.

The Chronicle of Fu Xi

9. Flotilla

"Demons in the water. Demons among us. The God of the Narim gave me sight only to recognize that which slithered in the deep. My poor, beloved Atamoda could see both." – Conversations with the Uros.

The Chronicle of Fu Xi

***

Ice enveloped Atamoda's arm. She snapped out of her stupor and yanked her arm from the water. She shook it as if it had been bitten, wiping the moisture off on her winter tunic. Atamoda bolted upright in bleary-eyed panic, unsure how she ended up in the bottom of this boat.

It is dawn.

She quickly looked about, trying to get her bearings.

I fell asleep!

Horrible reality washed over her like the cold flood smothering the world. Atamoda's arms sagged under the realization that she'd passed out.

How long?

She peered into the water, afraid of what she would see. Nothing stirred. She leaned over and sniffed the water, testing to see if it carried the now familiar scent that accompanied a demonic attack.

When the demons swarmed, the water released a faint, but noxious odor. Acrid and coppery, she could only describe it as a mix of blood and vomit.

The demons turn the water to venom with their very presence.

Water, her people's nourishing life force, became their enemy.

No foul reek wafted from the flat surface this morning, but Atamoda took no comfort. The demons withdrew with the dawn, as they had on the previous mornings. She knew the danger abated only temporarily.

Atamoda squinted against the dull sunlight filtering through the overcast. The light hurt her eyes, but was welcome nevertheless. The heavenly curtain which descended in the wake of the thundering star seemed thicker this morning, robbing the dawn of color and washing the world in a lifeless gray. Atamoda felt as washed out as the sky, as cold as the sea.

She fingered her chest, searching for her missing li-gi.

Aizarg, where are you?

Far across the water only a few remaining tree tops poked above the water, the last vestiges of the marshy coast. Beyond them, the sea stretched endlessly north, occasionally dotted by floating chunks of ice. She scanned the horizon, hoping to see Aizarg, somehow, some way, sailing toward them.

A dark, little voice hissed in her mind. *Where would he get a boat?* She quickly pushed it aside. Doubt tried to strip away her hope, to expose her, naked and defenseless, before remorseless fate.

Setenay is with him. They are alright. She railed against the madness. She had to believe it. If she didn't, madness as deep as the water beneath the flotilla would claim her.

Her arms burned, her shoulders ached. In an attempt to stretch her legs, Atamoda shifted in the bottom of the boat, careful not to disturb Su-gar lying asleep at the other end of the small reed boat. Little Ba-tor cuddled between the young woman's legs like a newborn. Seeing them helped calm her nerves.

Atamoda needed sleep, too. Days of relentless demonic onslaught weakened her defenses. But, at least for now, the demons were quiet.

She turned right and looked south. Like a forest in the dead of winter, naked masts and rigging filled her vision. She hoped to see her oldest child, Kol-ok, approaching across the lashed decks that formed the floating island. Across the Lo flotilla, blanket-covered mounds crowded the decks where families huddled for warmth. Weary eyes, shrouded in misty breath, peered out from beneath the blankets.

The men cower with the women and children. Atamoda knew it wasn't from cowardice, but from the realization they could do nothing to protect the flotilla.

Spears meant nothing against the enemy which tormented the remnants of the Minnow and Crane Clans. Only two women stood between the festering schools of demons and what remained of the Lo nation.

Here we are on the crest of our doom, the curse Setenay foresaw.

Su-gar groaned as if in pain, stirred and shook her head.

She's still fighting the demons in her sleep.

Neither of Su-gar's parents was known for their physical beauty. However, something about the combination of Ula and Ood-i, created a striking beauty in their daughter. Thick, black, and slightly frizzy hair framed a pleasingly round face. Her deep brown eyes, framed with lush eyelashes, topped generously pouting lips. Her pale, unblemished skin and ample bosom completed a young woman sought by men from across the Lo Nation.

Now Su-gar mourned. Her father accompanied Aizarg on his quest, trying to turn back the wrath of a nameless god and save the world. Her mother, Ula, fell to the demons the first day of the flood.

Su-gar stretched and bumped against Ba-tor between her legs. Her eyes flew open and darted about.

"Mother!" Su-gar screamed and shot upright in the boat. "Demons! Demons in the water!"

"Shhh!" Atamoda leaned over and stroked her hair. The girl's deep, soulful eyes made Atamoda's heart ache. "We fell asleep. It is dawn. The demons are quiet for now."

"I am sorry, Atamoda. I did not mean to fall asleep!"

"You could not help it. Neither could I. Fortunately, the enemy did not strike. Dawn appears to halt their torments, at least for a little while."

"Xva has not returned?" Su-gar arched slightly higher, peering out over the flotilla. She swallowed hard, voice cracking. "Did we lose any more last night?"

"I don't know," Atamoda whispered.

Su-gar adjusted her sitting position, trying to get comfortable, while doing her best not to disturb Bat-or.

Atamoda insisted Ba-tor stay by her side and not with the rest of the children huddled in the center of the flotilla. She wanted her little one close to her, nearest the source of her protective magic. With Aizarg gone and Kol-ok helping Xva protect the flotilla, Atamoda needed reassurance. She needed her baby boy next to her.

"Get some sleep, Atamoda. If the demons return, I will wake you."

Atamoda did not hear her, her mind wandering over the terrible events since that day Ula died.

Kus-ge and boats from the Minnow Clan had arrived shortly before dawn the day after the marshes vanished under the flood. Enormous islands of ice, borne by the deluge, plowed under their arun-ki. Kus-ge led the survivors on rafts and boats to the Crane Clan.

They found Atamoda and her people already in boats and rafts, tied off to the submerged köy-lo-hely, the meeting platform in the center of their arun-ki. The slithering demons began to assemble in greater numbers, but had yet to attack the boats and rafts. The Minnow Clan and Crane Clans quickly lashed their boats and rafts together, creating a flotilla of nearly one hundred vessels carrying over two hundred people. That was as far as their unity progressed.

With their sco-lo-ti gone on the quest, discord immediately descended on the two clans. Many of the Minnow's men and elders were killed under the ice floes. After Atta's death, the Crane naturally fell under Xva's leadership, but Kus-ge stubbornly refused to acknowledge it. The two patesi-le stood face to face in the center of the flotilla, the fate of their people resting in their hands.

Kus-ge adamantly argued they continue west along the vanishing coast looking for survivors from other clans, or perhaps even sailing east to seek the shelter of the distant Adyghe Mountains. Xva and Atamoda told the assembled people the coast would likely soon vanish under the floodwaters and they would become hopelessly lost in the powerful current. If they allowed themselves to be swept to sea, the Uros may never find them, and death would surely be their reward. As the sun rose, so did the heated words.

And then the fireball cut the sky in two.

As if waiting for the fiery signal, the demons rose in force from the depths. A black slick of ice and hate encircled the flotilla, ripping boats' hulls and dragging screaming victims into the depths. Men hurled spears into the water with no effect. Women grabbed children and fled to the center of the flotilla.

The two patesi-le formed a hasty strategy to employ ancient warding magic passed down to both of them by Setenay. Atamoda took the northern flank where the ropes secured the floating island to the submerged köy-lo-hely. Kus-ge positioned herself on the southern end of the flotilla. Atamoda's and Kus-ge's combined magic protected most of the flotilla from the unrelenting demonic attacks, but only if they focused all their attention on the warding chants. Any time either one of them lost concentration, the demons swirled in and claimed another boat, another victim.

Atamoda hadn't left her boat or talked to Kus-ge since the assault began. Her world shrank to the stretch of water immediately in front of her. Her only news of her people was carried to her by Xva, who wandered the flotilla and tried to keep order.

Most of the time the demons turned away, but sometimes they didn't. While the majority of boats were lost during the nights, some were snatched when Atamoda tried to eat or drink or even relieve herself, deepening her sense of guilt. Between the horrible screams of her people being dragged to their doom, and the constant crackling of the demon ice, Atamoda's sanity began to slip away.

The demons sensed Atamoda's exhaustion, and took delight in tormenting her. In her heart, she knew the demons could take them anytime. The flotilla became their plaything, something to be toyed with until they found other sport. Knowing the demons would take Kol-ok and Bat-or if she failed, kept her fighting.

During the long, terrible nights, the patesi-le blindly chanted into the starless void, arms extended, for hour after grueling hour. The crackling of ice and occasional scream painfully reminded Atamoda that her magic was too weak to protect everyone.

The demons relented briefly at dawn. That's when Xva returned to their boat bearing the grim tally of the dead and number of boats lost.

Now Atamoda scanned the surrounding boats, searching the weary faces of her tribesmen for Xva. A gnawing fear burned through the numbness in her spirit.

"Get some sleep, Atamoda," Su-gar repeated.

"I will, when Xva and Kol-ok return,"

"What if they don't come back?" Su-gar fretted.

"They will!" Atamoda snapped. "They will! And so will my husband!"

Su-gar shrank back. "I am sorry."

Tears welling, Atamoda shook her head and waved her hand. Pressing fingers against eyelids, she willed the emotion and despair back into the dark recesses.

How many are already dead? The voice in her mind whispered again.

She took several deep breaths and opened her eyes as control returned.

"He will return, and so will Aizarg. I know this," Atamoda said. "Xva must also attend to Sahti." Xva's pregnant young wife, helped care for the children in the center of the flotilla.

Since Atta's death at the hands of the demons, young Xva stepped into the role as leader of the arun-ki, a role surprisingly unchallenged by the older men. Perhaps it was the trust Atta once placed in the young man, or the overwhelming fear generated by the demons. Perhaps it was the hard look in Xva's eyes since Atamoda pulled him from the demons' clutches. Something in the young man's spirit demanded others follow. For that, Atamoda was thankful.

As if in answer to a prayer, Xva and Kol-ok stumbled from beyond the huddled mounds and collapsed into the boat between Atamoda and Su-gar. Atamoda threw her arms around Kol-ok's neck.

Xva laid his spear across the bottom of the boat, closed his eyes, and drew a deep breath. Sugar leaned over and handed him a water skin and a piece of dried fish. Xva inhaled the food and gulped down the water.

Xva looked years older. His long sandy hair fell lank over his brow, obscuring what were once piercing hazel eyes. Dark shadows below his eyes mirrored the sky.

"How are you holding up?" he asked Atamoda.

"I fight until the Uros returns." It was the only answer she could give without breaking down again. "What of the flotilla?"

"With first light I tallied seventy-three boats and rafts."

Su-gar gasped and pulled sleeping Ba-tor protectively to her bosom.

"How many of us remain?" Atamoda whispered.

"Eighty-five."

Atamoda turned away, overwhelmed by a staggering sense of failure.

"The children?" she finally found the courage to ask.

"Safe on the center rafts. We lost only men last night; Minnow Clan mostly, from the southern flank. The demons ravaged the outer boats until almost dawn. Without your magic, patesi-le, all would be lost..." Xva opened his mouth to say something else, but held back. Atamoda saw fear behind his exhausted expression.

"What is it you fear to say?" Atamoda demanded. "Why only the Minnow Clan? Tell me."

"Kus-ge collapsed before dawn. We cannot revive her. Her magic no longer shields our people."

Atamoda slumped down into the boat.

Sleep. I just want to sleep.

She caught a faint odor wafting from the north.

Venom.

Xva sat up and looked about. He pressed his hand against the bottom of the boat. "Did you feel that?"

Atamoda's heart sank.

Kol-ok looked over the side where the ropes anchored the flotilla to the Köy-lo-hely.

"They're gnawing the ropes again."

10. Giant Rising

Wise men will one day dismiss those dark days as myth. Such things could never be, they will say. Their doubt will be understandable. When the inevitable Age of Disbelief comes to pass, I will not condemn mortals for their ignorance.

I will rejoice in it.

The Chronicle of Fu Xi

***

The day wore on and so did the wailing from the masses packed on Hur-ar's rooftops.

The water, choked with all manner of debris, relentlessly inched up walls and turned the streets into muddy rivers and the Grand Market into a lake.

The King and his court surveyed the disaster from the palace balconies. The last regent of the City of Gold ran from one edge of the lush rooftop gardens to the other, staring in disbelief at his forsaken city.

Black claws yanked under all who swam or waded through the muck. Those who tried to row through the streets on makeshift rafts fashioned from doors and tables capsized and vanished.

On a few rooftops, warriors tried to establish some semblance of order. In most places, however, the strongest preyed on the weak, as the city spasmed in its final moments of life.

Yet, even in Hur-ar the last bright sparks of love glowed brightly. In isolated pockets, husbands reassured wives, mothers comforted children, and lovers embraced against the coming doom. Beggars and feral children, the forgotten of Hur-ar, clung to high stairwells. Some succumbed to the black claws, while merciful hands pulled others up to their last refuge.

Along the city's edges the strongest struggled to scale the cliffs which, for centuries, shielded the City of Gold. Now those cliffs formed prison walls, confining the damned to their tomb. Above it all, the Black Fortress stood impassively, offering neither judgment nor hope.

The survivors felt the glacial wave before they saw it. A bass pulse throbbed through the mountains, felt more in the bones than with the ears. Rocks jiggled loose and tumbled down the cliffs, hurling the climbers to their deaths. The vibration strengthened to tremors and tremors swelled to a roar. The roar transformed into a shock wave ripping the roots of the earth from their foundations.

All of Hur-ar turned west and witnessed the end of all things. Beyond the city parapets and newly formed Black Sea, a sinister line piled above the horizon. It thickened into a wall and merged with the clouds. A sudden blast of cold wind swept the city as if the atmosphere fled in terror.

The Hur-po spent their last moments in astonishment, possessing no context for what they now witnessed. The world to the west became blackness and simply ceased to exist. For those brave enough to gaze upon it, details of the approaching mile-high wave became discernible in the last seconds. The impossibly black water carried in its vertical face the shattered remains of a scoured continent.

The glacial wave slammed against the face of the Adyghe Mountains, instantly flattening millions of acres of forest, before exploding into the canyon.

In seconds, filthy, boiling froth piled against the Cliff Road and transformed Hur Canyon into a lagoon. Beyond the lagoon's mouth, the glacial wave rampaged south, a ravenous beast flattening, shredding, and submerging anything in its path. Inside the lagoon, the water rose and swirled about, robbed of much of its energy.

Hur-ar vanished under tons of debris and mud, eternally lost to history.

Water, the enemy for which the Black Wall had been truly built, climbed higher and higher up the Cliff Road until it sloshed against the outer gate. The bronze bell clunked dully in the current before falling silent forever. The flood pressed against the outer gate's pitch-sealed kupar logs. Reinforced by a massive interior ramp constructed from layers of Lo reed bags filled with sand, the wall didn't budge under the intense pressure. Only a trickle penetrated into the holding area between the gates. Tamed by the Black Wall, the flood slowly filled the holding area between the gates. Finally, it crested the inner gate as a gentle waterfall and streamed into the Black Fortress. Repelled by an unseen force, no water demons slipped over the wall into the compound.

The Black Wall transformed into a dam, the double gates into a lock. The Black Fortress bent the floodwater to the will of the Nameless God.

A tranquil pool rose around the silent, sealed Ark. The morning's cooking fire hissed into extinction. Water filled Noah's stone cottage and covered the wooden supports beneath the Ark. As the water crept up, weight shifted until the Ark's side boards creaked and popped.

Almost imperceptibly, the giant rose.

Borne on the shoulders of the Deluge, the Ark floated higher and higher until the Black Wall itself vanished under the waves. Without so much as bumping the canyon walls, the giant drifted into the lagoon. With seven slow, lazy spins, the Ark passed beyond the two islands that were once the tops of the canyon walls, to join the Black Sea. The current snatched the Ark and carried it swiftly south to its fate.

Ahead, the clouds thickened.

11. Demon Dawn

In the time before my immortal body attained manhood, Mother led me deep into the evergreen forest beyond the Lotus Bridge. On a gray winter day we ventured beyond her domain. After many hours wandering the fern-carpeted eternal twilight, Mother took my hand. Ahead of us sinister growls echoed among ancient the ancient forest, as burly shadows darted beyond the trees.

She casually spoke, as if we strolled through Nushen's market, "Do not be afraid. As long as you hold my hand, you are hidden from all harm."

We emerged into a bright clearing where a pack of gray wolves cornered a doe and her fawn. They paid us no mind, though we stood in plain view at the edge of the forest.

Instinctively I pulled away, but she held me there, her face impassively locked on the unfolding drama.

The doe's wide, unblinking eyes are forever burned in my memory. Pinned against a cliff, she shielded the trembling fawn behind her. Ragged wounds painted her fur crimson. She darted about, striking out with her front hooves. The doe still possessed the strength to run, but she held her ground, prepared to give her life for her offspring.

The pack could have taken them both at any time, but they seemed to take pleasure in tormenting the doe. My stomach knotted at the inevitable outcome.

The wolves withdrew and began to circle in unison, preparing for the final assault. Their almost sexual excitement permeated the clearing like the prickling heat before a thunderstorm. On some unheard signal from the pack leader, the hunters plunged inward like a bolt of lightning.

Guttural, wet, ripping echoes haunted our footsteps as we slipped away.

"Why did you bring me to see this?" I asked.

"To witness the power of a mother's love, and to know evil lives in all things, not just man."

The Chronicle of Fu Xi

***

Atamoda focused to her right, where four heavy ropes anchored the flotilla to the submerged köy-lo-hely. The current streamlined the flotilla toward the south and out to sea. One of the lines vibrated heavily, like a fishing line with a carp just starting to nibble the bait. A moment later it popped, went limp, and floated to the surface. If the demons cut the remaining lines the flotilla would quickly drift to sea...

...and away from Aizarg. He will never find us.

Rage exploded in Atamoda's heart, reinvigorating her will.

"Damn you, hideous spawn of heli-dar!" She shouted. The patesi-le waved her arms over the water and uttered the ancient warding chant taught to her by Setenay all those years ago; a chant she'd almost forgotten, a chant she'd thought she'd never need.

Like falling leaves, the submerged shadows drifted away, but not before another line fell limp. The demons lazily fluttered about until they gathered about two dozen yards from the flotilla. There, they massed.

The reek of venom became overpowering as the surface flattened into an oily sheen. The water seemed to thicken before it hardened into ice. This time, it wasn't the usual thin crust which often formed wherever the demons swam. Instead, it formed a thick, icy callous that warped the water to their will.

"What are they doing?" Su-gar whispered.

"Massing," Xva said as he grasped his spear and stood in the boat. He turned to the flotilla and shouted. "Here they come!"

Screams rippled through the flotilla.

Tears welled in Su-gar's eyes. Ba-tor woke up and began to cry. Su-gar pulled the little boy closer and reached out to encircle Kol-ok's neck, but he gently pulled away.

Su-gar reached out again, but the boy picked up his makeshift spear; the same crude stick he carried everywhere since Aizarg departed on the quest. He considered the demons and then turned to Su-gar.

"I am the son of a sco-lo-ti, son of the Uros."

"You know that spear will do no good!" she cried as the building fear finally overwhelmed her.

"I know," Kol-ok replied.

At that moment Atamoda saw Aizarg standing upon the köy-lo-hely, defiantly shouting *No!* into the darkness.

Before I perish, I see my husband's spirit dwelling in my son.

Through her pain and exhaustion Atamoda smiled. Pride and love flooded the spaces in her heart hollowed by despair.

Kol-ok met his mother's eyes and smiled tenderly. He leaned over and kissed Atamoda on the forehead. He then straightened, hefted his spear, and turned to Xva.

Xva merely nodded as an unspoken understanding passed between the boy and the man.

"Men to the perimeter!" Xva shouted. "Women and children to this side of the flotilla, where Atamoda can protect them!"

A sense of doom and determination simultaneously gripped the remnants of the Lo nation. Spears clattered and bristled as men dashed from boat to boat towards the perimeter. The last few days had taught that the Lo spears were useless against the demons, but, like Kol-ok, they prepared to fight nevertheless.

Atamoda's boat rocked back and forth from the activity on the flotilla behind her. The waves slowly rippled outward toward the ring of ice. Despite the rocking, Xva and Kol-ok stood tall, spears cocked at the ready, in the center of the boat.

Su-gar clutched Bat-or tightly and pressed herself all the way to the stern, while Atamoda knelt over the bow.

One woman stood between the Lo and annihilation.

The patesi-le shook her arms vigorously and prepared to begin her chants anew. Without Kus-ge she could not protect the entire flotilla. She knew that those on the other side would surely die. As she watched the building ice only a few yards away, she doubted she could protect any of them for very long.

The demons massed under the ice like fish gathering under a dock. Now there were thousands of them, perhaps tens of thousands. They twisted, slithered, and intertwined in a knotted frenzy, as if waiting for a signal to plunge inward. Pulled along by the demonic undercurrent, the noose of ice groaned and began to rotate.

They are gathering power.

Atamoda began her chant, slowly at first and then faster, with more inflection. Grim resolve reinforced her will.

I will not die in fear.

As if in response, cracks suddenly formed in the ice ring. Shards splintered and drifted away. Several demons shrank farther back under the rotating rim.

Atamoda suddenly remembered a sunny day so long ago, when an old patesi-le instructed a young girl on a warm dock over a friendly sea. Setenay made her recite the ancient chants over and over until they were seared into her mind.

***

"Where does a patesi-le draw her power? From Psatina?" she asked Setenay

"A patesi-le draws her power from love, child. Psatina only taught us how to channel it. Love flows from a woman's soul like warmth from the sun." Setenay lifted her face to the midday sun and closed her eyes. "The wellspring of a woman's soul is bottomless and only deepens with time. Never forget that and your magic will be limitless."

***

Atamoda's heart swelled with new confidence. Her voice and arms strengthened.

The ice sheet popped and crackled under her magic's renewed assault.

Feel my power!

"Mother!" Kol-ok gasped. "The demons falter!"

A white wisp flickering in the water immediately before her caught Atamoda's eye. Her cadence faltered, and her arms sagged as the drifting object drew her attention. At first she thought the demons had snapped another rope, its frayed end billowing in the current. She lowered her face and peered down, drawn to the sharpening image, as everything around her faded.

***

Atamoda paused her chanting to readjust her legs, which began to ache against the rough dock. She looked back at Setenay, lounging against her father's upturned boat, eyes closed and sunning herself on the dock

"Old Mother, is there anything as strong as love?" she asked.

A cloud passed over the sun and cast a shadow over the old patesi-le's face. The old woman opened her eyes and let her gaze wandered off to the water. A chilly, unexpected breeze swept off the sea.

"Fear," Setenay whispered.

***

A clawed fist clenched a knot of waving, gray hair. It thrust the lifeless head toward the surface. The corpse's hair billowed back like seaweed.

Setenay's dead eyes stared back at Atamoda.

Atamoda shrieked and collapsed backwards into the boat. The demons' hissing transformed to cackling. They lunged en mass toward the flotilla.

Atamoda's trembling arms finally seized in agonizing cramps as her world blurred into darkness.

Fresh screams penetrated her thoughts, accompanied by the sickening sound of ripping and tearing reeds. She felt a sudden lurch, the world shifted, and then freezing cold gripped her lower body.

"Ko-lok!" she heard Xva scream.

Warmth caressed Atamoda's cheek. It increased to raw, almost painful heat as light penetrated her close eyelids.

Did Aizarg call a council? Someone must have lit the brazier atop the Köy-lo-hely? It feels good.

Atamoda briefly cracked her eyelids to a world on fire before the water and darkness took her.

***

"Wake up."

Atamoda didn't want to obey, but the familiar voice beckoned her.

Darkness lightened to gray, and gray congealed into a ghostly image. A blurry face slowly materialized, its details stubbornly refusing to focus. She squinted, unsure if her eyes lied.

He filled her vision, eyes brimming. She reached up and tenderly explored the familiar curves of his nose, cheeks and forehead until she plunged her fingers through his hair.

His hair.

Only one logical thought occurred to the patesi-le, one explanation for what she saw.

Am I dead?

She caressed her own cheek, wanting to know if she was still made of flesh.

She knew those eyes, the same eyes which greeted her after hours of bloody labor bringing Kol-ok into this world. He wore the same expression after saving Ba-tor from nearly drowning last spring. Sweet tears and a trembling smile painted a mosaic of relief and ebbing fear across her husband's face.

The flesh and spirit are still one.

Atamoda closed her eyes, slowly wrapped her arms around his neck, and deeply inhaled his sweaty scent. With silent sobs, Aizarg tightly enveloped her. She savored each of his hot tears rolling down her shoulder and back.

From behind, little arms encircled her, soft breathing caressed her ear.

"Daddy is home, Momma! Why is your hair all white, Daddy?" Ba-tor asked, the horrors of the last few days banished in a single moment of joy.

Another set of arms hugged them as Kol-ok rested his head on Atamoda's other shoulder.

Great Mother Psatina, if I am dead, then what a blessed death this is!

And then she remembered Setenay's face in the deep.

"Aizarg!" she moaned and surrendered to racking sobs. Horror and relief clashed like the competing tides of the Black Sea.

In the bottom of a small reed boat, on the edge of a brittle flotilla of reed and wood afloat an endless sea, a family embraced.

12. Crest of Our Doom

"For virtue or sin, trial or torment,
That demon and god test mere mortal soul so?" — Amiran, Song
of Atlas

The Chronicle of Fu Xi

***

Ba-tor clung to her leg as Atamoda searched for answers.
She recovered enough strength to stand and collect her wits,
but events moved too quickly. Tendrils of smoky mist
danced on the water, carrying the venomous odor away on
the wind. The demons and ice vanished, though how, she
had no idea. She eyed the water suspiciously, unwilling to let
her guard down. Aizarg's presence didn't bring the expected
relief, only a different sense of fear.

Atamoda knew she'd never feel safe again. All illusions of
control were washed away, replaced with constant
uncertainty and a gnawing coldness in the pit of her
stomach.

They stood on one of the two wedding barges Aizarg and the quest party returned upon, now secured to the edge of the flotilla. The boat where she battled the demons lay partially submerged, one end ripped away, the other end still tied to the flotilla and filled with water. Atamoda's gaze kept returning to the shredded boat, wondering how she survived.

Aizarg surveyed the floating island as the people crowded around them in a crushing semi-circle. Frightened and exhausted faces, from both Crane and Minnow Clan, pressed in. Some cried out for news of the quest. Others asked when the flood would end, and when the fish would return. Some beseeched the Uros if they were safe from the demons. Atamoda wanted answers, too.

But before she could ask any questions, Aizarg held out his arms and raised his voice. "We will convene a Council of Boats in due time. Until such time, prepare your boats and rafts for sail. Secure your gear and make your knots strong and true." Aizarg glanced at the darkening sky. "Rough seas await us."

After days of sleepless hell, she expected the Lo to demand answers. To Atamoda's surprise, the people quieted and listened to their leader.

They share my hope. Perhaps Aizarg's return signals the end to this nightmare. Atamoda pushed back the nagging feeling this was a fool's hope.

"Above all," Aizarg said, "We must stay together. Cling to one another, hold on and do not let go. Together, we will persevere and live to see the sun again. Separated, the Great Sea..." he paused, took a breath and resumed speaking, "...this Black Sea will claim us. Now go, and do as I ask."

Black Sea?

Without a murmur, the Lo turned, quietly gathered their children, and returned to their boats. Atamoda leaned against her husband, fatigue rapidly overtaking her. His arm encircled her waist, supporting her with welcomed strength.

She turned her attention to the quest party disembarking the barges one-by-one.

Levidi stepped forward and handed Aizarg a staff encircled with a strange, beautiful red metal.

He's changed, too.

Beneath Aizarg's best friend's carefree and optimistic veneer, she detected a new hardness, as if Levidi aged a hundred years in only a week.

Haven't we all?

Levidi kissed Atamoda on the cheek and gave her a squeeze. "Alaya?" he asked breathlessly.

Atamoda smiled wearily and nodded to the heart of the flotilla. "She cares for the children aboard the center raft."

Levidi looked expectantly to his Uros.

Aizarg grinned and jerked his head toward the flotilla. "Go!"

Atamoda grasped Levidi's arm. "Take Ba-tor with you and place him with the rest of the children. I need to talk with my husband."

"Come, little man!" Levidi snatched Ba-tor under his arm and dashed across the crowded boats.

"Hurry back," Aizarg called out after him. "We have much to do."

Several men stepped off the wedding barge from behind Aizarg. They swayed across the bobbing deck in an alien manner, obviously unaccustomed to life at sea. A small, bald man with furs heaped over his shoulders, almost to the point it appeared he had no neck, approached her followed by six mountains of men with long, black hair and beards, and equally covered in furs. The small man reminded her of a marsh fox, the large men of wolves.

A-g'an.

Unconsciously, the wife of the Uros quickly straightened her hair, smoothed her tunic, and prepared to greet the guests entering her arun-ki.

The fox, sharp snouted with hungry eyes, smiled and bowed low. Atamoda remembered the demons' toothy snarls and shuddered.

Virag! All thoughts of hospitality evaporated. Though she'd never met the marsh trader, she knew enough of his reputation to recognize him.

"You must be Atamoda, Patesi-li of the Crane. I am honored and humbled."

"You brought Virag the Slaver here?" she spoke in a low voice through clenched teeth to her husband. "You brought *him* among us?"

Aizarg placed both hands atop the strange, red-metal staff. His gaze hardened on her in a way she'd never witnessed before.

My husband returns a stranger. Sadness swept over her as she battled to control her emotions.

"They *will* be welcome among us." Unfamiliar power filled his voice. He leaned in, voice finally softening to its old, familiar tone. "I will explain everything. Trust me, wife." He straightened and spoke louder. "Virag, take your men and go to the center of the flotilla. You will be safest there."

Virag nodded and spread his arms in supplication. Atamoda recoiled as the a-g'an lurched past, stumbling with each swell.

They are more helpless than children, worthless. Why did he bring them?

Okta stepped lightly off the raft, closely followed by a young man dressed in only a loin cloth. The boy walked the decks like an a'gan; his sandy hair and piercing gray eyes bespoke an unfamiliar tribe.

With a wide grin, Okta embraced Atamoda, lifted her off the deck and spun her around. "I knew it! No flood can kill the Lo." Wrung with exhaustion, Atamoda's head spun, but she steadied herself. For a moment Okta reminded her of Atta, and the sadness threatened to overwhelm her again.

Okta surveyed the flotilla. "Excellent, a floating arun-ki! How many clans?"

Atamoda looked back to Aizarg. "Minnow and Crane, but..." she began to speak of their losses.

"And the Carp?" Okta interrupted.

Atamoda shook her head.

Okta waved his hand dismissively. "No matter. I'm sure my people are afloat upon the goddess's womb, waiting for my return."

Atamoda heard doubt lurking beneath his bravado.

"I see familiar faces, Atamoda," Ba-lok stepped up. The young sco-lo-ti's bruised and battered face sparked more questions in her mind. "The Minnow are here. Where is my wife?"

She pointed south. "On the far side, among most of your arun-ki. She collapsed during the last assault, I know nothing else."

Ba-lok dashed off across the decks without another word.

"Okta, inspect all the vessels," Aizarg said. "Make sure they are securely tied to one another, but they use proper slip knots in case we need to quickly disband. Also, make sure each vessel is individually seaworthy."

Okta nodded. "If I find any improperly pitched, they'll have to be moved to the perimeter. We can't have a waterlogged boat weighing down the center."

"Agreed," Aizarg said, and then cast a worried glance over his shoulder. "Does anyone hear that?"

"I hear nothing," Okta said.

Aizarg shook his head. "I am tired, as are we all."

"And you are?" Atamoda asked the grey-eyed boy.

"I am Ezra of the Hur-po, my lady." Perhaps two years older than Kol-ok, Ezra bowed low and spoke in a strange, guttural accent.

A man's will floats upon a sea of boyhood tenderness. Empathy and instant liking filled her heart.

Aizarg placed a hand on Ezra's shoulder. "My wife, I bring you..." Aizarg clenched his eyes and struggled for control. Atamoda placed her hand over her mouth in response to his pained expression, all thoughts of her battles with the demons vanished,"...I bring you a *friend*. He saved my life." Aizarg struggled to finish.

What happened to them out there?

Without a second thought, Atamoda warmly embraced Ezra. "Thank you, Ezra of the Hur-po."

Ezra stiffly allowed Atamoda to embrace him, but looked back to Aizarg as if seeking permission.

Atamoda turned to Kol-ok, who waited patiently, makeshift spear in hand. "Ezra, this is my son, Kol-ok."

The two boys eyed each another, taking one another's measure. Xva materialized from a nearby boat and dropped his spear before Kol-ok.

Aizarg cocked his head at Xva.

"Uros," Xva said with determination. "Your boy is dead. Before you stands a man. If Atta were here, he would say no less."

Aizarg turned to Atamoda. "Atta?"

Atamoda shook her head, tears beginning anew. "So many, Aizarg. So many have perished."

Aizarg gripped Kol-ok's shoulder and clenched his jaw, fighting back conflicting pride and sorrow.

"Two new men are forged upon the sea," Okta nodded to Ezra.

"Yes," Aizarg smiled and brought Kol-ok and Ezra under each arm. "Two new Lo men!"

"We need men, Uros," Xva said. "We have so few."

Atamoda caught her breath as a tall, dark girl, perhaps fourteen summers, stepped from the raft.

A Scythian!

Aizarg followed her gaze and motioned to the girl. "I present Sana, Princess of Scythia. She, too, is welcome among us. This was Setenay's will. She placed her in Ghalen's charge until we can decide what to do with her." Aizarg paused and took a deep breath. "Setenay..."

Atamoda placed her hand on his chest as she remembered the face in the water. "I know."

Sana bowed her head slightly. Her dark beauty reminded Atamoda of Kus-ge, but without the arrogance.

"Welcome, Sana." Atamoda gestured to the center of the flotilla. "Make your way to the center raft and find rest and food."

Ghalen emerged behind Sana. "You heard her. Get moving," he barked.

Sana scowled at Ghalen.

He carries wounds on his heart. They all carry fresh wounds.

"Father?" Su-gar brushed past Atamoda toward the wedding barge, searching its empty deck. She turned pleadingly to Aizarg. "Where is my father?"

Atamoda scanned the empty wedding barge and then looked to Aizarg. His expression told her everything.

Su-gar crumbled to the deck.

"The demons took Ula first," Atamoda said to Aizarg as she knelt to comfort Su-gar. Su-gar's mother, Ula, dove into the water to swim to Atamoda's hut, only to be killed by the water demons. When Atta, a village elder, dove in to save her, the demons took him, too.

Su-gar sobbed face down on the deck as Atamoda rubbed her back, unable to find words of comfort.

"Atamoda, take her to the center raft with the others," Aizarg whispered.

"Give her a moment!" Atamoda snapped. She regretted her tone the minute the words escaped her mouth.

"Our moments are running out."

Sana stepped around Aizarg and knelt next to Su-gar and Atamoda. The Scythian considered Atamoda as if asking permission. The patesi-le nodded, curious as to the girl's intentions.

Sana lifted Su-gar's chin and stared into her eyes. The Scythian brushed the wet strands of Su-gar's dark, wavy hair from her cheeks as the girl's sobbing subsided.

Sana whispered into Su-gar's ear, though Atamoda could not hear the words.

Su-gar considered Sana quizzically as her sobs vanished. She nodded, and then Sana leaned in again and whispered something else. Su-gar stared off into the distance, listening intently.

Is she casting a spell on her? For a brief moment Atamoda considered intervening.

Su-gar's breathing slowed. She wiped her eyes and nose and refocused back on Sana as a hint of a smile touched the Scythian Princess' mouth.

Su-gar sniffled and straightened her hair. "Help me up, Atamoda."

After standing, Su-gar turned. "What is your name?"

"I am Sana."

"Sana, come with me, and I will show you where there is food and rest." Su-gar locked arms with Sana and led her to the flotilla center.

Everyone, including Ghalen, looked on in stunned silence. Ghalen's gaze lingered on the two women, his expression softer.

"Ghalen," Aizarg said. "Much needs to be done. Go fetch Levidi. I need him."

Ghalen hurried away as Atamoda turned to Aizarg. "Tell me what happened."

"The demons led us to you. I knew we'd find someone in danger if we followed them." Aizarg hefted the staff. "This banished the demons."

Atamoda finally took a good look at the staff. The alien red orb, like glittering metal blood, tapered and wrapped around a plain wooden shaft.

"It's your boar spear!"

He slowly nodded, never taking his eyes off hers. The staff and the grim expression on his face frightened her more than any demon.

"You've been touched." No, she knew that wasn't the right word.

He's been called.

Somewhere on their quest a strange god transformed her husband into an instrument of divine will. She reached out to touch it as her husband considered her intently. Atamoda's stomach knotted. Her fingers trembled as they drew closer to the strange metal.

"You should have seen it, Mother!" Kol-ok interrupted, coming between them and breaking the spell. "A giant pillar of fire! It surrounded us and..."

Aizarg shook his head and raised his finger. "Kol-ok, I need you and Ezra to do something." Aizarg point to where the remaining ropes anchored the flotilla to the submerged köy-lo-hely. The anchor boat's bow began to dip as the water deepened with each passing minute. "Cut the ropes and free this floating arun-ki," Aizarg said.

Panic flared again within Atamoda. "That will cast us adrift. We will never find our way home!"

Aizarg squeezed her hand. "Home is forever gone."

"Heli-dar lies to the south. The bosom of the Great Mother is the realm of the dead."

"I've already walked the realm of the dead. We trust our fate to the current and the God of the Narim." Aizarg removed one of the two li-ges around his neck and placed it around her's. "We are together. We are home."

Aizarg suddenly peered over his shoulder at the darkening northern horizon.

"What is it?" she whispered.

"Dark clouds, do you see them? They rush from the north to meet the ones approaching from the south. When they clash I fear it will not bode well." He nudged her toward the center of the flotilla.

Kol-ok and Ezra knelt down and looked back to Aizarg for confirmation. The Uros nodded. "This Nameless God promised us a new world. The only way to find it is to cut loose the tethers that hold us to this one."

Ba-lok reached to cut the line, but hesitated. "Father, the rope is no longer tight."

Atamoda watched as the ropes bent limply and began to slide under the boat. Boats and rafts creaked and popped as they shifted and jostled against one another. Reed scrapped against wood as the deck beneath her slowly began to shift and rotate.

"The current reverses," Aizarg said.

The flood is receding!" Atamoda gasped.

The tethers suddenly yanked tight, and the entire flotilla lurched around the pivot point. Atmoda held Aizarg to steady herself. Confusion and screams spread across the flotilla.

The flotilla accelerated toward the tree tops along the submerged shore.

"Cut the lines! Quickly!" Aizarg shouted.

"But the flood is receding. If we stay here the water will pass us by," Atamoda said, unsure why Aizarg still wanted to cut the lines.

"Cut the lines, now!" Aizarg commanded, eyes locked on the approaching line of clouds.

Kol-ok's line quickly succumbed to his flint blade. Ezra's rope, however, floated closer to the bow and had too much play for Ezra to simply sever it with one hand.

Only Atamoda saw everything unfold. Aizarg and Kol-ok were not watching the a-g'an boy as he tried to cut the line. Ezra ignorantly wrapped the rope around his wrist, which quickly slipped under the boat.

She reached for him. "Ezra, no!"

The rope snapped tight and ripped the prow off the boat, yanking Ezra into the water. The boy vanished under the flotilla.

Without hesitation, she leapt in after him.

Bone chilling numbness embraced her as she plunged into murky shadow beneath the flotilla. Atamoda frantically fought the current, chasing Ezra's struggling image. He seemed to become more tangled in the rope anchoring him to the köy-lo-hely far below.

If he does not cut himself loose, I will not be able reach him!

Over her head, wobbling bubbles clung to the bottoms of rafts and boats. The speed at which the flotilla accelerated overhead gave the illusion she swam at an incredible speed. Atamoda knew better, knowing the current flowed faster than she could swim. Ezra's image slowly faded, his form less animated.

I cannot save him.

She switched her attention to the flotilla overhead, trying to gauge how long until the opposite side passed over. She planned to snatch the underside of the nearest vessel and work hand-over-hand until she pulled herself up.

She looked down just in time to see Ezra's face, cheeks puffed out, eyes bulging in terror, hurtling toward her. He drifted just under the hulls, a frayed rope wrapped around his left wrist, knife still clutched in the other hand.

She caught him, snatched the knife, and tucked it into her drawstring. The knife became a dangerous liability now that he'd freed himself. She'd seen enough panicked children to know Ezra teetered on the brink of losing control.

His lungs are beginning to burn.

Kicking against the current, she cradled Ezra with one arm and felt along the flotilla bottom, ready to grab the last boat.

Ezra began to thrash, clawing at the hulls.

The water lightened ahead, she sensed the edge of the flotilla approaching.

Just a few more moments, hold on Ezra!

The boy began to claw at her, trying to poke his face into the voids and cracks between the boats and rafts. Expertly tied Lo knots secured the Lo fleet together with flexibility, snug enough to prevent each vessel from bumping and damaging one another. If he tried to cram his face up between them, he would likely get trapped and drown.

His thrashing erupted into blind violence. If he prevented her from grabbing a passing boat, they would both die. Atamoda did the only thing she could to save both their lives. With a sudden thrust, she rammed the top of his head into the underside of a passing raft.

Ezra passed out with a thud.

I'll worry about clearing his lungs topside.

For a moment she hung suspended above the blackness, the flotilla passing just over her head. Memories of the demons bubbled up in her mind as she suddenly found herself fighting for control.

The last boat rapidly approached as Atamoda's lungs began to ache. Gently cradling Ezra's waist, she kicked hard with the current and caught a handhold on the reed keel.

And then her hand slipped.

Frantically, she flailed for the boat. Above the water, she knew the wind pushed the flotilla faster than she could swim with the current. She'd never be able to catch them, especially towing Ezra's limp body.

She made one more lunge, but the boats' edges slipped farther away. Atmoda abandoned the flotilla and kicked for the surface. A strong arm snatched her around the waist and pulled her with great force toward the flotilla. She turned to her left and saw Okta winking at her, his left arm firmly holding the side of a boat.

"Help us!" Okta gasped, exploding up out of the water dragging Atamoda and Ezra with him.

Ba-lok and another man from the Minnow Clan plopped Atamoda and Ezra in a boat next to the unconscious Kus-ge.

"Okta, what happened?" Ba-lok said.

"The current suddenly shifted. Ezra was pulled under trying to cut us loose. Atamoda dove in after him. I told the Uros I'd get both of them."

Aizarg sent Okta instead of jumping in himself?

"Ba-lok, please help me up." Shivering and coughing, Atamoda struggled to stand. "Aizarg is on the other side of the flotilla, likely worried about me. I must go to him."

Ezra suddenly coughed and began to stir.

Okta leaned over him. "He will be fine. He didn't swallow too much sea." He examined the swelling bump on the boy's forehead and chuckled. "I saw how you calmed him, Atamoda. We'll have to teach him to swim."

Atamoda turned her attention to Ba-lok's wife. "How is Kus-ge?"

"Exhausted. We cannot wake her," Ba-lok said

Atamoda envied her. She wished she could fall asleep and put this unending nightmare behind her forever.

"Let her sleep," she said. "Take care of Ezra, let him sleep, too. I'll be back to check on both of them."

Atamoda looked off to the northwest. The tree tops were close. In a few more minutes they would find themselves caught up in the branches.

She faintly heard her and Okta's names being called along the edges of the flotilla.

They are looking for us.

"Aizarg needs me." Atamoda stepped out of Ba-lok's boat and onto the adjoining raft, ready to make her way through the crowd across the flotilla.

Then the deck shifted under her feet.

What now?

A faint rumbling from the north made Atamoda stop in her tracks.

"What is it?" Okta gasped.

"I hear it too," Ba-lok stepped next to her.

Atamoda lifted her ear to the north. "There it is again. I am not imagining it." *Is that what Aizarg heard?*

Across the flotilla, all the Lo turned and faced north. A hush settled over the flotilla. A frigid blast of air swept across the decks, making Atamoda shiver.

"The northern sky darkens. The clouds are so low!" Ba-lok said.

"The current shifts yet again," Okta looked around at the water as it began to retreat from the shore again.

"Sco-lo-ti, what do you hear?" voice quaking, a man from the Minnow Clan asked his leader. "Do the demons return?"

"I don't know." Ba-lok shook his head.

The rumbled strengthened, steadily growing louder until a low vibration pulsed deep through her chest and rattled her bones.

Atamoda turned ashen; her mind finally comprehended the horrible magnitude of what her eyes witnessed.

"It's not a cloud."

Across the entire northern horizon, the sea rose to join the sky.

Run to Ba-tor!

Screams rose over the thunder as Atamoda fled toward the flotilla's center.

13. The Courtyard of Stone

I wasn't the only refugee from the Deluge climbing the ragged spine of the world. Through mountain mists and torrential rain, omnipresent companions shadowed my every footstep. To my right, the future floated as a cold specter holding aloft a dim torch. To my left, the past dogged each footfall, snapping at my heels.

In the courtyard of stone they become one.

The Chronicle of Fu Xi.

***

Forever is a cold, unchanging twilight.

Fu Xi thought he knew the meaning of forever. The clouds thickened, and the sky darkened until mist and rain, day and night, melted into one. Time ceased.

He did not know north or south, dawn or dusk. Fu Xi only knew trudging up or down. Trails, canyons, ledges, and peaks all blurred together, only pressing forward into the wall of water mattered.

Occasionally, Fu Xi found ledges and caves deep enough to shelter him and the horse from the relentless downpour. Starting a fire wasn't possible, what little timber he could scavenge was waterlogged or rotted. These respites were only brief affairs, a chance only to wring out his clothes, inspect his gear, and catch some needed sleep. Without fail, the rising deluge drove them from their resting places and higher into the mountains.

As the days passed, rot began to eat away at Heise's tackle. The oilskin kept Fu Xi's armor and food dry, but the reins and straps securing them to Heise's back began to bleach and crack. The apples and grain long gone, only mold lined the empty food bags.

Heise's ribs poked out along his flanks, but his eyes were still clear. Sores began to appear where disintegrating leather rubbed his hide. Fu Xi spent a great deal of time readjusting the load to keep the condition from worsening.

He also spent a great deal of time scavenging for scrub grass, never passing up a solitary blade. Often, Fu Xi climbed sheer cliffs to pluck hardy tufts from among stubborn rocks to feed his horse by hand.

Unless he could find more food, he knew doom awaited his beautiful black stallion. Heise provided the demigod a tenuous toehold in this world. The horse became an hourglass, marking the passage of time. All thoughts of his mother's prophecies, finding the man with white hair, or his mysterious half-brother washed away.

Only his horse mattered. Fu Xi even abandoned all thoughts of himself.

***

Tiejiang crouched before a collapsible iron rack over a small fire. A clay pot filled with rice porridge, a kettle of tea, and a loaf of freshly steamed bread atop the rack made my stomach growl louder.

He must have been waiting in the hayfield since before dawn, his presence here wholly unexpected but entirely welcomed.

Carrying my sandals, I let the dew-covered grass caress my feet as I squatted next to Tiejiang. The young man nodded deferentially, gingerly offering the delicate ceramic cup with hands more suited for pounding iron than serving tea.

I tapped two fingers against the rack's corner and offered my thanks. Respectfully and patiently, Tiejiang waited for me to sample the tea to ensure it met my satisfaction.

"The tea is delicious. Thank you, Honored Student."

Tiejiang still did not pour himself a cup. Instead, he prepared me a bowl of porridge and generous portion of bread.

Only after I smiled and nodded, did he prepare himself a cup and small portion of food. Carefully, he turned the spout away from both of us as we settled in to eat.

The Chronicle of Fu Xi

***

Fu Xi's shirt had rotted off days ago, exposing a sunken, empty belly. His divine blood kept him strong, regardless of his burning hunger. Separating seams and gaping holes in his cotton trousers testified they would soon follow the shirt's example.

The demigod's skin grew pale, soft, and wrinkled like an old man's. Occasionally, he considered his own flesh, amused at the illusion of aging.

He plodded forward, reins in hand, down another mountain trail, along yet another cliff, when a woman's scream rose from somewhere ahead.

Fu Xi cocked his head to one side as the sound penetrated the thundering wall of rain and wind. Just when he thought his sanity was washing away with the rain, the scream echoed again.

The trail widened ahead, allowing him to lead Heise at a trot. As the trail descended, thundering rapids congealed from the downpour and hemmed them in on the left. Ahead, a wall of sheer granite blocked their way. The trail widened into what appeared to be a narrow defile to his right and vanished into the rainy curtain.

To the right it is.

Fu Xi led Heise up the trail, the excitement energizing the otherwise lethargic steed.

Less of a canyon and more like a wide crack in the mountain, the defile afforded space enough for both man and horse with room to spare. The gray walls vanished into the rain high over his head. Fu Xi's horse kept a sure footing despite the small streams gushing down either side of the trail.

Another high pitched shriek echoed down the defile, cutting through the rain's background din. Fu Xi stopped in his tracks. A beast lurked somewhere beyond the rainy curtain.

Fu Xi turned and reached under the oilskin blanket on Heise's back and withdrew the orichalcum blade. Fashioned for gods, the Red Sword and the neatly packed Red Armor were both untouched by rust or rot.

Blade extended in one hand, and reins in the other, Fu Xi cautiously inched his way deeper into the narrow defile.

***

We appeared roughly the same age, two men in their early twenties dressed in simple cotton trousers and tunic. We squatted before the fire as old friends do, slowly enjoying our steaming tea and watching the sun come up. For fifteen years, this is how we spent our mornings before stoking the forge and beginning the day's lessons.

"The cooking rack is new, isn't it?" I examined the collapsible iron rack, admiring Tiejiang's handiwork. "Don't let the village women see it, or they will be pestering you for one."

"They already have. The main rack breaks down into two pieces, the legs fold in. It can easily be stored in a backpack."

I nodded my approval and took another sip. The rack was beyond anything I taught him. Tiejiang long ago developed into a master smithy. Mortals often blossom beyond the dreams of their divine mentors.

"Why are you not with your new bride?" I finally asked.

"She sleeps in our hut."

"Do not let her sleep in too much, or she will become a lazy wife."

"She's not lazy, only exhausted. I let her sleep out of pity." The briefest of smiles touched his lips.

"And you are not exhausted?"

"A good smithy knows when to let the metal cool. Besides, I'm hungry." Tiejiang held the cup to his lips to hide his smile. "Are you exhausted, Lord Fu Xi? It is my sincerest wish that my cousin pleased you."

I cleared my throat. "Her ancestors would be proud."

"Good, because I have many more cousins asking to sleep with you," he said with a straight face. "They are lined up behind the haystack, shall I get them now, or do you want to finish your breakfast first?"

I threw a crust of bread at him as he abandoned all pretense and fell backwards laughing, holding his stomach.

Oh, I miss his laughter! Perhaps more than anything in this world, I miss his laughter.

The Chronicle of Fu Xi

***

Heise whinnied and tugged against the reins.

"Yes, I'm sure you can smell them. Stay behind my sword."

In a few minutes the defile veered right and then widened into a large, almost circular opening. At first glance it reminded Fu Xi of a natural courtyard with the defile continuing on the opposite side.

A solitary, scraggly tree stood in the enclosure's center, gripping naked rock with gnarled roots. High in its bare clutches, a thin, nude girl clung desperately among twiggy branches. Two burly shapes circled the trunk, high muscled shoulders rising and falling with smooth fluidity. Even with their soaking, spotted fur matted against their skin, the big cats were half as large as his horse. Long, curved fangs extended far below their lower jaw. Even in the dull light, their pale eyes gleamed with primal hunger. The cats' attention fully locked on their prey, they didn't notice Fu Xi's approach.

Dagger teeth!

A shredded human body, throat ripped open, lay crumpled at the base of the tree among shattered tree limbs.

Fu Xi released the reins and placed himself between Heise and the predators. The horse reared back and whinnied, drawing the cats' attention.

They stopped pacing and turned toward Heise, ears perked forward. Fu Xi crouched with sword extended over his head. Maddening hunger burned in the animals' eyes, and the demigod knew they would fight until the death.

The dagger tooth on the left slowly paced farther left, the other one extended right.

They are famished, but not stupid. They sense my power.

Fu Xi quickly ascertained that the cat on the left was dominant of the two juvenile males.

Kill him and the other may bolt.

A purring sound tickled his ear. Instinct forced his head right where gleaming eyes peered from a narrow ledge immediately above them. A third giant cat leered down, legs bunched underneath.

***

"If you're not here to offer up your female relations to me, why did you come? How did you know where to find me?"

The laughter died, as did Tiejiang's smile. He stood and walked behind the haystack. In a few moments he returned carrying a well-worn, bulging, leather backpack, my scabbard and conical hat securely fastened to its side. Tucked under his other arm were my heavy boots, sturdy cotton trousers and tunic. He bowed slightly, placed the pack and clothes at my feet, and resumed his place next to the fire.

I stared at the pack and my fate before glancing up at Tortoise Mountain. It shone impassively in the morning sun.

"Uncle Heng did not come down for the wedding. His visits from Tortoise Mountain are rare these days, so when he knocked at my door this morning, I knew it must be important. He handed me those and said I'd find you here with my cousin."

"Let us finish this excellent breakfast before I depart," I said. The sun finally crested the trees, ushering the day's heat and banishing the dew.

The Chronicle of Fu Xi

***

The beast leapt as Fu Xi sliced upward.

Half of the dagger tooth slammed fully into Heise's back, the other piece falling into a twitching mass on the trail. The panicked horse bolted past Fu Xi into the stone courtyard where the cat on the right leapt after him. Fu Xi cursed under his breath and committed to battle.

With a soul-curdling scream, the dagger tooth on the left flattened its ears and swiped at Fu Xi with both claws. Heise raced around the edge of the enclosure at full gallop as the other lion pursued, occasionally swatting at Heise's haunches, trying to bring down the horse. Every time Fu Xi shifted to intervene, the other lion blocked his path.

They're trying to separate us.

Fu Xi grudgingly admired the beasts and knew only one option lay before him. He lunged at the cat ahead of him, trying to pin it against the cliff. Surprised by the attack, the cat rose on its haunches and lashed out in a flurry of claw strikes. Claw and sword blended in a crimson blur. Agonizing gashes opened across Fu Xi's torso, arms, and legs as he absorbed the frenzied assault. Gashes also opened across the cat's hide, wounds the mortal beast could not sustain.

Finally, the Red Sword found the cat's neck. Fu Xi turned just in time to see Heise vanish into the darkness of the opposite defile, the other big cat close on its heels.

Clenching his bleeding abdomen, Fu Xi turned to pursue when he heard a moan to his right. The girl in the branches moaned again and began a slow tumble from the upper limbs.

Fu Xi looked down the defile, where the dagger tooth's screams echoed off the canyon walls. He leaned forward to pursue his horse, but the girl in the branches moaned again.

She's going to die anyway. He took two steps down the defile and stopped.

The demigod closed his eyes, turned and faced upward to the rain. His shoulders relaxed as the pain in his abdomen abated. Making peace with his decision, he turned and walked under the tree just in time to catch her before she struck the stony ground.

***

We ate in silence. After breakfast I changed behind the haystack while Tiejiang covered the fire with earth, poured water over his rack to cool it, and packed his cookware.

"Where will you go, Lord Fu Xi?" Tiejiang called to me over the haystack.

"East." Mother warned me a new quest awaited me following the wedding, though I did not take her so literally. This quest was like no other she'd ever bestowed upon me. I carried no new craft, art, or skill to teach the Tall Men of Cin. Her orders were simple.

"May I inquire the nature of your quest?" he called.

"Dragons."

The clanging shuffling on the other side of the haystack paused momentarily and then resumed.

I rolled up my formal attire and stepped from around the haystack, more comfortable in my traveling clothes.

Tiejiang stood before me, boots on his feet, a freshly stitched leather pack over one shoulder, walking stick in hand. My heart sank.

The Chronicle of Fu Xi

***

For her size, perhaps a child of twelve, she barely weighed that of a six year old. Fu Xi gently laid her down among the broken branches and examined her.

Starvation gripped the child, only a collection of bones and skin. Thighs and arms reduced to sticks, knees and elbows bulging. Fu Xi then realized that she wasn't a child at all, but a severely famished young woman. He looked back at the body of her companion, an older man, his flesh nude, and limbs equally thin.

The demigod's heart ached for the two mortals.

Neither of them would have afforded even a snack for the lions.

Something around her neck caught his attention. Fu Xi fingered a thick metal collar, black and rusted.

It's welded.

He looked over at the man, who wore a similar collar.

Slaves.

His heartache changed to uneasiness.

Though sallow, she shared Fu Xi's own light yellow complexion and normal eyes. The dead man's eyes were round, his skin pale with death, but clearly white. Unlike any man in Cin, he had a hairy face.

Fu Xi swallowed hard and examined the woman's body. A thick callous encircled her neck under the collar. Faded lash marks crisscrossed her flesh. And then he saw it on her right shoulder.

Fu Xi leapt up, sword in hand, as if the woman's body had burned him.

It cannot be!

He paced around the stone courtyard as if someone, or something, may attack at any moment. Fu Xi ran his hand through his soaking hair, mind reeling at the implications of the ragged brand burned into the woman's right arm. He approached the man's body and found the same brand on his right arm...

...a sea serpent, twisting around a trident.

How did they get here?

The woman stirred.

Fu Xi knelt down next to her, trying to shield her from most of the rain.

Her eyes fluttered open and looked about until they focused on Fu Xi. Her face summoned images of balmy jungles, sugar white beaches, and a small, gentle people of far southern Cin.

"Rantaian...Rantaian..." she gasped in a hoarse whisper. Fu Xi understood the tongue, but it wasn't one of Cin's.

"Rantaian..." she kept repeating for a few more moments, until her eyes closed and her breath ceased.

Rantaian...The Chain.

Fu Xi stood, still staring at her body. How these two escaped he didn't know. If they were here, then another beast, one far more dangerous than a dagger tooth, lurked somewhere beyond the rain.

This beast hunted Fu Xi.

He examined the Red Sword, an artifact of his journey to Wu. His armor and his horse, other legacies of his quest beyond the Sunrise Sea, were somewhere out there in the Deluge. Now more than ever, he had to find them.

***

I picked up my own pack and strode past him, unable to meet his pleading, eager expression.

"And what of your bride?" I asked, picking up my pace toward the cool, dark forest only a few paces ahead.

"All those years, working together at the forge, you told me of your many quests. I dreamt of going with you and seeing the wonders of the world beyond Nushen!"

"You are a man now, with responsibilities. Your duty is to your wife. My duty is to the Goddess Nuwa. Go home."

"I am your Honored Student. My home is with you."

My heart torn, I stopped and took a deep breath before I turned around.

"You are, and always shall be, my Honored Student. Now you are also a husband. Soon, you will be a father. If I have taught you anything, isn't it the importance of duty?"

"I am afraid," he said as the pack slipped from his hand.

I placed my hands on his shoulders and tried to smile. "Why are you afraid?" He didn't look like a young man anymore, but the boy I took by the hand and led out of the garden of stone.

"You will be gone many years. I may be dead before you return."

He gave voice to my fear, too.

"This may be true, maybe not. The only thing which is important is what you do with your life while I am gone. You are the smithy, the heart of the village. Instill love into all you do and the village will prosper; the Goddess will be pleased. Put your wife and your children at the center of your heart, and you will be a content man."

"I do not want you to go." His tears flowed freely.

"Goodbye, Tiejiang." I picked up my pack and turned around, the sanctuary of the trees only a step away.

I'd never departed on a quest through the forest across the fields, usually taking the path from the central avenue. The dark shadows embraced me. I slipped through last night's fog still dancing between the ancient trunks, letting its wetness mix with my own tears.

"Farewell, my Honored Teacher," his fading voice followed me into the forest.

I turned and saw him for the last time, standing alone in the bright sunshine beyond the trees. The short, green grass behind him sloped up across the field to Nushen's bright red tiled roofs.

"Goodbye, my son," I whispered and turned east toward my destiny.

The Chronicle of Fu Xi

14. Between Worlds

When the waves ride high, the Lo hug their boats. - Lo Proverb

The Chronicle of Fu Xi

***

Here, at the end of all things, the sky and sea merged into one. To Atamoda, it was as if the gods rolled up their sleeping mat and shook humanity off the firmament as if they were no more than bed lice.

A lifetime of prayers, and we are no more than lice?

The wave's terrible grandeur paralyzed her as screaming men and women blindly stampeded past, Virag and his a-g'an henchmen among them.

Where will they go? There is nowhere to run.

Okta rushed by against the crowd, perhaps trying to get back to Aizarg before the wave swallowed them.

And the monster would swallow them. It grew vertically, reaching to the sky, seemingly without getting any closer.

Atamoda knew, however, only seconds remained before it crushed them.

Atamoda also knew she could not reach Aizarg and Kol-ok before the monster swallowed them.

Ba-tor.

She pushed against the crowd in Okta's wake, toward the flotilla's center and her youngest child. Faces blurred past, eyes wild with panic. Some fell into boat bottoms, only to be trampled underfoot.

Atamoda passed them by, abandoning her patesi-le duties. Terror of dying alone inoculated her against the mob's panic. Her baby boy needed her. She needed him.

Atamoda dashed from raft to boat, over and around those who instinctively knelt down in their rafts or in the bottom of their boats.

A moment later she found Bat-or clinging to Sana. Roughly a dozen Minnow and Crane women huddled with twice that many children on the center rafts. Su-gar knelt apart, mesmerized by the wave.

"Give him to me!" Atamoda commanded.

Sana obeyed. Atamoda stroked Ba-tor's hair and hummed softly, trying to ease her baby's terror.

"Ba-tor, look at Mother." She faced him away from the wave, wiping tears and mucus away from his dirty face. It broke her heart thinking of the terrors he endured over the past few days.

She kissed him all over his face. "All of this will be over in just a moment, and then you and I and Daddy and Kol-ok will all be together in the sunshine."

Shaking uncontrollably, the child closed his eyes and buried his head into his mother's bosom.

She looked around, desperately trying to find her husband and Kol-ok.

Where is Aizarg? Why isn't he trying to find me?

"Patesi-le!" A young Minnow woman clutching her baby begged. "What shall we do?"

"Hold on," Atmoda replied. "Hold on....hold on...hold on...," she repeated until the gale tore away her words.

The howling wind stripped blankets and mats and sent them flying into the sea spray. Ropes and rigging popped and snapped with frantic force. The wave's thunder enveloped her body and became deafening. Those who stood, knelt. Those who knelt, lay flat.

Sana's hand found hers. Atamoda turned and saw the Scythian Princess staring defiantly at the wave, her lips moving rhythmically, though she could not hear her words. Atamoda squeezed her hand.

Now the wave's scale and speed suddenly registered in her mind. Countless tree trunks and gigantic mountains of ice suspended in the wave's churning face, gave testament to ruined lands she never knew existed, all wiped clean by the Nameless God of the Narim. To Atamoda, it was as if the earth vomited up all the foulness of the g'an and sent it hurtling to the sea.

She spied Aizarg and Levidi side-by-side across the flotilla, defiantly facing the wave. Their garments rippled in the powerful wind as Levidi held the staff high. They seemed to glow against the wave's inky backdrop.

What are they doing?

The wind instantly reversed with such force Atamoda thought someone had hit her, slamming her and Sana forward against the deck. A mast snapped next to them, barely missing the two women. Atamoda screamed in agony as her ears felt like they were going to burst. Shrieking, Bator squeezed the sides of his head. She looked up in time to see a misty shock-wave ripple over their heads and hurtle past Aizarg and Levidi toward the wave at unimaginable speed.

How can Aizarg and Levidi still be standing?

Immediately in front of the flotilla, the wave fell backwards, transforming from a vertical wall into a steep slope.

The decks shuddered as the wave struck.

Atamoda experienced the most terrifying of sensations, as if an invisible hand pressed her against the deck. Struggling against the force, she barely managed to roll over on her back so as not to smother Ba-tor. Her child pressed hard against her chest as if he weighed as much as a man, making each breathe a battle.

Pinned by the invisible force, she stared straight up at the clouds. The deck buckled wildly beneath her; each log, rope, and reed fiber stressed to the breaking point.

Atamoda sensed her head rising and feet falling. The flotilla slanted at an insanely steep angle, like an insect clinging to a wall. Craning her head back, she saw the wave vanish into the clouds above her. Fighting for each breath, she barely managed to lift her head and peer between her toes. Below her, the unseen hand pinned the Lo flat against the decks. Beyond the edge of the flotilla, the wave stretched far below her.

We're riding the wave! Her heart raced as fear and elation became one. Atamoda closed her eyes and surrendered to the pressing hand. Washed in dizziness, she battled the urge to vomit. When she found the courage to open her eyes, the clouds appeared closer, accelerating toward her.

Then the world went gray. Cool mist enveloped her as the wave's deafening roar lessened. She hung suspended in the mist, Ba-tor pressed against her chest, and the raft hard against her back.

We are dead. We are between worlds.

Then blinding brightness enveloped the world. Sunlight, powerful and warm, bathed the flotilla.

Everything grew quiet, and the invisible hand pinning her down evaporated. The deck ceased its shuddering, and she felt light, almost as if she could float. Atamoda shielded her eyes as her vision adjusted to a crystal-sharp blue sky.

Suspended between heaven and hell, the flotilla floundered atop the giant wave's crest, and Atamoda's fear turned to euphoria. She'd never seen a sky so blue, a sun so bright. To their left and right the wave rose above the white, fluffy clouds like a black glass mountain. Overwhelmed with beauty, she realized the wave carried them closer to the sun, to paradise itself.

We are above the clouds. Psatina carries us home to Father Sky!

The patesi-le stood and stretched her hand toward the sun, knowing heaven was almost in her grasp.

"Please, Psatina, forgive us. Carry us home!" she sobbed.

She wanted to grab onto the warm yellow orb and hold on, letting the flotilla with all its nightmares fall back into mist without her and Ba-tor. With a subtle shift, she felt the flotilla gently fall away under her feet. Her stomach fluttered, as if lifted by a hundred butterflies. For the briefest of moments Atamoda believed the gods had spared her.

But the sun remained cruelly beyond her reach. That's when she saw the towering clouds.

The titans stood shoulder-to-shoulder, horizon-to-horizon, in opposition to the great wave. Their grotesquely flattened heads reached for the sun and devoured the sky. With purplish-black bellies, bloated and engorged, the storms gave birth to jagged streaks of lightning. The bolts danced up and down the tempest's leading edge like ill-begotten harbingers, only to be answered by even more brilliant flashes deep within the storm.

She knew the wave carried them to the storms, to Helidar and the underworld itself.

The gods offer us as a sacrifice to hell. There would be no forgiveness, no salvation, no hope.

"No, no, no!" she screamed, clutching Bat-or as tightly as she could with her left arm, while still desperately straining upward with her right.

Heaven rejected the flotilla as her feet settled firmly back onto the cold deck.

Despair as deep and black as the sea filled her heart. "Great Mother, let this end! Take us home. No more, no more!"

The blue sky remained mute; the creaking rigging and groaning deck the only sounds as the flotilla slid backward over the wave's crest and descended once again into the maelstrom.

A strong hand snatched her to the deck.

Sana, eyes full of determination, shouted above the gathering wind, "*Fight!* Fight and live!"

With a shudder, the flotilla lurched right and began to slowly spin. Knots and ropes creaked as the screaming among the Lo resumed. People clung to reed and wood and twine as the flotilla spun faster and faster. Sun, sky, and mist alternated and blurred until nausea overwhelmed Atamoda. The cold mist enveloped them once again as she succumbed to the disorientation and vomited. She wiped off her mouth and opened her eyes, only to be surrounded by a world of howling, unnatural violence.

Mountainous waves, black and covered in brown foam, teetered all around them, choked with logs, ice, and splintered timber.

A Minnow man she did not recognize stumbled from behind her and grabbed the hand of the woman with the baby. "Glania, come! We stand a better chance in a smaller boat on our own." He lifted her and dragged her away. Glania looked back at Atamoda with trepidation.

Through the crowd, Atamoda saw them stumble into a boat at the edge of the flotilla. Glania, baby crying in her arms, never took her eyes off Atamoda. In the confusion and chaos no one other than Atamoda witnessed the man pull the knots and release the boat from the flotilla. He pushed away into the violent sea and began paddling between the waves. Neither Glania nor her husband saw the enormous tree trunk tumble out of a nearby crest, but Atmoda did. With leaves still attached, the trunk slammed into the tiny boat, dragging it below the water, never to surface again.

Atamoda closed her eyes against the horror, opening them in time to spy Ghalen shepherding women and children toward the flotilla's center. Atamoda's heart lifted as she saw Kol-ok with them. Even with all their skill, the Lo had difficulty remaining upright in the howling gale and undulating decks.

Kol-ok dropped to his knees next to his mother. "Father commands all to the center! I am to stay with you." Atamoda wrapped her arm around his neck and held him tightly.

Arcs of lightning, only glimpsed by the Lo in times past with utmost rarity, traced long, ragged tendrils across the boiling sky.

Through the spraying mist, she caught glimpses of men running across the decks, desperately fighting to keep the flotilla together. Occasionally, she spied Aizarg with Levidi and Okta by his side, issuing commands from a nearby raft.

She wanted him with her, with his children. Atamoda knew the thought irrational, but it didn't matter.

The sea's power wreaked havoc faster than the men could work. Knots held, but ropes snapped, and deadly space formed between the boats. The sea splintered hulls and swamped boats. Atamoda looked on horrified as the flooded hulls began to pull down the surrounding vessels.

She heard Okta's voice rise on the gale. "Release the flooded boats!"

Men pulled knots and kicked away the ruined hulls as gaps in the flotilla multiplied.

Ghalen appeared next to the women, rope in hand. "Secure this to the decks and hold on to it!" he shouted, barely audible above the wind.

Atamoda handed Bat-or to Sana, and with Kol-ok and several women, tied the rope in a long line across several rafts. Everyone grabbed on, wrapping their hands, but careful not to tie themselves to the rope. The rope came not a moment too soon as muddy waves broke over the decks, trying to wash them away and spreading a thick layer of silt across the flotilla.

Women clutched children and held tightly to the rope. Filthy water washed over them, swamping more boats and driving their occupants to the crowded rafts. Dozens more packed around them, shivering and clutching the rope.

Large swaths of the flotilla vanished at a time under the waves. Atamoda held her breath until she saw the decks reemerge, wondering in horror how many of her people had been washed away.

At the edge of the flotilla Atamoda heard a wet ripping and popping above the wind. An enormous tree trunk invaded a gap between two boats. Its upended roots stretched outward like a hundred deformed claws, shredding ropes and ripping apart boats and rafts. People leapt out of the juggernaut's path as it plunged deeper into the flotilla's heart, forming a watery chasm. Ai-dar, a Minnow elder, could not dodge quickly enough. The old man stumbled over the lip of a boat and fell face-first onto a raft. The tree trunk crushed the boat behind him as its roots snared his legs. He dug his fingernails into the wood, but the tree dragged him into the water. Horrified, she watched the trunk roll over Ai-dar before it sank beneath the waves, leaving the two halves of the flotilla joined only at the two center rafts.

Several men, led by Okta, threw ropes across the widened gulf and struggled to pull the two halves together against the invading waves. As they worked, peels of deafening thunder joined the howling wind, making it almost impossible to hear the screams.

A strange wave rose high above the others in the distance. It collapsed, rose, and collapsed again in an odd manner that immediately drew Atamoda's attention.

The wave thrust upward, closer now. With each flash of lightning, it came ominously into focus. Only one wave removed from the flotilla, she finally saw its white sides streaked black with silt.

An island of ice!

The giant ice shard loomed larger than the entire flotilla. If it struck them, all was lost. As if drunk, the berg bobbed vertically. Then, a wave suddenly thrust it high until it teetered precariously over them, lightning dancing off its jagged tip in ear-splitting explosions. For what felt like an eternity, the iceberg thrust vertically above the water, as if defying the forces of nature. Slowly, it twisted and fell backwards toward them.

"Down!" Atamoda shouted.

She shoved Kol-ok to the deck and threw herself over both her children. Atamoda buried her head into Kol-ok's back as a muffled boom shook the deck. She wrapped her entire arm around the rope just as a blast of frigid water slammed against them. The rope snapped tight, trying to rip her arm out of its socket. Kol-ok, with a strong grasp on the rope, stayed firmly at her side. The powerful current sought every nook and cranny, trying to lift her from the deck as if seeking her other child beneath her.

Silt filled her mouth and invaded her nostrils. Bodies slammed against her as the current ripped her people from the decks. Atamoda tried to open her eyes to see Bat-or, but closed them against the stinging grit.

She felt Bat-or slip in her left arm. Desperately, she tightened her grip, but the water's unrelenting force capitalized on the growing gap between her and her little boy. Bat-or's little fists tugged her tunic, desperately trying to cling to his mother. His tugs turned to flails, interfering with her tenuous grip around his waist.

The water didn't relent. Atamoda's fingers cramped, her bicep burned, but his slippery skin slid farther down her arm.

Another body slammed hard against her shoulder, jarring Bat-or from her hand.

Without hesitation, Atamoda let go and followed her child.

Atamoda tumbled violently, rolling and slamming against decks, masts, and other people as the current rocketed her along. She fought to remain conscious as her head repeatedly struck the decks. Atamoda felt herself cartwheel upside down as water rushed into her nose. Suddenly, the deck erupted from the water, and her tumbling ceased.

Coated in a layer of silt, she struggled to stand. Atamoda found herself on the edge of the flotilla, the deck slick with slime. Had the deck breached only a moment later, she would have been washed overboard. Her legs quaked uncontrollably as she scanned the decks around her, praying Bat-or might be caught in the rigging or in the bottom of a boat. Across the flotilla she only saw silt-covered bodies beginning to stir and cough.

"Bat-or! *Bat-or!*" she screamed across the waves, tears cutting channels in her mud-caked cheeks. In the lightning flashes, she spied dozens of men and women bobbing in the water, slowly drifting away. Some clung to logs, others to shattered reed hulls.

Some floated face down.

"Atamoda!" Aizarg appeared next to her.

"Bat-or!" She pointed to the sea. In a matter of moments, he secured a rope around his waist, tied it off to the deck, and leapt in. Aizarg swam from one floundering person to the next, sending them back toward the flotilla along his rope. Atamoda and Kol-ok helped pull each from the water, but Bat-or was not among them.

Soon, Aizarg could find no more. Still, he repeatedly dove into the water, searching for his son. The waves began to diminish, even as the sky darkened, and lightning proliferated across the heavens.

Okta came alongside them. "The waves begin to subside. We have to repair the flotilla the best we can while we have a chance. We need the Uros." Okta reached down for the rope to pull Aizarg back in. Atamoda shoved him back.

"He searches for my son!"

Okta grimaced. "I am sorry, truly. Many have been lost. But we need the Uros, or many more will die this day. The ice island did not strike us, but it washed many of our people overboard." Okta pointed across the flotilla. "Even now, Ba-lok, Ghalen, and Levidi are leading rescue efforts on the other sides."

Kol-ok began to sob as the realization of his brother's fate became real.

"I will rescue my son if you men will not!" Atamoda gritted her teeth and turned to dive in. Okta grabbed her arm.

"Dive in and you will die! Bat-or is dead. Many are dead!"

Atamoda yanked away as Aizarg lifted himself out of the water. He approached Atamoda, eyes red-rimmed with tears, and wrapped his arms around her.

Atamoda shrugged him off and tugged at the rope around his waist. She tried to untie the wet knot, but her trembling fingers would not obey.

"Atamoda...he's gone," Aizarg whispered.

She slapped him with full force. He staggered back and rubbed his cheek.

"If the Uros will not save his child, I will!" She tugged and tugged, but the knot wouldn't budge.

"I do not need a rope." She turned to dive in, but Aizarg grabbed her from behind, pinning her arms to her side.

Atamoda kicked and screamed, fighting her husband with all her strength. "He's not dead! Let me go! He needs me."

Husband and wife sank to the deck.

She gazed out across the restless water and thought of Setenay's lifeless face. *The demons. The water is full of demons.* The thought of her baby boy floating among the demons drove Atamoda to the brink of madness. "We cannot leave him out there. He was so afraid, Aizarg. I cannot bear thinking of him being afraid." Aizarg squeezed her tighter.

"I need you!" he whispered urgently into her ear. "Kol-ok needs you. Bat-or's journey is over. Come, we must attend to the living."

"Mama," a tiny voice called from behind.

Atamoda's heart fluttered as Aizarg pulled her up.

"Mama," the voice called again.

She turned to see the Scythian girl, completely covered in silt, standing behind them. Bat-or rested on her hip with his little hands outstretched. Only his eyes and lips weren't caked in silt.

"The water washed me to the end of the rope," Sana said with her strange, fluid accent. "He tumbled into me a few moments later, and I was able to snatch him. I think we passed out."

Atmoda rushed to embrace Bat-or, and in the process, embraced Sana, too. She held the Scythian girl close, sobbing and repeating "thank you" over and over.

Sana nodded and pulled way, relinquishing Bat-or to his mother.

"Hmm," Okta grunted.

"Sana, you have my undying thanks," Aizarg said.

As the wind died, moans and cries became audible across the flotilla. Silt covered forms were lying on the decks, or stumbling about in a daze. Some called for loved ones; others began sifting through the debris, trying to put their vessels back in order.

At the edges, men with ropes tied to their waists repeatedly dived into the choppy water, dodging floating debris as they searched for those washed overboard.

Something struck Atamoda's shoulder with a warm, wet heaviness, soon followed by more wet impacts on her head.

"Mamma, water!" Bat-or pointed upward as the fat rain drops fell harder.

"What is this?" Kol-ok asked.

"The Tears of Psatina," Aizarg held his hands up, letting the rain wash away the filth. "It is as Noah promised."

15. The First Council of Boats

Where there is purpose, there also is hope. — Lo Proverb

The Chronicle of Fu Xi

***

Atamoda huddled among the survivors, shielding Bat-or against the driving rain like a mother bird protecting her fledgling. Each flash of lightning peeled back the darkness, revealing the shivering, desperate faces around her.

Cold rain poured off her bare skin, making her wish for winter garb. Every few minutes Ba-tor shivered, despite her best efforts to warm him with her own body.

"I'm cold, Momma," he said.

"Shhh. Daddy is going to fix it."

Exhausted and in shock, the remnants of the Lo nation crowded around the Uros and his inner council like a wall.

Beneath a sail hastily stretched into a leaky canopy, the council laid their grim tally before their Uros.

"The sea took fifteen Minnow, along with a third of my boats and three rafts." Ba-lok had to almost shout to be heard above the wind and flapping canopy.

Aizarg turned to Levidi. "And the Crane?"

"Nineteen lost, including four men. Eight boats and two rafts are destroyed. Three might be salvageable...maybe," Levidi shrugged.

"What is our final count?" Aizarg asked Okta.

Okta laid down a handful of broken sticks and hastily arranged them on the deck in the center of the circle.

"Thirty-four rafts survive. In addition to the two wedding barges, we have thirteen large rafts and twenty common rafts, with thirty-nine boats scattered all around. I count twenty-six men, not including Virag and his worthless henchmen. As for women and children, they number almost fifty.

Okta pointed to the largest sticks. "The wedding barges are here, the rest of the flotilla stretches out in a long line, mostly Crane vessels, until they transition to Minnow vessels. The arrangement is lopsided and unwieldy. We lurch from one swell to the next, the Minnow vessels whiplashing at the end of the procession. How we survived so far is a miracle." Okta's eyes briefly flashed up toward the staff. "We must reorganize the fleet before the next big wind hits."

Ghalen spoke up. "Reorganizing will be difficult. The boats fill with this infernal sky water as fast as we can bail, not to mention the waves. But it's the confounded silt that's sinking them. And what doesn't flounder, the sea rips apart. Debris and ice slam against our outer vessels even as we speak. " Ghalen shook his head. "Most of our poles have snapped, so now the men use masts and sticks to deflect the debris."

Ba-lok leaned in and tapped the sticks. "We have to separate the flotilla, and quickly. We stand a better chance of survival one boat at a time."

"And how do you intend to keep our people together?" Okta snapped.

"The same way we keep a fishing fleet together in fog, with lines and torches."

"Torches?" Okta flicked his finger under a stream of water leaking through the canopy. "Bah! This is no wind storm, or even ice mists. There is no shore to paddle to, no home star to guide upon. We've never dealt with waves like this, or floating ice and debris. *Never.* If we do it your way, rafts will shatter, boats will swamp, and people will die."

"A Lo man knows his boat! No one knows how to tend this jumbled mass of vessels, it's completely unwieldy," Ba-lok countered.

"I must agree with Ba-lok, Uros," Ghalen said. "We may not last the night."

"And who will man the boats, Ghalen?" Okta said. "We don't have enough men to tend each vessel. Do we abandon women and children to their own skill against *this* sea? And how shall we divide our food and supplies?"

Ba-lok glared at the older sco-lo-ti. "We have no other choice."

"We have a choice!" Okta turned to Aizarg. "Ba-lok wants us to take our chances one boat at a time because that is what he knows. But if this deluge lasts as long as the Narim foretold, then we will perish *one boat at a time.*"

"Okta, there is merit to what you say, but our odds at riding the storm are better one boat at a time." Ghalen said. "We're being ripped apart."

Levidi nodded. "If we untie the vessels, I doubt we'll keep the fleet together longer than a few hours. The storm is separating the flotilla whether we wish it or not. We're unraveling along the edges like a piece of cloth. Water drenches everything. Precious supplies have been washed overboard, and what's left will rot if we can't keep it dry. The men need sleep, and the women and children are cold."

"Ghalen and Levidi speak wisdom. We sit here and jabber while boats are crushed. Separate the fleet, save our people" Ba-lok insisted.

Atamoda saw fear masked as determination guiding Ba-lok. For that, she did not blame the young sco-lo-ti. Even with his faults, she knew he cared for his people. But in Okta's face she saw a different expression.

Purpose? Or perhaps inspiration?

More than any Lo clan, the Carp held a magical attachment to the sea. They considered land taboo, often living their entire lives without dust touching their heels.

She knew something gripped Okta's mind like a wolf seizes the throat of its prey, locked and unwilling to release it. Atamoda knew Okta desperately wanted to make the others understand his vision for the flotilla, whatever it may be. She hoped Aizarg would give him a chance to voice his thoughts. The idea of riding out the deluge bobbing amongst these towering waves in a solitary raft terrified her.

Her gaze drifted to the staff cradled in her husband's arms. The men droned on as her mind drifted, and her eyes grew wide. With every flash of lightning, the red metal orb seemed to swim with a dim glow originating from within.

Another tendril of lightning arced across the sky accompanied by a rolling clap of thunder and a terrible epiphany. A dark thought sank its teeth into her mind, shaking Atamoda from her trance. She looked up to see Aizarg staring at her.

"Atamoda, you wish to say something?" he said.

She pointed to the staff. "I believe this totem is a gateway to the Nameless God. Truly, I dread drifting too far from its power. You men consider only the waves and wind, but if the demons return, Kus-ge and I cannot protect a scattered fleet. They fear the staff, not us."

Okta grinned and wagged his finger at her excitedly. "Yes. Yes! We must also consider this."

Before Aizarg could say anything, Okta quickly rearranged the sticks and splintered pieces of wood. "Before us exists only two constants, storm and sea. Unless we can stabilize the flotilla, we cannot exist in harmony with either. We must cease fighting." Okta paused as a hint of a smile touched his lined face. To Atamoda, he almost seemed to grow younger. Okta slowly raised his hand and closed it into a fist. "We must become one with sea and storm."

As Okta spoke, Atamoda sensed the flotilla slowly spinning, directionless, with no other purpose except to endure. Occasionally, tremors shook the flotilla as debris assaulted the edges. Decks rose and fell with sickening groans as lightning sizzled throughout the inky sky. Yet, the Lo ignored the dying world and hung on each word uttered by the Sco-lo-ti of the Carp. Soon, those in the inner council were nodding and asking questions.

Atamoda could not hear every word, nor did she understand everything Okta spoke of. But she recognized the light of hope beginning to take root in the hearts of the council and her people.

Finally, the questions ran out. Okta looked about, unable to suppress his smile.

Aizarg turned to his inner council, "You've heard Okta's plan. Speak your thoughts."

"What Okta proposes has never been done. To attempt it in the best of times would take days. Now..." Ba-lok shook his head. "...now, it's impossible."

"I don't know, Aizarg," Levidi stared down at the collection of sticks. "I don't know."

Ghalen tapped the center of the sticks. "If the seas grow any rougher, I can't see how this can be done. If the Nameless God grants us a reprieve, perhaps."

Aizarg closed his eyes and lowered his head.

Is he praying?

Atamoda found the sight of a man in communion with the spirits jarring. So much had changed. She wondered what thoughts, what prayers, raced through his mind. At that moment the patesi-le realized how much she mourned for the lost gods that no longer filled her spirit.

Could I ever commune with this Nameless God?

The people stared at her husband, waiting on their Uros to pronounce their fate. Heavier than the rain, she felt anxious fear radiating toward him, a dark light more imposing than the giant wave.

Aizarg took a deep breath and handed Levidi the staff. "Wedge it there." He pointed to a small gap between two logs in the center of the wedding barge.

Levidi obeyed as Aizarg stood to address his people. "If we separate, our people will drift alone in the veil of darkness. Our light will be extinguished forever, one boat at a time."

Aizarg's voice rose above the thundering rain as he gestured to the inner circle. "The flotilla is our arun-ki, this inner circle our köy-lo-hely. We are Lo. One people. Let our light begin here."

As Aizarg spoke, the red metal orb began to glow like the previous night's embers being rekindled just before dawn. Gasps went out among the Lo, including Atamoda. The Lo held their hands toward the staff as the glow slowly intensified, infusing washed out faces with color and life.

Once again, the Nameless God displays His power.

Bat-or stretched his little fingers toward the light. "It's pretty, Mommy."

Aizarg continued, "The Deluge is the will of the Nameless God, but so are we! The Lo will unite and become one with sea and storm. Crane, Minnow, Carp, and Turtle will turn Okta's words into reality and link this flotilla into an unbroken chain, which will carry us across the Black Sea."

Rays of light extended to the arun-ki's embattled edges, where the men fighting the sea turned to witness its brilliance.

At opposite ends of the crowded circle, the Fox and the Snake averted their eyes from the wondrous light. Unnoticed by all, they shrank back into the shadows behind the curtain of rain.

16. The Little King

In my quest for dragons, I traveled east along paths and trails crisscrossed throughout the millennia. The land of Cin had changed dramatically since my last journey. The Icelands had retreated north, and once familiar landmarks vanished. I lost my way on several occasions. Cold lakes and new forests blanketed lands where impregnable glaciers once stood. Not only was the natural world transforming; the most dramatic changes were in the world of men.

I revisited settlements established on previous journeys. Many were gone, but some survived. A few remained simple villages where they still praised Nuwa's name. However, several had grown into cities of hundreds, even thousands, of people. They possessed crafts I never taught them, such as the wheel and the bow. These people forgot Nuwa and lifted up mortals they called 'kings,' as gods. These kings raised armies and made war upon one another. In them, I sensed the influence of the Corruptor and began to doubt my purpose.

As for dragons, they had faded into legend. With a heavy heart, I continued east until I came to the place where Cin met the Sunrise Sea. I could go no farther and made a bonfire on the shore.

The Chronicle of Fu Xi

***

No sleep, no food, only rock and rain and the fruitless search for Heise. Days and days had passed, with no sign of his horse.

Fu Xi's mortal half gasped for life, eating away at its own flesh. It fizzled away like hot grease on an iron pan, leaving only pure divinity clinging to this world's rocky soil.

Naked and raw, he crept forward across stone and crevice. Long ago, though how long he didn't know, cotton and deerskin had rotted away. Cloaked only in the daggertooth's fur, he crawled from rock to rock, orichalcum sword tied to his back with twisted strips of daggertooth skin. Like macabre armor, the cat's skull covered his head, long canine teeth resting over his cheekbones.

Fu Xi sensed the predator's spirit stirring in him, a ghostly remnant clinging to the uncured hide. The beast's hunger stirred like a fire in his belly, its powerful restlessness coursed through his limbs. Now he smelled roasting meat wafting up from below.

Somewhere below, men ate.

His tortured stomach twisted and growled.

Fu Xi slowly made his way down until he heard voices. A ruddy glow outlined the top of a ledge below him. Smoke wafted around the ledge, misty fingers crawling toward him through the rain. After three days, his feet finally found enough purchase to allow him to let go with his fingers.

Fu Xi listened to voices echoing in the night, a series of hacks and grunts for which he had no reference.

Four? Perhaps five.

No matter, they had food. He found their deep, satisfied laughter unnerving in the cold grayness.

There were several tribes of mountain people throughout Cin, hardy stock who thrived where rock and glacier scraped sky. Perhaps these were such men, who stored meat inside glacial ice.

He peered over the lip and looked down. A generously wide ledge spread out about twenty feet below. The firelight danced over the smooth rock, yet he still couldn't see them.

His mother's words echoed in his mind. *There will be no other men.*

And yet, here they were, and they possessed a fire where Fu Xi could not create one. They ate generously where Fu Xi could find no sustenance.

Fu Xi strained to understand their words, but only heard unintelligible noises over the rain and wind.

One of them passed gas, provoking an explosion of laughter from the rest.

I understand that. Fu Xi chuckled, but his laugh emerged as a husky croak.

Like a cat, Fu Xi leapt the remaining distance, landing in a crouch and facing five of the squattest, hairiest, pug-nosed fellows he'd ever laid eyes upon. Judging by their reaction they didn't think much of Fu Xi, either.

They stumbled backwards away from their roaring fire, deep-set, beady eyes darting about in shock. They scuttled away from Fu Xi until they bumped up against a massive brush pile, reminding Fu Xi of fat field mice seeking the protection of a haystack.

Wrapped in goat hide from head to foot, they wore fuzzy, conical hats with long ear flaps that looked like donkey ears. Each sported dangling, oiled moustaches that looked like whips hanging well past their chins.

Donkey Men.

"Nyah!" the one closest to Fu Xi screamed and dropped his wooden bowl. Thick, brown stew full of meaty chunks spilled out onto the ground.

It then dawned on Fu Xi how he must look.

"Excuse me, but this isn't what it looks like." He lifted the dagger tooth skull from his head.

"*Nyah!*" The five Donkey Men screamed in unison. Judging by their petrified expressions, he might as well have removed his head.

Fu Xi held up his hands. "I only want something to eat, and then I'll be on my way." It suddenly dawned on Fu Xi how short these Donkey Men where. He thought they were recessed farther back in under the ledge, but as his eyes adjusted to the firelight, he realized that the tallest barely came up to his sternum.

The one closest to him, most likely their leader by his haughty expression, seemed to relax, understanding Fu Xi wasn't an immediate threat. He twirled his moustaches with tiny, sausage fingers.

"Well, my Little King, may I trouble you for a bite to eat?" Fu Xi motioned to one of the bowls and pretended to eat.

"Ah! Nya*hhh*!" The Little King nodded with fresh understanding.

He glanced back at his compatriots and pointed at Fu Xi with a sly grin. "Nyah."

As one, they looked at Fu Xi with equally sly grins, nodding and speaking in perfect unison. "Nyahhh!"

Then the Little King proceeded to hold court before his rapt subjects. He spoke at length in a high, squeaky voice with great inflection and grand hand gestures, occasionally turning and bowing to Fu Xi with an irritatingly ingratiating smile, as if not wanting to appear rude to his visitor.

To Fu Xi's ears, he only repeated the same word, *nyah*, over and over. Sometimes, he barked the word and stamped his feet as if issuing commands. Other times he lowered his hands, palm down, as if making a reasonable appeal for calm.

His subjects reacted accordingly. Occasionally, they turned to one another and nodded excitedly. A few times, they gasped in shock. More often, they appeared agitated and twisted their moustaches nervously.

Fu Xi spoke a thousand tongues and could make sense of a thousand more. Yet, here he stood, stymied by apparent gibberish.

Nyah? Even the Icemen's grunts made more sense than these Donkey Men.

While the Little King held council, Fu Xi studied the ledge.

Wide enough for several elephants, deep enough for several horses.

The ledge turned out to be a massive, but shallow, cave no more than twenty paces deep. The ledge's overhang stretched high above, creating a cathedral arch vanishing into the shadows above his head. An ancient brush pile rested against the sheer cliff that served as the cave's back wall.

He thought what a good shelter the cave would have made for Heise.

A loud *nyah* brought Fu Xi's attention back to the speech. Finally, the Little King finished with a flourish of the wrist and a slight bow to his subjects.

And they applauded with a jolly chorus of "Nyah!"

Of course.

The Little King snatched a wooden bowl from one of his subjects, not much bigger than a cup to Fu Xi, and extended it. He stretched his little arm as far as he could without stepping forward, as if Fu Xi might bite it off.

Fu Xi bowed slightly and reached for the bowl. He then realized that the rotting smell he briefly detected came from the Donkey Men themselves, not any carcass lying about.

The Little King's grin widened, revealing a row of filed, needle-like teeth.

***

Alone at the edge of the world and the end of a fruitless quest, I listened to the pounding surf and contemplated all I had seen. Under the stars, with only despair for companionship, I thought of the wicked cities and my failure among the Ice Men. My thoughts wandered to Tiejiang and the acolyte of Nuwa, and I knew the time had come for my wanderings to cease. The tutelage of the Tall Men had come to an end. With the rising sun, I swore to let mortal fortunes fall where they may.

Perhaps my mother knew this. Perhaps my destiny lay elsewhere besides beloved Nushen.

I awoke before dawn, eager to watch the sunrise and start a new life. A black form emerged from the rising sun. My heart pounded in my chest as I thought at first a dragon skimmed low over the water. As it drew closer, I rubbed my eyes, spellbound by a sight no less glorious.

An enormous ship, more massive than a hundred elephants, with crimson sails like sunset thunderheads, upon masts higher than the tallest oaks rode a sparkling sea. Spellbound, I watched until it dropped anchor beyond the breakers. It lowered several small boats. They assaulted the breakers in a spear-tip formation, and rowed toward my bonfire.

Dozens of creatures, which I first took as demons, swarmed onto the beach like angry red ants. Their hair was as black as mine, yet their eyes were strangely round. They wore dazzling metal armor over crimson skin.

Wielding graceful white metal swords, they immediately set upon me. After seven of them fell under my blade, the rest withdrew to the water's edge, chattering like angry squirrels. I instantly disliked this alien tongue. Their leader studied me with eyes like black glass. While he attempted no parley, we had come to a fundamental understanding: I knew they were not demons, and he understood I wasn't mortal.

They may have been mere men, but they fought magnificently, with more skill and ferocity than any in all of Cin. Their prowess and grand vessel deeply disturbed me. More troubling still, their white metal swords had seriously damaged my bronze blade.

Sword resting between my legs, I stood between the red men and my beloved Cin and waited for them to make the next move. Then the lieutenant cautiously approached me with the hyena's grin. I held my blade as he chattered and pointed to another boat approaching from the ship.

Until that wonderful and terrible sliver of time fell upon me, my life had been a granite mountain where the years fell like raindrops, but washed away not the first pebble. The conqueror stepped from his boat and cast a mighty shadow across my beloved land. In him I saw the mountain, the ocean, and the sky for the first time. Upon that beach I diminished and rejoiced.

I, Fu Xi, Lord of Cin and son of the Queen of the West, stood before another god and knew awe.

How can I describe glory with mere ink and parchment? Even the dragon's tongue fails to do justice to those who've never seen the sun.

Obsidian skin and eyes round like harvest moons, the giant strode forward wielding a blood red sword not unlike that of the Offering Blade. His eyes, gray and sharp as winter's first snow, captured me and held my feet firmly to the sand. He laughed as if greeting an old friend, deep and rich and bubbling with glorious power. His red armor, polished and unadorned, captured the sun's radiance. But his shadow is what I remember most. It fell away from the rising sun, stretching and undulating across the beach until it touched me, breaking the spell.

His laughter transformed into a war cry as he fell upon me with the blood sword. I had never encountered such an assault and fell back beneath the onslaught. Gouged and weakened from the white swords, my bronze sword proved no match for his blade. Needing to preserve its integrity for an opportune moment, I dodged and ducked, leaping away from the crimson edge.

The Chronicle of Fu Xi

***

The attack erupted with a knife in the back.

How did they get behind me?

With stunning speed, all five Donkey Men piled on, knives and teeth ripping and shredding his flesh, all to the sadistic chant, "Nyah!"

Fu Xi spun about, trying to yank two of them off his back. One of them stuck him behind the knees, sending him slamming against the ground. Tiny limbs and tiny blades blurred in the firelight, penetrating hide and skin.

Fu Xi rolled over, pinning the two who clung to his back. He endured their assaults while concentrating on the other three.

The smallest one, possibly a woman, gnawed on his ankle like a dog, even growling while sinking her teeth into his tendons. This irritated Fu Xi to no end, so with a hard kick, he sent Dog Girl hurtling over the cliff.

With a wet crack, he smashed together the heads of two on his chest, of which one was the Little King.

In short order, he rolled over and snatched one off his back. Kicking and screaming, he tossed him over the cliff to join Dog Girl. A moment later, the last Donkey Man kicked and pedaled over the chasm, Fu Xi firmly clenching him by the scruff of the neck. He spit at Fu Xi and clawed at his arm with sharp, filthy nails.

Fu Xi had seen many things in his immortal life, but he didn't think he'd seen anything quite as sneaky and vicious as the Donkey Men.

"What are you?"

The Donkey Man hissed and swung with greater ferocity.

"You're heavier than you look. Utter one word, any word, other than *nyah,* and I'll spare your life!"

"Nyah! Nyah!" He tried to kick Fu Xi, apparently indifferent to the fact his stubby legs hovered over the abyss and certain death.

Fu Xi let go and wiped his hands. He walked back to the fire, listening to the fading *Nyahhh!* echo down the canyon.

There will be no other men, his mother had said.

"I certainly hope there won't be any more Donkey Men," he laughed.

***

Confident at first, the black god pressed the attack, but he grew frustrated as his sword met only air. He retreated a few paces, assessing me.

I studied him, too, examining the red armor for gaps and weaknesses. Glorious or not, I would not accept defeat at the hands of this alien god and his red warriors.

He became like fire and I, air. Together, we transformed into a storm of sand and spray along the beach. He employed the blood sword with a direct, unrelenting fighting style. My body became a weapon as I probed for an opening to strike with my inferior blade. My kicks and

156

punches, powerful enough to snap the back of an ox, only served to delay his next attack.

Such exhilaration! Such reckless, untamed power! For centuries I took my immortality for granted. Could he slay me? In my passion, I didn't care. My blood coursed like a wild river. For the first time, I understood what mortals felt when dancing with death...Alive! For that fleeting dance upon the sunrise beach, I would have traded the previous eternity.

With a spinning kick I struck at his neck, but missed. He whirled about, and I felt the blade kiss upon my thigh. I leapt backwards in a somersault, my wound sealing before I touched the sand. Crouched beneath his next slash, my sword thrust up and found his right forearm. Shocked, he withdrew and examined the wound. It sealed in seconds, his blood evaporating off the sand in a barely discernible sizzle.

He flexed his hand several times in amazement, perhaps shocked. The red warriors exchanged worried glances as they stepped back a few paces.

Had they ever seen their god bleed?

The black god lunged again, fueled by careless rage.

Another opportunity presented itself, and I thrust my blade into a gap below his armpit. He pivoted at the last moment as the tip snapped away with a hot spark, my sword deflected downward.

Off balance for only a blink of an eye, I fell forward, and he slashed at my neck. I yanked up my sword to block, but the red metal cut through the bronze as a scythe slices through the harvest wheat. My sword lay in two pieces on the sand, its edges glowing and molten.

His red blade halted a hair's breadth from my neck.

The black god didn't press his attack. Instead, he sheathed his sword, pulled me up, and hugged me as if we were long-lost friends, laughing the whole time.

With questioning brow, he tapped my chest.

"Fu Xi," I answered.

"Foo-Zi..." My name rolled off his lips slowly, as if he tested it, perhaps searching his thoughts for any glimmer he had heard it spoken before.

The black god slapped his chest and proclaimed his own name, each syllable dripping with glorious pride and power.

"Leviathan!"

The Chronicle of Fu Xi

***

Fu Xi tossed the cured goat hide pot full of cooked human flesh over the cliff.

Bandits and cannibals, I should have guessed.

Fu Xi felt his wounds close and then reopen as he searched the Donkey Men's camp for food and supplies. He touched the gashes and sniffed.

Poison.

Already weakened, his body could not fully reject the poison and seal his wounds.

Perhaps it will take longer than usual. Fu Xi pressed on through the pain and continued to search the camp. Leather bags full of rotted leather, furs, bone trinkets, and primitive tools comprised their meager treasures. Keeping a bag and a few of the most promising furs and scraps for himself, he left the rest. Other than a crusty, green copper knife, he found nothing of use.

A pile of human bones, some freshly picked, sat just under the ledge and out of the rain. A few looked as if they'd been gnawed on. Too exhausted to feel outraged, Fu Xi simply used a stick to sweep the remains over the edge as well. Soon, only the brush pile and fire remained.

He knew by the relative absence of refuse, this wasn't the Donkey Men's normal hideout. The flood likely pushed them into the mountains, as it had Fu Xi, where they preyed on other refugees.

Fu Xi conducted a cursory search of the cave's edges and found the narrow goat path the Donkey Men took up the cliff to the cave. If any more of this vile band lingered in the storm, they'd have to approach from this direction. Satisfied, Fu Xi returned to the fire and took off his lion skin, laying it as close to the fire as he dared to dry it out.

He pulled a few large branches off the pile. The wood, completely dry and desiccated, almost crumbled in his grip.

This is beyond dry rot. Old, perhaps even ancient, the dry mountain air had preserved the timber from decomposition.

Jabbing pain penetrated his side. Fu Xi examined his abdomen where a trickle of blood still leaked from one of the knife wounds. It wasn't healing as fast as usual.

He dabbed his finger in the blood and sniffed it.

I'm not familiar with this kind of poison.

He needed to rest. His immortality could only sustain flesh for so long. Without food he may cease healing at all.

He broke off a few more pieces of wood, light as the papyrus he'd seen in Wu, and laid them on the fire. The limbs blazed brilliantly and were gone in moments. Thankfully, they created a lasting coal bed.

Fu Xi's eyes soon grew heavy. Eventually, the lion skin dried out. He wrapped himself in its warm embrace and laid down his head on the smooth, bare rock.

It's so smooth, like a river stone. Something about the brush pile and cave floor gnawed at Fu Xi, but the nagging thought lost to his weariness.

"'Nyah'...what the hell does that mean, anyway?" the demigod whispered before sleep finally found him.

***

A cheer went up from the red men. Leviathan motioned me to come with him back across the sea. I acquiesced, my curiosity piqued.

In truth, I willingly succumbed to his spell, fully and without reservation. Euphoric from the battle, I climbed aboard Leviathan's great ship. I only looked back long enough to witness the red men stripping their dead and abandoning the bodies on the beach.

Thus began my long, self-induced blindness.

The Chronicle of Fu Xi

17. Arun-ki

"My men may have bravely rearranged the vessels in treacherous seas, but it was the Lo women who stitched them together. On that day, we ceased being a flotilla and truly became an arun-ki, if only for a little while." – Conversations with the Uros.

The Chronicle of Fu Xi

***

Wind whipping his soaked tunic, the Uros leaned into the gale upon the bow raft. He stared out across the water, as if oblivious to the flurry of activity transpiring behind him. Atamoda knew the wind pushed them backwards, but the wind and waves painted the illusion that they plowed headlong into the waves with great speed, as if the hand of the Nameless God drove them onward.

The Uros grasped the top of the anchor pylon, the thick cypress log lashed to the bow raft's deck by seemingly endless rope loops. Two ropes, both thicker than a man's bicep, led away from the pylon. One trailed a few feet to where Ghalen busily organized a team of men around the new sea anchor; Ba-lok, Ezra, Levidi, and Kol-ok among them.

A collapsed bag, wider than two men were tall, ruggedly constructed of tightly woven reeds, and reinforced with rings of thickly twisted ropes, Okta promised this sea anchor would grip the waters like a mighty claw.

By contrast, the old sea anchor, barely managed to keep the flotilla pointed into the wind. A temporary collection of stitched sails, its thin and knotted line had broken numerous times, sending the flotilla floundering dangerously and forcing Ghalen to take a boat to retrieve it.

The team would haul in the old anchor immediately before deploying the new anchor. Both could not be simultaneously deployed, Okta warned, lest they tangle and collapse. The transition would be perilous and must go exactly as planned, or the flotilla could turn broadside into the waves.

The other cable secured to the anchor pylon ran in the opposite direction, straight down the center of the flotilla.

The Spine.

My rope. Atamoda allowed herself a brief, self-satisfied smile as she admired the women's handiwork. She waited under a meager line of canopies with the rest of the Lo women, including Sana, looking on as the men prepared to fulfill Okta's vision.

"Where is he?" Kus-ge huffed. "Let's get this over with."

Atamoda peered over her shoulder, searching for the Master of Boats beneath the patchwork of reed canopies erected over the center rafts. "Okta had business to attend to at the stern. He'll be along shortly."

"Why can't they just toss it in?" Su-gar asked.

"Aizarg wanted the Master of Boats here for this moment," Atamoda responded.

"This *moment* is cold and wet," Kus-ge said. "I want to dry off."

"The sooner the bow is reliably pointed into the wind, the sooner we can raise the remainder of the canopies. Until that time, we can't start a fire in our braziers," the old Minnow woman Ro-xandra said from Kus-ge's right.

Except for those tending the children on the Supply Barge, all the women were present. Atamoda studied the line of faces she'd worked shoulder-to-shoulder with since the council meeting. In that time, the flotilla had transformed from a collection of logs and reeds into a floating village, an arun-ki. She shook her head, amazed at how much had changed in only a short time.

It feels like an eternity.

To Atamoda, the mighty cable they called the Spine symbolized the Lo's salvation. For two straight weeks the women had labored, at first under driving rain, and then under hastily erected reed canopies. Day and night, Okta paced the decks shouting like a Sammujad slave master, "More cords!"; "Make it thicker!"; "More, more, more!" Only the constant lightning and pitching decks kept the women from outright mutiny. They feared the sea more than the Master of Boats. Slowly, they transformed heaps of reeds, scooped from the sea, into fiber cords. In turn, they bound and wrapped the cords into the mighty cable, perhaps the strongest rope ever woven, which now lay at her feet.

Now her knees throbbed, and her hands and joints were swollen to the point she could barely bend them. Weariness filled every inch of her aching bones, but only pride and satisfaction mattered now.

The Spine formed the flotilla's centerline, binding and aligning the five largest rafts, the core rafts, end to end. At the heart of these rested the two wedding barges, the Supply Barge, and the Köy-lo-hely. Heavy rope joints secured the Spine at three points on each raft, while normal mooring lines attached all the rafts along the corners. The Spine bore the brunt of the sea's assault, while distributing the waves' violent jolts evenly across the length of the flotilla.

The men, including Aizarg, were shocked when Okta, contrary to all the Lo knew of seamanship, demanded small gaps, slightly less than a man's stride, between the rafts' fore and aft sides. Okta carried the day, but only after reluctantly agreeing to Ba-lok's demands that tightly bound reed bundles be secured to each raft's corners. Okta insisted these bumpers were unnecessary but wouldn't interfere with his design.

Seven slightly less robust cables ran perpendicular to the Spine, attached along its axis at the rope joints. Okta dubbed these "ribs." They linked seven rows of rafts, radiating laterally from the Spine. Each rib consisted of three to seven rafts, largest toward the core with the smaller rafts at the edges. This arrangement gave the flotilla a roughly oval appearance. Okta insisted the ribs must run centerline across each row, and the gaps in each row must align, even if it meant excessive gaps between rafts.

Atamoda remembered how Okta explained it to the council. "The sea anchor aligns the Spine with the sea. The Spine binds the core and lessens the sea's anger. The ribs wrap the flotilla to the Spine." He held his palm up flat and then bent his knuckles. "The hand's joints work as one, fingers aligned for strength and unity. If the joints and ribs are not aligned, they work in opposition."

Atamoda couldn't shake the unsettling feeling that it was all for naught. She could not see the fruition of Okta's vision, and suspected, neither did the men. Yes, perhaps the flotilla crested the waves with slightly less whiplash, but now the water sloshed excessively up through the gaps, spreading silt and flotsam across all the decks, not just the periphery. Also, now that the flotilla had more of an oval shape, it wanted to spin atop the waves, as opposed to aligning with them. This put tremendous stress on the spine, corner mooring lines, and even the wedding barges.

While perhaps the strongest rope ever fashioned by the Lo, the Spine jerked uncomfortably left and right against the attachment knots. Sometimes it bunched up with too much play, only to suddenly snap tight when a large wave rolled beneath the decks. Even Atamoda knew, after a few more days of this unrelenting lateral motion, the Spine would begin to fray and inevitably snap. In fact, the obvious progress Atamoda saw in Okta's design lay in the flotilla's prow, which absorbed the brunt of the sea's fury.

The prow consisted of three large rafts and one common raft, arranged into a curved bow. Unoccupied barrier boats, turned sideways and firmly lashed to the rafts' leading edges, were piled head high with tightly cinched driftwood. The barrier boats, in turn, were protected by a line of heavy driftwood logs, tied two deep to the windward flank. Together, the logs, boats, and wall formed a crude barrier Okta called the *storm wall*. Ideally, all the boats secured along the flotilla's flanks would be shielded in the storm wall's shadow.

But so far the flotilla wallowed too much for the storm wall to serve as an effective shield.

And now they waited for Okta, the Master of Boats, before deploying the sea anchor.

"How much longer will Aizarg wait?" Levidi's wife, Alaya, asked. "Shouldn't someone fetch Okta?"

Pale and drawn, Sahti stood next to Alaya, rubbing her swollen belly nervously. Atamoda told Xva's expecting wife to wait under the canopies, but she insisted on seeing the sea anchor's deployment. Sahti's baby, and their dwindling food supply, had become constant sources of worry for the patesi-le.

Sahti, a meek girl who rarely spoke, seemed to read Atamoda's thoughts. "I am well, patesi-le. Do not worry."

Atamoda pushed the uncomfortable thought from her mind and once again looked to the stern. "If the Uros can wait, we can wait."

***

"There! It's done." Okta beamed as he finished lashing the tiny boat to the flotilla's stern, straddling the boundary between the Crane and Minnow Clans.

"What are you so happy about, Marsh Man?" Virag croaked, fighting not to vomit again.

Okta shot him an evil look. "Your new home was the final boat I had to secure. The flotilla is complete."

"I'm happy for you," Virag sneered.

Okta ignored him and rattled off a series of instructions on basic seamanship, most of which Virag ignored. With white knuckles, the once mighty Sammujad slaver gripped the raft's mast as the rain pelted him unmercifully. Okta quickly secured a tattered reed mat over the little boat to keep Virag and Spako somewhat dry.

Spako, the only surviving remnant of Virag's Sammujad body guard, knelt on all fours at the edge of the raft, heaving his breakfast into the water. The giant man's back arched like a cat.

Okta casually stepped around Spako and continued to issue instructions. He handed Virag a clay jar. "Use this to bail out the boat. Keep the canopy tight and the sides cinched down, or the wind will get under it and blow it away. Remember, the canopy will not only keep out the rain, but most of the sea. The vessel is now your responsibility."

"Answer me this, how are the both of us supposed to fit in there?"

"This arrangement is the Uros' will, not mine. A proper Lo man must learn to build a boat before he can command one. If this vessel sinks, you'll have to sleep exposed on a periphery raft with nothing to protect you from the elements." Okta's barely suppressed grin infuriated Virag even more.

Virag leaned against the mast, fighting to control his lurching stomach. He watched horrified as the frail craft repeatedly slammed the adjacent raft.

"We'll be smashed to bits! That toy won't last an hour."

"We're about to deploy a larger sea anchor. If the line holds, it will dampen most of the whiplash here at the stern. You're..." Okta flashed that damn grin again, *"...downstream. It's the safest place in the entire flotilla. Trust me."*

Virag grew suspicious.

That bastard is playing me for a fool.

He wanted to complain, but lacked the will. Clinging to a mast day after day in fear of being swept overboard, continuously pelted by sea and rain, drained him of the strength to fight.

Okta nudged Spako with his foot and pointed to the boat. "Get in," he commanded.

Like a beast, Spako crawled the few remaining feet and slid his enormous bulk under the canopy. The boat sank several inches.

Okta lifted part of the canopy and motioned for Virag to enter. The slaver felt like a piece of livestock being led to the slaughter pen. The little vessel would either be a sanctuary or a coffin. Right now he was too tired to care which.

Resigned, Virag crawled in after Spako.

Spako's enormous bulk raised Virag's end several inches. Up and down, side to side, Virag's head snapped sideways in an unending whiplash. He'd once seen a Scythian break a wild horse, and he'd wondered how the warrior stayed atop the bucking beast without breaking his neck. Now Virag rode the bucking horse, but gripping the boat's sides did nothing to stabilize the world.

Again and again, he lifted the tarp and vomited over the side. He cursed Okta. He cursed Aizarg. He cursed Spako, now blissfully asleep. Virag cursed the entire Lo nation and his mother for bringing him into this world.

***

"Here comes a big one!" Ghalen shouted and pointed off the bow. A rogue wave poked above the line of storm-driven crests. Everyone braced as it slammed against the storm wall. Spray washed across the entire flotilla. Water gushed over the sticks and drained away between logs and boats. The Spine twisted back and forth with creaks and pops as rafts slammed against one another. Atamoda felt the flotilla lurch sideways down the backside of the wave, almost ninety degrees to the wind. Only with agonizing slowness did the old sea anchor slowly draw the bow back into the wind.

Ghalen marched to Atamoda, "Where is Okta? We're sliding around like a pig in the mud." Ghalen kicked the Spine. "If we get hit like that again, the only thing this will be good for is tangling us up."

"Okta said he needed to finish some work at the stern. He will be here," Atamoda said.

Ghalen exhaled and turned to rejoin the men on the bow raft. Aizarg hadn't budged, even with the wave. He still guarded the narrow gap in the storm wall, grasping the pylon, staring out to sea.

"Let's deploy it without him," she heard one of the men say.

"Yes, deploy the anchor," Kus-ge shouted through cupped hands. Soon, other Minnow women joined her in a chorus of frustration.

"We wait for the Master of Boats." Aizarg called over his shoulder.

Perhaps I should go find Okta.

She turned around to see Okta standing behind her, grinning broadly.

"Where have you been? We've been waiting."

"I had to find a boat for the a'gan. I can't have Virag and that oaf of his wandering about forever, vomiting all over my decks.

"Where did you put them?" she asked, intrigued.

Okta grinned even broader. "I think I found a boat worthy of the rat."

"Okta, what did you do?" Atamoda looked at him from the corner of her eye. Before he could respond, Ezra bounded over.

"Okta! We're ready. Come on, I can't wait to see how well it works." He tugged at Okta's tunic like an eager child.

"Alright! Alright!" he laughed.

Ghalen spread his arms out and shook his head as if to say, *"We're waiting"*.

Another wave struck them slightly offset, and the flotilla lurched sideways again. Atamoda grabbed on to the nearest mast and held on. Unfazed, Okta strode to the bow raft.

How can he be so confident? Atamoda knew in the next few moments she would either witness something amazing, or Okta's failure.

"Ba-lok, haul in the old sea anchor!" Okta bellowed.

Aizarg stepped back away from the bow raft, allowing Ba-lok's team to move forward. Ba-lok nodded and signaled to Ezra, Kol-ok, and several other men. Together, they repeatedly pulled in unison, until a pile of rope and sail lay in a heap at Okta's feet, the three stitched sails now reduced to a tattered mess.

Ba-lok clucked softly. "It's no wonder we couldn't hold true into the wind anymore."

Okta lingered a few moments over the old anchor. When deployed, the rope and sail were the light yellow color of denuded reed fibers. Now the sails and rope were stained dark green with black streaks.

Okta squatted next to the old sea anchor. Atamoda saw the confidence drain from his face.

"Okta, the flotilla turns. Are you ready?" Ghalen asked.

As if shaken from a trance, Okta looked up. "Deploy the sea anchor."

Together, the men lifted the collapsed bag onto its side. The rope rings woven into its skin gave it a somewhat rigid shape, but the men struggled against the wind to push it over the sea wall. Several times, the wind blew the anchor backwards. Once, it partially inflated and almost slammed into the canopies.

Critical moments passed. The raft under her feet began to groan as the flotilla began a slow turn to starboard.

"Wave!" Ba-lok shouted. Off the bow, several crests away, another dark rogue rose.

"Get it in the water, now!" Okta seized the leading edge of the anchor, trying once again to drag it over the storm wall.

Atamoda looked back at the women staring in horror.

"What are you waiting for?" she shouted. "Get over there and push!"

The women surged forward, lending dozens of hands to the effort. The flotilla turned farther right, the storm wall now almost nighty degrees to the oncoming wave. The anchor teetered precariously on the edge of the wall for what seemed like an eternity before splashing into the sea.

The bag opened immediately and began to sink. The line quickly played out, guided by Ghalen through the storm wall aperture.

Atamoda looked left and saw the rogue wave towering above them.

It's going to flip us!

The anchor line popped out of Ghalen's hands as the bow snapped left, squarely into the wave. Several people, including Atamoda tumbled to the deck.

Atamoda scrambled to her feet as the rogue wave struck the arun-ki. With a deep bass thump, the Spine snapped tight. The decks buckled upward in a rapid, orderly succession down the length of the arun-ki. Instead of water sloshing from between the gaps, it sprayed straight upward. The jets shot up highest at the first rib, but each successive row of gaps shaved off more of the wave's energy, until it produced only a little splash near the stern. Each row rose and fell in perfect harmony until the arun-ki gently slid down the wave's backside.

The Lo stared in awe as the arun-ki molded itself perfectly to each successive wave. The Spine no longer lurched from side to side, but held straight and true like an iron bar. All rolling and sliding motion instantly ceased, and seventy rafts and boats pitched up and down as one. To Atamoda, the decks almost felt like solid ground.

A cheer went up from the crowd. Ghalen embraced Okta, slapping his back, followed by the rest of the men. Led by Atamoda, the Lo women surrounded the Master of Boats, smothering him with hugs and kisses.

Aizarg made his way through the crowd and embraced the sco-lo-ti of the Carp. "Blessed will Okta's name be for all time, the Master of Boats."

Okta turned red, obviously uncomfortable with all the attention.

"There is still much work to do," he said in a gruff voice. "Kus-ge, Atamoda, now that we are true to the wind, we need more canopies."

Aizarg laughed, and Atamoda relished the sound. "We can make canopies later." He turned to the men. "Ba-lok, Levidi, secure the braziers atop the core rafts. I want fires tonight, let there be some warmth in this arun-ki for a change!"

Another cheer erupted from the Lo. Aizarg returned to the shelter of the canopies, followed by his people.

Atamoda lingered, watching as the Crane and Minnow dispersed to either side of the Spine, chattering excitedly and patting Okta on the back as they passed by. Still standing over the old sea anchor, Okta merely nodded and grunted, never taking his gaze off the stained heap of sail and line.

"Are you coming?" Alaya called to Atamoda.

"I want a few moments alone," she said.

Alaya smiled and turned to join the others. A Lo never had to explain to another the need for solitude.

Atamoda strolled to the pylon. She needed a few moments to herself before returning to the Köy-lo-hely and all its duties. In all her life, she never thought solitude would be such a precious luxury.

She closed her eyes, surrendering to the wind and rain.

Now the sea has a rhythm!

The tension ebbed from her shoulders. The ever present knot in her stomach, her constant companion since Aizarg departed on his quest, relented.

Atamoda blew out a long, slow breath and opened her eyes.

"North." Okta stood next to her, the old sea anchor and line heaped over his shoulder like some disemboweled sea monster. He sounded tired, his face pale and washed out under the rivulets of rainwater.

"What?" she asked. His expression concerned her. This wasn't the look of a man who had just saved his people.

He pointed off the bow. "That is north. The wind and current work as one and carry us south."

"How can you be so sure?"

"I still smell the stink of the g'an."

***

Levidi flopped down on the deck next to Ghalen, who reclined on a partially destroyed boat with his fish ration resting upon his stomach.

Alaya tended the nearby brazier, throwing twigs and sticks scooped from the sea onto the coals. The heat felt good, but Levidi wished it were hotter.

He yearned for the sun, but wouldn't voice his complaint aloud, except perhaps to Alaya later that evening.

"Amazing, isn't it?" Levidi remarked through a wad of dried fish stuffed in his mouth. "The way the deck no longer buckles wildly."

"How do you have any energy to talk?" Ghalen grunted. "I'm too tired to even eat."

"Always enough energy to eat, always enough to talk." Levidi considered how the firelight highlighted the fullness of Alaya's bottom. "Always enough energy for other things."

Ghalen chuckled, never opening his eyes. "Here we are, adrift on an endless sea, with no promise for tomorrow, and you think about mounting your woman!"

"Hard work makes me restless."

"Hard work makes me tired. Okta was merciless today, but it's good to be dry and not sleeping packed together on the wedding barge."

After a few backslaps and congratulations following deployment of the sea anchor, Okta had them working again.

Stacks of mats and fresh rope the women had woven over many days were strung in short order across the arun-ki, finally shielding the majority of the flotilla from the pounding rain. People quickly spread out to either side of the Spine, taking possession of rafts and boats.

The fact that the Minnow took one side and the Crane took another wasn't lost on Levidi.

Sana assisted Alaya and several Minnow women in tending to the children, including many orphans. Levidi considered the children sitting cross-legged around the brazier. Their large, mournful eyes followed Sana, Alaya, and the old Minnow hag, Kirabol, warming their rations on sticks over the brazier, struggling to keep the crumbling strips from falling into the flames.

So many.

The warm feeling of accomplishment ebbed away.

Sana reached into the fire, trying to pluck bits that fell into the iron pan.

"Stupid a-g'an!" Kirabol scolded. "Wrap it in a wide reed and tie it to the stick like this."

How did that old strip of leather survive the wave? So many strong, young Lo had been washed away, yet this old humpback survived.

Levidi knew little of Kirabol, other than that the Minnow said the old woman rivaled Setenay in age. Her broken, bent body and twisted nose reminded Levidi of an old snapping turtle.

Ba-lok said the old spinster was mad and lived alone in a hut on the Minnow arun-ki's downstream edge. Setenay dutifully cared for her until the day she left for the quest. For some reason, Kirabol now spent more time with the Crane than her own clan.

Now the snapping turtle wanted a piece of Sana.

Kirabol snatched a piece of reed from the overhead canopy and grabbed the end of Sana's stick. "Like this."

Claw like fingers danced for a moment, and then the fish clung dutifully to the stick.

"Don't stick it too long in the fire; you only need to warm it enough to comfort the children."

Levidi saw the defiance simmering in the Scythian girl, but he admired the way she held her tongue.

The women warmed the food and then broke it into pieces and handed it to reaching little hands. The scene reminded Levidi of mother birds feeding their chicks.

Once the children were fed, the women affixed their rations to sticks and roasted them.

The faint hint of roasted fish lingered. Levidi's stomach growled, and he wished he hadn't gobbled his food so quickly, regretting the lost opportunity for warm food.

Alaya sat down next to him, gingerly popping crispy flakes into her mouth.

Mouth watering, Levidi gave her a longing stare.

"You ate yours!"

He continued to stare.

Alaya rolled her eyes. "Oh, alright, just stop looking at me that way! Open your mouth."

She popped a steaming chunk into his mouth. The fire seemed to unlock juice trapped in the fish, softening it into a delectable morsel.

"You're pitiful," she whispered with a seductive smile.

Levidi bestowed a long thank-you kiss, squeezing her bottom in the process.

Always enough energy for that.

Levidi sensed the newly born fires already warming the arun-ki beneath the canopies. They beat back the rain and cold only a few feet, but enough to create a delicate cocoon of life.

He looked to his left to see Ghalen sitting up, staring at Sana, who sat next to Ba-tor, feeding him.

She has a great deal of food. The other women had already finished their rations and were preparing the children for bed. Yet Sana still fed the children rations.

Then Levidi realized the Scythian girl was feeding Ba-tor her rations.

"Scythian," Ghalen barked.

Sana looked up, eyes narrowing.

"Ghalen, she's..." Levidi tried to interrupt, but Ghalen ignored him.

"Scythian, come here," he repeated.

Glaring, Sana stood and approached.

Ghalen held out his ration. "Make yourself useful and cook this for me."

Everyone stopped eating and watched the drama unfold.

Ghalen and Sana stared at one another with iron resolve.

"Ghalen," Levidi whispered. "Alaya can do that for you."

Ghalen held up his hand. "She needs to carry her own weight."

Levidi thought about how much Sana had cared for the Lo children.

Sana crossed her arms. Levidi saw the fire in her eyes and suddenly remembered how she battled them on the g'an.

The Nameless God help us, she's a Scythian.

"Good luck with this," Levidi whispered and slid right to get some distance, pushing Alaya with him.

"What's he doing?" Alaya said in a low tone.

"Being an ass."

"Cook it," Ghalen commanded again.

As if the wind changed directions, something suddenly shifted in Sana's demeanor. She smiled warmly and took the fish cake from Ghalen's hand.

In a few moments, Sana secured the fish to the stick just as Kirabol had instructed. Relaxed, she turned the fish back and forth over the brazier. She smiled at Ghalen in a way Levidi thought perversely seductive.

"How does the Lo lord prefer his flesh?" She slid one hand down to her thigh, slowly pulling back the deerskin to reveal where her smooth, muscled thigh joined her bottom's round curve. She held out the stick with the steaming fish. "Does he prefer it warm when he puts it to his lips, or perhaps too hot to touch?" She waived the stick back and forth over the fire.

Back and forth, back and forth...

Alaya elbowed Levidi in the ribs. "What are you staring at?"

He shrugged innocently. "What? I'm still hungry."

"Keep staring at her, and you'll go hungry tonight!"

Levidi sighed.

Ghalen gazed at her with a guarded expression. He leaned over to Levidi. "See, she only needs a firm hand."

"If you say so." Levidi wasn't sure who manipulated whom at the present moment.

Sana withdrew the fish from the fire, steaming with a blush of golden brown. Sana brought the stick only inches from her pursed lips, softly blowing on the tip, steam dancing around smoky eyes locked on Ghalen.

She nibbled on the tip. "I think it's ready, my lord."

Ghalen looked downright smug as he signaled her forward with two fingers extended downward.

Levidi couldn't even hear the rain as Sana stepped around the children, sliding left and right, hips swaying. Before she exited the ring of children, only a few paces from Ghalen, she knelt down before the two little Minnow orphans, Toma and E'laa. She pulled off the fish and handed them each half.

"Thank you, Sana!" they said in unison. Beaming, the children began to eat.

Ghalen shot up. "What are you doing?"

"Feeding the children, of course" Sana said innocently. "I'm sorry, do you want it back?

"Children, Lord Ghalen wants his food back." She held out her hands. "Hurry up, we can't let it cool. He likes it hot, you know."

The twins raised pitiful, soulful eyes to Ghalen, lower lips trembling.

Alaya stifled a laugh. Several other giggles rippled among the women.

Ghalen turned red as the coals in the brazier. He shook his head and grimaced. "No...I mean they can keep it," he stuttered.

"Tell Lord Ghalen thank you, children," Sana said, grin dripping with contempt.

"Thank you, Lord Ghalen," the twins said in perfect harmony.

"And quit calling me 'lord'!" Ghalen huffed.

Levidi bit his inner lip to keep from laughing.

Sana returned to the brazier, breaking the green stick in several places with a slow series of agonizing *pops*, but keeping bark attached. She held up the limp branch and playfully wiggled it, letting it flop lifelessly above the fire.

Ghalen folded his arms, eyes like flame.

"This one isn't good anymore, is it? No worry, plenty of sticks around here."

Kirabol cackled, slapping her thigh.

Too bad we don't have any of Virag's wine; Ghalen needs it.

With a look of complete control and satisfaction, Sana turned her back to Ghalen and strutted away.

What happened next, Levidi didn't see coming.

In a blur, Ghalen leapt over the children, dodged around the brazier, and swept Sana over his shoulder. The Scythian girl didn't even have time to shriek before he catapulted her into the Lagoon.

"I like my flesh *wet*, and freshly caught from the sea!" he shouted down at her.

Sana thrashed in the water, unable to keep her terrified face above water.

Alaya gasped. "Levidi, do something!"

"What? I think it's best they work it out themselves."

She struck him in the arm and leapt up, springing to Ghalen's side. "She can't swim. Jump in and save her!"

Ghalen didn't budge. "She needs to learn."

"Oow! You damn men are all the same!" Alaya hit him in the shoulder too, and then dove in after Sana.

Alaya dragged the coughing Scythian onto the deck as Ghalen stormed off past Levidi.

"I tried to warn you," Levidi said as he passed.

"Shut up," Ghalen hopped onto the adjoining raft and vanished into the arun-ki."

***

Thick, sticky air suffocated the slaver, sending him into a panic. The rain thundering against the leaky canopy did nothing to ease his nerves. Virag wanted to be back on the raft, tied to the mast in the open air. If he didn't escape this coffin, he would die; of that he was certain. He tried to crawl from under the canopy to the adjacent raft, but the violent rocking kept knocking him into the bottom of the boat. His panic began to transform to madness as he briefly contemplated throwing himself into the sea.

And then, he felt the boat lurch forward and quickly cease its violent side-to-side motions. In only a few moments, it settled into a slow, relatively gentle, vertical shuffle.

Virag slumped into the bottom of the boat, his grip on the side relaxed.

Mysteriously, the boat transformed from stifling prison to sanctuary.

Okta must have done that anchor thing he kept babbling about.

Spako's continuous stream of snores seemed louder, the rain less threatening. Virag kicked Spako to make himself feel better, but the bodyguard didn't stir.

He gazed up at the water dripping between the tightly packed reeds, wondering why Aizarg spared his life.

To the sound of distant thunder, sleep eventually stole over the slaver.

18. The Dragon's Mark

Except for the captain, only red men crewed the ship. While they walked in fear of Leviathan, the captain did not.

A thick, grim fellow, he wore black wool from head to toe, and carried a whip the way other men carry a sword. Buried deep underneath a bushy brow, he possessed the same strange round eyes as Leviathan and the red men. While the men of Cin sometimes sported thin, wispy beards, this man's black whiskers were like a bristle broom. I fought the urge to touch it the entire journey.

Perhaps their round eyes fascinated me the most. I'd seen eyes like this before, though it took me a day to make the connection. These Tall Men shared the same round eyes as the Ice Men. I pushed this fact aside, determined not to let the physical similarity prejudice my opinion.

We sailed east across what I had once assumed an endless ocean, but two days later we sighted a lush, mountainous land replete with cool mists and dense forests. The ship steered south along its western coast for several more days until we rounded a peninsula and turned north.

I felt I had nothing to fear from Leviathan or his men. I spent those days wandering about the floating village, this glorious blend of timber, rope and canvas, woven into a magical sculpture gliding across the waves. Mother never hinted that such a wonder was even possible.

Something new! Oh, how can I convey to the gentle reader how powerful a spell discovering something new can cast on an ancient heart.

On the morning of the third day, Leviathan took me by the arm and escorted me to the bow. The ship paralleled a massive sea wall of boulders, each as large as the ship. It originated from basalt cliffs and protruded a mile into the sea.

How could even gods fashion such a wonder? I made no attempt to hide my unabashed awe from Leviathan. He tapped me on the shoulder and pointed ahead to a wide opening in the sea wall. We turned west and entered the Harbor of Wu.

Nothing could have prepared me for what I beheld.

The Chronicle of Fu Xi

***

Fu Xi awoke with a startle and snatched up his sword.

Dragon!

He crouched naked beside the dead fire, Red Sword at the ready.

The odd brush pile, the abnormally smooth ledge... evening's slumber cleared the mist from his mind, revealing morning's truth.

Breathe. Relax. Fu Xi's heart pounded as he forced himself to admit that if a bull dragon still dwelt in these mountains, the Donkey Men would not have camped here...

...at least not for long.

Fu Xi donned the lion skin, slid the Red Sword over his back, and walked to the edge of the cliff and into the rain. Turning and taking in the cave's grand sweep in the gray daylight, it all made sense.

Almost.

It isn't deep enough.

He returned beneath the ledge's shelter. His feet slid over the granite floor, sanded smooth by armored scales over a span of centuries.

Fu Xi approached the brush pile, seeing it in a new light. The stack of dry rotted timber, possibly here for hundreds of years, didn't arrive on this ledge naturally. Judging by the size of the vegetation pile, the bull dragon couldn't have been more than adolescent, perhaps two centuries old, when it last hibernated upon this ledge.

He craned his neck back, scanning the cave wall until he saw another cavern recessed high above, almost hidden in the shadows near the ceiling. The ledge only served as the dragon's porch, above lurked the beast's true lair.

After a few minutes of digging in the brush pile, Fu Xi found a stick that didn't crumble in his hands. Scrounging a few scraps of cloth from the Donkey Men's loot pile, he fashioned a makeshift torch. He stirred the fire's ashes, rekindling enough dormant sparks to light the torch.

Fu Xi placed the torch between his teeth, found a handhold, and began to climb the cliff.

***

The scale of the city overwhelmed me, the details lost in the overall impression washing over me like a wave. My first thought became my lasting thought - nature bent and subdued in ways I'd never witnessed before. The city, vast and overwhelming, dominated the hill rising from the harbor, smothering whatever natural features the Emperor of Heaven once placed there.

The cities in Cin were walled and in constant danger of being reclaimed by the surrounding wilderness or attacked by neighboring settlements. This city existed boldly, without fear, open and bright. At the tall hill's base, a long stone jetty protruded far into the harbor. Wooden buildings, storehouses, and moorings packed its half-mile length. More people crowded onto that jetty than existed in Cin's largest settlement. Thousands of buildings blanketed the hill and lorded over the harbor. Squat wooden and mud structures crammed along the harbor, while ever more glorious structures adorned the hill as it climbed away from the waterfront.

The ship anchored in the harbor for several hours as small boats came and went. I didn't understand the nature of the delay, but I surmised they were preparing for Leviathan's arrival.

Eventually, we docked, and Leviathan escorted me into the bustling city. His warriors formed columns on either side of us, clearing a path through the throng of humanity. People threw flower petals and dropped to their knees as Leviathan passed. His lieutenant, the foul-looking red man from the beach, marched ahead of the procession shouting and wielding a whip with cruel indifference to the people's adoration.

We marched up an avenue composed of stone blocks joined so tightly a knife blade could not slide between them and so wide ten men could walk abreast Yet, for all its width, the crowd pressed in so relentlessly I thought they would sweep the bodyguards aside.

Even I, a god, found it overwhelming. Wu wasn't a city so much as a hive, engorged with breeds of humanity I did not know existed. Red, black, and olive faces strained around, over and between the guards to catch a glimpse of Leviathan. A few even possessed skin pale as moonlight and hair like fire.

With the exception of red men, who wore either white armor or finely adorned red robes, the mortals of Wu dressed in simple linen robes with varying degrees of color, quality, and cleanliness.

We marched higher up the hillside until we left the frantic bustle of the wharves behind us. The columned marble buildings grew in size and stature as did the spaces between them. Now, only red men and women of various color and garb (or lack of it) strolled among isolated structures of stone and marble. These magnificent palaces ascended above the trees and dotted the mountainside high above the city.

In the distance, I saw thousands of men disemboweling the mountainside above the sea. Now I knew where the stone came from for the sea wall and the city. Wooden scaffolding stretched hundreds of feet up terraced cliffs. From several miles away I heard the clink of thousands of hammers and picks. The quarry cast a pall of yellow dust over the city.

Leviathan's palace dominated the hilltop. It possessed an uncanny similarity to Nuwa's Second Realm, but its scope far exceeded Mother's temple. A hundred columns supported a structure of astonishing dimensions, a man-made mountain of polished limestone, granite, and marble. Frescos and carvings lined the entablature above the main colonnade. Scenes of ships, porpoises, dolphins, and the creatures I would soon come to know as horses, stretched over my head. Leviathan waved off the bodyguards, and together we entered the palace.

While I let the wonders of Wu sweep me away, Leviathan studied me. I try to imagine what Leviathan thought of me, this strange god who gawked in unabashed wonder at his city.

He led me to a sunken rotunda as grand as the Place of Perfect Sorrows. Instead of a view of the sky, I looked high above at a dome decorated in exquisite, lifelike murals depicting battles and great feats. I will never forget my shock as I beheld a painting of a sky full of dragons.

The Chronicle of Fu Xi

***

Fu Xu held the torch high as he stepped into the dragon's lair. Except for water dripping somewhere deep in the cave's pitch black bowels, absolute silence permeated the cavern. A thick, unbroken layer of dust covered the perfectly smooth, wavy glass, coating the entire cavern. The black glass removed all doubts that Fu Xi stood in the former lair of the mountains' lord.

He knelt down, wiped away the thick dust and caressed the glass. It felt as smooth as ice yet almost warm to the touch, as if retaining the memory of the fire that birthed it.

Holding the torch high, Fu Xi craned his head back and peered up at the roof. Glass coated stalactites extended from the darkness.

No guano, no bats.

Nor did he smell the characteristic mustiness associated with the dark, deep places in the earth. Once a bull dragon staked claim to a cave, he sterilized it with fire, converting rock to obsidian glass. The glaze sealed every crack and crevice, and rendered the cave inhospitable to vermin. Bull dragon's kept their lairs immaculately clean, not even dragging prey into their sanctuaries.

Fu Xi felt like an intruder in a sacred place. No less holy than his mother's inner sanctum, this cavern still held power long after its lord had vanished.

Fu Xi wrapped another rag around the torch and made his way deeper into the cave. He ran his hand along the wall, feeling for the tell-tale ridges and bumps he hoped to find. It did not take long.

He stepped back and held the torch toward the wall. Elegant wiggles, curves and dots covered the wall, each melted into the glass by what must have been incredible heat. They formed intricate patterns from just above his head until they disappeared into the blackness above.

The Dragon's Mark.

These mysterious designs adorned every dragon's lair he'd ever explored. Their purpose remained a mystery, one his mother never would discuss.

How did he die? Fu Xi couldn't imagine a great bull dragon dying. But die they did, slowly vanishing over the course of the centuries. Yet, in all his travels, never did Fu Xi find one bone, a single tooth, or even a scale.

Perhaps they faded so men could rise.

The torch flickered, signaling to the God of Names the time had come to leave. Fu Xi turned toward the entrance's dim beacon as terrible sadness enveloped him. Dragons were already rare when his mother brought him into the world so long ago. Now, all that remained to testify of their existence were these wondrous caves.

Must I fade, too?

***

Four tall, narrow windows in the upper dome focused beams of sunlight down upon an enormous marble statue dominating the rotunda's center. A strange god stood in lifelike splendor atop a device I would come to learn they called a chariot. Hurtled forward by two powerful horses, his beard and hair flowed back over perfect shoulders. Boldly naked, face stern and fierce, the god gripped a strange three-pronged spear in his right hand, as if ready to strike.

Leviathan halted a few paced before the statue and bowed slightly in deference. He turned to me and pointed to the statue.

"Poseidon."

He touched his chest. "Leviathan."

I nodded, understanding Leviathan had sprung from this god called Poseidon as I had from Nuwa.

I, the God of Names, Son of The Goddess of the West, felt suddenly small. A much greater world, ruled by a powerful god, and his offspring lurked at Cin's very doorstep.

And, until this moment, I knew nothing of them.

I wanted to examine more closely the colored, inlaid tiles decorating the polished black granite floor, but Leviathan gestured I should follow him. As we walked deeper into the palace I glanced back at the tiles radiating from under the chariot's wheels. They spread across the entire floor in unusual patterns and shapes that, at the time, appeared random and meaningless to me.

Nothing about this Son of Poseidon could be random or meaningless.

He escorted me to a spacious chamber near the main entrance. A luxurious wooden bed rested in the chamber's center, painted bright red and raised on a spotless white marble floor by four bronze posts. Dark wood cabinets, carved with fish and unfamiliar birds, lined the opposite wall. Each held dozens of silk and cotton robes, blouses and tunics. A spacious marble tub sat atop a ceramic tile platform. Beyond, a gracefully arched window on the southern wall opened to a breathtaking view of the harbor city. Murals and frescos adorned the other walls, depicting everyday life in places far more glorious than the city out the window.

As I strolled around the chamber, a parade of serving women bustled in carrying pots of steaming water. They filled the tub, then surrounded me and attempted to strip off my clothes. At first I resisted, but eventually I surrendered to their gentle persistence and delightful giggles. Without too much effort, they pushed me into the tub.

Leviathan departed, his hearty laughter lingering in the corridors beyond.

After my bath, breads, tasty cheeses, and exotic fruits were brought to me. I spent the rest of the evening alone, sitting in the window and gazing at the city below.

Upon the ledge, admiring the tens of thousands of lanterns which rivaled the stars above, I decided patience would be the best course of action.

Even after nightfall, I heard the distant pounding from the quarry.

The Chronicle of Fu Xi

19. The God's Burden

A bearded mortal with midnight skin and eyes as deep and mysterious as the Sunrise Sea awakened me. Blacker than Leviathan, his thickening body, balding crest, and gray-streaked beard spoke of both privilege and one taking the first steps into life's autumn.

Ah, but his eyes sang of one who'd lived a thousand lifetimes! He stood at the foot of my bed, arms crossed, considering me, not as a man looks upon an immortal, but as if I were a curious phenomenon to be studied. Something in his expression vaguely reminded me of Mother, and I found the experience uncomfortable.

He wore fine white linen wrapped and folded in the most puzzling of fashions around his body, a dark purple band falling gracefully down the center. He knew enough of the coastal Cin dialect to converse with me, introducing himself as Amiran, a member of a caste of learned mortals known as 'Scholars'. He bowed low, and on behalf of his master, welcomed me to the Palace of Leviathan, Prince of the Great and Glorious Empire of the god Poseidon. As a god and honored guest, I would be treated well. However, by my host's command, I must not leave my chambers until I could converse directly with Prince Leviathan, who in due time would personally answer all my questions.

I'd never heard a Cin dialect spoken in so rich and deep a voice. It reverberated in his throat like captive thunder, but spilled forth like spring cream. I enjoyed listening to him, impressed by his grasp of my language's subtle tones and inflections.

Every morning for two weeks Amiran came to my chamber for language lessons. An exotic, and I must admit, pleasant odor always accompanied him; warm like autumn's first wood smoke, yet slightly sweet. Its presence would precede the scholar by a few moments and linger long after he left.

More often than not, Quexil, Leviathan's lieutenant from the battle on the beach, accompanied him. Quexil stood in a corner, leaning against the wall, arms crossed. With hair cut as if someone had put a bowl on his head and trimmed around the edges, his beady eyes and large Adam's apple gave him the look of a foul tempered vulture. He kept a silent vigil on the old scholar, though for what purpose I could only guess.

I took delight in shocking Amiran with my rapid mastery of their tongue, which they called "The Song of Atlas." I found the name laughable, though I politely withheld this opinion. An oddly crude language for such a glorious civilization, full of abrupt halts and stuttering sounds, it lacked the melodic grace inherent in Cin's many tongues. Eventually, I could converse well enough with Amiran without accidently spitting when speaking.

I found myself intrigued with this amazing mortal. I greatly desired to ask him questions, but he would only cast a wary glance toward Quexil, stating, "Prince Leviathan will address these concerns, my lord. I humbly beg we continue with your lesson."

I began to feel like a prisoner and resolved to confront Quexil the next morning.

However, Amiran and Quexil didn't return at dawn. Instead, Leviathan burst into my chamber, dressed in a flowing white robe. Intricate gold earrings dangled from his ears, each finger encased in silver and gold rings. Several jewel-encrusted necklaces hung from his thick neck. He joyously embraced me and expressed his pleasure that we could finally speak to one another.

Questions tripped over questions, but he insisted on showing me the palace first.

"Now that you can speak our language, you can command as a god rightly should." With that, he whisked me away on a grand tour of the Imperial Palace of Wu.

The Chronicle of Fu Xi

***

Like an unrelenting predator, the waters claimed the dragon's cave and chased Fu Xi up the mountain. He shambled along a ridge, spirit driving his failing flesh onward.

Gnarled pines, forever bent with the wind, reached up to the heavens in a tangle of black and gray. Along the mountain's spine, they clung to lichen-stained boulders and thin mud as if terrified they could slide off the mountainside at any moment.

This mountain is ancient, it has secrets.

Until now, the rocks and cliffs had been sharp, new, and thrusting boldly into the heavens. Now the landscape felt worn, old. Twisted limbs begged the heavens for mercy, or perhaps forgiveness, but the sky answered only with more rain.

Time no longer mattered, the passage of day and night a concern for the past age, not this one. Fu Xi's universe consisted only of a pebble or a boulder within his immediate sight. His only goal the next handhold, his only hope another footstep.

Fu Xi's weakened flesh couldn't reject whatever venom had tipped the Donkey Men's blades. His wounds wouldn't fully close, and they festered in the rain. The poison seared the demigod's blood, trying to pry divine spirit from muscle and bone. He felt his flesh slowly boiling away.

The lion's skin had begun to rot, too. Fu Xi had already cut strips to reinforce the straps holding Red Blade to his back.

Five mangy hyenas may bring down the lion.

Fu Xi laughed deliriously at the thought.

He looked about only to discover the downpour had transformed into snowfall. The wind ceased as heavy wet flakes softened the jagged gray mountain with an unbroken white blanket.

Silence, so strange and alien after days of unceasing rainfall, filled his ears. His own heartbeat pounded in his chest so loudly Fu Xi felt certain it could be heard for a thousand miles. The silence also gave birth to voices. Children laughed and acolytes shouted his name. Sometimes, Tiejiang's hammer rang out against the anvil, slicing clearly through the snow without echo. Fu Xi almost felt the forge's heat, and heard Tiejiang's laughter. More than once, a horse's neigh made him spin about.

"Heise, you are a lazy horse," he croaked at the snow drifts, almost too weak to speak. "You can come out now. I promise I won't make you carry me." Breaths came in ragged puffs, each word heavy as an iron ingot. "You were very selfish to leave me. I would have killed the other lion, if you had..." he wheezed and steadied himself against a boulder. "...if you had only waited a few moments. Come out so I have someone to talk to."

Soon, the snow piled deeply all about. Bare feet numb and icicles dangling from the daggertooth fangs, Fu Xi trudged forward, seeking any path that would support his weight.

Snow turned to drifts, and drifts to white waves frozen in mid-crest.

So white, so soft. Perhaps I could lie down, if only for a little while.

Lungs scraped the thin air with every ragged wheeze, reminding Fu Xi he still lived. His mind began to drift as his eyes grew heavy, and warmth spread through his limbs.

***

As we walked, Leviathan told me this was the farthest outpost of the Empire of Poseidon, and I could dwell there as long as I desired.

Glorious. In how many tongues can I say this word? It is the only word the God of Names can summon to describe Leviathan's domain.

A city unto itself, one could enter the Palace of Wu and never find their way out. Walls of the whitest marble and gilded ceilings lined endless halls, staterooms, sleeping chambers, dining halls, gymnasiums, baths, brothels, and pleasure gardens. Half a dozen kitchens fed Leviathan and his staff of warriors, servants, and concubines. Gardens bursting with a dizzying variety of exotic flowers and trees, imported from every corner of the empire, blanketed the grounds. Pools and fountains flowed from crystal clear springs throughout the estate.

My questions melted under Leviathan's radiance. Every time I presented an inquiry, he distracted me with a new wonder. Before I realized it, evening's end found us upon gilded thrones, side by side, in Leviathan's great hall.

He held court among a thousand of his best warriors, the red men I came to know as Olmecs. Wearing headdresses overflowing with colorful feathers, they reclined across the hall's expansive floor upon cushions and blankets. Even without their white armor, the jagged red and black body paint covering their squat bodies made them appear grim and eager to kill, even as they celebrated.

The Olmecs reflected the throne room's unexpected savagery. Instead of airy, refined columns and tapestries common to the rest of the palace, the throne room felt tomb-like, a man-made cavern of dark gray lava stone. Geometric gold and silver designs covered the ceiling. Every few feet along the long walls, a stone head, topped with a plumed headdress, glared out into the hall. Black iron braziers cast malevolent shadows across the giants' ruby eyes and menacingly gaping mouths.

Leviathan pointed to the heads. "This hall honors my elite Olmec Warriors, the Obsidian Guard. These statues memorialize their great captains who have served me in ages past. They hail from deep jungles in the narrow isthmus between two great continents. More loyal warriors, you will never find."

I glanced at Quexil lurking alone in the shadows, a living reflection of the stone heads. He nodded and smiled, mouth filled with the same sinister points.

These Olmecs would bear watching, Quexil included.

"Bring the feast!" Leviathan commanded.

Clad in white silk like my host, we dined on tender meats, richly stuffed eggs, and roasted snails. Music of string and horn, so extraordinary that I cannot describe it, made my soul ache. Their wine, made from a fruit called a 'grape', must have been fermented in Heaven itself. And the women!

At Leviathan's command, a tapestry of nude women in every hue, every color, paraded before us to the beat of a lone, sultry drum. I recognized that a few were from coastal Cin. Some were like Amiran and Leviathan, with ebony flesh and long, lean, legs. Then came forth women with dusky flesh, rich, flowing locks, and delicious mysteries in their eyes. Finally, there came the most exotic women of all.

Three ivory-skinned women danced before the thrones, one with hair of gold, one with hair of coal, and one with hair of fire. At first I thought they may be ice women, with skin so white it must be cold to the touch. The redhead leapt into my lap like a cat, straddling me with urgency. I found nothing cold about her.

"Enjoy, brother," Leviathan laughed. "But be cautious with the white ones. They bite."

Then I noticed a raised patch on the woman's arm. A second glance revealed it to be a brand, a serpent wrapped around a spear. My heart skipped a beat as I fingered the delicate scar, and I realized she was a slave.

She burrowed her face into my neck, seeking lips and darting tongue. Red wine embraced sweat, blending and becoming one in my blood. I closed my eyes, leaned my head back and surrendered to the fire haired woman.

I caught glimpses of the ceiling, with its exotic geometric patterns, that wrapped around skulls and dancing skeletons brandishing clubs and spears.

If not a throne room, then what purpose did this place serve?

Images replaced reflection, instinct replaced thought. A chorus of drums joined the lone beat, pounding faster and faster. Air stifling, heart pounding, passion rose against my will. I caught only a glimpse of the women as they danced, sweating bodies throbbing to the beat. The Olmecs rose, pounding bare feet against stone in time to the beat. Wide, lustful gazes feasted on the line of women, now separated from the warriors by only a narrow strip of floor. The women turned their backs to the men and faced Leviathan, undulating as if taunting the warriors. The men howled in response and sliced their chests with obsidian blades, smearing blood over their war paint. The air sizzled as blood, music and passion built to unbearable levels.

Leviathan sat impassively staring at the throng and ignoring me as I struggled against the spell. The skeletons on the ceiling seemed to come alive, tormenting my spirit as the throne room transformed into a dark temple, the feast now a sacrifice. I drowned in pleasure, unable to heed my hearts warning call as I felt her tongue run over my neck...

...and then her teeth.

Before darkness took me, I recall Leviathan raising his hand and dropping it. The Olmecs surged forward, snatching the women into their midst; grabbing, pulling, taking...

...screaming.

"For this is why the gods came to earth," Leviathan smiled from behind his goblet.

Skeleton's danced above my head, and mute giants looked on as the world vanished in fire and flesh.

The Chronicle of Fu Xi

***

Thunder rumbled in the distance.

The snow is soft, and not so cold. I will be stronger with a nap.

It rumbled again, sharper, closer.

Will I die? Or perhaps I shall only freeze, and reawaken with the spring.

Fu Xi's eyelids grew heavy, warmth spreading through his limbs.

A tremendous boom shook the mountainside, snapping Fu Xi from the deadly stupor, and he began to shiver anew, life surging through his limbs again.

The boom transformed into a low, rumbling growl, and then a primeval roar.

Disbelief stirred the demigod to action. He groped for the hilt around his shoulder like a dog chasing his tail, before falling into the snow in a heap. He seized the hilt, only to find the sword had frozen to the lion hide. Summoning his strength, he ripped the sword from his back. Patches of frozen fur clinging to its edge; what had once been magically light, now felt like lead.

He staggered up.

It's close.

To his left the beast growled again, a cat's purr magnified a thousand fold.

It knows I'm here.

The expectation of battle heated his blood, reawakening nerves already raw from the venom's fire. The pain reminded Fu Xi how close he'd come to giving up.

The air thickened, as the heavy, lifeless snowfall suddenly swirled in silent vortices.

Could it be the beast from the cave? Fu Xi thought that doubtful, the lair had appeared abandoned for centuries.

He looked up in hopes of spotting the creature. The gray momentarily darkened as something ominous swooped overhead, just out of sight, just out of reach.

It's toying with me.

Fu Xi didn't like being the mouse, but if it wanted him, he could do little to thwart its attack.

A tremor shuddered underfoot as it landed close by, just beyond the white curtain.

"Mother," Fu Xi whispered, unable to contain a smile. "I have found your dragon."

***

Naked, I woke alone in the cavernous throne room. Only a few torches lit the dim chamber, now cold as a tomb. I stood, my feet covered in wine or blood, which I knew not. The chamber had been swept clean, not even an overturned goblet remained. The giant heads stared mutely into the emptiness, granting neither approval nor condemnation.

I caught a whiff of a smoky, sweet odor and caught Amiran scrutinizing me from the shadows. Even in the darkness, I could not mistake his disappointment. He pointed to a white garment draped across a stool.

"Your robe, my Lord. A hot bath awaits in your chamber."

With that, he turned and departed, leaving me alone with my shame.

The Chronicle of Fu Xi

***

Sword supported by unsteady arms, Fu Xi trundled toward where he suspected the dragon waited.

It's a bull, I know it!

The snow under his feet thinned, and Fu Xi sprinted headlong into the blizzard. His grin expanded into a maniacal mask. Fu Xi didn't care that he lacked the strength or armor to defeat even an adolescent female dragon, let alone a fully mature bull. He took the dragon's presence as a gift.

Let it end this way.

On this day the son of Nuwa would meet this great beast in battle; a blessed avenue to a glorious ending, an ending fitting for a god.

The snow thinned to a meager flurry as the air grew even colder. White transformed to gray, gray to an enormous black form looming above him. As he sprinted toward the beast, Fu Xi let loose a war cry and struck the Red Sword against a nearby boulder, neatly cutting a swath off the granite and purging the blade of ice and hair.

The snow parted and Fu Xi faced a cliff.

Panting in great misty heaves, he touched black rock. A growl bubbled up from behind him. Fu Xi wondered how the beast maneuvered around him so quickly, so quietly. He also realized the dragon had now trapped him against the cliff, cutting off any escape.

He's an old beast...a crafty beast.

Fu Xi extended his sword and prepared for his final battle.

"Lord of the Mountain, I am Fu Xi, Son of Nuwa!" he shouted and rattled the sword against the cliff. "Show yourself, and let us get this over with."

As if in response, a fresh growl echoed around him.

The snowfall slowed to only a few drifting flakes. The world fell still. Fu Xi's eyes darted left and right, waiting for the attack. Perhaps it would descend from above, trying to impale him with claw spikes. Maybe the dragon would charge, wings pulled back like cat's ears, and snatch him up in iron jaws. Or the dragon may simply deliver a bolt of fire against the cliff, incinerating Fu Xi without honor.

Instead, human laughter, like melodious chimes, rang out from the mist.

***

A hot bath and warm breakfast didn't cleanse my spirit. My heart felt as if bathed in venom.

A jovial Leviathan found me sitting on my window ledge, staring at the city. As morning waned to afternoon, we strolled through one of the palace's many gardens. While Leviathan talked of his far off land, my thoughts drifted to the feast and the brands on the slave women, and the savagery I witnessed.

I stopped and interrupted him. "Many of these mortals are slaves, are they not?"

Leviathan crossed his arms and nodded, as if he'd been expecting this question. "The feast, it disturbed you?"

"Yes."

"The mortals or your behavior?"

"Yes."

"You will get used to it. Such rituals are for their benefit, not ours." His grin reminded me of Quexil's. *"It only overwhelmed you because you were unaccustomed to its intensity. The Obsidian Guards hold such feasts to honor us. Quexil says your behavior last night greatly honored them."* His grin only grew wider. *"They can't wait until the next celebration."*

"You should have warned me. My conduct was unworthy of the Son of Nuwa."

He considered me as if I were a fool. *"By what measuring stick do you judge yourself? By mortal man's? Does a lamb judge a lion? Free yourself from such obscene notions, brother. Gods make their own rules."*

"Were any of the women hurt?" I demanded.

Exasperated, he poked my shoulder where a barely noticeable blemish remained from last night. *"Which one bit you?"*

"The redhead...I think."

"Like a cat that purrs before biting the hand that strokes it." Leviathan chuckled. *"Did she die?"*

"I remember nothing after she...serviced me. But you know tasting our blood will kill any mortal creature."

He continued his stroll. *"She knew that. Her people hail from an island of cold mists on the edge of the Icelands. They believe it's possible to attain immortality by drinking a god's blood. When they can't get god's blood, they're quite content drinking each other's."*

"Does this superstition condemn her and her people to slavery? Perhaps they are better served with enlightenment."

"She would rip open your throat and die feasting on your blood before she would succumb to 'enlightenment.' She cannot rise above her breeding. No mortal can."

I thought of Tiejiang and my beloved Nushen.

"What of your Scholars? Amiran is a remarkable fellow."

"The Scholars are my father's dogs!" Leviathan snapped, his rage taking me aback. He quickly composed himself. *"My father graciously provided Amiran to assist me in exploring the Cin's coastal areas. His service has been invaluable. Let me express my point a different way.*

"All men are slaves to their own weakness, to death. Am I right?"

I searched my mind for one instance where mankind lifted themselves to enlightenment without my intervention, but could not find one example.

"Yes," I confessed.

"No matter how high they fly, they will always succumb to the weight of their petty desires. We must not teach them, we must lead them. Only in this manner, can they be truly fulfilled.

"A god's brand is a symbol of life and liberation, our collars, rungs by which they climb from darkness. The Sons of Poseidon call it The God's Burden. Brother, never forget they are only a step above the animals, ready to tear out our throats for the slightest taste of immortality. On whatever shores the Sons of Poseidon make landfall, we find them as mere brutes. Is it so different with Cin?"

His words fell across the soil of my heart, waiting for the right moment to germinate.

"Are all of them slaves?"

"All mortals are slaves to a god's will, but warriors and sailors carry no brand and wear no collar. Olmecs are naturally gifted to the natural order of the universe. Of all mortals, they are the most loyal."

"Slavery is against all Nuwa has taught me. It is forbidden in Cin."

"Did you not tell me the ways of Nuwa are vanishing? Didn't you tell me the kings in Cin make war on one another?"

"I did."

"A strange reward for so many millennia of service, I should think."

He held out his arm in a great sweeping motion, as if he could behold the entire world with a single glance. "Where the Eleven Princes reign, men do not starve or make war on one another. The Palace of Wu is only a shadow of Poseidon's greater glory. Tell me, Son of Nuwa, what have you to show in your lands?"

In that sliver of time, I doubted an eternity of service, and the seeds took root.

"Do not be sad. I know everything you and the great Goddess Nuwa did for the land of Cin, you did for love. I only offer another way, no less steeped in love."

He patted my back as if consoling me. "If the slave girl still lives, I will see she is punished." Leviathan continued his stroll.

"There is no need to punish her."

His voice darkened again. "Mortal bites come in many forms, some nibble like sweetest honey, others snap with a viper's fangs. Do not trust to your immortality for protection. Love them, but never trust them." He raised his finger. "They will worship you. They will fear you. They will serve you. But mortals will never love you. The God's Burden is simple: From men, take what you want. For men, give what they need."

He stopped again and considered me again. "I see doubt."

"It is not my intent to offend you. It is only that you have shown me things I've never considered."

"Consider this...Serve or rule, a god must choose."

His mood lightened, and he hugged me around the shoulder. "My long lost brother, you are now one of us. The days and pleasures of this world are endless..." He clenched his fist. "...ours for the taking! Fu Xi, you belong among the Sons of Poseidon."

My doubts melted away, or perhaps I merely suppressed them. For the first time in my immortal life, I wasn't alone.

I belonged.

The Chronicle of Fu Xi

***

A moment of crystal lucidity washed over Fu Xi's famished mind.

I'm going mad.

He stepped away from the cliff, sword outstretched.

"What does the mighty Fu Xi have to fear?" A voice danced beyond fog.

"What do you want?" Fu Xi shouted, stumbling once again into the deep snow.

A shadow darted to his left. Fu Xu ducked and slashed, but slew only a few unfortunate snowflakes.

"Does the God of Names fear death?" the voice spoke from his left.

Fu Xi whirled about, but saw nothing.

A black-clad figure gelled from the fog and passed to his left, hands casually behind his back. High, proud cheekbones framed obsidian eyes. The man's features reminded Fu Xi of the tall tribes who dwelt east of Nushen.

Fu Xi whirled about, but the stranger vanished. The snow stretched unbroken

"Show yourself!"

"Here I am," a breathy, frigid voice whispered in his ear.

Fu Xi spun to face the little woman who died in the courtyard of stone. She stood motionless several yards away, clad only in her rusty iron collar. Her bare feet hovered just above the snow.

"Your mother betrayed you," she said, face slack and pale as the drifts.

Fu Xi turned and fled the way he came, following his own footprints away from the cliff. He glanced back, but the figure had vanished. Fu Xi turned about and came face to face with a Donkey Man.

The grubby creature considered him with the same dark eyes as the woman had. "How many quests did Nuwa send you on, all the while denying you the pleasures your flesh so desired?" he hissed.

Fu Xi fled in the other direction, terror routing his pride. He lunged into the gray, slogging through the snow, leaving a jagged, white trail in his wake.

Laughter followed him.

Thick pines materialized ahead. Without realizing, Fu Xi had plunged headlong into a forest, but the arboreal sentinels offered no sanctuary.

A child's voice drifted among the trees, "She dragged one mortal husband after another into her lair, afraid of being alone, feeding her carnal desires one victim at a time."

Fu Xi glanced right and saw Lian. Nuwa's final earthly shell appeared just as he remembered her on that final Offering Ceremony, her white silk acolyte gown melting into the snow.

"How many did you watch her slaughter, Fu Xi? She sent you to save them, yet she used their bodies as playthings."

"Lies!" Tears of rage streaming down his face, Fu Xi lunged toward the child but fell headfirst into a snowdrift.

"She failed, and so did you."

Fu Xi looked up and came face to face with Quexil. The Olmec's red skin and jagged war paint clashed violently against the snow.

"I've watched you for quite some time, as you scurried back and forth from Tortoise Mountain on her little errands. You've crossed Cin again and again, dragging the Tall Men from caves, teaching them fire and how to sprinkle a few seeds in the mud. Was it all worth it?"

Like a daggertooth, Quexil circled in a wide arc, brandishing a steel sword and poison words, each syllable slashing open a new wound. Doubt sawed its way into his spirit.

"I wonder how you felt when you spied our ship that morning, or what thoughts raced through your mind as you beheld Wu for the first time. I think you felt inadequate when you learned how grand the world truly was...and how small a part you played."

"Depart, demon."

Quexil stepped closer. "It is you who tread in my realm."

He took a step closer. Fu Xi heard the snow crunch beneath his feet, saw misty breath emerge from Quexil's mouth. "You could have joined us."

A step closer.

"Leviathan laid a banquet before you. He embraced you."

A step closer.

"He called you 'Brother'."

"Silence," Fu Xi whispered.

"In gratitude, you conspired with a mortal, a *slave*."

Fu Xi tightened his grip on the Red Sword.

"You repaid your host with betrayal, but one could only expect as much from the Son of Nuwa." Quexil hissed.

"No!" Fu Xi shouted and thrust the Red Sword at Quexil's heart.

Red and white metal clashed in a blue flash.

20. Downstream

Surrender the thief to the marsh. Banish the murderer to the g'an. Pity the fool and madman, but lodge them well downstream. – Lo Proverb

The Chronicle of Fu Xi

***

In what seemed like only a blink, Virag awoke to the reek of excrement. He craned his neck, thinking Spako had shat himself.

His bodyguard hadn't moved. The slaver had no idea how much time had passed, but the gray light peaking under the tarp looked a little brighter.

Above the rain he heard women's voices and then a clumpy splash beyond the hull very close to his head. The reek suddenly intensified.

Virag untangled his legs from Spako's and tumbled from under the canopy, struggling to make sure he didn't slip into the gap between the raft and the boat.

He quickly noticed that someone had erected makeshift poles and canopies almost up to his boat, providing much welcomed shelter from the rain on the adjacent rafts.

When he finally found his feet, he faced four women bearing heavy clay pots with brown-stained rims. They wore the haggard expressions of those who hadn't slept in days.

"What are you doing?" Virag demanded.

"What do you think we're doing, *a'gan?*" A young woman with thick curly hair and sharp, olive features replied incredulously. "We're dumping our families' night soil."

"Not next to my boat you don't! Dump it somewhere else."

"This is downstream. If you don't like it, move your boat."

"Toss it over there," Virag pointed to the raft behind her where a man and two small children huddled in the shadows.

She looked over her shoulder, and then considered Virag as a patient adult speaking to an ignorant child.

"That is my cousin's raft. I couldn't even think of dumping our refuse there."

"Then dump it over there!" Virag pointed to the opposite side of his boat, where a cluster of lashed boats bobbed between two rafts.

The woman's jaw dropped, as if Virag just asked her to kill her first born. "Those boats are Minnow Clan; to dump our refuse there would be a grave insult."

The other women covered their mouths and snickered.

Virag's rage intensified. A few weeks ago this woman would quake in fear in his presence. She would be perhaps only suitable to service his bodyguards.

"Do not throw your shit next to my boat." Virag inched closer, moments from cuffing the insolent bitch across the face.

"Move your boat." She stepped toward him, unfazed by his aggressive posture.

The other women backed off.

"Do you know who I am?" Virag seethed.

"Yes, you are an a'gan fool who lashed his boat downstream."

Virag slowly slid his right hand down to the small of his back, where he kept a hidden dagger.

As if sensing the growing danger, the other women stepped farther back.

"Alaya," one of them said. "Let's get Ghalen."

The woman called Alaya locked eyes with Virag and stepped to his left. She lifted her pot next to the bow of his boat and slowly began to tip it.

"Spill it and I'll gut you from ass to mouth."

Virag grinned as he saw a spark of doubt cross Alaya's face, but the woman kept tipping.

His hand crept toward the hidden hilt.

"Is everything in order, Alaya?" Ghalen's voice rose above the rain from behind Virag. The slaver slowly moved his hand back down to his side.

"Yes, Ghalen." A wry smile crossed Alaya's face. "I was just dumping the night soil when this a'gan came along. He speaks in gibberish. I think he still suffers from wave sickness."

The women, obviously infused with fresh courage, giggled again.

"I will not be made sport of. Stop these hags from dumping their shit next to my boat!"

Ghalen laughed. "You are downstream, what do you expect? That is where we rid ourselves of night soil. Do not fret; the current will carry it away soon enough."

Virag grabbed onto the mast to avoid falling over. "Okta planned this! I will not stand for it. Where is Aizarg? Bring him here, let him decide."

The tall, fair-haired marshman crossed his arms and laughed. "Judging by the way you grip that mast, you do not stand very well at all. By the Uros's own decree, the Master of the Boats decides who goes where in this arun-ki. If this is where he wanted you, this is where you'll stay."

"Put me on the wedding barges, *my* rafts. You would not have them if it were not for me."

"They are not your rafts, or did we not make that clear?"

"Then put me on the other side of the arun-ki, away from this offal."

"Very well!" Ghalen grinned broadly, and Virag knew instantly he'd made a mistake.

He snatched Virag by the arm and dragged him through the heart of the arun-ki, from raft to raft, past masses of Lo huddled around glowing braziers, until they arrived at the storm wall.

Virag shielded his face from the blinding rain and stinging spray as Ghalen pushed him ahead through the wall's opening onto the bow raft, naked before the sea and storm.

"I do not want to go out there!"

"Come on, slaver," Ghalen shouted over the howling wind. "Let me show you where we will move your boat. The air is very fresh here, you will like it. I know the Master of Boats would approve."

Exposed to the roaring elements, the terror of the first day returned with a vengeance. Virag clung to Ghalen like a child, shame and rage forgotten, as waves sloshed over his calves and threatened to pull him into the water.

Ghalen steadied himself against the stout pylon and pointed to the rope. "That is our new sea anchor. Without it, we would eventually flounder and die. It keeps *your* boat sheltered in the arun-ki's wake.

"No one can live here, on this side of the wall. If you continue to make trouble, you and that Sammujad beast of yours will find yourselves camped here. Do we understand each other?"

Only wanting to escape this place, Virag nodded vigorously.

"Good." Ghalen shoved him to the other side of the storm wall under the sheltering tarps.

Virag stumbled back to his boat, the Lo snickering as he passed.

Let them laugh. Okta will pay. Ghalen will pay. They will all pay.

Virag slid into his boat, kicking Spako as he settled in. The sleeping Sammujad didn't even stir, making Virag even more furious.

Outside the tarp, slop splattered against the hull as the stink of shit and women's laughter invaded his boat.

21. The Dragon's Shadow

Naturally, Leviathan asked me about Cin. Perhaps I should not have been so forthcoming, but my host openly discussed his home.

He told me of his father, the god Poseidon, who came to earth and took mortal lovers, just as Nuwa had. At first, Leviathan took me as a long lost brother, a bastard from one of his father's trysts. He was genuinely shocked when I told him of Nuwa, as Poseidon had made no mention of other gods. He also took interest when I described the Offering Festival.

"How does Poseidon choose an Offering?" I asked.

"My father does not share the affairs of his inner temple with his sons."

Unlike Nuwa, Poseidon begot not one child, but six pairs of twins. Ten males were born of Poseidon's first mortal queen, Cleito. Leviathan and his sister, whom he refused to speak of, were born to a beloved mistress.

Poseidon established an earthly kingdom in his mortal queen's native land, an island continent between four greater continents. He divided this dominion among the first ten princes and anointed his firstborn son, Atlas, king over all. To the eleventh prince, Poseidon gave dominion over the seas. Much as Nuwa had done, Poseidon tasked his offspring with earthly affairs and retreated into his temple.

Everything I had accomplished in Cin paled in the light of their greatness. In the Children of Poseidon I thought I had found my answer, my true purpose. In them, I saw all I tried to build in the Tall Men.

Perhaps my centuries of wandering were over.

And yet occasionally, when the wind blew just right from the harbor, the faint clink of hammers and stench of blood briefly stirred me from a waking dream. In those times Leviathan appeared as if magically summoned by my stirring doubt, to distracted me with every possible pleasure.

And I relished Leviathan's company like a boy seeks out his older brother. Perhaps I sensed Leviathan seducing me, co-opting me, corrupting me...but in the end, I permitted it.

Only I am to blame.

The Chronicle of Fu Xi

***

Steel and orichalcum danced amongst the trees, breaking the silence with sharp clangs. The demigod summoned all his remaining strength, pitting his rage against the Olmec. The Red Sword should have immediately sliced through the steel, but somehow Quexil fought on.

The warrior effortlessly dodged Fu Xi's best attacks, countering with mighty blows. Soon, Quexil transformed into a blur darting from tree to tree. Trunks splintered and limbs fell as Fu Xi pursued his foe.

His enemy slipped behind a tree and vanished. Fu Xi halted, wheezing for breath.

"Fu Xi the Betrayer," a deeper voice rumbled. "Fu Xi the Failure. Were I merciful, I would slay you and end your suffering."

The voice reverberated as an enormous shadow expanded and stretched beyond the trees.

Fu Xi took a step backward.

"Merciful."

The word echoed, transforming to a rumbling purr.

"Merciful!"

The purr swelled into a growl.

"MERCIFUL!"

The growl thundered into a mountain shaking roar as the forest erupted into sizzling flames.

An eternity of courage drained away. What he faced terrified Fu Xi far more than a dragon, more than death. Damnation incarnate pursued the demigod.

Fu Xi fled downhill, unable to see more than a few yards. Flames licked his back as he burst from the tree line, chased from the snowy heights by the stink of charred wood and crackle of burning green wood.

He crashed through saplings and brush, as snow became rain. The beast's words burrowed into Fu Xi's soul, like worms seeking a soft spot in the apple's skin.

Another brilliant, exploding flash of light erupted behind him, this time seemingly farther away. The flames cast long shadows through the trees, flickering fingers pointing the way for Fu Xi's escape.

Another boom echoed, this time fainter and from ahead.

The demigod did not slow as the slope steepened, and the trees fell away on both sides.

Fu Xi recognized the deadly drop off ahead barely in time. He skidded, but the slick mud gave way and he fell on his bottom. Sliding downhill even faster, he snatched at branches and saplings, but they either snapped or pulled free from the mud. He spun about on his stomach, clawing for any handhold as the Red Sword slipped from his grip. His feet met air as he found himself dangling from the cliff, gripping a nub of icy rock. Fu Xi looked over his shoulder in time to see the Red Sword vanish amongst jagged boulders and pounding surf far below.

***

Seasons were difficult to reckon in Wu's evergreen eternity. My unease following the dark feast melted away as the days passed, and I sank deeper under Leviathan's spell.

One day Leviathan found me wandering hedgerow mazes overlooking the sea, a slave girl on my arm, and a goblet in my hand.

"Come, I want to show you something."

I abandoned the pouting woman and my wine and followed him into the gentle valley stretching north behind the palace.

We strolled down a winding, narrow lane into a place that reminded me of home. Misty forests and lush green meadows blanketed one rolling hill after another. The smell of fresh grass filled my nostrils and made my heart glad.

From time to time, strange tracks made by an unknown hooved animal crisscrossed our path. When I queried Leviathan, he only smiled and said I would soon see. We crested a hill overlooking a large meadow enclosed by an extensive split-log fence. That's when I saw the creatures from Poseidon's statue.

I abandoned Leviathan's side and ran to the fence like a child abandons his father's hand at the first glimpse of a new wonder. Timber rails shook beneath my hands as they galloped by with speed only surpassed by the winged dragons of my youth. Grace inspired these creatures. Grace captured in flesh, the sacred imprint of the Emperor of Heaven's hand.

"What are they called?" I asked Leviathan.

"Father dubbed them 'horse' when he named all things at the dawn of time."

"Whore-ssaha." The word's crudity left my mouth sour. Once again, the language of Poseidon disappointed me. And I knew there were many things in the world Poseidon did not name.

Leviathan put his hand on my shoulder. "When I watch you, I see myself when Father first sent his sons forth to tame the world."

"My people call them 'so-qui-li'." A red man approached from my right, taller than any Olmec I'd yet seen. He wore deerskin trousers and

nothing else. A long, jet black braid fell down his back. Exuding quiet power, he struck me as being apart from the other Olmecs.

"Great Lord Leviathan, the stables are ready." He bowed deeply.

"Sunalei Ostu is my master of horses. I call him Sunnah."

Sun-nah-lay-i Ohs-tuh. So many strange languages! Leviathan opened an entire universe I ached to explore.

The Chronicle of Fu Xi

***

He didn't remember pulling himself up, but somehow found himself lying along the edge, panting for air. Two muddy sandals stood before him. He looked up to see the acolyte he'd bedded in the haystack those years earlier, the gown she wore that night plastered to soaking skin. She rubbed a grotesquely swollen pregnant belly. The silk gown had split open, exposing sickly purple and varicose skin stretched to the breaking point. The rain slackened as the apparition loomed closer, long, wet hair plastered against her pale face. Hatred replaced the gentle warmth he once saw in her eyes.

"No more!" Fu Xi shouted. Covered in mud, he sat up and slid backwards until his back encountered immoveable rock. His right arm dangled over the cliff.

She kissed her palm, and then held it flat towards the cliff's edge. Lips pursed with the utmost tenderness, she softly blew a foul kiss into the mist. Like a curtain swept aside by a giant invisible hand, the rain suddenly pulled back. A thin sheen of clouds still cloaked the sun, but the entire horizon now lay exposed. An unending ocean stretched before Fu Xi. Angry white-caps mercilessly assaulted a handful of rocky promontories poking above the stormy sea, stretching away toward the horizon.

"Have I journeyed so far beyond the Roof of the World that I gaze upon an unknown sea?" he whispered to himself.

Fu Xi squinted at the rocky outcroppings, trying to snare an elusive thought fluttering like a moth just beyond reach.

And then he knew.

There will be no other men.

"No."

The apparition cackled.

"Look down from the roof of creation, Fu Xi, and behold a murdered world, drowned by the Heavenly Emperor and his lap dog, your mother."

"Lies." He closed his eyes as despair's cold venom finally reached his heart.

She giggled. "No lies, Fu Xi. Lies are unnecessary servants where darkness and death reign. Despair and fear will suffice nicely.

"Nushen lies buried under a mile of water and mud, along with every village you ever set foot in. Gone. Cursed. Forgotten. Abandoned...*like you.*"

He opened his eyes and beheld a nude Erubian girl, barely a woman, with long hair like dirty water. Fertility's perversion, she cradled an equally grotesque pregnant belly, eyes brimming with vacant hate.

"Your quest has failed." Blood began to trickle down the inside of her thigh. "The man with white hair is dead, his people swallowed by the flood."

She pointed accusingly. "Forsake your mother and the Emperor of Heaven, and I shall raise you higher than any who have come before or after. In the coming age, the greatness of the Eleven Princes shall pale compared to your glory."

Eyes like a snake, she advanced on him, blood gushing from between her thighs.

"Choose, Son of Nuwa. Serve or rule."

"No," he mouthed.

"Then abandon all hope. The past is dead, the future, stillborn."

Mud and stone gave way, and the God of Names fell.

22. The Peaceful Walk

"*Lord Fu Xi, come,*" *Sunnah spoke in short, choppy sentences as one not comfortable with the Song of Atlas.*

He hopped the rail fence. Swallowing hard and heart pounding, I followed. We strode into the meadow as horses thundered by so close I thought they would knock us down. The heat radiating off their bodies warmed my skin. I glanced back at the railing, but Leviathan had vanished.

"*Soquili have powerful spirit, almost as strong as god. My people live in harmony with Soquili since Edoda made them from lighting and thunder.*"

"*Are they...magical?*" *I asked.*

The red man frowned at me. "*All life magical. I thought gods know this.*

"*Stay here, don't move.*" *Sunnah whistled faintly, and a chestnut stallion broke away from the herd toward us. Galloping at full speed, I thought for a moment it might trample us. At the last second, Sunnah pivoted and leapt onto its back. They merged into a single, fluid entity. Slightly supported on his knees, Sunnah sat arms crossed and bottom barely off the horse's back. I wondered if he controlled the creature, or if it merely permitted him to ride.*

The horse bolted right, and accelerated toward the fence. It arced gracefully over the rail before hitting the ground at full gallop. Sunnah appeared to speak to the beast and nudge its mane. In response, the horse wheeled about and galloped back at the railing, accomplishing another beautiful leap before trotting toward me.

I stepped back as Sunnah slid off its back.

"What must I do?" I asked him.

"My people walk two paths to become one with Soquili. First is Do-Hi, the Peaceful Walk, which begins as child." He placed his hand palm down, two fingers extended to indicate perhaps a toddler walking. "It is way of listening, watching, and wisdom." He pointed to his ears, his eyes, and his heart. "Path of patience last lifetime."

"Is this the path you took?"

Sunnah nodded.

"As a god, I have as many lifetimes as necessary. What is the other path?"

Sunnah smiled and produced a green apple in his right hand. "Bribe."

The Chronicle of Fu Xi

***

He tried to take a breath, but his lungs refused. He tried again, but it felt like sand filled his chest.

I am dead.

Fu Xi pushed himself onto his elbows and gagged until gouts of sour water gushed from his mouth. The spasms receded, and he inhaled a gulp of sweet air.

I must be alive, or I wouldn't feel so terrible.

He found himself sprawled across a huge oak trunk that was stripped of most of its branches. Limbs quivering, he pushed up onto all fours and somehow sat up.

Fu Xi shivered in the cold drizzle, naked amongst a massive timber pile, washed up on a strange shore. The shattered forest stretched into the fog in both directions.

Waves sloshed between the timbers and splashed around his feet.

Fu Xi looked at the knobby bulbs he once called knees and the twigs that used to be his legs. Hands shook as if palsied, his skin, only a modest veil for a bashful skeleton. He touched the dagger wound, surprised to feel a scar. The venom no longer burned in his veins.

Fu Xi vaguely remembered clinging to drifting logs and the passing of days and nights, but nothing more. He knew he should get up and keep moving, but didn't know where to, or even if he could. He craned his head about to look behind him.

The timber piled up against formidable cliffs, mighty walls stretching in both directions and ascending into the fog. Climbing them would be impossible. He could not stand, let alone climb off the timber pile.

He lowered his head into trembling hands.

"Mother, forgive me."

He laid back on the trunk, letting the rain wash over him. Fu Xi wanted to surrender and end the humiliation of his failure. An alarming chill settled into his bones, as if the rain leeched a divine essence from his spirit and flesh.

One more journey awaits the God of Names.

Yet, another voice inside shouted, *No!*

He tried to suppress the voice, command it to accept its fate. He'd fought the good fight, carried on as far as his flesh could carry him. The time had come to surrender.

No! The voice shouted again.

Fu Xi suddenly recognized this voice. It had always been there, so long eclipsed by divine blood's blinding light. This cry came from his mortal half, kicking and screaming against the darkness enveloping it.

Where there is purpose, there is hope. Fight!

Fu Xi steeled himself for the impending struggle. Taking a deep breath, he forced himself back into a sitting position, head swimming from the effort. The deathly chill ebbed, but he knew it would return if he didn't get up.

He tried to stand, and the world went black.

He awoke with a face full of wet sand. He rolled onto his back as pain raked ragged claws over his chest. He coughed and felt something warm trickle down on his chin. He wiped it away and discovered bright red blood covering his fingers.

I've broken my ribs.

Fu Xi looked up and realized he'd passed out, tumbled off the timber pile, and now lay at the base of the cliff.

Icy fingers crept back into his flesh. This time, his mortal half remained mute.

***

He placed the apple in my hand. It reminded me of the green apples in Mother's orchards.

"Hold toward herd, see who hungry."

I offered the apple, trembling in anticipation. The horses galloped by, seemingly uninterested in my gift. Then a gray horse peeled away and trotted tentatively in our direction.

"Hmm," Sunnah grunted.

"What?" I asked, concerned about his tone.

"She not one I expected."

Another horse, this one with a beautiful black coat, separated from the herd and trotted toward us, but hung farther back.

Sunnah laughed and crossed his arms. "Where gray goes, so goes black." He pointed at the gray horse. "He loves her. The master will be amused."

"Why?"

"He say 'Sunnah, whatever horse choose Lord Fu Xi, teach him to ride.' Two Soquili choose Lord Fu Xi. Two very different soquili, this make more work for Sunnah."

The gray mare pulled back her lips and took the apple. I expected her to pull away, but she continued forward and nuzzled me. Except in combat or a hunt, I'd never been so close to a beast. I never thought man and animal could bond, and yet such a thing had just transpired.

"What's her name?"

"Don't know, she not tell me. Maybe one day she tell you."

216

She stretched out her long neck and nuzzled Sunnah.

"Can you talk to them? What is she saying?"

"She want another apple, promise to teach Fu Xi to ride." He rubbed her snout. "No more apples until you earn them!" he scolded.

I mimicked the way Sunnah stroked the animal. The corded muscles beneath her bristly fur felt like iron, potential power ready to be unleashed at my command.

Command? I don't know if that is the correct word. Perhaps request might be more appropriate. This beast and I were about to enter into a partnership whose dynamics I could only begin to imagine.

"What about him?" I nodded to the stallion as it pawed the dirt and snorted, bobbing his head impatiently up and down. "He doesn't sound happy."

"He jealous, wants us away from mare." He shrugged. "Or maybe he want apple, but too proud to be nice. She give herself, but him you must take.

"Come," he said. "We go to barn, get bridle. Much to do. Lord Leviathan want to ride with you soon."

He grimaced, face intense. "Lord Fu Xi must not fall, make Sunnah look bad."

As we walked through the meadow toward the gray wooden and stone structure in the distance, I noticed Leviathan's brand on Sunnah's arm.

"You are not Olmec?"

Sunnah's mood darkened. "No."

"Tell me of your people."

"My people ride ponies."

"What is a pony?"

"Like horse, but small, strong, fast. Horse bred for gods. Ponies wild and free, like Sunnah's people."

Sunnah wouldn't look at me, the twinkle evaporated from his eyes. I decided not to press the conversation, so it surprised me when he continued to talk.

"Gray mare see your spirit. You are god, but not like god. Gods and Olmecs come up Old River in ships, take ponies. Take Sunnah's people. Ponies gone. Sunnah's people gone.

"World belong to gods. World belong to Olmecs."

I glanced up the hill toward the palace. In the distance Amiran stood alone, watching us.

The Chronicle of Fu Xi

***

Fu Xi closed his eyes, this time he felt sure for the last time. Perhaps a day passed, or only a moment, before he heard the voice.

"Take my hand," he said in perfect Nushen Cin.

Fu Xi's eyes opened to a broad, stocky shadow standing over him. The stranger rested against a spear, hand extended.

For a moment Fu Xi hesitated, wondering if the Black Dragon had returned to torment him, but then relented and offered his hand.

The stranger hefted him up, supporting Fu Xi's arm over his broad shoulder. Each step summoned dagger-like pain in Fu Xi's side. The stranger partially carried him towards the cliff wall only a few paces ahead, where Fu Xi spotted a vertical crack, perhaps only a few feet wide, partially obscured by a large boulder. Together, they entered the narrow ravine.

The walls stretched so high, the sky looked like a thin, crooked line, and the light dimmed to an eerie twilight. They sloshed through rainwater streams cascading down the granite corridor toward the sea.

We're walking uphill.

"Where am I?" Fu Xi coughed, but the stranger didn't answer.

Fu Xi squinted in the darkness, trying to focus on the man helping him. The stranger's long brown hair and matted beard seemed to melt into the thick, wet furs heaped on his shoulders. Fu Xi hadn't seen fur like that in an eternity.

Mammoth.

The man stared ahead with a calm, knowing smile. Fu Xi peered harder, trying to make sense of the stranger's face.

Something is wrong with his brow.

"You're an Iceman!"

The Iceman grinned warmly at Fu Xi, with twinkling hazel eyes so generous and full of love it stole Fu Xi's breath.

"Morning Star?"

"Come, Fu Xi, let us walk together for a while."

"You're dead." Fu Xi looked about, letting this realization sink in. "Am I dead, too?"

"You are immortal, though you seem to have forgotten."

Fu Xi rested most of his weight on Morning Star's shoulder, which felt as real as the stony ground beneath his feet. He dared not speak further to this apparition, fearing Morning Star would vanish and leave him alone again. Fu Xi didn't fear death as much as being alone again.

But Morning Star kept talking, voice brimming with kindness and patience. "I was born in a high, cold place like this. Deep in a cave, warmed by an enormous fire, my mother birthed me and died. I should have died, too, but another woman took me to her breast. Our clan was bigger then, we had more food."

"You can speak," Fu Xi whispered, finding strength in Morning Star's words. "I couldn't even teach you to grunt, though I know you tried."

"Does my voice please you, Fu Xi?"

Fu Xi realized this was the voice he always imagined Morning Star would one day possess; one to match his beautiful cave paintings, one which nourished Fu Xi's spirit more than any earthly feast could ever satisfy his body.

"It does," Fu Xi choked back a sob, pressing his fingers against his eyes.

"We searched for you, across the glacier and into the low-lands. Our people prayed for your return, and forsook the taste of all human flesh. Along the way, we found others, both Tall Men and Icemen. We shared your gifts and became one people as we followed the mammoth east across the Ice Lands.

"And we never ceased searching for our long lost god."

Fu Xi sobbed, surrendering to overpowering sadness and joy.

His voice is a place of safety where all my burdens are taken from me...

"Along the way, we left our story on the walls of a thousand caves. One day, others will enter the dark places and find the pictures we left behind."

...Let me feel this way every moment for the rest of my life, come what may...

"In time, our descendants followed the last of the mammoth herds across an icy land between two great seas. There, we found new lands, warm lands. We learned to speak, and to sing and dance and tame the wild ponies. We did so many wonderful and terrible deeds."

...His voice is a promise fulfilled. His voice is...

"You believed in us. You did not forsake us, and one day the world will know, we were seeds not stones. Know this, Fu Xi. Even a god such as you cannot see the entire weave, where the ends are joined to others by the Master's hands."

...Hope.

Morning Star halted. Fu Xi looked up and saw the ravine ended in a narrow fissure, through which poured blinding light. He held up his hand to shield his eyes, and felt warmth caress his palm.

"Go," he commanded and pointed to the crack.

"I cannot! There is nothing left, I am empty."

"Then be filled. You carry a god's burden, Fu Xi, but you do not carry it alone.

"You have other children to save. Bring them to this place of safety, so they may lay their burdens down. You are the answer to a prayer they have yet to utter. Like me, they must not be forgotten."

Fu Xi gazed upon the crack, doubtful he could squeeze through. He turned to Morning Star, but the Iceman had vanished, as did the rain.

"Do not leave me!" Fu Xi cried, but only echoes answered him.

Summoning the remainder of his strength, Fu Xi wedged himself into the narrow gap as a faint voice called from behind.

"A land of promise lies beyond this darkness. The way home is always forward."

Naked and alone, Fu Xi slipped through the crack and fell into sunlight.

23. At the Weave's Edge

Soon after the men departed to fish, the women and children would congregate in shore camp to gather reeds. By mid-morning, their rafts piled high with lush stalks, they sailed to the köy-lo-hely. While the children played around them, the women would sit and chat while stripping stalks into soft, yellow fibers. After the mid-day meal, they hung the strips over long cross-poles to dry for several days. These eventually would be used for cloth and rope.

As the shadows stretched east, the patesi-le would lay out strips of raw reeds lengthwise, signaling to others weaving time had begun.

The women knelt in a long line facing the sea and began to arrange their reeds. Each arun-ki had its own distinct pattern, a mark by which clans recognized one another. As they weaved, they slapped the stalks flat where weft and warp embraced. Soon, the women pounded the deck in perfect unity. The arun-ki's unique weave gave birth to its own harmony.

It only took a birdsong, a breeze, or perhaps a cricket's chirp for one of the women to begin the ai – the reed. Her voice chased the natural sound the way a child gleefully pursues a firefly. Immersed in

*the weave's rhythm, the other women joined in. They inched forward
across the köy-lo-hely, weave and song edging toward the sea. Then, far
away, the first halah – the wood, answered them.*

*The Home Song called the men to shore and bound the arun-ki into
one clan, one family.*

The Chronicle of Fu Xi

***

Ghosts of the dead drifted through Atamoda's thoughts
as the arun-ki slid from one wave to the next.

Lace under, lace over, slap. Lace under, lace over, slap...

The sound of palms striking stalks rippled left and right
across the Supply Barge. Every time the women developed
some degree of rhythm, someone would slap out of time and
destroy the harmony. The line of Minnow women kneeling
to her left could not sync with the Crane kneeling to her
right. What should have been a comforting ritual, now
devolved into a necessary, but disjointed noise.

The urgency they shared over the past two weeks had
evaporated. Thanks to Okta, death's visage transformed
from an angry sea trying to rip the arun-ki apart, to a
growing ache in their bellies. Now the people had time to
reflect and think. After the new sea anchor, laughter could
occasionally be heard above the rain. But now the women
worked in glum silence, thoughts on their hunger, the dead,
and the long journey ahead.

Atamoda tried not to think of the dead, but as the rainy
days passed, their faces did not diminish. Instead they grew
clearer in her mind. Friends washed away, children ripped
from mothers' arms, fathers swallowed by the sea; all of
them reminded Atamoda that her family lived. If she wasn't
thinking of the dead, she worried about the living.

She glanced at Sahti. The young woman's dirty blond hair
cast a lifeless shadow over her pale face and dark circles lined
her eyes. Atamoda always gave Xva's wife the biggest fish

cakes, and Xva gave her most of his ration as well. Atamoda told her to go lay down, but she wouldn't listen.

"It makes me forget, and it keeps Xva from worrying over me," she had told Atamoda.

She'll likely deliver in the next month. She closed her eyes and offered a silent prayer to the Nameless God. *Please, no more pregnancies until the fish return.*

The rain continued its relentless assault as curtains of water poured off the makeshift canopies. She differentiated night only by its absoluteness. Lightning, which once terrified the Lo, was now welcomed as little slices of daylight.

Her hands slid in and out of the weave in time with the only reliable rhythm, the rocking deck. Atamoda lifted the canopy section and inspected it as Su-gar dumped a fresh pile of soggy reeds between her and Kus-ge.

Su-gar put her hands on her hips and exhaled through puffed cheeks. "The sea is choked with reeds and about every imaginable log and stick. I doubt we'll ever run out. Why does Okta insists we gather more?"

"I wish the sea was choked with fish," Kus-ge said. Atamoda wished her fellow patesi-le had said nothing, as it only served to remind everyone of their empty bellies.

Trying to quickly turn the subject, Atamoda considered the pile of ripped and crushed hulls lying behind them. "The men will use the rest to repair the old hulls and build more."

"But we have enough boats and rafts," Su-gar remarked. "Canopies cover the arun-ki end-to-end."

Because if we don't keep busy, we will think of food. If we don't keep our hands occupied, we will turn them on one another.

Atamoda knew solitude flowed in the Lo blood as much as the sea. With the two clans cooped up together, nerves would soon fray.

"Because we don't know when the next storm will shred a canopy or when a wave will snap a line," Atamoda said. "Each destroyed boat represents our world growing a little smaller. When we repair a boat, our world pushes out a little farther."

As restless as the sea, Su-gar paced back and forth. "I am so sick and tired of scooping grass out of the water."

"*I* am so tired of listening to you complain!" Kus-ge snapped. "Sit down or leave. You're driving me crazy."

Su-gar shot Kus-ge a stare every bit as venomous as the water demons could muster. "You don't tell me what to do."

Kus-ge rose from behind her pile of reeds, stretching in a slow, threatening manner. She reminded Atamoda of a panther. Despite the wet, clammy atmosphere, Kus-ge wore summer garb – a simple loin cloth and deerskin covering her breast.

The slapping ceased as the line of Crane and Minnow women on either side of the Spine stopped to watch.

Atamoda stood and stepped between them.

"Su-gar, our need for rope is as great as our need for shelter." She pointed to a large pile of unattended reeds. "Please start stripping those into fiber."

Su-gar obeyed, never taking her eyes off Kus-ge. Finally, Kus-ge returned to her place next to Atamoda.

A smattering of palms slapped the deck, and the weaving resumed, along with Atamoda's uneasiness.

Atamoda's reed pile slowly transformed into a stack of square mats, each about twelve square feet. Once each woman completed her pile, she would begin joining them into sections of varying sizes, depending on where they were needed.

Atamoda reached for two of her mats and a handful of reeds, ready to join their ends by splicing the weaves. She glanced offhandedly at Kus-ge's mats.

Now the disjointed slapping made sense.

Why didn't I realize it earlier?

"Kus-ge, your sections are double weaves. I thought we discussed this."

Kus-ge didn't look up from her work. "Minnow double weaves keep the rain out. Crane single weaves leak."

Atamoda looked down the line of Minnow women on the other side of Kus-ge. All their mats were double weaves.

"Single weaves keep us dry enough. Double weaves use far too many reeds. Every day fewer reeds float in the sea, and most of what we find now is already starting to rot. We agreed on this."

"I changed my mind," Kus-ge shrugged.

"It requires twice as many strips to join a single to a double weave. You've wasted half our reeds," Atamoda exclaimed.

Kus-ge tossed a completed mat onto her pile and crossed her arms. "If the patesi-le of the Crane desires single weaves on her side of the Spine, she is welcome to them. The Minnow side will be dry."

Once again, the line grew quiet. The Crane women looked on intently.

Atamoda took a deep breath and put on a patient smile. "We do not have enough reeds for double weaves. We will use single weaves."

"Is this your will or the will of the Uros?"

Atamoda felt herself flush. She measured her words with great care. "They are one and the same."

With a crooked smile, Kus-ge stood, arms still crossed. "Then the Uros and his wife can weave them." She strolled away like a cat. The Minnow women silently filed in behind her.

Atamoda remained kneeling after they vanished to the far side of the arun-ki, flexing her hands and taking deep breaths.

Su-gar knelt next to her, touching her arm. "Are you alright?"

"Yes." She patted Su-gar's hand and glanced up at the rest of the women.

My women.

"Go to your boats. Our work is done for the day. The hour of rations is almost upon us."

"Are you sure?" Alaya asked.

"Go, yes, I'm fine. I need some time alone."

Su-gar and Alaya helped Sahti to her feet and, with the other Crane women, left Atamoda alone with only the rain and unfinished piles of mats as company.

Difficult enough before the Deluge, Kus-ge grew more confrontational with each passing day, as if purposely driving a wedge between the Minnow and Crane. The more Atamoda tried to collaborate with her, the more Kus-ge resisted. Atamoda knew she had to handle this herself. Aizarg's power only extended so far, no matter how touched by a god.

Before the Deluge, Atamoda had little respect for the young woman who could not assume her patesi-le duties until Setenay's passing. But following Kus-ge's performance during the battle against the demons, Atamoda no longer doubted her power.

Atamoda knew a confrontation loomed ahead. She needed to talk to Kus-ge alone, without the pressure of onlookers, where she could delve into the emotions driving the young woman away.

From beyond the brazier's flickering shadows, a familiar figure emerged. By the silhouette's graceful, gliding stroll, Atamoda thought Kus-ge might be returning.

Perhaps she wants to talk.

Instead, Sana stepped onto the raft, Bat-or dancing around her feet.

The Scythian has learned to walk the deck like a Lo woman.

Seeing her little one with the Scythian girl lifted Atamoda's spirits. She readjusted herself to a cross-legged position and patted the place beside her invitingly.

Bat-or plunged into the reed pile and then rolled into his mother's lap. "Momma, I have a secret!" he whispered breathlessly.

Atamoda's eyes grew wide. "What is it?"

Ba-tor leaned in. "Sana doesn't know how to swim."

Atamoda turned red. "I apologize for my son. He's only a child and doesn't know what he says."

Sana sat down and shook her head. "I don't understand?"

"To the Lo, telling someone they cannot swim is a grave insult."

Sana placed her hands on her hips and gave Ba-tor a scolding look.

Bat-or's eyes grew wide. "It's okay, Momma. I'm going to teach her. And when I grow up, I'm going to marry her."

Sana's mock scowl melted into a stifled giggle. "If you are going to marry me, then you need to learn how to ride a horse. A proper Scythian bride must be carried away on a horse."

Bat-or scrunched his face up, as if giving the subject deep thought. "Momma, do we have a horse?"

Atamoda's stomach growled. *If I had a horse right now, I'd eat it.*

Atamoda shook her head. "I think we forgot to bring one."

"Sana, may I carry you off in a boat, instead?" Ba-tor asked.

"Of course, my brave warrior." She giggled again with a smile so warm it made Atamoda question everything she knew about the Scythians.

"I'm going to find Daddy! He has to teach me to make a boat." Ba-tor leapt off her lap and bounded toward the Köy-lo-hely.

"Tell you father and Ghalen I will be there in a moment to help dispense rations," she called after him.

"Is it safe for him to go alone?" Sana asked.

"I don't think he'll go near the edges again." Atamoda paused and watched her boy scamper away. "He's taken quite a liking to you. I hope he isn't being a pest."

Sana grinned. "He's wonderful. Other than you, he is the only one here who has shown me kindness."

"I am sorry. My people will come to accept you."

"Their hatred is understandable. My people grind our enemies into soil, including the Lo. We preyed on you even to the end."

Atamoda did not know what to say, so she said nothing. Atamoda liked the way Sana's voice sounded. Unlike Ezra's guttural, halting accent, Sana's voice flowed low and smooth like a deep, steady stream on a warm day, almost lulling her into a trance.

Sana picked up a mat, toying with the frayed hem.

"Bat-or reminds me of my little brother."

Thankful for an insight for further conversation, Atamoda almost opened her mouth to ask about her family, but then remembered the fate of Sana's people.

"I'm sorry."

Sana turned to Atamoda. "Do not be. Death is a part of Scythian life. We prepare for it at the moment of birth. We don't hide from it, but chase it like the wind across the open steppe. This death," she motioned her head up toward the rain pounding on the tarp, "is different. There are no songs to sing which steel the heart and calm the trembling hand. It is a cold death sent by a cold god." She gazed off into the distance. "I stay away from the edges, too."

"Okta fashioned a small lagoon near the stern on the Crane side. The water there is tranquil enough, and the edges always in arm's reach. Perhaps I can teach you."

Sana cleared her throat. "Someone already acquainted me with the lagoon."

Atamoda stifled a smile.

Sana sat quietly, considering her hands. "It is hard for a Scythian to admit we fear anything, but I fear the water...the demons."

"The demons are gone. Aizarg has assured us of this."

"How can he be sure?"

"Let me tell you a secret. The demons are never truly gone. They were here before the Deluge, and I suspect they will be here after this is all over. There are demons everywhere, in the sky, in the earth and within us. There are those we should fear and those we simply imagine."

Sana lifted her head and considered Atamoda. "How do you know the difference?"

Atamoda thought of the image of Setenay's face in the water. She paused to choose her words with care. "Fear those that separate you from what you love, and dismiss those that bind you to what you loathe. All of them feed on the same thing, fear. Take away the fear, and you unmask the demons for what they truly are.

"All my life, we Lo feared the demons that rode horses and carried bows. I feared those demons far more than those that hid under the docks and crept below the ice. Yet, here is a Scythian before me, revealed not as a demon, but a beautiful young woman."

Atamoda patted Sana's knee. "You have a home among us, and I hope we become good friends. I will always be in your debt."

Sana stared at her hands resting on her thighs.

As Atamoda stood and brushed tattered bits of stalk off her dress, she spied the glint of sharp metal poking from underneath Sana's loin cloth.

Sana caught her eye and adjusted the flap to conceal the knives.

Atamoda suddenly remembered the stories she'd heard about the ruthless Scythian women, of cold steel slicing warm necks in the dark of night. She forced herself to remember this woman-child saved Ba-tor.

"I must go and disperse this evening's rations. Are you coming?"

"I will stay here," Sana replied.

"As you wish." Atamoda turned to go, but stopped. "I am patesi-le...I have to ask you..."

"My blades are clean." The girl said in a voice as cold and sharp as the iron between her legs.

Atamoda walked away, suddenly doubting herself and wondering if Setenay had done the right thing...

...and if Ghalen would be safe around the Scythian.

***

Sana sat alone listening to the rain, doing what she always did during the call for rations; waited until everyone else had taken their allotment. If any remained, then she would eat. Sana didn't want to endure their stares as she stood in line, slowly shuffling from raft to raft, from one dripping canopy to the next.

Mostly, she didn't want to see Ghalen, who the Uros had placed in charge of the food and supplies. He reminded Sana too much of her failure.

More than once she'd considered breaking her oath to her grandmother, the Lady of the Water, and take her own life. Only the fact that she no longer possessed Death, the dagger for just that purpose, kept her alive. To kill herself with another dagger doomed her for eternity.

The Scythian princess considered the reed mats scattered about her. Out of curiosity, she picked one up, admiring the handiwork. Steppe women worked in crafts of leather, skin, and fur.

She turned the mat left and right, letting it flop this way and that, studying each individual weave, amazed at their rigidity. Its toughness reminded her of cured leather. The pattern didn't look too difficult to mimic, either.

She picked up a few a reeds and played with working them between the loose ends, starting and then undoing the pattern until it made sense.

Soon, her hands moved in rhythm with the waves, and she forgot the hunger burning in her belly and the loneliness burning in her soul.

24. The Four Gifts

I spent much of my time learning the Kingdom's craft and lore. Not only did I learn to ride horses, I mastered the white metal they called "steel", far superior to bronze and iron in every aspect. In the armories and gymnasiums, I sparred with the Olmec war masters until steel became an extension of my essence.

Never far away, Leviathan watched me, Quexil always by his side. Perhaps Quexil most of all raised the warnings in my heart. The warrior had his fingers in all matters, his obsidian eyes seemingly everywhere, watching all. Fawning and overly deferential in his dealings with me, I recognized his sycophant's heart. Why one as powerful as Leviathan, who ruled merely by inherent divinity, would desire one such as Quexil at his side, eluded me.

Leviathan's will radiated over me like a dark sun. I basked in his presence, craving only to hear him call me "Brother". Never knowing one of my own, I could not help but measure all I had accomplished against his standard. For thousands of years I lived among mortals, like one of them, yet apart. Like the great palace on the hill, Leviathan stood above and separate from his people.

Where I taught, he conquered. Where I guided, he commanded. Where I mentored, he reigned.

The Chronicle of Fu Xi

***

So long unacquainted with raw sunlight, Fu Xi's sight remained a glittering blur. He knelt in golden sand, so hot it almost burned.

Let it burn.

Warmth trickled into his muscles. Like a tender shoot, he seemed to draw strength from the sunshine. Finally, tall grass and sparkling water crystalized in his vision. Shaking, Fu Xi stood and surveyed the land spread before him like a feast.

Low sandstone ridges, eroded by time, lay all around like lions basking in the sun. They gave way to a band of sandy dunes, which then transformed into golden grasslands rippling in the warm breeze. Beyond, crystal waters sparkled at the feet of a pale blue sky.

Distant thunder rolled behind him, where a wall of mountains held back towering thunderclouds, seemingly guarding this land from The Deluge beyond.

He staggered downhill and waded into the grass, stretching out his arms and letting the soft stalks caress him. Antelope lazily eyed him as they shambled past and continued grazing. Here and there, locusts hopped from his path. Fu Xi halfheartedly snatched at them, but they proved too quick. The thought of an insect crunching between his teeth, its juice squirting down his throat, reignited Fu Xi's maddening hunger. Trying harder to catch a grasshopper, he began to laugh deliriously and lurched toward the shimmering water.

"Come here, you little devils, and let me pop one of you into my mouth." But they easily eluded him, parting before the once mighty god like the grass. Unable to quench his searing hunger, Fu Xi fell face down into wet, sandy soil.

After resting several moments, he spotted a fat worm snaking toward a puddle. He pounced, pinched it between his fingers, and began to slurp it up. That's when he came face to face with a ghoul.

Forgotten, the fat little worm dropped away. At first, Fu Xi thought the terrible visage another demonic apparition. Bulbous, bloodshot eyes blinked at him in disbelief, as if Fu Xi were the monster. Skin stretched over its skull like a drum and cracked, bleeding lips pulled back over shriveled gums barely able to retain their teeth.

Horror and sympathy filled Fu Xi's heart for the suffering creature, obviously closer to death and in worse shape than himself. "I had a worm," he said, patting the ground. But his prey had already burrowed into the soft loam. "It was very fat, and I would be glad to share it, but I believe it has escaped.

"I think we may be able to dig up another, maybe you can help me. If I can get my strength back, I may be able to fashion a weapon, and we can hunt antelope."

The ghoul smiled at him. He reached out to touch his new companion, but his new friend vanished in muddy ripples. Like the last wave from an ebbing tide, a moment of lucidity washed over Fu Xi.

I will go mad before I starve.

He rolled over and stared at the sun. A flicker of grey caught his eye. Fu Xi turned his head to see snarling teeth. A wolf protruded from the tall grass only a few feet away.

***

"Let me come with you!" I followed Leviathan outside onto the grand promenade where a host of Obsidian Warriors waited, commanded by Quexil.

"Patience," Leviathan turned, replete in the Red Armor and long crimson cape he had worn when I first encountered him. "I must sail north on urgent business. I insist that you remain here."

"Why? Are we not brothers? Is there any task, any burden you cannot share with me?"

He leaned in and whispered where the others could not hear, "There are big brothers, and there are little brothers."

I would have been insulted if it were not for his playful nature.

"The duties of the Empire are mine alone. I must be seen by my subjects as solitary in the administration of Imperial rule. You must be properly presented to Poseidon before you can assume the duties of a god beyond Cin's borders.

"Would you have me running about your lands, giving those in Cin the impression another god held imperium?"

"I understand now. How long will you be gone?"

"A month, maybe two. Autumn storms may delay me longer." He winked. "What is a month to a god?"

To be alone again for a month, without the company of my kind, filled me with dread.

"What would you have me do in your absence?"

He laughed and grasped my shoulder, leading me to the edge of the steps overlooking the palace grounds. "Enjoy! Live like a god. No pleasure will be denied you."

He led me down the steps. "Before I sail, I give you four gifts."

The Chronicle of Fu Xi

***

Fu Xi became the worm squirming in the sand. This wolf wasn't an illusion, a trick of the mind summoned by a dark god or starvation. It intended to make an easy meal of him.

With only moments left to live, Fu Xi began to laugh. "You might not like the way I taste. I don't suppose I could talk you into helping me dig for worms?"

Looking about for danger, the wolf inched forward, jaws dripping. Fu Xi turned back to the sun, thankful to view it one more time before he passed into true eternity.

A dark blur erupted from the nearby grass. Fu Xi squeezed his eyes against the dirt and grass being thrown over him. He heard yelps and felt shaking ground before passing out.

***

Leviathan nodded to Quexil, who clapped sharply twice. Sunnah strolled from behind a hedge, leading the black and gray horses I'd learned to ride.

My beloved horses were the first two gifts.

Leviathan then drew a crimson sword similar to his from the scabbard tied to the stallion's flank. He offered it as if it were holy.

"This is an orichalcum blade, wielded only by the gods. You've seen its power; you know what it can do. When the world was young, Father Poseidon crafted one set for each of his children from dragon fire. This sword and the matching armor," he nodded to the bundle on the stallion's back, "belonged to my sister. I now give them to you."

"Why?" My astonishment at the majesty of these gifts was immeasurable.

Leviathan grasped me behind the neck, his grip like steel. Foreheads touching, he held my face close to his. "Because you called me, "Brother" and asked nothing in return." He stabbed his finger at the distant horizon. "I have ten blood brothers who would gladly remove my head for one more ounce of power. My sister tried.

"You are worthy of the Red Sword, Fu Xi…," He embraced me and whispered in my ear, "…as long as you never betray me, Brother."

Glory and red metal blinded me, as Leviathan forged me into a tool serving his naked ambition. My heart shouted for me to throw down the Red Sword, to dig in my heels against the unrelenting tide that was his will.

Instead, I rejoiced.

He relaxed his grip and placed the hilt in my palm, tenderly closing my hand over the silken grip. "Brothers. Two gods, born to rule."

"Brothers," I nodded and embraced him.

Leviathan seemed to fight for composure as he gestured to the horses.

"Practice both horsemanship and combat until my return. Together, we will make plans for an expedition next spring to complete your quest for dragons. They are sacred to my people, too. Perhaps you will let me accompany you to Nushen, where you can present me to the Goddess Nuwa.

"Afterwards, we will return to Father's empire. On that day, we shall ride side by side into Poseidon's Temple. On that day, my brothers will remember what it once meant to be a god."

Quexil stepped forward and bowed. "Great Paqua, the tide will only be with us a little longer." A name only the Obsidian Warriors were permitted to call him, Paqua meant 'Flat Nosed God' in the Olmec tongue.

Leviathan ignored him. "It was no accident we found each other. It could only have been destiny, set in motion by Nuwa and Poseidon themselves. The world was put here for us to take." He grasped my forearm. "Do you understand?"

"I understand," Did I see greatness or madness in my brother's eyes?

On the jetty I watched Leviathan's ship sail beyond the sea wall. His spell seemed to fade as the crimson sails vanished over the horizon. Quexil escorted me to the palace as emptiness settled in my soul.

In retrospect, I am both ashamed and unapologetic regarding my affection for Leviathan. I was one who'd never known the taste of water, and now could not live without its life giving elixir. For thousands of years I walked alone, neither true god nor mortal. I never wanted to walk alone again.

"Lord Fu Xi," Quexil called as I climbed the stairs into the palace. "Great Paqua bid that I obey your word as if it where his, but with one exception. You are not to leave the palace grounds."

In the days that followed, I busied myself on horseback, with swordplay, and concubines. Sometimes, I ventured out to explore, but Quexil always appeared to remind me of Leviathan's edict, or distracted me with 'urgent' matters needing my immediate attention.

Eventually, wine and women kept me in the palace as the days and nights became one. Soon, the quarry, the city and my home were all but forgotten. And so it would have remained if it had not been for Amiran.

The Chronicle of Fu Xi

25. The Fox and The Snake

When the red moon first kisses a Scythian maiden's thigh, her mother bestows upon her the four daggers she will carry for the rest of her life. If she is of royal blood, she will receive five. The first dagger is named Vengeance, and must taste an enemy's blood before the girl can taste the lips of her betrothed.

A Scythian maiden must take life before she can give it.

The Chronicle of Fu Xi

***

The slaver stewed in his own hate; rage rekindled against the Lo with every swell and each flash of lightning, a hot, irrational hate in a coldly rational man.

Why did he save me?

That question infuriated Virag more than his perpetual sea sickness, Spako's snoring, the unceasing rain, or the excrement dumped an arm's reach from his head every few hours.

Why did Aizarg spare my life?

A few weeks ago he would have attributed the Uros's mercy to weakness, but now he wasn't sure. Maybe it wasn't a sign of weakness, but it was still a mistake.

Virag pushed thoughts of Aizarg out of his mind and peered from under the canopy, occasionally wiping the water from his eyes and trying to forget his misery. His head pounded in a never ending headache. The contents of his stomach, a few chunks of rancid fish, banged against his gut, begging for release.

Spako groaned, curled into a ball so tight Virag would not believe it if he didn't see it. Spako's enormous bulk forced Virag to pull up his restless legs, desperate for relief from the occasional cramp. He would order Spako out to fend for himself among the Lo, but he needed the brute. Without Spako, he'd be defenseless. Spako was a witless oaf, but also the only leverage Virag still possessed.

The more you walk the decks, the faster you'll grow accustomed to the sea, and the sickness will pass, Aizarg had said.

Another of the man's lies.

Virag wanted nothing to do with walking the decks. All his warriors, save Spako, had walked the decks. Now they were gone, taken by the waves.

Sickness or no sickness, I prefer this hell to the one exposed to the sea.

He hated the tiny boat, but he loathed the thought of drowning even more. Virag had come to hate many things and many people since Aizarg appeared at the outset of the flood.

The days following Virag's confrontation with Ghalen blurred together. He ventured forth very little, dividing most of his time between vomiting and bailing. He passed the days doing exactly what he did now, peering out from under the canopy, watching the coming and goings on the adjacent rafts.

The nations surrounding the Great Sea, from Lo to Sammujad to Scythia, all knew him as the Marsh Fox. Before the Deluge, secure in his cocoon of power, the title amused him. Now he clung to it like a lifeline. The title held salvation. Virag must now become the Marsh Fox if he were to survive and exact his revenge.

Safe in his soggy den, the Fox listened and watched and waited.

Be quiet, be still. Let them forget I am here.

His stomach rumbled. Judging by the dimness of the light and restlessness of those on the surrounding rafts, the hour of rations drew near.

He kicked Spako. "Get up!"

The giant stirred, rocking the boat uncomfortably.

"Wake up, you idiot."

Spako's eyes glinted in the darkness. "Lord?"

"Make yourself useful and draw our rations. And be quick about it."

Spako slowly crawled from under the tarp and slipped on the nearby raft with a thud. Virag noticed how much weight his body guard had lost since the Deluge began.

If he starves, he won't be of much use to me.

He also instructed the oaf to listen and watch, but Spako wasn't terribly useful in that regard. Virag needed news from beyond the cesspool, of what Aizarg and the men were doing. He also told Spako to bring back any reeds he could manage to steal.

No one knew when the rain would end. No one knew when they would make landfall. And no one knew when the fish would return. Rations grew thin, and bellies began to ache. Fear would soon take root among the Lo.

Virag counted on it.

He stretched his legs into the warm void left by Spako's absence. Blood filled his knobby legs, and his joints cracked. The slaver lifted the blanket off the bulge he'd been reclining against and patted the carefully wrapped horde of dried fish.

Virag horded three-fourths of his ration, and half of Spako's. Food would soon become the most precious of commodities. Virag grew up hungry. Famine was an old friend, and he'd come to relish the burning in his belly, a fire to keep his mind keen and hatred hot.

The sound of women's voices approached above the noise of the rain. The Fox peeked from his den's shadows. The wind and waves did carry most of the excrement way from Virag's boat, but that didn't matter. The women took pleasure in dumping their refuse as close to his boat as possible. Green slime and flecks of brown, peppered the bow, regardless of the unrelenting rain. Now, he didn't care.

The closer, the better. I can hear them more clearly. His razor-sharp mind cataloged every person, each passing event. In only a few days, he knew every Lo woman by sight. The Lo women often spoke freely among themselves, forgetting the slaver reclined unseen only a few feet away.

They think of me like a dog.

Now the Fox waited in eager anticipation for the unsuspecting herd to come to the watering hole, carelessly dropping morsels along with their filth.

He quickly recognized the two approaching women as Minnow Clan, each bearing a clay pot on their hip.

A tall woman clothed in long, winter garb glided effortlessly over the rolling decks. Wild, gray hair framed her sunken, downcast eyes.

That hag is Ro-xandra, Ba-lok's aunt. The Great Wave swept the barren widow's husband, a Minnow elder, overboard. She's quiet, but the Minnow bitches listen to her. Her bitterness may prove useful.

Behind Ro-xandra a short, frumpy girl, barely a woman, followed along, chattering incessantly. Clothed only in a summer loin cloth, her dark features and long, black hair hinted at a strong streak of Sammujad blood.

Ahh! Doinna, my stupid little songbird. He'd learned more gossip from this girl than any other Lo wench. Engaged to a Crane man taken by the demons, her fate was now very much in doubt. Virag's ears perked up, trying to pick out her words from the rain.

"You don't think he likes her, do you?"

Ro-xandra shrugged. "She's beautiful and wild. Men often desire the exotic. Perhaps Ghalen is one of those men, I do not know."

"But she's a-g'an..." Doinna sputtered and looked down insecurely at her small breast and formless hips. "*A Scythian!*"

Ro-xandra's lip lifted, as if she were too tired to manage a full smile. "Yes, but a penis doesn't care about that, does it? And you are not the only eligible young Lo maiden in the arun-ki. Ghalen spends much of his time with the Crane. His loyalty lies with Aizarg and not Ba-lok. Su-gar is also beautiful and unmarried. When she ceases mourning, she may win Ghalen's hand."

"What does Su-gar have that I don't?"

Virag stifled a laugh. Squat Doinna would have barely been suitable as a serving wench in his yurt.

Su-gar, however...I could have fetched excellent trade from any Scythian lord for a night with her.

"Anyway," Doinna shrugged and stuck her nose up in the air. "I hear tell Su-gar has eyes for another man."

Ro-xandra raised an eyebrow. "Be careful what you say, girl."

"It's true! Everyone knows it."

"Atamoda owns the Uros's heart."

"I wish Ghalen would notice me," Doinna sighed and poured her pot into the sea.

Ro-xandra put a hand on her hip and considered the girl with contempt. "We're running out of food, the men struggle to keep the arun-ki afloat, and all the young worry about is what is between their legs."

Doinna harrumphed, and then turned back toward the Minnow Clan's rafts. "At least what's between my legs still works. Anyway, there isn't anything else to do, so I might as well find the pleasures of a man to keep me busy." She walked away, leaving Ro-xandra staring incredulously after her.

Ro-xandra spoke softly, never taking her eyes off Doinna's receding figure.

Virag heard every word.

"Laugh and love now, foolish girl. Let Ghalen, or any man for that matter, drop his seed between your thighs. I hope you enjoy it. When your belly swells like Sahti's, and your stomach burns with hunger, you will curse every second of that pleasure. When you hold your emaciated infant to your dry breast, do not come begging me for morsels."

Ro-xandra spit into the water and slowly followed Doinna into the crowd.

She knows the food will soon be gone. Virag sensed deep bitterness dwelling in Ro-xandra, and, if properly bent to his will, it might prove useful.

He smiled to himself, taking pleasure in turning Okta's insult into strength. He was about to recede into the boat's depths when she emerged from the arun-ki's warm heart, small pot in hand. Judging by the way she casually swung her arm, he knew it wasn't full. The dark beauty gracefully traversed the pitching decks, casually glancing everywhere except toward his boat.

She never comes here.

He planned to eventually seek her out, but it pleased him she made the first move.

The slaver recognized a fellow predator. Like him, she had no place among the gentle Marsh people. She slithered in plain sight for all to see, but only Virag recognized her.

"She wants to know what I'm doing," he muttered to himself. "I want to know what she is doing, too." The Fox leaned forward, barely sticking his snout from the den.

She held the pot out into the rain and dumped its meager contents into the water. Their eyes briefly met before she looked away and disappeared into the ruddy light, never looking back.

The Snake slithered away while the Fox crept back into the den.

Perhaps it's time I learn a thing or two from the Snake.

Virag's stomach growled. Irritated, he wondered what kept Spako.

***

The Sammujad giant towered over the Lo at the end of the line snaking into the arun-ki's center, where the holy woman they called Atamoda doled out the daily food ration. The decks buckled more than usual as he cast a wary eye on restless white caps, which seemed to glow in the gray twilight.

The decks shuddered as another enormous wave broke over the storm wall, spraying mist over everything and momentarily dimming the braziers. Those ahead of him in line barely flinched and continued to talk casually to one another. Spako trembled, his empty stomach heaved. He only wanted to slink back into the boat with his master, curl up and die.

He closed his eyes and hugged the mast even tighter. Spako wanted the nightmare to end, dreading whenever the Master commanded him to fetch their rations. Once a mighty warrior, he now felt as helpless as a child.

He did not know why the strange Lo god spared him and took the rest of his Master's henchman. Master said Spako was good for only two things, looking fierce and killing.

Spako knew how to look fierce, that was easy. But killing, he didn't like killing. He'd do it if he must, but it made him feel bad, like the sea did now...sick inside. Thankfully, Master said Spako was too clumsy to be a good killer, so usually Spako only had to stand behind Master's couch with a spear and look fearsome.

Now the others were dead and Master told Spako to do many things he wasn't good at, like listening and remembering. He hoped Master didn't ask him to kill, because he felt sick enough.

The deck below lurched and dropped with greater frequency. Spako had walked the deck when it had been worse, but now it frightened him more. He gripped the mast even tighter, trying to catch his breath.

I cannot breathe. He wanted to run, but fear paralyzed him. He hugged the mast tighter, knowing any minute the raft would disintegrate below him, sending him into the depths where the demons awaited. Spako slid down to the deck, desperately wanting something solid to make the world stop shaking.

Several women and children ahead of him in line began to giggle and point.

"Look at the mighty Sammujad!" One of them said. "He cowers like a baby."

Thunder boomed and another wave jolted the flotilla. Too terrified to even feel shame, Spako hid his face. Once, they would have trembled in his presence, but now he played the fool for their amusement.

"The Sammujad is going to soil himself!" one of the women cackled before the rest joined in.

"Leave him alone!" A woman shouted. Spako heard pushing, a wet slap and someone yell, "Ouch!"

"Get back in line and leave this poor soul alone," her voice came again. He wanted to open his eyes, but couldn't. The mast was safe, and that was where he would stay.

"He's just a stupid a'gan, Su-gar," an older female voice said, perhaps the woman who cackled. "He knows nothing of the sea. Why do you care?"

"He is alone, and afraid. What do we really know of the sea? Were you not afraid when the demons came?"

Silence.

"Imagine how one only accustomed to the land must feel. Where is your pity?"

A tender touch lighted on his shoulder. She smelled the way all Lo women did, like fresh spring air.

His heart slowed, and his fear subsided enough for him to open his eyes. She had a face filled with love and goodness. Peace suddenly washed over his heart.

"Do not be afraid."

Spako nodded dumbly.

"The waves are frightening, but you are safe."

The old woman crossed her arms and turned her back to them, moving up in line. "Stupid Crane girl, wasting your mercy, if you ask me."

The girl with the eyes deeper than the sea ignored her, never taking her gentle gaze off Spako.

"Stay here," she said. "I will get your ration and bring it to you."

The line moved on without him as she returned and knelt down next to him. "A portion for you, and a portion for the one you share your boat with."

She held out two crumbling handfuls of dried fish wrapped loosely in leaf, but Spako could not remove his hands from the mast. She sighed, put down the fish, and began to gently pry his fingers from the mast.

"The waves will take Spako," he whispered.

Su-gar looked out across the whitecaps. "Is that your name...Spako?"

He nodded.

"Spako, take my hand, and I will lead you to your boat."

Unable to take his gaze off of her face, he surrendered to her will. Her touched calmed him as if under a trance. Gently supporting his elbow, Su-gar scooped up the leaf and led him across the pitching decks. The Lo gave the lady and the giant odd looks as they stumbled by.

"Spako does not walk on water," he stammered. "The ground should not move."

She smiled. "The waves will tell you what to do with your feet if you listen to them. Do not fight it, flow with the water."

"Spako will try."

She patted his hand.

They came within sight of Virag's boat. Su-gar stopped, her warm expression evaporated as she considered the boat. She looked up at the giant. "You can make it the rest of the way. If you need help getting you ration, look for me. I will help you."

Her hand slipped away, and the trance evaporated. Sadness fell over Spako. The decks seemed to pitch higher, the rain was louder, the air colder.

The girl called Su-gar smiled and turned away. Spako looked at the reed tarp covering the boat. Now it didn't look like sanctuary.

He knelt down and crawled into the humid, stifling boat. It stank.

Virag kicked him. "What kept you? Give me the food.

"The portions are smaller, fool! Next time, make sure they give you the same size allotment." Virag tossed him a small chunk as if he were a dog at his feet. "Eat."

The slaver took one small bite for himself and then carefully wrapped the rest and tucked it under the blanket.

"I see they gave you a leaf. Ask for two next time. I figure they'll become expensive commodities as soon as all the debris begins to sink."

Spako pulled himself into a ball and shrank back into his corner of the boat. Instead of closing his eyes, the Sammujad turned and cracked the tarp on the side facing the sea.

For reasons he could not understand, he wanted to look at the sea and smell the fresh air.

It smells like her.

Soon, the waves rocked the giant to sleep.

26. The Kingdom of the Mind

The sultry morning breeze woke me from my wine-fueled slumber. The sea breeze carried the promise of rain, and the faint pounding from the distant quarry. The wind became a messenger for my conscious. I stared at the gilded ceiling, trying to ignore its call.

Two slave girls shared my bed, one ebony, the other as pale as the gossamer curtains dancing over my window. They snuggled close to me as I lightly caressed their brands, wondering how much pain they had felt under the iron's kiss.

Then a familiar, smoky scent tickled my nose. Across the room someone cleared his throat.

I craned up to see Amiran standing patiently beside the door.

"I bid you good morning, Lord Fu Xi. I am here to ensure your needs are met in Lord Leviathan's absence."

"My needs?" I considered the two girls, one under each arm. "I think my needs are already taken care of."

Amiran clapped twice and barked, "Be gone!"

The girls slid from my bed without so much as a pout or a glance backward. No blessing asked, none given. Last night's pleasure forgotten, diminished.

Amiran stared at me with that same penetrating gaze.

"Give me your thoughts, Scholar. I've suffered that damnable look on your face more than once since my arrival. Why do you disturb me?"

Amiran grinned and bowed slightly. "It isn't my intention to be disrespectful; it is only that you are so different from the Princes of Poseidon." Amiran caught himself as if he'd been speaking out of turn. "Would you care to join me for breakfast?"

Eager for the food and conversation, I quickly donned the garment they called a toga, relishing its comfort and simplicity. Following Amiran through the palace, I realized he'd been speaking in my native tongue.

"You're speaking Cin in my own dialect."

"Does it please you, Lord? I've been practicing. Your language is exquisite."

"Do you attempt to ingratiate yourself?"

His backbone stiffened. "I do not ingratiate."

I realized I'd insulted him. "I did not mean to offend."

His demeanor softened. Grinning wide, he rubbed his round belly. "No offense, Lord Fu Xi, only hunger. We will dine in the library." The contrast between his white teeth and black skin gave the impression his smile might swallow his face if it grew any wider.

Plump, with delicate hands like a woman's, yet possessing iron's glint in his eyes, Amiran presented a quandary. Neither king nor vassal, how do I classify this slave who spoke like a god?

"What is a 'library'?" I asked as I followed. I'd yet to hear Leviathan or Quexil speak of this place.

He spoke over his shoulder. "Perhaps we should stop in the rotunda first?"

Like Mother, he answered questions with questions.

"You irritate me," I said bluntly. "You speak in a free manner with both me and Lord Leviathan. No other mortal I've encountered here does this, even Quexil."

"I overheard you tell Lord Leviathan you often live among mortals as one of them, teaching them. Why, then, Lord Fu Xi, would my manner irritate you?"

I held my tongue, realizing all in Nushen spoke to me with easy familiarity. Why, then, did it disturb me now?

We entered the rotunda, where Poseidon's statue greeted all who entered Leviathan's palace.

"The Caste of Scholars enjoys special privileges bestowed by our master, The Glorious God Poseidon. Collectors of the world's knowledge, we are slaves to the truth, and the truth must never be afraid to speak."

"Why are you here, serving Leviathan?"

"As Expedition Scholar during the exploration of Asu, which you know as Cin."

Amiran motioned to the floor where I stood, with its intricate, if puzzling, tile patterns. "Do you know what this is, Lord Fu Xi?"

I shook my head. "I've passed it by many times, but there are still many questions I have yet to ask. Leviathan has kept me occupied with sword and horse."

Amiran grinned and winked. "Yes, I see. It's a wonder you find time for wine and women."

"You aren't afraid to speak, are you?" I warmed to this odd, fearless man. I never saw this side of Amiran during my tutelage following my arrival. But then again, Quexil wasn't here.

He circled the outside of the tile pattern, never stepping inside the black inlaid border. "Your right foot treads the western coast of the continent we call Olma Major." He pointed. "Your toe touches a star, which represents the Imperial Colony of Nazcu. Your left foot rests in the Ocean Gadeirus, named for Leviathan's half-brother and Ruler of Olma Major."

I knelt down, touching the tiles, unsure exactly what Amiran meant.

"To your left, across the Ocean Gadeirus, is Wu, that tiny crescent off the coast of the Continent Asu, what we call the New World. To your right lies the continent of Olma Minor. Farther right, the Ocean Atlas, and then the continents of Alkebulan and Ereb."

Then it all formed in my mind, an overwhelming truth. I reeled under its power.

"This is the world, Lord Fu Xi."

The Chronicle of Fu Xi

***

Fu Xi opened his eyes to find a leather strap, cracked and bleached almost white, resting on his chest. He followed it up until he came eye to eye with what must be the first creature to greet him in the afterlife.

He frowned, unsure if he finally faced madness, death, or salvation. He held out a tentative hand. Hot, wet breath caressed his fingers. A broad, warm nose nuzzled his palm.

"I beg your forgiveness if I don't rise," Fu Xi croaked. "I don't mean to offend, but I'm not sure you're real."

He looked to where the wolf had been and saw nothing. The soft ground all about had been torn up, as if a battle had taken place. Fu Xi looked in the opposite direction and saw the wolf's trampled body heaped several yards away.

"Thank you," he whispered tearfully. He reached up and caressed his horse's snout. Too exhausted to guess how his beloved horse survived, Fu Xi merely accepted it.

Heisè nuzzled Fu Xi's cheek, and then nudged his side.

"I can't stand," Fu Xi answered his friend's unspoken question.

Heise's saddle and bags were gone, only his bridle remained, but his flanks appeared fully healed.

"I can see by your healthy coat and fat belly, you have been eating well. You've obviously been enjoying yourself while I've been trying to save the world."

Heise bobbed his head and pawed the ground.

"It's good to see you, too."

Fu Xi gulped. "Perhaps you can assist me in digging for worms?"

Heise neighed and shook his head.

"I didn't think so."

***

I'd never seen a pictorial representation of land. Its simplicity, its brilliance, stunned me.

Amiran enjoyed this, of that I had no doubt.

"What is this called?" I tapped the floor.

"A map."

"I've never seen a map."

"A god never forgets. Your kind has no need for such things. Mortals, however, with our limited intellect, require crutches in many forms."

In my many thousands of years, I never had to explain to a mortal how to go somewhere. It was I who journeyed from place to place, committing valleys, fields and streams to memory. Such an abstract representation was simply unnecessary.

Amiran smiled patiently, the way I would smile at a befuddled mortal.

"Gods may rule the world, but mortals administer it. A map keeps the wandering heart from losing its way home."

After a few questions regarding orientation and methodology, reading the map became easy. The scope, however, implied staggering scale.

"How big?"

"That is a good question, and one subject to serious scientific debate. Some of my colleagues say the world is endless, infinite in all directions. Others say it drops off and spills into the abyss. The prevailing theory holds the world is encircled by a wall of ice." The corner of his mouth lifted slightly. "I have my own theories."

I motioned him forward, curious about a feature on the map, but Amiran didn't move.

"Only gods may straddle the world," he said grimly.

Suddenly self-conscious, I joined him. The world within the circle wasn't mine.

Four straight lines stretched from the perimeter to the center, where Poseidon's statue loomed. Beneath the chariot wheels, the lines intersected in a smaller continent, composed of golden tiles.

"What is this place?" I pointed.

"The Kingdom of Atlas, the center of the Universe, the very heart of Poseidon's Empire." He gestured to the scattered islands surrounding it. "These are Realms of the Eleven Princes.

"Ten islands for the ten sons of Cleito, with the oceans and seas bequeathed to Leviathan. He is Master of Fleets, Regent of the Waters."

"And the twelfth, Leviathan's sister?"

"I am forbidden to speak of her, other than to say she is a traitor."

"There is much Leviathan hasn't told me."

"I'm sure he will in time, Lord Fu Xi." Something about the flatness of his tone suggested otherwise.

Squiggles fashioned from fragmented red tiles littered the map. "What are these? What lands do they represent?"

"I will show you over breakfast." With that, the Scholar turned and strode deeper into the palace. We passed familiar halls and entered dull, unadorned corridors I'd yet to explore. No longer light and airy like the rest of the palace, these dim, smoky passageways were lit by crude torches. The mundane palace business occurred here. We passed kitchens, storage, pantries and slaves' gawking stares.

"They have never seen Lord Leviathan here. They've never seen a god tread such lowly places."

We turned a dim corner and came face to face with Quexil.

The Chronicle of Fu Xi

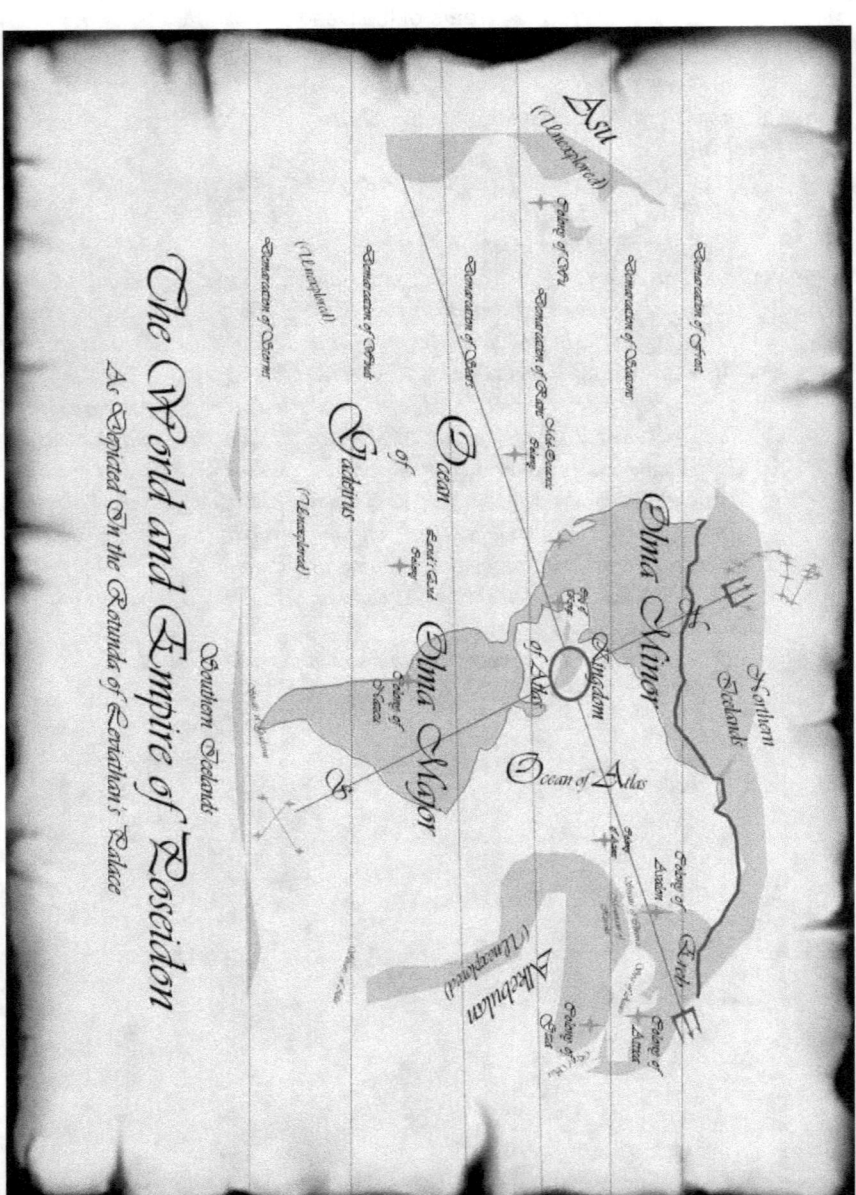

The World and Empire of Poseidon

As Depicted On the Rotunda of Leviathan's Palace

***

Fu Xi remembered the wolf, and knew what he must do. But he didn't have the strength to drag himself to the carcass.

"I am too weak to crawl, but you can help me." Fu Xi wrapped the reins around his arm, feeling the knot he tied on that rainy cliff long ago. He found searing pain in his abdomen, reminiscent of the agony he'd experienced when the reins had sliced into his flesh.

"Drag me, Heise. Take me to the wolf." Fu Xi would devour the beast, as it would have feasted on him.

Heise seemed to understand and began to back up, dragging Fu Xi easily over the sand, but away from the carcass.

"No! Take me to the wolf, or I will die."

Heise ignored his pleas and pulled him into the tall grass, away from wolf's cooling flesh and his last hope.

"Stop!" Fu Xi tried to free his hand, but the horse dragged him faster, and his arm burned anew.

They entered a clearing where the grass had been flattened around a small mimosa tree. Heise stopped under the tree and dropped his head, letting the reins loosen from Fu Xi's hand.

Fu Xi looked up and saw Heise's saddle and saddle bags. The Red Armor, still tightly bundled and lashed firmly to the cracked leather, lay on its side.

Within arm's reach, a saddle bag lay, flap partially open. Fu Xi peered at the bag, and, with a shaking hand, lifted the flap. A single green apple rested just inside the otherwise empty bag.

***

"Where are you taking Lord Fu Xi, sorcerer?" Quexil hissed.

Amiran folded his arms and stared down the warrior. "To the Library, Olmec. What of it?"

The Scholar's tone betrayed not a shred of fear. I'd seen Quexil spar, and he had no equal among mortals. I had yet to see Amiran handle a weapon.

"I forbid it!" the Olmec shouted.

"You have no authority over me." Amiran raised his sleeve, displaying the trident scar on his bicep. "You know who I serve."

"I want to see the Library, Quexil. Let us pass."

"Beware these Scholars, Lord Fu Xi. They are deceivers."

"Let us pass," I repeated.

Quexil's face screwed into a grimace. I knew it took all his self-control not to fall upon the Scholar.

"Great Paqua will hear of this upon his return, sorcerer."

"Of course," Amiran replied.

"Quexil..." My tone carried a warning.

Quexil bowed low and stepped aside. "As you command, Lord Fu Xi."

We stepped by, Amiran not looking back.

"That patch of burnt flesh can't protect you forever, slave," Quexil called from behind.

"Obviously, he wants to kill you."

"He wants to kill everything."

We climbed a flight of stairs into the tower which I'd only glimpsed from the gardens. A two story, gray protrusion from the outside, it always struck me as a wart, an ugly afterthought to the otherwise glorious structure. Until now, I thought it a granary, not worthy of a second glance.

Amiran produced a jingling set of keys from somewhere in his toga, dangling them close to the lantern hanging beside the door.

"Ancient edict dictates all colonies possess suitable accommodations for the Scholar's Library. Lord Leviathan insisted this one be built as far from the throne room as possible.

"Mind you, my predecessor, the Scholar Aric, built this one during the colony's founding over twenty years ago. It suited his tastes, not mine."

"*You mean to tell me this grand palace and the city were constructed that recently?*"

I remember supporting myself against the cool, damp stone wall as I grappled with the thought of the sprawling city and enormous palace being built in such a short time.

"*Yes,*" *Amiran said casually as he squinted at the keys.* "*Forgive me, lord. My eyes are not what they used to be. Ah! This is the one.*"

He fumbled with the lock, bronze scraping against iron, until I heard a click. I wanted to further examine the lock, as such things were also unknown to me.

It is difficult to admit, but I grew uncomfortable in Amiran's presence. It is one thing to be humbled in the presence of another god; it is quite another to realize one's ignorance compared to a mortal. Every corner brought a new discovery and a fresh reminder I knew nothing.

The door swung open, flooding the corridor with sunlight. I entered the Scholar's Library and left behind everything I thought I knew, or could even imagine.

I stepped into a honeycomb of mysteries and wonders. Thousands of cubbyholes covered the walls from floor to ceiling, each stuffed with tightly rolled tubes bound with a ribbon. Wooden ladders with wheels rested against these shelves. High above, a rickety scaffold led to a circular platform circling a domed ceiling. There, a large slit opened to the sky, allowing sunlight to pour into the great chamber.

Strange objects, like birds fashioned from wood and cloth, hung suspended from the dome. Mysterious trinkets and devices, incomprehensible in purpose, rested on several long tables.

I stood spellbound as he shut the heavy door behind me with a heavy boom. Several pigeons leapt into flight from hidden crannies and flapped around the dome.

Amiran stood next to me and swept his arm over the chamber. "*Each of these scrolls is a map, but not of distant lands or seas. They are maps of men's thoughts...ideas captured for eternity and transferred across time and distance. The symbols imprinted upon them we call 'writing'.*"

Amiran stepped around me into the ray of sunlight pouring from above and held his hands high.

"*Welcome, Lord Fu Xi, to my realm, the Kingdom of the Mind!*"

The Chronicle of Fu Xi

***

As if in a dream, Fu Xi closed his hand around the apple. Fat, firm, and heavy in his grip, it felt as if just picked. His stomach contracted and cramped, both frightened and excited in anticipation. He put it to his mouth and bit down, teeth aching against the smooth, tight skin.

Sweet, luscious juice squirted over his tongue, only to be instantly absorbed. After only a few chews, he tried to swallow but couldn't. He kept chewing and chewing, fighting the overpowering urge to inhale the food, knowing he would only vomit it back up. He could not let a drop of this precious gift go to waste. Too weak to eat, he suckled the apple, drawing juice and new life like a newborn. Tingling surged throughout his body, awakening nearly dead tissues. His vision suddenly sharpened, colors springing to vivid...

...*Life!*

His stomach heaved, and then relaxed. He took a bite. And then another, until nothing of the apple remained.

Supporting himself against Heise, Fu Xi rose on shaky legs. He patted the horsed flanks as large teardrops rolled down sunken cheeks.

"I searched the roof of the world trying to save you. Instead, it was you who you saved me." Fu Xi embraced the horse's neck.

He didn't know why he wept, only that he must. Perhaps he wept in gratitude for his own salvation, or his beloved horse's deliverance. Maybe he mourned for a dying world beyond the mountains, where distant thunder announced the continuing Deluge.

***

We leaned over a scroll as he attempted to explain the little marks and pictures covering the parchment. From somewhere in his toga's folds, he produced an odd device and placed it on his nose. A golden wire frame suspended two clear circles, like discs of ice, which rested on Amiran's nose just below his eyes.

He noticed my curiosity and handed them to me.

I placed them on my face as I'd seen him do and looked at the scroll. The symbols appeared twice as large. I took them off, and they returned to their normal size.

"Amazing!" I tapped the circles, partly expecting them to be cold.

"They are called spectacles. These," he tapped a clear circle, "are made of glass. Many years ago, a great Scholar noticed how his staff seemed to bend when he dipped it underwater. Light has physical properties that can be manipulated, bent by transparent material like water or glass."

I handed the spectacles back. "The Sons of Poseidon taught you this?"

Amiran smiled, the lenses magnifying his twinkling eyes.

"Gods are perfect, and have no use for such trinkets. Nor did the gods teach us writing, though all things born from the mind of man serve the gods' purposes."

He returned his attention to the scroll.

"A symbol can preserve a sound, a concept or an idea. A group of symbols, strung together in the proper way, can transport one to a different time, make you experience love like a swooning maiden, or step into the mind of a man dead a thousand years."

"I must learn this!" I could not wait for Amiran to teach me and wondered why Mother hadn't given me such an art to teach the Tall Men.

"I would be honored to teach you." As he spoke, Amiran removed a small cup, perhaps twice as big as his thumb, its opening blackened with soot. He pulled forth a long, hollow stem and inserted it into a hole at the bowl's base. From the within the toga's folds he withdrew a small pouch, opened it, and pulled out a pinch of dark, shredded leaves. This leaf was the source of the sweet, musky aroma I'd associated with Amiran.

Amiran he held it up. "Tobacco...the only damn thing the Olmecs are good for. I am overly fond of it." He frowned and looked up at the ceiling, as if considering something. "They are also good at growing coffee. Have you tried coffee yet, my Lord?"

I shook my head.

He snapped his fingers and grinned. "Tea! The people of Cin are fond of something they call tea. I have some, would you like a cup?"

"Yes! I haven't had any since I've been here. You are most gracious."

"I procured some during some of our tentative forays along the coast. I'm afraid I don't know how to properly prepare and serve it. Would you be so kind as to teach me?"

He didn't wait for my answer and hurried off. "We shall have tea, and I shall introduce you to coffee!"

Coffee. It sounded magical, but I quickly learned I would rather have a horse defecate in my mouth than drink another cup. Bitter mud is perhaps the best way I can describe the vile fluid.

"It's an acquired taste," he said apologetically, and despite my polite protestations, replaced my cup with a properly prepared serving of tea. I held a much different opinion of tobacco, however.

He passed me the pipe and instructed how I should breathe the vapor. After a few coughs, the silky smoke caressed my lungs.

We lounged with our feet up on the table, he with his coffee and I with my tea, passing the pipe between us in comfortable silence.

"I take it you approve of the tobacco?" he asked.

"I do. I do."

"Then perhaps you will approve of this blend," he winked and tapped out the pipe. From a different pouch he produced a pinch of a lighter colored weed.

"This herb grows at the edge of our Olma Minor territories where we mine copper near the Icelands. It's one of my favorites; I hope you enjoy it as much as I do." He lit it with a candle and took one long puff, holding it until his face darkened more than I thought possible. He exhaled in a long burst and then slumped deeper into his chair with a mellow grin.

He handed me the pipe, and I mimicked the way he inhaled. Instead of the rosy, sweet aroma, this tobacco possessed a sharp, acrid tang. I didn't think it as foul as coffee, but could not fathom its appeal.

"I am not sure I approve," I admitted to my host.

I remember staring up at the odd slit in the domed roof, watching doves flutter through sunlight shafts. Before I realized, a delightful numbness spread though my body. I found myself staring at Amiran, a broad grin glued to my face.

"On second thought, I approve."

"I thought so." He laughed.

I remember suddenly being hungry...

...and happy.

The Chronicle of Fu Xi

27. The Lost

The sea must be respected, for Sethagasi quickly claims those who don't. Sometimes the lost leave clues, like an empty boat washed into the reeds. More often, a fisherman never returns, and those who search find no trace.

Sethagasi, the Great Sea, whispers in the surf, "Remember your dead", and I will keep them safe, deep in Heli-dar. Woe to those who forget the lost, for at the end of all things I will disgorge them upon you, and the waters will be filled with the tears of the dead." – Lore of the Lo

The Chronicle of Fu Xi

***

He rarely leaves that spot, even to come to bed.

Recessed in the shadows of the adjoining Supply Barge, Atamoda watched Aizarg and Ba-lok take private council through the curtain of rain. Aizarg hadn't moved in what felt like an eternity; cross legged, chin resting on his fist, staring at the staff. It rested upright in a small hole carved out of the center log by the mast.

The black-iron brazier, the largest in the arun-ki, blazed on the other side of the mast, its three iron legs securely lashed to the deck. Several other braziers survived the opening days of the Deluge, and were dispersed equally across the arun-ki's core. Wood wasn't a concern. Sticks and logs scooped from the sea lay everywhere in piles to dry. But they never fully dried out.

Nothing ever really dried out.

The canopies dripped incessantly, but the Köy-lo-hely and Supply Barge were the driest. Their tall masts gave the canopies the best angle to shed water, which fell in sheets in the gaps between the adjacent rafts. Throughout the arun-ki, the drainage gaps created rain curtains between rafts. One could not move about without receiving a wet reminder of the continuing Deluge. They also provided welcomed privacy, a semi-transparent illusion of separation between families and clans.

Atamoda looked back at the Supply Barge's dark center. There, Kol-ok and Bat-or slept curled up under a rough blanket. The orphans also slept here amongst piles of salvaged reeds, sections of damaged boats, masts and rigging.

As Master of Boats, Okta directed that anything the Lo needed for keeping their world together would be stored here, only to be issued by Ghalen. The Uros and his family called it home.

Ghalen slept on a boat near the lagoon on the Crane side of the Spine, with Sana sleeping on the adjacent raft with Levidi and Alaya.

Atamoda wondered if Okta ever really slept. She assumed he would have been content with his victory over the sea, but since the deployment of the new sea anchor, he restlessly walked the decks, a scowl on his face, usually with Ezra in tow. When not fretting over something needing his attention, or chastising a man for not keeping his vessel in a manner Okta deemed seaworthy, he slept on the raft he'd constructed during the quest.

By some miracle, it survived with only minor damage. Okta spent many hours reinforcing the meek little craft of driftwood logs. Instead of placing it near the flotilla's center, Okta positioned it on the Minnow side periphery.

"I want it always touching the sea, open to the horizon," he told Atamoda. He never spoke it, but she knew he wanted a place to keep a lookout for his people, silently praying for a glimpse of them emerging from the unending storm.

Ezra rarely left Okta's side, but he never slept on the little raft. Atamoda suspected the Hur boy feared being so close to the open sea, terrified a rogue wave would sweep him to his death. All but two of Virag's party had already been swept away.

With dawn approaching, Okta and Ezra were aboard their raft, preparing for the impending ceremony.

Atamoda's gaze fell on the mast and the twenty-one gouges scarring its surface - one for each day since the rains came. Twenty-one days of scraping silt off of decks and out of boats, of mending rafts and patching hulls, of moving vessels and stretching canopies. Twenty-one days of rain, deadly waves, thunder and lightning. After three weeks of survival, the Uros deemed that this morning they would mourn their dead.

Face grim, Aizarg nodded. Without another word, Ba-lok rose and departed to the Minnow side of the Spine.

She wondered what matter demanded Aizarg's full attention outside a meeting of the inner council.

Atamoda hefted a small bag filled with wood ashes she'd collected from the braziers, and stepped through the watery curtain onto the Köy-lo-hely.

The heat from the brazier carved a warm, dry bubble from the clammy air. She curled up next to her husband and laid her head in his lap. For what seemed like forever, he didn't move. And then, slowly, she felt his presence slip back into this world. Aizarg tenderly began to stroke her hair, the firelight to lull her into a trance.

As her hand glided over his thigh, the rain took on a comforting thrum. A fresh, cool breeze occasionally penetrated below the canopy. Staring at Aizarg's staff, her eyelids grew heavy.

The blood red metal orb seemed to shimmer in the firelight. She tried to focus on the fluid-like metal spiraling down the wooden shaft, but her weary eyes refused to focus. Maybe the firelight or the rocking deck played tricks, but the spiral seemed to coil and uncoil like a snake. She wanted to shake her head to clear her vision, but numbing weariness chained her to Aizarg's lap. Atamoda wanted to close her eyes, but they would not obey. A first, she thought the other coil only a shadow. But in both light and darkness it wrapped around the staff, slipped down the rod, and merged with the staff's long shadow.

The blackness slithered and undulated toward her. She tried to stir herself to action, to scream and warn Aizarg, but her voice would not obey.

With a mighty crash, the darkness pounced on her.

***

To a clap of thunder, Atamoda awoke with a gasp. Sea spray covered her as the brazier sizzled in defiance. Aizarg stared at her with a mix of concern and interest.

She sat up and rubbed her eyes. The staff stood unchanged in its hole by the mast.

"I slept hard," she said as the dream's memory washed away, leaving only unease.

He gazed up at the tarp, where rain gave testimony to a dozen holes. "Dawn is here, and a fresh storm."

Melancholy washed over Atamoda as she straightened her hair and steeled herself for what the day's grim duties would surely bring. Lightning flashes illuminated people making their way across the adjoining decks toward Okta's raft.

"Come, it is time." Aizarg stood to go.

Atamoda picked up the bag of ashes and followed her husband. Before Aizarg slipped into the rain curtain onto the Supply Barge, he turned to her.

"You spoke a strange word in your sleep."

Atamoda shrugged. "I cannot remember having a dream. Have I spoken in my sleep before?"

"No," Aizarg said.

"What did I say?"

"Rantaian."

RAN-tay-ahn?

Atamoda shook her head at the nonsense word. "It was only a dream."

Without another word, the Uros and patesi-le slipped under the rain curtain to join their people.

***

The rain fell straight and heavy on a flat sea. The lightning and thunder remained at a distance, to what Okta swore was south, where the sky loomed darker. The Lo had come to understand these periods of calm were only gaps between the heavier storms. The wind may abate, the waves come and go, but the rain poured unrelenting.

"We need to get on with it," Atamoda heard Ghalen whisper to Aizarg. "The lightning is coming closer. We still have repairs to make from the last storm."

"Where are Ba-lok and Kus-ge?" Aizarg said.

Aizarg and Atamoda stood at the edge of Okta's raft, the tarp pulled way, exposing them to the downpour. The Lo gathered just under the canopies in the adjacent boats and rafts, waiting for the ceremony to begin. To their left, the Minnow. To their right, the Crane. In the middle waited Okta, Ghalen, Ezra and Sana.

"I commanded all to attend, even the a'gan. Where are they?"

"I will fetch them," Ghalen turned to storm off when the crowd parted behind them. Kus-ge stepped forward, followed closely by Ba-lok. In the dim shadows beyond, behind the crowd, she saw the giant warrior, the one called Spako.

Where there is Spako, Virag is nearby.

The two a'gan seldom ventured out of their boat, but the Uros commanded all to this gathering. Ba-lok and Kus-ge's tardiness irritated her. Atamoda grew weary of Kus-ge's games.

Okta stepped out into the rain. "We are all here, Uros."

Aizarg placed both hands on the staff, and stood with his legs spread slightly apart. "The Nameless God promised a new land, not a calm sea. We drift at this god's mercy, knowing neither which way the current drifts or the wind blows. The only power left to us, is our choices. The choice I make this day is that we remember the lost. Today, we speak for our dead."

Women wailed and men cried out as emotions, bottled up since the first demon attack, bubbled to the surface. Many fell to the decks, succumbing to their grief.

"Who speaks for the Minnow Clan?" Aizarg asked.

Ba-lok stepped forward into the rain, accompanied by Kus-ge. "I speak for my dead."

Kus-ge emptied her bag of ashes into the water before they returned to their places.

Atamoda stood dumbfounded.

She emptied her entire bag!

Last night, she gave Kus-ge specific instructions to only pour one third of her bag into the water. Both she and Kus-ge would have to perform the ceremony for Okta and Ghalen's clans, neither represented by a patesi-le. Ashes would also have to be poured for the a'gan, as called for by Lo tradition.

Neither Aizarg nor any of the men noticed the hard stares exchanged between the two women.

She did it on purpose.

"Who speaks for the Crane?" Aizarg asked the crowd. By tradition, an Uros must speak for all. In all ceremonial affairs regarding his clan, a surrogate must speak for him. Last night Aizarg selected his surrogate without hesitation.

Xva left his place next to Sahti and stepped next to Atamoda. "I speak for the Crane."

Atamoda carefully lifted her bag, releasing only a smattering of dust into the sea.

Aizarg raised an eyebrow, but Atamoda ignored him.

Xva sat back down next to his wife.

"Who speaks for the Carp?" the Uros called.

"I do!" Okta shouted defiantly. "And I do not know who lives or doesn't among my people. When I have an accounting of the dead, I will speak for them. Until that time, they all live in my heart."

Inside, Atamoda sighed in relief. Now she'd have enough ashes to complete the ceremony.

Obviously not satisfied with Okta's answer, the Uros pressed the issue.

"I understand your hope, sco-lo-ti. But we were spared by the hand of the Nameless God. Is your faith so strong to believe that *all* your people survived? Perhaps it would be wise to symbolically honor the dead, while praying for the living?"

Okta crossed his arms and would not be swayed. "If the Carp do not join our arun-ki before we reach land, I will mourn and remember.

Ghalen stepped forward next to Okta. "I echo Okta's sentiments. I speak for my brother, Ma-sok, sco-lo-ti of the Turtle. In my heart, my people live. I will mourn and remember when either my hope dies, or we reach land without them."

Aizarg nodded. "So be it."

Kus-ge glanced at Atamoda and the bag of ashes in her hands. "We must remember, we must mourn! Sethagasi demands it." *She knows I don't have enough ashes for the complete ceremony. She's trying to dishonor me in the eyes of the people.*

Aizarg looked out over the Black Sea. "Perhaps in this we should also break from the old ways."

The waves picked up, and the deck began to rock as Aizarg continued the ceremony. "It is I who speaks for the a'gan among us, lest we not remember them and their dead."

Atamoda looked to see if any of the a'gan were watching, but only Sana and Ezra looked on. Spako's head no longer bobbed at the back of the crowd and Virag was nowhere to be seen.

She hefted the bag, now filled with too many ashes for the rest of the ceremony.

Aizarg continued, "It is I who speak for the Lo. It is I who speak for the lost clans, and I who beseech the Nameless God to watch over them, keep them safe and bring us together where gentle waves lap against a sandy beach and green shoots reach for a warm sun.

"Mourn while the sea and sky allow." Atamoda turned the bag upside down and spilled ashes for those who were not of her people. The wind began to blow, carrying some of the ashes over the crowd.

28. The Boundary

The Scythians called it Limita, the Lo and Sammujad simply called it the Boundary. Predators dwelt where short, brittle grass met tall, lush reed. Some peered outward to the steppe, others inward to the marsh. Here, the meek timidly poked their heads from the undergrowth and sniffed the air for the scent of danger. Creatures foolish enough to leave their element usually met with death.

The Chronicle of Fu Xi

***

In the thundering midnight, Virag walked the deck.

At first, he crawled along the edges of rafts, between huddled groups of sleeping Minnow Clan families. Between the constant roar of the rain and hissing braziers, they did not hear him. Even if they did, they didn't bother to stir. Hunger began to take its toll, driving most to states of lethargy and sleep.

He knew this day would come, when he'd have to venture forth from his fetid cocoon. If she had not drawn him out, he would have delayed this day as long as possible.

Last night she strolled by again, excrement pot in hand. The Snake dumped the pot so close to his boat some of the excrement bounced off the hull. Before he could get angry, she leaned over, as if examining something in the water, and spoke just loud enough he could hear her.

"Tomorrow night, at the storm wall. Avoid the Crane side of the flotilla, leave your dog."

As he passed across the Minnow vessels, he found himself better able to stand. His nausea seemed to subside with each step. The waves possessed a rhythm. He could not dance to it, but he found himself able to at least tap his toes.

He stumbled forward past the last Minnow raft and stepped onto one of the barrier boats, steadying himself against the storm wall. It had changed since the last time he was here.

The Lo fashioned a crude covering for the wall of sticks, made of leaves interwoven with salvaged reeds. He guessed this would prevent water from collecting in the bottoms of the boats. They also fashioned a walkway from poles and sticks along the inside of the storm wall, precluding having to step into each boat as one made their way along the inside of the wall.

Like last time, the waves roared loudest at the bow, though he couldn't see them in the darkness. This time, however, he wasn't as afraid. He felt his way around the wall until he found the opening to the bow raft.

Virag squinted, trying to see if she waited here as promised.

"Step through the opening," she called from beyond the wall.

The Fox took a deep breath and inched his way through the opening and into the pitch blackness, one hand gripping the wall for dear life. Until now, Virag thought she chose this place because no one would see them together. Now he knew better.

She wants me at a disadvantage, to negotiate on her own terms. Damned if she will see me afraid.

He let go and stepped out into the pelting rain and sea spray.

***

Before the Cataclysm

Her breath came in gulps. The long, dry grass caressed her thighs as she sprinted along the no man's land separating the steppe from the marsh, the Lo from the steppe dwellers. Her long, black hair chased after her, dancing in eternal breeze that existed between the worlds of water and grass.

The Boundary held magic for her, a place few dared dwell. The *Limita* demanded caution.

This place is only for the strong. I am death. I am death.

Sweat poured between her breasts, covered only in a light deerskin scrap. The five iron knives tucked into her waist thong rubbed hard and cold against her bare skin. She pushed herself harder, delighting in the way her long legs felt as they stretched to their limit. The dark woman wanted to run forever, away from one life and toward another.

She imagined herself on horseback, flying across the steppe toward the distant mountains.

East, ever east.

She erupted through a hedge of tall, yellow grass into a clearing. A squat man with bear skin heaped over his shoulders bolted upright and spun around. He brandished a sagar in both hands, eyes wide in surprise above a thick, curly beard.

Sammujad.

He wiped the back of his hand across his greasy smile. "Hey, boys, come on out here. A little rabbit has stumbled into camp."

Sammujad emerged from the surrounding brush, each bearing a heavy sagar spear, the long shafts used to halt Scythian horse charges. Six in number, they casually surrounded her. She reached behind along her thigh and withdrew her longest knife, the bone handled beauty with a straight double-edged blade she called *Wrath*.

"I'd say you found yourself a pretty little mouthful, Bolian." A wiry man approached, licking his lips. She smiled invitingly, hoping he'd come closer so she could slice off his testicles.

"Back off, Wadim," the man named Bolian challenged. "I saw her first."

"And you can be the first to watch me mount her!" Wadim's nostrils flared in challenge. The two men lunged at one another, sager extended.

The fools will fight each other before they try to rape me. She'd seen it before, knowing how such animals thought. She also knew when wolves fight, the rats move in for a morsel.

She spun around just as another warrior tried to seize her. A moment later, he writhed on the dusty ground holding his neck, bright red blood spurting between his fingers.

The men stopped fighting and stared at her, jaws agape.

It wasn't the kill I expected, but it is enough.

She waved the dagger playfully at her pubic area before running her tongue over the crimson blade. "Anyone else want to try their luck?"

The two other men forgot their feud as they watched the last of their companion's life dribble way. They lowered their sagar toward her, finally united in purpose.

She narrowed her eyes and crouched, *Wrath* extended out ahead of her.

I am strong. I am death.

"Enough!" a high pitched voice commanded from the clearing's edge.

The bald man, small and lean, pushed his way through the undergrowth across the clearing. Naked except for a Lo-style loin cloth, he delivered sharp backhanded slaps in both directions as he passed between Bolian and Wadim.

She could never understand how small men could often dominate obviously stronger, larger men.

The woman lowered *Wrath*, and stepped over the cooling corpse.

Then again, maybe she could.

The bald man approached her, eyeing her as if she were a commodity.

Her blade rested against her thigh, pointed downward but ready. She fingered the hilt, wondering what the bald man would do.

He doesn't take unnecessary chances. I have that in my favor.

The Fox came agonizingly close, trailed by his giant henchman. Her blade hand twitched, he mind calculating the rewards of simply killing him versus letting him live.

The slaver leaned in. His stink assaulted her with a thousand terrible memories.

So close.

"Familiar situation we find ourselves in, eh?" he said. She smelled his sour breath and saw his blackened teeth. "Isn't this how I caught you the first time, a foolish girl treading The Boundary without a shred of caution?"

"I'm not longer a girl. Get out of my face or you'll see how foolish I can be."

He glanced her up and down, and laughed. "No, you are most definitely not a girl anymore. You're also late," he continued. "I thought I trained you better than that."

She slowly slid *Wrath* into the gap above the small of her back.

***

The bow raft pitched and bucked, absorbing the waves' assault and sparing the rest of the arun-ki the sea's rage. In a matter of seconds, his furs were soaked and heavy. He wished he'd left them in the boat as peered into the blackness along the wall, trying to see where the voice came from.

She came into focus a few paces away, a pale image against the darkness. She reclined against the wall, back flattened, legs and arms spread wide. The Snake wore nothing except for a waist string, where he discerned the dull glint of knives. Long black hair clung to her breasts, which rose and fell with each deep breath. Head tilted back, she let the spray wash over her with each wave, as if making love to the sea.

If the Lo could see her now, naked with only her daggers, they would know her as I do.

Virag swallowed hard and licked his lips at the sight, remembering the first time he'd seen the Snake, when he thought her only a stupid child.

She's thinks she can use her body to disarm me....she might be right.

Blood pounding, Virag grinned in the darkness.

On the boundary between arun-ki and the watery abyss, the Fox had just wandered into the Snake's pit. Virag knew he may have made a dangerous mistake, but he enjoyed the game nevertheless.

Gambling and combat both begin with an ante. So let it begin.

"Do you still want to kill me?" he asked, beginning dance of words. Whether it would become a dance of death he did not yet know.

"Yes," she said without opening her eyes.

***

"Where is he?" she demanded.

"He's late, too. He, however, has the gold, and can be as late as he damn well pleases." Virag chuckled and walked over to the body. "And the cost of replacing this man will be taken from *your* payment."

He pointed at the big man. "Spako, drag this piece of garbage into the open steppe so we don't have lions sniffing around."

His henchmen assembled in the center of the clearing, all leering at her. She'd been in the depths of the Marsh Fox's den before and knew some of their faces, including that of the corpse cooling on the ground. The rest of these men would also one day feel the *Wrath's* kiss. Today, she had to be pragmatic.

Patience. The instrument of her vengeance would soon be here.

Virag turned and gazed at her, as if wondering what she might fetch on the block. He pointed to her thighs. "You're leaner since I saw you last. I approve. Pity I had to let you go. You'd been far more comfortable in my yurt." He rubbed his cheek and examined her face. "I expected he'd buy you, but I never expected he'd set you free." He shook his head in genuine bewilderment. "No, I didn't see that one coming."

There is much you won't see coming.

All around them the brush erupted in an explosion of branches and leaves. Horses bearing warriors clad in glittering bronze galloped into the clearing from every direction. The Sammujad hastily formed a circle, sagar bristling outward, as Virag dashed to the center.

Her heart leapt.

The horsemen encircled the slaver's meager force. To her, the Sammujad appeared crude and barbaric compared to the magnificent armored warriors. They pointed black, polished lances down toward the Sammujad. Even their horses wore armor.

She whispered a prayer to her dark gods the horsemen would slay Virag and his men on the spot.

We don't need them anymore.

One horseman trotted to the fore, his breastplate sparkling like the sun, jewel encrusted sword dangling at his hip. A light chain mesh hung from his golden helm, covering all of his face except his eyes. She knew immediately it was him.

He dismounted and waved off other horseman, who dutifully lowered their lances.

"What is the meaning of this?" Virag demanded.

The towering warrior removed his helmet, freeing dark, curly locks which tumbled over broad shoulders.

To her, he might as well have been a god.

"Can't be too careful, slaver. We had to make sure it was you."

"Careful? Of course its me!" Virag spat and pushed his way out of the circle. The Fox and his wolves looked small, so helpless compared to the Golden Lion. She wanted to laugh with glee.

"Who else would be here, waiting on you? I have the goods, Prince Bal-eeb. Let's get this business over with."

The warrior threw his helmet at Virag, who barely caught it and stumbled back a few paces.

"We do business when I say we do business."

The warrior looked about, a sparkle in his eye, as if trying find something. "Where is my Marsh Flower?"

She pretended to pout and strolled forward. Horse and man parted for her.

Virag rolled his eyes.

Bal-eeb grinned and took her by the hand. He turned to the nearest mounted warrior. "Set up a picket in case any of Tuma's raiders picked up our trail. Send a message to our main force and tell them we made it, proceed as planned. Set up camp, no fire." He considered Virag dismissively. "We do business when I return."

Hand in hand, the Lion and the Snake vanished into high grass.

***

"He's dead," Virag stated flatly, wondering if she'd accepted that fact in her heart.

She didn't respond.

"The City of Gold is gone, perhaps even under our very feet. If the great wave came from the north, then Hur-ar met its fate before the steppe."

As his eyes adjusted to the darkness the raindrops pouring off her pale face became visible.

We're all pale now. No matter, I never much cared for the sun anyway.

An odd thought crossed his mind.

Has she been crying?

"If you invited me here to kill me, please get on with it. I'm cold and wet. I'd rather be cold and wet in my boat. Otherwise, I'm leaving." He turned to go.

"What would our dear Uros think if I told him why you had those wedding barges?"

Ah, so it begins.

He turned to face her. She now stood tall, balanced on the edge of a barrier boat, waves sloshing over her calves.

She's trying to show me she's in charge, comfortable on her turf, flaunting her power. Virag grudgingly admired her. He mentally kicked himself for even entertaining the thought she'd been crying.

"I think he'd be none too happy, witch. And I believe he'd be equally interested in your role."

She caressed the blades lined up across her right thigh, aching close to her magical place, each so slender and delicate and lethal. "Do you think I need these to slay you? You are only a push away from the edge and unable to swim."

"But I thought you were also of the g'an? Or have you finally accepted the humble ways of a Lo woman, *Marsh Flower?*" He used the last words as a dagger of his own, hoping they would reveal his suspicions. Anger flashed in her eyes and he knew still mourned.

For Bal-eeb or the power she lost?

"You better hide those daggers or you'll betray your true nature. Virag turned his back again. "You're wasting my time. I'm going back to my canoe before someone sees us together."

"No one will see us. I doubt anyone will notice our absence."

She paused. "I want to make a bargain."

He thought he heard a twinge of desperation in her voice.

He turned his head slightly, "A bargain? For what commodity? Unless you can wrest food from Aizarg's bitch you have damn little to bargain with."

"You keep our secret and I spare your life."

Virag laughed. "That is not a bargain, it's a truce. I hold your life in every bit as much peril as you hold mine. The same stone will sink us both." Virag shrugged and waved his hand dismissively. "Fine, a truce. Though I don't believe that's why you drew me here. Killing me would have kept you secret safe, and I know you would have enjoyed that immensely."

The Snake approached, her smile betraying a renewed confidence.

So dangerous and so beautiful. Yet, so predictable.

"The food will soon run out. He..." she paused. "*She* who controls the food will control the arun-ki."

"I'm listening."

Lighting flashed from the belly of a fresh storm far beyond the sea anchor.

29. Vengeance

In the language of killers, there is no word for "fair." – Scythian Proverb

The Chronicle of Fu Xi

***

He rolled off her into the soft grass. They lay side by side, both heaving for air. Dragonflies buzzed overhead in a narrow window of pale blue, framed by a high wall of reeds.

Her pleasure tingled far deeper than the physical warmth slowly receding in her belly. She rolled onto her side, supporting her head with her hand, and watched him.

Eyes closed, chiseled features relaxed, she wanted to touch him, but was afraid....afraid he'd vanish in a puff of smoke, like everything else she cared about - like her grandmother, her real brother, and her innocence.

She knew he wasn't asleep. Living gods never slept. She plucked a blade of grass and ran it lightly over his abdomen, tracing the lines of his fading battle scars, each only serving to heighten his beauty. Her fingernails left several new ones on his back.

The smell of their drying lovemaking mixed with the breeze and sweet smell of crushed grass. Underneath it all lingered his scent: sweat, iron and the exotic oils rubbed over his hair and muscles. She had no reference for the scent other than it was *him*.

This was *her* man, the deliverer given to her by the dark gods in return for a promise she'd soon fulfill.

"Tell me again, my prince. About Hur-ar. What does my palace look like?"

He scowled mockingly. "It's big, just like I told you before. Too damn big, and drafty. You'd hate it."

She pouted and slapped his belly. "Stop that! Tell me again. Tell me about the gold."

"As you wish," Bal-eeb put his hands under his head and stared up at the sky. "The walls are the finest alabaster. Two giant bronze doors open from the Avenue of Kings to a courtyard garden as lush and peaceful as the legendary Paradise of the Narim. A cool fountain, carved like a roaring lion, lords over the courtyard, fed by an ice-cold spring. Beyond, double doorways, gilded by the Royal Smith himself open to..."

She laid her head on his chest, listening to his voice reverberate deep in his chest to mix with his heartbeat. She closed her eyes and tried to image everything he described, though she had no idea what things like 'alabaster' and 'avenue' meant. She only knew they were grand and powerful things and would soon all be hers.

Bal-eeb ran his fingers through her hair as he spoke, as if the act seemingly hypnotizing both of them. After a few moments she noticed he'd stopped talking. She opened her eyes and found him staring at her with an uncertain expression.

She looked at him sideways, eyes narrowing. "You want to tell me something, but you fear to speak it."

He rested his head on his arms and stared up at the sun, perhaps thinking how he could conquer it. "My campaign against Scythia begins tonight. It will take many months. I will be away from Hur-ar several times until the snow falls on the Black Fortress."

"You aren't taking me to the golden palace? I am not to be your queen?"

"You are not ready to enter Hur-ar," he said flatly.

Her stomach dropped as her world, and hope, crumbled. She raised her chin defiantly and crossed her arms. "I have served my purpose? Is that it?"

Bal-eeb turned his head and cracked a devious smile. He held her chin. "Did I not buy you from the slaver? Did I not release you?"

She nodded.

"The Lion of Hur-ar keeps his promises. Come with me on my conquest of the world. Keep my tent warm. Share my bed and I will heap Scythian treasure around you each night. We will enter Hur-ar together, side-by-side on a golden chariot. No one will dare oppose me, no one will dare touch you. No one."

She lowered her head, unable to hide her disappointment. *Alabaster, it sounds so magical. I want to see it!*

He tenderly lifted her chin. "Understand this. If I leave you in Hur-ar alone, I cannot protect you."

She scrambled over to her knives lying in the grass beside her meager strips of clothing. Clenching them all in one fist, she shook them at her lover. "I can protect myself!"

He wrapped his big hand around her fist and gently lowered it. "To rule in Hur-ar one must spear the shadow, slay the whisper, dance with the lie. You must learn the ways of court before you can hunt the gilded halls. The Scythians call it the Place of Mazes for good reason." He took her knives and tossed on top of his breastplate with a clang. "Your wits must be your armor, your tongue a dagger coated in honey. My enemies are legion, but my allies present an even greater danger. They will seek to destroy you. You will become lost among a thousand smiling faces, a blade behind every back."

Bal-eeb propped himself up on one arm and paused, searching her face. She once again saw conflict swimming in her lover's eyes where'd she'd only seen unshakable confidence before.

He leaned over to his waist wrap crumpled next to them. From some hidden compartment, he retrieved something small and jingling. He turned his hand upside down and let a long, sparkling chain dangle before her eyes.

The golden chain's etched pattern twisted like diamond teardrops encircling a tendril of sunlight. A coiled pendent, shaped as a snake-like beast and forged from a strange red metal, hung on the end. A delicate lattice of etched gold crisscrossed obsidian wings as black as midnight. Sunlight reflecting off the dragon's ruby eyes peppered her face with flecks of bloody light.

"This is the *Kerubim*, a handsome gift from the High Priest of Ba'al himself. He said two powerful dragons forged it ages ago in the act of love. The red metal is love's flame eternally captured. The obsidian wings, forbidden passion. The sparkling gold represents the seed of creation, infused with starlight stolen from heaven itself by Ba'al, the Light Bringer."

Mesmerized, she reached for the pendent, but he pulled it back, snapping her from the trance.

"Shellbaz gave this me knowing I will one day be king. Two dragons made one, a god born to rule."

Her mind reeled. She straddled her man's chest, inching closer to the treasure, but he kept it just out of reach

"The Lion of Hur-ar takes what he wants. The Narim once said, 'That which is most pleasing is not what is taken, but given.'" Bal-eeb gently lowered the chain over her head. It fell across her skin, the dragon pendent settling between her breasts.

He touched her belly. "From your womb will come my son, his spirit wild and free like his mother's. A king born to rule."

She felt her spirit bounding free and joyful in her chest, as glorious as the dragon over her heart. She placed her hand over his.

"From your seed will come my son, his spirit as strong and unyielding as his father's. A god born to rule."

She mounted him again, filled and complete. She imagined herself drawing power from the pendent and prayed silently to the dark gods for him to plant a seed within her.

In a tiny glade, buried in the deep grass and hidden from view, the Lion and the Snake took refuge from their own ambition, content in each other's arms.

***

Between the arun-ki and the endless midnight sea, the Snake and the Fox birthed a conspiracy. As they talked on the stormy bow, Virag's unease ebbed as he grew accustomed to the rhythm of the waves. He didn't feel as cold, the waves didn't loom so ominously.

Virag meticulously laid out his plans, and the Snake's role in them. She listened without a word until he finished.

"Aizarg isn't ruthless. He won't do it," she scoffed.

Virag smiled. "Oh, he will. He must. If he doesn't, not even his god can help him. Fear festers among the Lo, something these once sheltered, gentle people are unaccustomed to. I manipulate fear like the blacksmith works in bronze. It will only take a nudge to heat it, cunning to bend it to open rebellion."

"The Uros commands loyalty. His inner circle is strong."

"We will isolate him with whispers."

"You cannot isolate him from Atamoda."

Virag smiled. "Patience. The sea is deep, the night is dark. Opportunities will present themselves soon enough to neutralize Aizarg's woman."

"She's like Setenay, she sees."

"Setenay is dead."

"The Uros also wields the power of the God of the Narim."

"Gods are crutches for desperate fools and luxuries for the rich. They do not fill bellies or bring back the dead. Simply do what we agreed upon and the flotilla will be firmly in our control in a manner of weeks."

***

The towering flames illuminated the entire lagoon as if it were high noon, affording the Lo no place to hide, no escape. Virag would have never believed it would have been this easy.

He sat cross-legged on the dock and watched in morbid fascination as the two enormous wedding barges drifted to and fro, silhouetted against the backdrop of flaming huts. Out of the original fifteen huts in this arun-ki, only this one remained unburned.

Fourteen stilted torches.

The stench of burning reeds and pitch stung his nostrils. Heat rippled across the lagoon as the flames licked the sky. Burning arrows blossomed from the barges like shooting stars as well-pitched boats erupted into flames. Lo bodies drifted everywhere, floating pincushions riddled with Hur arrows. In the distance, Virag saw the glint of armor as the warriors strolled up and down the narrow beach, killing or capturing those who made it to shore.

Less than an hour ago, the screams were deafening. Now the only screams Virag heard was that of the sco-lo-ti's wife in the hut next to him.

The Hur soldiers were having their fun.

The heap of bloody flesh next to him moaned and began to stir. The Sco-lo-ti of what only an hour ago was the Gar Clan, opened swollen eyes at the carnage. The chieftain groaned.

"Ah, he's awake. Prop him up," Virag commanded the Hur warriors looming behind them.

They lifted the nude, blood streaked sco-lo-ti and shoved him down on his knees. His arms and shoulders drooped at a sickeningly low angle, broken in several places. That didn't preclude the Hur from tying them behind his back. His blackened limbs had swollen to the point the skin began to split.

"I'm glad you're awake, Vi-nair," Virag said in a chummy tone, as if they were old friends taking the night air on the dock. "There is still business to attend to."

Virag looked back at the two Hur warriors standing behind them. "Go into the hut with your friends and enjoy yourselves. I want to take the air with my old friend."

They men looked at one another, unsure if they should follow the slaver's orders.

"He's harmless now. If you don't get in on the festivities in the hut, your friends probably won't leave anything for you."

One of them grinned at the other and motioned to the ladder leading to the hut's entrance. A moment later, Virag and Vi-nair were alone.

The low cries coming from the hut suddenly intensified, mixed with guttural laughter.

"Why?" Vi-nair croaked through a swollen jaw.

Virag said nothing for what seemed an eternity while the broken man beside him softly cried. The slaver's head cocked to one side, legs casually crossed and arms resting in his lap as if watching a macabre festival across the lagoon.

Finally, Virag took a deep breath, drinking deep the stink of slaughter. "They call him the Lion of Hur-ar, you know. When a lion hunts the Boundary, wolves and foxes go to ground. He approached me in the Grand Market, knowing of my relationship with Lo chieftains. I made a choice that fateful day, serve the Lion and prosper, or go to ground and die."

Virag considered the man suffering next to him. The hardness drained from his face, transforming into something that could be taken as pity. He gently patted the sco-lo-ti's back, careful not to touch his shattered limbs.

"I'm going to tell you something I've always wanted to say. If I could have lived as one of you, I would have. Your sheltered isolation, free to eat and make love and raise babies without fear, protected by a stretch of water no conquer has been able to breach...ahh! But I regret your way of life will soon come to a brutal end, especially when your people have been my best trading partners."

The slaver paused to gather his thoughts, and then continued, "You ask why this happened; because a Lion has strolled into our world. Like an antelope on the outside of the herd, yours is the most easterly arun-ki, far removed from the rest of your nation. *Conveniently* isolated.

"You monster!" Vi-nair spit, struggling to free himself despite the agony. But his shattered arms would not obey.

Virag leaned back as his veil of pity evaporated. "Blame me if you wish, but this isn't my handiwork. I'm a trader, not a conqueror. It really doesn't matter if I helped him or not, the Lion would have found someone else to give him what he needed, most likely one of your very own. Gold is like the sun, it blinds men to the light of their own conscious.

"One at a time, from east to west, the Lion of Hur-ar will quietly conquer the Lo villages. His army will leave no evidence, do nothing to raise the suspicions of the horse clans. Once your people are enslaved he can move on to his true objective, the Scythians. Unimpeded, his armies will sweep north from the marshes and crush the horsemen. He intends nothing less than ruling the world. I intend to make a healthy profit."

Finally, Virag turned and raised his finger, as if emphasize an important point. "If it provides any consolation, not all your people will die. Some will be carried away to Hur-ar, but my agreement with the Captain precludes me from taking any as booty. It's quite a lucrative agreement, mind you, but I'd be a liar if I didn't say I'm disappointed I'll get none of the slaves."

Vi-nair shook his head over and over, eyes clenched, mouthing "no" over and over.

Virag leaned in and gently placed a hand on his shoulder. The sco-lo-ti winced in agony at the touch. "Life is simply unfair. I've always wanted to say that, but to do so is considered weakness among my people. Be warned, this nightmare isn't over. In the fleeting moments before you die your life will drift so far from fair even the dark gods of Scythia will cringe at your fate."

Virag sprung up and faced the burning village, face demonic in the fire light. He pulled a crooked iron dagger from under his tunic and pointed it at the barges lumbering back and forth in the lagoon, picking off survivors.

"Without the wedding barges you ransomed for your daughter, none of this would have been possible! Isn't that ironic? Depending on how this goes, he'll move on to Aie-lok's village next, and then Aizarg's and so on and so forth. You get the idea. I've already purchased two more wedding barges from Ai-lok. His son delivered them to me no more than a week ago.

"That old sco-lo-ti will soon see his own handiwork turned against him, too. I was lucky to make that deal. That old bitch Setenay tried to talk him out of it. Luckily for me, I had someone on the inside."

Virag slowly looked down to Vi-nair, teeth gleaming, voice smooth with wicked pleasantry. "Didn't that ravishing daughter of yours marry Aie-lok's son not long after I ransomed her back to you? What's his name...Ba-lok? I must admit, I was a bit offended when I wasn't invited to the wedding. I thought we were better friends than that."

"Spare her! You said you wanted to keep her. Don't let them kill her. Virag, don't let these monsters kill my daughter!"

Virag ignored him, his devilish smile growing ear to ear. The slaver considered the barges as they lingered on the far side of the huts, which now had burned almost to the water line. The lagoon began to dim as warriors pulled bodies out of the water, occasionally slicing a throat or binding one which might prove a useful slave.

One barge began a slow turn towards the dock as the cries within the hut turned to frantic screaming. Virag kept talking as if they screaming didn't exist.

"Long ago, I thought you Lo a stupid race, soft and foolish. Those barges prove you are not stupid. Neither the Captain's army nor my men could bend the craft to our will, at least in the time afforded us."

From somewhere behind them there came a splash and laughter from the hut. Knowing his wife's fate, Vi-nair lowered his head to the dock.

Virag grabbed the sco-lo-ti's hair and yanked his head up, slapping him gently across the face. "I told you it would get worse. If it were up to me, I'd kill you now. I'd slice your throat from ear to ear and end your suffering quickly." Virag peered back at the approaching barge. "But you've been promised to another."

Vi-nair's sobbing abated as he peered at the approaching barge. Two shadows stood side-by-side at the front; one large, and obviously a warrior, the other slender and diminutive.

"It was no twist of fate my men captured her last spring," Virag continued. "She's a careful, clever girl, but she had a weakness.

"You Lo and your custom of mercy! It seems your father's fascination with that Scythian witch you called your mother has come back to haunt you. I guess she never truly accepted the Lo ways and filled her granddaughter's head with romantic images of the steppe."

Virag jerked Vi-nair's head toward the approaching barge. The sco-lo-ti's eyes widened with dawning horror.

"I was more than happy to exploit her illusions, her fantasies." Virag looked into the distance, his eyes focusing on a place of pain and pleasure and licked his lips. "It's easier to twist someone to your will when they hate you. Oh, does your daughter hate me! But, my friend, she hates you *so much more*.

"The little Marsh Flower I captured two summers ago was not the same girl I returned to you. I twisted her into a beautiful and deadly snake."

Virag drank in the horror on the sco-lo-ti's face when he recognized the form of Kus-ge on the front of the raft. "Your daughter approaches, sco-lo-ti. She comes to collect her reward for this night's bloody work. It is time for me to collect my payment as well."

Virag snatched back the sco-lo-ti's head and pried open his mouth. He knelt in front of Vi-nair, dagger in hand, blocking his view of the approaching barge.

"She thinks you abandoned her to my clutches, she thinks you were too weak to fight for her. I worked hard to make her believe you abandoned her because of her Scythian blood, because she wasn't a son." He looked over his shoulder at the approaching barge. "I imagine her feelings would be vastly different if she knew the barge she rides was paid as ransom. Lies are always sufficient to make one hate, but stronger magic is required to induce betrayal.

With a lightning cut, he sliced out the sco-lo-ti's tongue. Vi-nair lurched in agony, blood spurting from his mouth.

"The Captain did something even worse, he made Kus-ge think he loves her. For love, Vi-nair, your daughter has betrayed you."

Virag dangled the bloody organ. "I collected my payment, now it's safe for your daughter to collect hers. Can't let her know the truth, can we? That would ruin everything."

Virag considered the tongue for a briefest of moment before tossing it in the water next to the patesi-le's corpse.

"Truly important tasks should never be left to someone you trust. They should only be given to someone you've twisted."

Kus-ge leapt the remaining few feet from the barge to the dock. "Where is he?" she demanded.

***

She pulled a long, thin dagger from the band around her thigh. "There is another beside Atamoda we must eliminate," she said, toying with the blade tip. "Sana must die."

Virag raised an eyebrow at this unexpected turn. He'd considered approaching the Scythian as a potential ally.

"The Scythian girl is dangerous," Kus-ge said. "The longer she lives among the Lo, the closer she gravitates to Atamoda. She will only grow stronger among them."

Virag's eyes narrowed. "You fear her?"

"No." Kus-ge snapped too quickly. "But she has power, and she's too close to Ghalen.

"Ghalen hates her."

She barked a short laugh, "Men know nothing! He hates the way she makes him feel. She twists him, and he twists her. Soon, they will be entwined and it will be too late."

"Too late for what?"

"The cutting."

Virag held his face up to the downpour. "Dawn approaches. We must slip back to expected places.

"One enemy at a time," Virag said as he turned to make his way back through the sea wall. "Leave the Scythian alone for now. Raise no suspicion. Proceed with our plan."

***

Virag stepped out of her way as Kus-ge halted a few paces, face blank as she considered her father.

"What did you do to him?"

Virag shrugged. "He insulted me, so I cut out his tongue."

"He was mine. You lied!" she fell upon Virag, slashing at him with a straight iron blade.

"You bitch," he dodged backwards. "I only promised he'd be alive and conscious. Put that knife away or I'll cut *your* tongue out with it!"

Bal-eeb snatched Kus-ge back. She struggled, but only briefly. Bal-eeb considered Virag as if deciding whether or not to kill him. "We had a deal, slaver. Why do you break it?"

"I didn't break it. She gets to take her father's head while he still lives. You promised me one item of booty of my choice, which I took. I wanted his tongue. She gets her prize, and I get mine."

Bal-eeb nudged her forward. "The slaver kept his bargain, I keep mine. Take your vengeance, and let us be off before dawn to finds us here."

He turned to one of his men. "Fish out the rest of the bodies. Drag them deep into the marsh and bury them. Leave no arrows. Not one trace, we can neither give Prince Tuma nor the Lo any idea who did this."

The warrior nodded and returned to the barge.

Virag looked on intently as Kus-ge knelt before her father.

She held up the long knife inches from her father's face. "This is one of the five knives Grandmother bestowed to me in secret, after Mother refused to take them. She called it *Vengeance*. Grandmother did not give it lightly, making me swear an oath to one day to slay one of her enemies. This, I will do. But before it can feast on old hate, it must taste new hate...the hate I carried for you since you abandoned me."

Kus-ge lightly traced the tip across her father's neck. Tears filled Vi-nair's eyes. He shook his head and groaned.

She doesn't see her father's sorrow.

"I dreamt of asking you why...why you let me suffer at Virag's hands, and why you sent me off to that fool Ba-lok so soon after I escaped." Kus-ge scowled up at Virag. "I will add this insult to the long list for which you will one day pay."

The Hur soldiers looked on with lustful gazes, anticipating the evening's final bloodsport.

Bal-eeb considered the events with iron impassivity.

"I cannot ask why," Kus-ge traced the blade down Vi-nair's chest until it rested against his abdomen. "But I can make you suffer."

The blade darted and her father's innards spilled on the dock.

Bal-eeb grasped her arm. "It is done. We must leave."

"I must watch him suffer."

"He will die in agony. That must be enough."

Kus-ge pulled away only for a moment before succumbing to Bal-eeb's will. They turned and stepped back onto the barge. In a moment it drifted away across the darkening lagoon as the fires finally reached the water line.

Before Virag turned to enter his own boat along with his henchmen, he knelt down next to the sco-lo-ti one last time. His dagger flashed, ending a father's pain.

***

Virag cautiously made his way to his boat, finding his footing easier this time. He slipped into the boat and curled up, listening to wind and rain between Spako's snores. The slaver contemplated his new alliance, and the Snake's strange hatred of the Scythian girl.

She seeks control of the food for power. I seek power to control the food. She's always been an ambitious girl.

Tomorrow he would get out of this boat and walk the deck. Much needed to be done.

30. The Second Council of Boats

The Lo refer to those times aboard the arun-ki as "when sea and sky became one."

Some days wind and waves assaulted the arun-ki, and the rain pelted the canopy like a cloud of stinging hornets. In those times, the Crane and Minnow became one and fought the sea together. During the Days of Waves, the Lo were strong.

Other times the sea rested flat and lifeless under a heavy blanket of rain. During the Days of Rain, the Crane and Minnow bickered and were weak.

The Uros hoped for Days of Rain, but Atamoda prayed for Days of Waves.

The Chronicle of Fu Xi

***

The rain pounded so hard against the canopy, Atamoda thought it would crush it flat. The deck lay still enough she might have thought her feet rested on solid ground. The brazier burned too hot, and the air felt thick and fetid. She almost hoped for a storm to stir the suffocating air.

Crowded on the Köy-lo-hely, they watched intently as the Uros and his council discussed the future. Ba-lok and Kus-ge knelt on the right side of the Spine, their clan behind them. Xva and the Crane sat opposite. All faced inward, toward the brazier and the staff resting in its hole. Atamoda knelt to Aizarg's immediate right, next to Levidi, the Staff Bearer. This had become the order, the new way of things. Across from them, Okta sat with Ezra and Ghalen, with Sana kneeling in the shadows behind them. Atamoda sensed danger hidden deep in this arrangement, and in the hearts of those gathered around the brazier.

Her husband and his staff lorded over all. Elevated upon a low stool fashioned from driftwood and cloaked in fox furs, Aizarg's shoulders looked too large, too a'gan.

Aizarg rose and addressed the council. "Let us begin this Council of Boats with thanks to the Nameless God for delivering us from the flood."

"Are we truly delivered, Uros?" Kus-ge asked with sharp tongue and innocent eyes.

"We live, and carry hope in our hearts. That is enough. There is much to be done before we see the sun again. The sea comes first, so let us now hear from the Master of Boats."

Aizarg resumed his place upon the stool. Okta entered the council center and dropped a section of badly stained rope onto the deck.

"Rope, we've plenty. Canopy..." Okta waved over his head. "The arun-ki is covered from end to end. The sea anchor holds, and we reinforce the storm wall whenever we can. The water isn't as choked with driftwood and logs as it was only a day or two ago, but the flood has provided almost all we need to reinforce the arun-ki."

"Almost?" Aizarg asked.

"We've worked miracles in seven days, Uros. No doubt of that. We've found plenty of reed and pine floating in the sea, but what we can't do is boil pitch. Your clans boil pitch in the shore camps, mine in a giant bronze pan constructed in the center of our Köy-lo-hely. These tiny braziers won't work, not even close."

Levidi frowned. "Our boats are already pitched, as are our rafts."

"Pitched, but damaged. We've made repairs, but none of it is sealed. Chunks of unprotected wood and reed now lay bare to this filthy water."

He picked up the rope and held it high over his head with both hands. Okta turned to the crowd. "This is the line from the old sea anchor." With a quick snap, Okta yanked it in two.

A gasp went up.

Okta shook both ends. "This is pitched Minnow rope, fresh and strong when we put it in the water three weeks ago."

"The sea reeks like swamp water, and every fisherman knows swamp water rots unpitched hulls. *This* water rots everything, pitch or no pitch."

"How long?" Aizarg said.

"The outer boats, the ones along the storm wall, will waterlog first. Those are heavily patched or rebuilt from crushed hulls. As for the family boats along the rim," he paused as if calculating something in his mind, "I give them two weeks before they won't support weight. Those families will have to shift to the inner rafts."

"The inner rafts weren't as heavily damaged," Ghalen added.

Okta shook his head. "No, they weren't. The wedding barges are as stout as I've ever seen. They'll float almost forever. The other rafts are in various stages of seaworthiness."

Okta paused and rubbed his beard. He knelt down and tapped the thickly corded ropes banding the deck logs together. "These are the weak points. We'll have to keep a close eye on our ropes. They'll break before the logs sink. All our new rope isn't pitched, so whatever we use to mend will break in a week or two."

"So we inspect," Ba-lok shrugged. "We inspect and replace every day until we make landfall."

Okta shook his head slowly.

"It's not that easy," Okta said. "When the great wave struck, when the storms were their worst, our boats were strong. While we've reinforced the arun-ki in periods of relative calm, our underbelly is weak. One good wave and rafts could disintegrate without warning.

"It's the water, Uros!" Okta threw his hands up. "And all the while this infernal rain isn't helping. We're rotting from the top and the bottom!"

Atamoda thought about how she'd noticed their skins and flaxen weaves starting to rot under the unrelenting moisture. Even with the canopy, the water penetrated everything. Her thoughts drifted again to their food supply. Atamoda sensed a rot beginning to settle in their hearts, too.

"What do you propose?" Aizarg asked.

"As Ba-lok said, inspect, every day. And not just the decks, we need to dive under and look at the bottoms. From the rib gaps, we can dive under and inspect the inner vessels, while inspecting the outer vessels from the rim.

"The seas and rain seem to be their lightest at dawn, so, with your permission Uros, I'll organize inspection parties each morning once we have sufficient light."

Aizarg nodded. "Thank you, Master of Boats. Do what you must. Ba-lok, you will assist him in this.

"The arun-ki must have a sound foundation if we are to weather the storms to come. This is not only a foundation of wood and reed, of rope and sail. We must also attend to the needs of the flesh, and these questions are not so easily resolved.

"Most of us are Minnow or Crane, but all of us are Lo. As Lo we are unified. Ba-lok is my second; should I fall, he will take my place. Levidi is my Staff Bearer, chosen by the Nameless God to wield the symbol of His promise. Among us sits the brother of Ma-sok, sco-lo-ti of the Turtle. Ghalen, rise and come forward."

Ghalen stood, and entered the circle.

He's changed so much, like the rest of the men who ventured on the quest. The playful twinkle in his eye vanished with the sun, replaced with hard-edge seriousness. Ghalen became their lion, their warrior, leading the daily fight for survival. The Uros had come to count on Ghalen to carry out his edicts, including the unpopular policy of confiscating all the food and storing it on the Supply Barge.

"In times before, a man's catch was his, to share or not to share," Ghalen began. "No one, not even the sco-lo-ti, could take what a man caught or hunted. Now, the world is different. At the Uros' command, I collected all the food shortly after the great wave." Ghalen gestured to Atamoda and Kus-ge. "Our patesi-le inspected and rewrapped all the food and stored it aboard the Supply Barge. Thanks to their efforts, we salvaged more food than I expected, but it is still woefully inadequate."

Ghalen paused, crossed his arms, and continued. "I know your bellies ache, but we must cut the rations by a third."

A collective groan went up.

Sahti went pale and bowed her head. Xva put his arm around his wife.

Ghalen continued undeterred. "We must stretch our meager resources until we make landfall or until the fish return. When the seas allow, Ba-lok and Xva will lead men throwing nets along the rim. But I suspect, wherever they may have gone, the fish will not return until the debris and silt settle out." Ghalen nodded to Atamoda.

She rose and addressed the council. "Except for the children and Sahti, we will no longer issue a morning ration. Our expecting mother and the children will receive half a hand in the morning and at sunset. Women and elders will receive half a hand at sunset; men, one and a half."

"What of the a'gan?" Ba-lok said. "They are worse than children, totally worthless."

"Sana will receive a woman's portion. Virag and his giant will receive an elder's portion," Atamoda said.

"Ezra will receive a man's portion," Okta interjected, arms crossed and eyeing the crowd as if daring anyone to challenge him.

Dissatisfied murmurs floated about the barge as she sat down.

Ghalen continued. "Someone will be on the Supply Barge at all times to guard the food."

Aizarg stood again and motioned for Ghalen to resume his place. "The fish will return. The Nameless God did not bring us this far to abandon us to starvation. Until the seas yield their bounty again, Ghalen speaks for me in all matters regarding our common stores."

A shadow passed over Aizarg's face. "Until that time, we will be hungry. Be warned, if anyone is caught stealing food, or hording...that person will be exiled."

Atamoda's heart caught in her throat.

Why does he say this? To exile one here, afloat in the Black Sea carries a sentence of death. To sentence one to death, even for murder, was forbidden.

Levidi leaned in, "Uros, what you say..."

"I know what I say. To steal from one is to steal from us all, as it is to horde."

The Lo sat in silence, the Uros's words falling heavier than the rain. Atamoda knew each searched their soul. She expected Ba-lok to protest, but he only stared at the deck.

"The Uros is most wise," Kus-ge purred and bowed her head.

The Lo dispersed to their respective sides of the Spine, talking quietly of the council events. Atamoda held Aizarg's arm. "We must speak."

31. Flutterings

"How can a leader listen to the hearts of his people if he is deaf to his own?" – Conversations with the Uros

The Chronicle of Fu Xi

***

"Why?" Atamoda shouted above the roar.

"If we cannot control our food, we cannot survive."
Aizarg gripped his staff as if the wind would steal it away.

A fresh storm rolled in from the north, and with it a
spectacular lightning display raged overhead. They leaned
into the wind, enduring the pelting rain aboard the bow raft.
She insisted they talk here, the only place in the arun-ki they
could speak privately.

Why did he bring his staff here?

"You pronounce a punishment before a crime has been
committed, and now you have no room for discretion."

"There must be deterrents."

"There must be compassion."

"Unless the fish return, we will soon run out of food. We live on the edge. One slip and we will not make it. You must trust me in these matters."

"Then trust enough to consult me!" Atamoda raised her voice, pointing toward the Minnow side of the Spine. "You consult with Ba-lok, but you have no time for me?

"I cannot always consult with you on everything. I'm trying to keep this arun-ki together!"

"I am trying to keep *our people* together," she held her fist tightly clenched next to her chest. "And they are starting to tear themselves apart. Hunger may kill us, but distrust and fear will destroy us as surely as the strongest storm." She slid closer to him and grasped his hand, careful to avoid the heat radiating from the staff. It felt like a third person, an interloper driving a wedge between them.

"Our people have never known famine. I must rule with absolute authority. Not only should my edicts be respected..." She saw doubt swimming behind Aizarg's eyes with each lightning flash. "...they should be feared."

She pulled away.

"Your edicts? Or your god's edicts?"

She regretted the words the second they flew from her mouth. Aizarg's head bowed, as if she'd placed another weight on his shoulders. Atamoda tried to keep the tenuous bridge between them open.

"The Nameless God doesn't speak to my heart, though I wish he would. You still speak to my heart. I beg you, please talk to me. Let me carry some of your burden. Don't shut me out.

"You no longer come to our bed. I miss you, and so do the children. The Nameless God spared us, yet you make no time for us. Levidi spends more time with the orphans than you make for Kol-ok and Ba-tor.

"You stare at the staff from nightfall till dawn. I am thankful to the Nameless God, but there are other voices, *loving voices.*"

Aizarg leaned the staff against the pylon, reached out and took her hand. "The people are hungry. Fear begins to crawl along the decks like a water demon. Frightened people do things in the dark of night they would not do in the light. My rule must be firm."

"Didn't the Nameless God also promise the light will one day return?"

"He did."

"Then rule firmly, but with *hope*." Atamoda drew him close. "Save some hope for yourself." At the edge of storm, sea and darkness, they sank to the deck in a lovers' embrace.

***

Alaya had grown so used to E'laa and Toma, she couldn't imagine life without them. Their little eyes heavy, she tucked the two Minnow orphans under the blanket.

"I don't want to go to sleep," Toma rubbed his eyes and yawned.

"Levidi is going to teach you a game tomorrow," she whispered, "But only if you go to sleep."

"What kind of game?" the boy asked.

"Levidi and Ghalen made a swing rope on the Supply Barge. Levidi swears it will swing all the way to the Köy-lo-hely, but told me he needs a brave boy to test it first."

Toma's eyes grew wide, and he tried to sit up. "I will test it! Please, let me try it."

Alaya smiled. "I will tell him, but only if you go to sleep."

Toma snuggled next to his twin sister, whose eyes were already shut. Alaya placed another blanket over the raven haired children and turned to join Levidi in the adjacent boat.

"Alaya," E'laa timidly called after her.

Alaya turned to see deep brown eyes, loving and full of trepidation, peeking out from below the hem. "Will you lie down with me?"

Without a word, she curled up next to the child and placed her arms over the twins, drawing them to her bosom.

"Don't leave us," E'laa whispered.

"I won't," she said and prayed to the Nameless God the words would be truth.

Alaya listened to the rain and let the rocking deck sink into her bones. The children occasionally stirred at the nearby claps of thunder, but soon their small chests rose and fell in rhythm with the sea.

E'laa and Toma's parents were snatched under by the demons while the twins looked on. Since then, they lived with the other orphans on the center rafts, taken care of by both Crane and Minnow women. Alaya felt herself drawn to them more than the other children. She developed a bond with them, to the point they began to eat and sleep with her and Levidi. Levidi welcomed the twins, treating them as his own children and giving them part of his own rations.

Atamoda promised her she would talk to the Uros about adopting the children. Alaya sensed hope fluttering in the darkness like a tiny moth, so fragile even a breath of joy upon its delicate wings may crush it. It gave her spirit enough light to find a song in the storm. She ran her fingers through E'laa's long, midnight hair and began to hum.

***

They reclined in each other's arms beneath the leading edge canopy, snuggling under a blanket Atamoda borrowed from a nearby Minnow family. Atamoda watched the lightning snake across the sky.

"You spend a great deal of time with the Scythian girl," Aizarg said, the afterglow of their lovemaking loosening his tongue.

"I like her."

"That's natural, she saved our son."

"I'm teaching her our ways. She's already making rope and weaving. Alaya says Sana is good with the children, but..."

"But what?"

"Sana has secrets." Atamoda rubbed the inside of her thigh. "She carries four daggers tucked in a band around her thigh, hidden under her loincloth."

"It is the Scythian way."

"I know, but it makes me uneasy."

"Should I be concerned?"

"No, but I'm not sure I fully trust her yet."

Aizarg paused for a moment. "Did she tell you anything about her past, about her parents?"

"She won't open up, other than telling me about her brothers and sisters."

"What does your heart tell you, patesi-le?"

"My heart says we should bring her into the Crane."

"Setenay wished for her to be in the Turtle Clan."

"She didn't know Ghalen would *be* the Turtle Clan." She sat up on her knees and giggled. "By the Goddess, Aizarg, they hate each other!"

Aizarg laughed, perhaps the first time she'd heard him laugh since he returned from the Valley of Beasts. "I know I shouldn't think it's funny, but it is."

"A few nights ago he told her to 'make herself useful' and cook his ration. She gave his ration to the children!"

"Ghalen didn't tell me about this," Aizarg smirked.

"He made Levidi promise not to talk about it."

"A promise never stopped Levidi from gossiping about anything. What did Ghalen do?"

"He tossed her into the lagoon. Alaya had to fish her out."

Atamoda paused for a moment. "While we're talking about this, the others should be placed, too. Ezra is easy, he is practically already Carp."

Aizarg nodded. "He has formed quite a bond with Okta."

"And then there are the orphans. They've mourned enough. Now they need homes. I believe the time for an adoption ceremony has come."

"Agreed. We will discuss it further with the inner council."

"Alaya and Levidi are particularly fond of the Minnow twins."

"They've wanted children from some time," Aizarg nodded. "You'll have to discuss it with Kus-ge."

Atamoda sank back down into his arms. "She raised no objections when Alaya took the twins from the Supply Barge; neither did anyone else in the Minnow."

"Hmm," Aizarg grunted.

Atamoda took a deep breath. "And then there is Virag..."

"Ba-lok has already approached me regarding the two a'gan. Virag and his henchman will be placed with the Minnow."

Atamoda's blood suddenly coursed hot. "No."

"Ba-lok thought it best we keep a closer eye on them, and I agreed. As much as I despise Virag, they cannot remain isolated downstream. Virag and his giant must be brought into the fold. He is willing to bring them into the Minnow."

She stood and paced back and forth beyond the canopy, arms wrapped tightly around her shoulders as the rain found her once again. "Kus-ge rules the Minnow. Kus-ge rules Ba-lok." She turned and faced Aizarg. "Virag slinks on the opposite side of the Spine, no longer content to hide in his boat. Whispers fester there. If Ba-lok wants the a'gan closer, it is only because Kus-ge wills it."

Aizarg stroked his beard. "She is a difficult woman; he is a difficult man. But he is my Second, and she is his patesi-le. They are part of our chain, as is Virag."

"Aizarg, the Spine has become a wall between the clans. Ill will spreads through the Minnow against us, against you. There are too many whispers floating among Ba-lok's people."

"I've heard no whispers. The journey is hard, the people are hungry. Nerves are frayed."

"It's more than that. We need to consider new ways..." Atamoda closed her eyes, searching for the right words. She couldn't, so she said what stirred in her heart. "Abolish the clans. Make us one."

By the way he frowned, she knew the idea didn't settle well with him.

"Integrate the clans, mix our peoples. That is the only way to build trust."

"There are few foundations left to us, and you ask me to rip them from beneath our feet?"

"Isn't that what you did with your decree? If you give Balok's council such weight, what of mine?"

Aizarg stood, donned his clothing, and picked up the staff. Atamoda followed, trying to keep touching him.

"If a wound turns the flesh sour, beyond the reach of root or tonic, would you not severe the limb to save the body? Rot has settled in on the Minnow side. It will spread if you don't act."

He turned and her hand slipped away. A cold gust embraced her, and she felt the wall between them reassert itself.

"I will consider what you've said." If her plea met fertile soil or bounced off her husband's heart, she did not know.

"I have much to attend to before I can sleep." He peered over her shoulder into the darkness. "The storm is closer." Aizarg turned to go.

"Your god does not speak to me," Atamoda called desperately after him. "How does he speak to you?"

Aizarg stopped, but did not turn around. Atamoda feared she may have crossed a forbidden threshold, a wall the strange god erected between her and her husband.

"He consumes me."

"I am afraid, not only for our people...but for you...*for us.*"

Aizarg stepped out from beneath the canopy, joining her in the rain. He tilted her head up and kissed her, rainwater pouring into her mouth. In the lightning she saw him smile.

"The inner council still has business, but I will come to bed tonight."

He turned to go, but then hesitated and looked back at her. "Do not be afraid, my love."

Atamoda watched her husband vanish among his people, huddled under the canopies. "I am afraid, but I will serve. I will wait. I will trust."

She turned away from the arun-ki to face the wind and endless darkness. The rain washed away her tears as she remembered that night, an eternity ago, when Setenay sent her to fetch Aizarg's boar spear. The same loneliness and isolation from that night filled her spirit now.

She gazed up at the spider web of silent lightning bolts crisscrossing the sky high above. "God of the Narim, is there room in his heart for both of us?"

She leaned against the storm wall, but then pulled away, repulsed by the slimy fungus coating the stacked timber. Atamoda frowned and wiped her hands off on her tunic.

She followed her husband into the canopy's shelter and the warmth of the arun-ki. Unnoticed behind her, just inside the storm wall, the farthest forward binding rope on the bow raft snapped.

***

Alaya slid under the tarp into the boat next to Levidi, careful not to lift the blanket too much and wake her husband. She snuggled deep into the hull beside him, drawing warmth from his smooth skin.

She listened to Levidi's breathing, her eyes unable to shut. *The rain is louder now.*

"You're thinking about something." Levidi broke the silence. "I can always tell when you're thinking."

"I thought you were asleep."

"Your singing was too beautiful. I haven't heard you sing since the day we left for the quest. What made you find your voice?"

She didn't answer, content to listen to Levidi's heartbeat mixing with the distant thunder.

"Did they go to sleep alright?"

"E'laa is still afraid to be alone. She'll probably wake up screaming again."

"I'll get up with her tonight."

Alaya smiled in the darkness and caressed his chest. They tried to bring the children in the boat with them the first night, but E'laa would not come near the raft's edge. When she woke up screaming, one of them would stay with her until she fell asleep again. Sana, who also slept on the raft, offered to comfort E'laa, but Alaya did not yet fully trust the Scythian girl.

They will be my children, therefore they will be my responsibility.

Toma, however, mourned differently from his sister. He acted out, fought with the other children, and occasionally bit. As if knowing the child needed a strong hand, Levidi spent a great deal of time with him when not attending to his duties as Staff Bearer. Those duties usually meant simply sitting at the Uros's side.

She traced her finger lightly over her belly, letting her mind drift with the waves. "What does it feel like when you hold the staff...when the Nameless God makes His presence known?

Levidi took a deep breath and placed his arms under his head. She sensed him staring straight up at the canopy only inches above their head.

"Whole."

She frowned and lifted her head. "And you don't feel *whole* with me?"

"Not like that...different." Levidi's voice wandered, as if he began to drift away. "Like a promise has been fulfilled. As if I've come to a place of safety, and all my burdens have been taken from me. When Aizarg places the staff in my hands, I am not afraid. I want to feel that way every moment for the rest of my life, come what may."

He sighed. "But the longer I am away from the staff, I feel the cold creep back into my mind, into my soul."

"What is the staff?"

"I can't put it in words," he whispered.

"Try," Alaya said, tracing her belly again.

"An answer to prayer I have yet to utter, a promise to a question I don't know to ask, let alone *how* to ask. It is..." She heard the frustration in his voice. He brought his hand up, as if trying to grasp an idea fluttering around his head.

"Hope?"

"Yes!" Levidi clenched his fist closed, his tone satisfied. "That is it, *hope*."

"I watched Atamoda cut another notch in the mast today," he said. "The mast gives me hope, too. Every scar in the wood is another day we're alive. She'll be cutting another notch in only a few hours, so we should get some sleep."

Levidi kissed her, then closed his eyes and soon filled the boat with light snores.

Alaya listened to the rain, unable to sleep. She didn't need to count the notches on the Supply Barge's mast to know how long they'd been at sea. Her body told exactly how much time had passed.

She caressed her belly, excited and terrified by the occasional flutters deep inside her abdomen.

"I'm hungry, Levidi," she whispered, but he didn't hear her.

From outside the boat, she heard E'laa's long, mournful wail. Careful not to wake Levidi, she slid out of the boat and lay down next to the child she needed to call 'daughter'.

***

Atamoda watched Aizarg once again, unseen in the shadows of the Supply Barge. Her bed remained empty as Aizarg resumed his place on the Köy-lo-hely.

Did I ever truly reach him?

He stared hard at the staff, as if it would bend and break, or buckle under the weight of a thousand questions, a thousand prayers, swimming through his mind. She wished the mysterious red orb would crack open and spill its secrets and tell him what to do.

She sighed. *It would probably tell him to go to sleep.*

She needed sleep, too, and started to turn away when she caught a glimpse of a man, spear in hand, approaching Aizarg from the far end of the Köy-lo-hely.

"Father?" the man asked.

Surprised, she looked back at the bed roll to see Bat-or sleeping alone.

What is Kol-ok doing?

Aizarg motioned his oldest son to come forward.

"Father, can you help me make a better spear." Kol-ok held out the spear; really nothing more than a crooked stick sharpened on one end. A few weeks ago, it looked too big for him. Now it looked too small. "There is plenty of good driftwood, and we have sharp flint."

Aizarg took the spear, turning it over in his hands. Atamoda looked on, fingernails finding her teeth.

"Yes, you need a new spear. This is a child's toy, only good for spearing frogs."

Aizarg handed Kol-ok back the spear. "But I cannot yet help you make a new one."

Kol-ok nodded, trying to hide his disappointment. But anger swept over Atamoda unchecked.

Now he is pushing Kol-ok away, too.

She began to step through the rain curtain between the Supply Barge and the Köy-lo-hely when Aizarg stood.

"A man needs a proper boat before he can wield a spear. Come, I think there are still enough good reeds on the Supply Barge to craft a boat."

Leaving the staff behind, Aizarg led a gleeful Kol-ok through the rain curtain, winking playfully as he passed by Atamoda.

"We'll start small, a craft suitable for a man and his nets. Never start with rope and reed, but with the wood for the center line which will anchor both. We must also find a piece of wood suitable for the mast and mast block."

Throughout the night and into the morning two Lo men built a fishing boat. They talked and laughed, oblivious to the rain and thunder.

Nearby, Atamoda slept, content in a dreamless sleep.

32. Wisdom's Scent

Life settled into a comfortable routine. I spent the days riding horses with Sunnah or sparring with the Olmec war masters in the gymnasium. When the sun dipped into the haze rising off the quarry, I usually found myself wandering toward the Library.

Quexil eventually abandoned his protests and stayed out of my way. The kitchen slaves grew accustomed to me and no longer gawked as I plied the palaces deep recesses toward the Gray Tower.

Perhaps it is the Library that I will associate most with Poseidon's Empire. The Library held a special magic, one previously incomprehensible. Now I understand how frustrated the Ice Men must have felt when trying to speak. I have been a deaf mute for thousands of years, and thought myself wise. What a fool I am!

In the short time we had together Amiran seemed almost frantic, trying to transfer as much of his civilization's collective knowledge to me as he could. I was barely able to decipher the art of writing, so the nights usually started with him reading from a single scroll. Sometimes, we leapt from subject to subject. Other times, we dove deeply into one that struck my fancy. As the evenings progressed, scrolls piled up around us, as did my questions.

For centuries, I taught men how to measure the dimensions of a hut. The Scholars created mathematics, and measured the dimensions of the world. Where I showed a village how to plant wild grain along stream banks, the Scholars bred new plants, resistant to locust and drought, to feed an empire. Amiran flooded my mind with science, engineering, medicine, alchemy, and a thousand other concepts and ideas.

One morning before dawn's light, I pushed away a scroll on metallurgy the way an engorged man pushes away a half-eaten meal. "Scholar, I am simply overwhelmed. What else is there left to learn? What have you not shown me?"

"The best! This Library is but a seed, cast far from the mother tree in hopes of finding root. This is merely the pitiful collections of two expedition Scholars, the essentials painstakingly shipped to a backwater colony. I've only shown you the sciences."

He scurried up a ladder to the highest shelves near the dome and returned with a velvet bag, richly adorned in golden braid and tassels.

"You've not seen our art, heard most of our music, nor have you read our poetry."

"Poetry?"

He opened the bag and withdrew a thick scroll bound with a golden cord. He unrolled it to arm's length, his eyes drinking in the tightly packed symbols as if he'd just opened a treasure vault.

"Poetry transcends song or saga. Through poetry, our souls rise above the lowly dust from which we were formed."

He lovingly laid the scroll on the table. "This poem is called 'The Song of Atlas'."

"I thought the Song of Atlas was your language."

"They are one and the same. This is the first scroll ever written by the hand of man, commissioned by Poseidon at the dawn of time to commemorate Atlas's birth. Over the centuries it evolved into so much more. It tells our story, our dreams and our nightmares.

"To be even considered to become a Scholar, a child must memorize and recall each of the ten scrolls, verbatim and with exact inflection, before attaining the age of sixteen."

"That is a daunting feat, even for a god!" I gasped. "You did this?" He nodded. "At eleven."

"How many opportunities did you have to pass this test?"

He frowned. "A candidate is only afforded one chance. Fail and he spends the rest of his days as a common slave. Pass and the universe is spread before him like a banquet."

"How many of these works were penned by the Eleven Princes?" I asked.

"The sciences and arts are below them, they consider it no different than toiling in the fields. The Princes pen their deeds in blood, not ink."

Throughout the remainder of that night Amiran recited selections from the Song of Atlas. I pictured him as a young boy, far away in that glorious city, nervously facing a panel of wizened scholars. This man must be exceptional among the exceptional.

Gentle reader, know this: everything I have previously said regarding the language of Atlas I fully recant. Through poetry, this wonderful dance of words, their tongue became as beautiful as any to grace my ears.

Surrounded by scrolls and Amiran's poetry, I smoked, sipped tea, and glimpsed a future without the gods.

***

The next evening the air hung heavy with the promise of rain. Warm firelight flickering through the open library door greeted me. Freshly brewed tea and tobacco smoke blended with parchment's musty odor to create an aroma I will fondly and forever call 'Wisdom's Scent'.

Amiran seemed distracted and somber. He fretted about the coming rain as he closed the dome's doors using a series of pulleys, gears and chains. That evening we also had company.

Two children, clad only in pure white linen loin cloths, joined us. Both possessed olive skin, flowing black locks, and soulful brown eyes framed by lush lashes. At first, I thought they were twin boys, but soon detected the faintest hint of breasts on one.

I assumed they were kitchen slaves, as they served us platters of fruits, cheeses and bread. But when Amiran doted on them, calling the boy Ercole and the girl Elda, it became apparent he held considerable affection for them, which they returned.

Bent over a dark stained table, chin resting on my fist, I ate and enjoyed a pipe, while Amiran instructed Ercole regarding a scroll's contents. He set Elda about cleaning the library.

Would they have shared some trace of Amiran's black skin, I would have entertained that they could be his children. He caught my eye and laughed in that deep, rich way of his.

"No, my lord, they are not my children, though I would be proud to call them son and daughter. Elda and Ercole are Prince Leviathan's personal slaves. I am their tutor."

My heart skipped a beat, remembering that night in the throne room and knowing what some of the more vile kings in Cin did with children.

As if sensing my concern, Amiran waved his hand and shook his head. "They are under his protection and will one day serve as craftsmen of sorts. Their small hands are ideally suited for delicate work. Extraordinary work."

I looked about at the many intricate devices scattered about the library and could understand the need for small, steady fingers. That's when I noticed several large objects resting on the library's long center table, each concealed under white linen sheets.

Amiran sat beside me and, with a small dagger, cut a piece of bread, dipped it in the oil, and popped it in his mouth. He slid a single sheet of parchment in front of me, displaying the same world map I saw in the foyer. Donning his spectacles, he used the dagger as a pointer and drew my attention to the coastal area along a continent.

"Ercole and Elda hail from the southern coast of Ereb, a land of emerald waters and white cliffs called Attica."

"They are fortunate to have a teacher such as you," I said.

"Perhaps," he grimaced.

"Are you well?"

"I am." He looked up at the dome and pointed to the scaffolding beside the dome's sealed door. There sat a brass tube resting on a tripod. "I intended to show you something tonight, but the coming storm had other plans."

"What was it you wanted to show me?"

"Truth." He put his glasses away. "And now that time is past, perhaps never to come again. Other truths await you, God of Names."

"You act as if a terrible burden weighs upon you."

"We all have our burdens. You have yours," he pointed to the children. "And they have theirs."

"*Will they be Scholars?*"

He snorted a laugh. "*The Eleventh Prince places no value in the Academy or Scholars. However, Ercole might one day wear the white toga, but not Elda. Only men who take a vow of celibacy may study the Song of Atlas.*"

"*You take such a vow willingly?*"

"*It's a small price for enlightenment. Celibacy refines the intellect, forcing the Scholar to channel sexual drives to other pursuits. It's an easy choice: privilege granted as reward for natural talent; or a life of poverty and servitude, never reaching one's true potential.*" He raised a finger to emphasize his next point. "*And Poseidon decrees death by crucifixion for any Scholar sharing the pleasures of a woman or a man.*"

"*A god's passion is no less diluted than a mortal's,*" I scoffed. "*I do not know how one can so easily dismiss the body's needs.*"

Amiran laughed. "*We do not dismiss it easily, trust me. We are encouraged to adopt other diversions.*" He tapped the fold in his toga where he stored his pipe.

"*If Elda is not to be a Scholar, why are you tutoring her?*"

His laughter died. "*Her value to Leviathan is singular.*" He took a deep breath as if collecting his thoughts, or perhaps preparing to plunge headlong into an unpleasant task. The air seemed suddenly charged, as if I stood on a precipice of a great, yet unseen truth.

"*I have listened to your tales of Cin, of your mother the sacred Goddess Nuwa, and of your quests. You have been mankind's teacher for countless ages, Lord Fu Xi. What I am about to reveal, I do so humbly. I know my place, and harbor no illusions that I am anything more than a speck of dust compared to your glory, or the glory of any immortal. But I beg you indulge me. Allow me to be your teacher, if for only the remainder of this night. Open your mind, and ignore your heart when it begs you to stop listening.*"

With a dull echo, distant thunder penetrated the bronze dome.

I'd grown accustomed, numb perhaps, to the ongoing revelations this land had offered. I craved them, eagerly seeking doors to all worlds Amiran opened to me. Yet, now I feared what he might say.

"*I have been your student since the moment we met, friend.*"

Once again he brought forth his spectacles, breathed on and polished the lenses with his toga's hem before inspecting them in the candle light.

"You wear the Red Sword Leviathan gave you around your waist tonight," Amiran remarked.

I shrugged, thinking it an odd observation. "The sword feels natural. What is your point?"

"My point is that before dawn that sword will taste blood. Perhaps even mine. I will not ask you to spare my life. I only ask for your promise to listen to what I am about to divulge before fury overtakes you."

The children ceased their cleaning and looked on with trepidation. "Are you mocking me?"

He put away his spectacles and considered me, a hard edge in his voice. "Who do you serve?"

"I serve the Goddess Nuwa."

"And Lord Leviathan, whom does he serve?"

"The God Poseidon."

"By the way your heart spills forth the words, you believe them truth. Let me tell you another truth. Leviathan has kept many secrets from you. He wishes to join your quest for dragons. Did you ask him why?"

"To honor me."

"What do you make of the dragons painted in the rotunda?"

"Glorious. Dragons are sacred. They adorn my mother's temple as well."

"Thirty years ago, Prince Gadeirus led an expedition to the frozen waste in far northern Ereb, where the Icelands bear down on the Dark Continent. There, he slew the last dragon seen by man or god."

I could not mask my horror. "The Sons of Poseidon hunt the sacred beasts?"

"Oh, yes! For both sport and orichalcum. Only fire-bile can transform iron into the Blood Metal, the lord of all other metals, even steel. Orichalcum is the most precious substance in the world." He pointed to the sword hanging by my side. "A thousand years ago King Atlas himself slew the bull dragon whose firebile forged your Red Sword.

"The Empire likely played no small role in the demise of the dragons, perhaps even in your lands."

I tapped the map stiffly. *"Cin is far from the lands of Poseidon. I don't see how this is possible."*

"A doe dragon must travel for hundreds, even thousands of miles to find a mate. Once a bull stakes his territory, there he remains until death or vanquished by another bull. Does are far easier to find and slay than bulls, and countless numbers fell to the Princes over the centuries. I suspect bull dragons in your land could not find mates and died off centuries ago."

Amiran's words were like heavy stones.

"Elda, come here."

The child put down a broom and approached.

"Give me your hand."

She obeyed, and Amiran held up her fingers.

"Only a child's fingers are small enough to fit between a dragon's neck cartilage and remove the delicate firebile bladders. Even in the largest bull, a man's or woman's fingers may not fit. The duct running from the gland sac to the throat is small and must be pinched off, sealed before the bile sac can be removed. Do you know what happens when fire bile makes contact with air?"

I nodded, remembering the terrifying heat from my few close calls with the beasts. I could not hide my disgust. *"Dragons are sacred, orichalcum be damned."*

Amiran's demeanor settled into an unfamiliar somberness. He motioned for her and Ercole to leave. The door shut with a hollow thud.

"Judge if you must, but the lamp of mankind's knowledge is lit with dragon's blood. Without firebile, the Eleven Princes would not have lifted men from savagery."

"Slaying dragons is savagery."

"One small bile sac is worth more than the colony of Wu. The entire ceiling of The Temple of Poseidon is gilded in orichalcum, harvested from thousands of dragons. Before Poseidon established his kingdom, beasts filled the skies. The god's lust for orichalcum drove the search for dragons, which led to the building of mighty fleets and the Great Age of Exploration."

He picked up the map and dagger and walked to the wall. I slumped in my chair, the horror of Amiran's tale stirring up Mother's stories of how dragons of old saved Creation. Memories from antiquity flooded my mind's eye, of watching majestic beasts dance between mountain peaks and skim across glacial lakes, listening to bulls' roars echoing for miles, and of doe's gossamer wings twinkling high in the sunset like rainbow stars.

"Every new land where the Eleven Princes made landfall in their quest for orichalcum, they encountered barbaric men, only brute animals. Poseidon, in memory of his mortal wife Cleito, swore to bring mankind enlightenment. And thus the Imperial Academy was born, to collect the world's knowledge and gather it in the shadow of Poseidon's Temple." Amiran shrugged, the sadness in his voice turning aside my anger. "Or at least that's how it began."

He idly toyed with a contraption, an odd piece of art, fashioned from several small wooden balls of various sizes and colors, all supported on metal arms extending from a large, yellow central ball.

He lightly slapped the balls, one at a time, sending them rotating around the central sphere. "The centuries drifted by, and the Empire grew powerful. Dragons became rare, forcing the princes to abandon their quest for orichalcum and seek other treasures to occupy their lusts."

Amiran stopped the third ball and, with a quick jab with the dagger, pinned the map to the blue orb. He closed his eyes, as if far away.

"For vanity, the Sun strikes down the lowly dust, lest it conspire with the wind to hide His glory."

He turned to me.

"What the Eleven Princes once did to the race of dragons, they now do to the race of men…and you are helping them."

The Chronicle of Fu Xi

33. Judgment

"A great chieftain is quick to the cut. The wind will carry away his mistakes, leaving only the memory of victories. His grandsons will grow tall and strong. A weak chieftain hesitates and knows only anguish. Remorse is his progeny, misery his funeral song." – Scythian Proverb

The Chronicle of Fu Xi

***

A man in name only...a hungry boy, that's all he truly is.

Aizarg swallowed his bile, knowing the sobbing youth kneeling before him faced a man's judgment.

"Who accuses this man?" Aizarg looked across the faces of those he thought he knew. Skin drawn tight, bellies beginning to cave in, they reminded him of a pack of wild animals.

They look like a'gan.

It wasn't long after Aizarg heard shouting from the Minnow side of the Spine that he had found Ghalen and Ba-lok standing over the frail looking Minnow boy they called Alad. A man for only one summer, his father being long dead, the demons took his fiancé, and a giant wave took his mother. A reclusive and quiet young man, Alad seemed an outsider even among his own.

Kol-ok and Alad had become friends, however.

Face downcast, rubbing one arm uncomfortably as if she couldn't warm herself, Doinna's accusation sounded more like a confession. "Alad sat next to me around the brazier after evening rations. He stole my portion while I looked away to feed sticks to the brazier. When I looked back he hurried to his boat, and my rations had vanished. It could have only been him."

"You lie!" he screamed. Ba-lok shoved him back to the deck.

"Alad?" Aizarg asked.

"I swear by the Nameless God, I did not steal! I thought about warming my portion, but was too famished. I ate it quickly and retreated to my boat to sleep." Tears streamed down Alad's face. "Doinna, why are you lying? I've done nothing."

Kus-ge turned to Ro-xandra. "Search his boat."

"Go with her," Aizarg commanded Ghalen.

As Ghalen went to investigate Alad's boat, Atamoda came running from the other side of the arun-ki, Sana and Alaya following close behind. "We heard shouts."

Aizarg pointed down to Alad. "He's accused of stealing food."

Atamoda grew pale. "What are you going to do about it?"

"Find the truth."

Ghalen and Ro-xandra returned only a few moments later. Ghalen held out his arms, burgeoning with wads of leaf-wrapped fish.

A stone settled in Aizarg chest. The moment he feared, but hoped would never pass, had finally arrived.

"Ba-lok, he is one of yours. What do you recommend?"

Aizarg wanted Ba-lok to say something, anything that would allow him to spare Alad's life. But the sco-lo-ti's unsure expression gave Aizarg no hope.

Kus-ge touched her husband's arm. "The food belongs to all the clans. Perhaps it's best to let the Uros decide."

"Yes," Ba-lok nodded quickly, obviously relieved. "The food concerns all clans. I defer judgment to the Uros."

A shadow emerged from behind the mob. "Did not the Uros decree any caught stealing or hording faced exile?"

"Be quiet, a'gan!" Kus-ge hissed at Virag. "You have no say here."

"Contrary, patesi-le, I do have a say. My belly growls as loudly as any. Alad stole from me as much as he stole from you. The Uros was clear. We all heard him. Exile should be his fate."

"No, Aizarg!" Atamoda beseeched. "Don't do this. Confine him to his boat. Cut his rations to the bare minimum. Do anything, *anything*, but do not do this. Have we not endured enough pain?"

"Father," Kol-ok stepped forward. "Alad is my friend. I believe him. Is there another way?"

Arms outstretched, Virag pleaded to the crowd, as if advocating the most reasonable course of action. "Did Alad not know the decree? Is his belly any more important than the orphans? Because that is what he did, he stole from orphans." Virag raised an eyebrow toward the heap of fish in Ghalen's arms. "And it appears he's been stealing for quite some time."

Tears rained down Alad's face, mucus running from his nose, as the man-child search Aizarg's eyes for any sign of mercy.

Aizarg knelt down. "Why did you steal?"

"I didn't! Please believe me, Uros. I don't know how that food got there. You must believe me."

Aizarg turned to Ghalen, Okta and Levidi, who stood behind him. "What do you counsel?"

"We're all hungry. If we let one steal, what will stop others?" Okta whispered.

"I have men guarding the food day and night, but Alad was one of them." Ghalen said. "He must have taken the fish during one of his shifts. I should have been less trusting. I am partially to blame for placing you in this situation. I am sorry, Uros."

Aizarg shook his head. "Alad's choices are his own."

"I support you regardless of your decision." Levidi put his arm on Aizarg's shoulder. "But the fish will return. We should remember that."

The eyes of the Lo nation fell upon him, their weight every bit as heavy as the power in the staff.

Aizarg realized he'd left the rod on the Köy-lo-hely. He flexed his right hand, craving the staff's weight.

If I delay, the decision will only become more difficult.

Alad stole the food, of that Aizarg had no doubt. The people wanted a decision, a quick resolution. If he delayed there would be grumbling, and judging by the rage on their faces, perhaps even violence.

"I will return this to the Supply Barge," Ghalen said turning away.

"Stop." Aizarg took three fish cakes from Ghalen. "After you return them, ready the most seaworthy boat you can find."

Alad released a mournful wail and pressed his head to the deck.

Atamoda slid between him and Aizarg, as if shielding the boy. "Reconsider! This is irreversible. There is no exile to a marsh teeming with life, a meal as simple as an upturned root, or a fate as a Scythian slave." She pointed to the Deluge beyond the canopies. "This is death."

"There is no other way." Aizarg summoned all his strength under her withering gaze.

"There is always another way." Atamoda sank to the deck and cradled the boy's head in her lap. Alaya and Su-gar joined her, but Alad drifted beyond consolation. Wrapping his arms around her waist, he sobbed into her lap.

"The mighty Uros lets the sea do his dirty work." Atamoda glared up at him. "You might as well take a knife and slice his throat now."

Never before had Atamoda looked upon him with scorn. A great weight settled on his chest, a dreadful pressure squeezing his heart.

"The Uros has spoken." With an impassive expression, Kus-ge turned away. Without a word, Ba-lok and the rest of the Minnow filtered away, abandoning one of their own to his doom.

Virag grinned and bowed before melting into the shadows.

Aizarg knew he'd made a mistake, one from which he could not escape.

And neither could Alad.

Someone brushed against him. He looked down to see Sana staring up at him, steel in her eyes. She whispered forcefully where only he could hear. "If you love your people, show no remorse!"

The Scythian girl vanished through the rain curtain.

***

Ba-lok pushed Alad's boat away into the rain with only three fish cakes, a canopy, and a small bailing pot. By Aizarg's decree, they denied Alad a paddle or a sea anchor, anything which could provide him steerage to return to the arun-ki.

Kol-ok held his mother, who would not look at Aizarg. Silent tears streamed down Atamoda's face as the boat slipped away into the downpour.

Alad's screams floated across a flat sea for two days, penetrating the rain and settling across the arun-ki like a vengeful spirit. At first, he begged for mercy, calling upon the Uros to take him back. As the first night fell, his pleas turned to curses against the Uros, Doinna and the Lo, each accusation a dagger.

Crying unceasingly, Atamoda never left the Supply Barge, trying to shut out Alad's voice. Furious at Aizarg, she could not eat. Occasionally, Su-gar or Alaya kept her company, but little conversation ensued. Even Bat-or spent most of his time with Sana.

Throughout the second day Alad's voice faded, perhaps to the south, perhaps the west, Atamoda could not be sure. In the end, Alad only repeated his mother's name over and over.

A prayer, a hope, a delusion...Atamoda did not know.

A powerful storm rolled down from the north, finally summoning the Uros from the Köy-lo-hely. The men fought wind and sea throughout the night and well into the morning. By dawn, the tempest had washed away three stormwall boats and two Minnow boats, though no one perished.

While others settled to sleep, hungry and exhausted from the night's battle, Atamoda knelt on the downstream edge, straining to hear Alad's cries. But the storm had washed the Minnow boy away.

To her left, a boat slipped away into the rain. She couldn't see the fisherman clearly, but knew by the way he paddled, it could only be Aizarg.

Sana joined her and put her feet in the water, softly splashing with her heels. They both sat in silence until Atamoda finally spoke.

"You think we're weak, don't you?"

"I am not Lo. My ways are different."

"Your people embrace death. You are hard."

"My people did what was necessary to survive. You have been kind to me, Atamoda. I will not speak ill of you or your people."

"Then why are you here?"

"Because he cannot be here." She pointed to Aizarg's ghostly figure in the distance, throwing and retrieving his net.

"I see." Anger flashed in Atamoda's heart at the haughty girl who assumed she could council a mother and wife.

"You are angry at me."

"I am not."

"You are also a bad liar." Sana grinned in a knowing way, with eyes far older than her young, strong body deserved. "All of you Lo are bad liars..." her grin suddenly vanished. "...almost all of you."

Sana pointed to Atamoda's necklace. "What is that?"

"It is called a li-ge." Atamoda lifted it from her chest.

"May I touch it?"

Atamoda hesitated for a moment, wondering why the a'gan wanted it. Then she lifted it over her head and placed it in Sana's palm.

The Scythian lightly traced the stone where the white and black symbols intertwined into one complete circle. "'There is peace when the souls of man and woman flow together like water.'"

The Scythian's knowledge of the Lo proverb surprised her.

Sana held the amulet tenderly, almost lovingly, before giving it back to Atamoda.

"I did not mean too insult you by interloping in your affairs," Sana said. "I am your captive and have never known a man's love."

"You're not our captive, I've told..." Atamoda interrupted.

Sana held up her finger. "I *am* a captive, but I have come to call you friend. I have come to love Ba-tor like a brother and will lay down my life to protect him. This is why I tell you these things.

"I am the daughter of Sawseruquo. A mightier war chieftain has never lived, nor a wiser one. A Scythian war council is a gathering of wolves, men who kill as easily as others breathe. To lead such men, my father had to be a wolf among wolves." She leaned closer to Atamoda. "My father killed hundreds, perhaps thousands of men. Many skulls rattled against his saddle. But he killed not for conquest, or gold, or pleasure, though many of my people did just that.

"My father killed to protect what he loved, his family and his tribe. The Uros killed to protect what he loves. He is a great man.

"He killed to protect you. He killed to protect Ba-tor, Kol-ok and everyone aboard the arun-ki.

"Great men only truly fall when abandoned by those they love."

Atamoda's knees suddenly ached, arms heavy with the memory of her battle against the demons. The screams rose in her mind, fresh and terrifying, as did the terrible decisions she made during those dark days.

"I've hurt him," she whispered.

"My father once told me that demons cannot rend what forgiveness has fortified."

Atamoda couldn't reconcile such a hope-filled message with a people as bloodthirsty as the Scythians.

"A Scythian war chief said that?"

"My grandmother did. Her wisdom was cherished among my tribe."

Atamoda reached out and took her hand. "I would have liked to have met your grandmother."

Sana smiled and stood to go, but looked back at Atamoda.

"Kus-ge..."

"What of her?"

"She walks like a Scythian."

***

From a patched boat, he tossed the net into a sterile sea. Skin numb and clammy under the rain's torment, Aizarg

327

needed to throw the net. With every breeze, Aizarg imagined he heard Alad still crying in the distance.

Levidi tried vainly to discourage him from taking a boat alone, asking what they would do if something befell their Uros.

He'd sent enough men out looking for fish, he told Levidi. Now came his turn.

Obeying his own edict, Aizarg remained within a spear throw of the arun-ki. The braziers flickered brightly through the sheets of rain. The arun-ki seemed to sit lower in the water than he remembered. The raft and boat deck lines seemed closer to the flat surface.

He heaved the net, watching the stones spin outward into a nearly flat circle. Aizarg kept the tag line just slack enough not to interfere with the spinning net.

Down the net sank until the line pulled tight.

Twenty feet and no bottom.

He wondered if it even had a bottom.

The rain continued its unending dance on the water. Many of his people hated the Days of Rain, because the unending roar on the flat water grated on their nerves, stoking tempers.

Hand over hand, he retrieved the empty net, dangled it over the side and gave it a little shake to clear any snags.

Sana's words still haunted him. Those were the first words she'd spoken to him since they reunited with the clans. He knew she'd been spending a great deal of time with Atamoda, but her uninvited counsel surprised him.

Setenay's voice. He'd yet to tell anyone of Sana's relationship to the Isp.

Atamoda still didn't know. Aizarg wasn't sure if he should tell her.

Once again, the stone went spinning. Once again, the net emerged empty.

Sarah's voice.

The Mourning ceremony did nothing to salve the wound in his heart. Aizarg didn't talk about the girl who would have been Atamoda's daughter, and she didn't ask. Aizarg wanted to talk about her, tell her about the girl who should not be forgotten. The proper time, the right moment, never materialized.

Pull.

His thoughts drifted to Ba-lok and Kus-ge. He knew plots festered with those two. To what purpose he didn't know, but suspected Kus-ge wanted control of the food.

And then there remained the question of Virag.

Why did I spare him?

Aizarg asked himself that question every day since finding the slaver.

Throw.

Aizarg wondered if mercy had a place in this new world.

Pull.

The stone sank and the line pulled tight, the empty net collapsing somewhere below the boat. Aizarg didn't pull it in this time. He stared at the raindrops dancing off the water, the memory of Atamoda's scorn cutting new gashes in his spirit.

She hadn't spoken to him since Alad's banishment, sleeping on Levidi's raft.

He saw more than scorn in her eyes.

Disgust.

A gust of rain shook him from the trance. Aizarg looked up to realize he'd drifted a considerable distance from the arun-ki. The downpour slackened to a drizzle, and the rain curtains parted. For a moment Aizarg had an uninterrupted view of the entire expanse, horizon to horizon. He slowly turned about, searching the horizon for any sight of land.

The arun-ki appeared as a piece of flotsam adrift on an eternity of water. The view overpowered him, much like the great wave had, though now he didn't have the power of the Nameless God to save him.

Shaking, Aizarg slowly sank to the bottom of the boat, which had begun to fill with rainwater. Head in trembling hands, he began to sob.

"God of the Narim, take this burden from me. I am only a man. I cannot do this, not without her! Take everything, but don't take her."

To the south, a peel of thunder answered his prayer. The rain intensified and cloaked the arun-ki from his sight.

***

Sana departed and Atamoda returned her attention to Aizarg's boat.

He had drifted considerably farther in the time she'd looked away. Her stomach twinged as she made her way to the arun-ki's southeastern corner where she could better see his boat.

Thunder rumbled to the north, the light shower transformed into a blinding downpour and Aizarg vanished.

***

Aizarg sat in the boat, now filling with rainwater like a tub. He knew if he tried to paddle blindly, he could end up farther from the arun-ki. The same current that carried the arun-ki also carried him. Aizarg picked up the small clay pot floating at the bottom of the boat and began to bail. As fog formed from the downpour, it enveloped him like a white, featureless wall.

The rain slowed to a light mist, and the fog pressed in.

Aizarg ceased bailing and looked about, his breath floating away in heavy puffs.

Somewhere in the mist he heard a loud *huff*, like a sudden deep exhale.

I am not alone.

"Okta?" Aizarg thought for a moment and called out again in both hope and fear. "Alad?"

A strong musky, animal smell assaulted him. At first he couldn't place it, but, as with many odors, it instantly transported him to another place and time. He remembered

330

being a young man, crouching in the reeds, watching unseen as a Scythian raider wandered the edge of the marsh seeking easy prey.

A horse!

A billowing image transformed against the foggy curtain. The shape slowly gelled into the gray silhouette of a man on horseback.

How can this be?

"Who are you? What do you want?" Aizarg shouted.

Where the figure's eyes should have been, two blue lights blazed into existence. Aizarg covered his eyes, the terror of the ice fog rekindled anew.

He found the courage to look up. The shadow rider had vanished, the air once again clean and as sterile as the sea.

The fog parted, revealing the arun-ki floating only a few yards away.

***

Atamoda watched as Aizarg tied his boat alongside Okta's raft.

She snared him in a tight embrace. "You vanished in the rain! I thought I'd lost you. I'm sorry. Please forgive me."

He ran his hands through her hair and considered her as if seeing Atamoda for the first time. "Forgive you for what?"

"For not supporting you. You are not alone, husband." She wrapped her arms around his neck and buried her head into his chest.

Aizarg lifted her chin and kissed her.

He held her hands, rubbing them, gazing down at his feet.

"Wife, I want to talk about something. Something we haven't discussed."

"Anything." She searched her husband's eyes, thankful for this second chance the Nameless God had given her.

"Sarah..."

34. The Traitor's Arms

"Leviathan treated me like a brother. You bring me here, seduce me with scrolls and exotic herbs in hopes I will betray him. I should strike you down!"

I wanted to strike him down, to forget all Amiran said and never hear him speak ill of Leviathan again.

Amiran stepped toward me and crossed his arms, just as he had defied Quexil. "You are starting to sound like him. Does the delightful venom of this place infect your heart so completely?

"I listened to how you speak of Cin and your beloved Nushen. I took a chance you spoke truthfully, that you were different than the Sons of Poseidon. I am a servant to the truth. If my words offend you, great god, then I was wrong, and my life is of no further consequence."

He paced around the long table, caressing the linen covered objects.

"Most of the clever contraptions you've seen thus far, like my spectacles, are toys Scholars fashion in our spare time; amusements and diversions. Let me show you the true fruits of our labors, why Leviathan and his brothers suffer our existence."

One by one, he yanked away the linens.

I didn't understand the objects' workings, but their jagged forms betrayed malicious intent.

"These are models of actual war machines. They inflict death on a grand scale." He pointed to one with a long lever attached to a four wheeled wagon. "This is called a "catapult". It can hurl a five hundred pound stone over three hundred yards with uncanny accuracy. In the siege of Combrogi, I saw one blast through a five foot thick wall, allowing the Olmecs to swarm into the Erubian city and slay all within. Prince Gadeirus wasn't too merciful following that battle; the enemy defied him too well." His eyes narrowed on me. "We only took a few slaves, the rest he permitted the Olmecs to eat."

I didn't want to hear anymore. But Amiran kept talking, his words burrowing into my soul, leaving me nowhere to hide, no refuge from the truth.

"We rarely employ catapults, they are only required against the most sophisticated of foes, like Attica. Leviathan insisted I oversee the construction of only one for the Cin expedition."

Thunder shook the Gray Tower as he pointed to a long, log-like contraption suspended from chains inside a cage on wheels. "Based on what you've freely told Leviathan, I think battering rams will be sufficient against Cin's bronze swords and primitive stockades."

Even now, I find it difficult to speak of how I felt that night. Coldness settled into my belly as I contemplated the depths of my blindness. Perhaps I felt more confusion than anger. Amiran left me with a stark choice: believe him or Leviathan.

"Go to the harbor if you don't believe me. See for yourself the ten thousand Olmec warriors bivouacked along the shore. Better yet, inspect the quarry and glimpse what awaits your people."

He touched another device, which looked like a shield on wheels with dozens of arrow protruding from it. "You will find forty of these down there, waiting to be loaded. This is a new weapon, never before employed in any previous campaign. It simultaneously hurls thirty spears over one hundred yards, propelled by tension stored in knotted ropes. Quexil wants to test it on captives, but Leviathan is saving it to use against your villages."

I'd laid Cin wide open to a monster.

Finally, he came to a model of a ship with enormous masts and a hull like a pregnant belly.

"This ship is called a "carrack", specifically designed for transporting heavy cargo during long ocean voyages. Thirty of these ships rest in the harbor, laden with supplies for a prolonged military campaign. Once they disgorge the necessities of war upon your shores, they will transport booty, including slaves, to the Kingdom. One such ship can haul over three hundred slaves in the most miserable conditions imaginable, Lord Fu Xi."

"He is my brother!" I shouted.

"He isn't your brother!" Amiran slammed his fist against the table. The model fell over and shattered.

Never had a mortal raised their voice to me.

"Leviathan wants to corrupt you, to numb your senses like the bitter weed. He needs to convince you to stand aside while his legions rape your homeland. He wants to use you and Cin's pillaged wealth against his half-brothers, and seize the throne from Atlas."

I drew the sword from its scabbard and held it in my hands. "He gave me the Red Sword."

"Leviathan both loves and hates you. In you, he sees what he should have been, how far he and the Eleven Princes have fallen. In you, he sees his sister, the Gray Eyed Queen." He pointed to the blade.

"That was his sister's sword, as is the armor. We call them The Traitor's Arms. If and when the time comes, in his mind it will make it easier for him to kill you."

I sank into the chair. "Why are you telling me this?"

"Because once I serve my purpose, Leviathan will kill me, and upon his return, destroy the Imperial Academy.

"Do you know who I am, Lord Fu Xi?"

"You are Expedition Scholar."

"I am Amiran, Master of the College of Metallurgy, Grand Scholar of the Imperial Academy." He pulled up his toga sleeve displaying his trident brand. "But what I really am is a slave. The Academy no longer serves truth, but instead builds engines of war to enslave our own race. Where once Scholar's served enlightenment, we now fashion machines to break, burn, and slash. Scholars do not wear the slave collar, we forge them.

"And that is what Leviathan is doing now; crushing a revolt in Wu's north and capturing more slaves to serve as pack animals for the continental invasion."

"I will see the harbor for myself." I turned to go, fury against Amiran rising. "If what you say is true, I will confront Leviathan when he returns."

"You are our last hope, God of Names," he called after me. "Only you can stand against them. Gods were created to serve mankind, not rule them. What now transpires is perversion. If Leviathan succeeds, mankind will fall into eternal darkness."

I fled the Library as Amiran's voice pursued me down shadowed halls. "Can you hear the quarry, Lord Fu Xi? CAN YOU HEAR THEIR CHAINS?"

The Chronicle of Fu Xi

35. The Uros Has Spoken

"Forging the chain that would become a new tribe depended on changing one heart at a time. It began with tough choices, hard truths, and soft words." – Conversations with the Uros.

The Chronicle of Fu Xi

***

Aizarg pointed to the Supply Raft. "Thirty-three gouges upon the mast, thirty-three days since the mighty wave swept us away, and the power of the Nameless God spared us."

As if answering for a crime, Virag and Spako stood in the center of the Köy-lo-hely under the stares of the Lo nation.

"I've called us together to address the whispers floating across the decks." Aizarg let his words sink into the two main clans on either side of the Spine. "Some of you question my decisions not only to bring a'gan among us, but to allocate them rations.

"For weeks they've been exiled downstream, isolated. 'We cannot have a'gan among us', you've whispered around the braziers. 'We cannot give our precious food to strangers', you've mumbled in the ration line. Your Uros has heard you...and you are correct. From this day forth, there will be no more a'gan among us."

The crowd looked at one another.

Aizarg nodded at Ba-lok. "The Sco-lo-ti of the Minnow will speak."

Ba-lok glanced uncertainly at Kus-ge, who gave him a nod and a nudge. He stood and cleared his throat.

"I, Ba-lok, Sco-lo-ti of the Minnow, accept Virag and Spako into my clan."

Virag bowed low before the Uros. "My thanks, Uros, and thanks to Ba-lok, my new sco-lo-ti. And my thanks ahead of time to the Master of Boats, who I'm sure, will assist in moving my boat closer to my new clan."

Laughter rippled throughout the crowd as Okta scowled. Virag unceremoniously turned and shoved Spako toward the Minnow side of the Spine. The assembled clans chattered excitedly as Virag and Spako settled in among the Minnow.

"Stop!" Aizarg commanded. "Virag will go to the Minnow, but Spako will join the Crane."

Virag approached the Uros, hands out in supplication. "He needs me, Uros. He is but a fool, despite his size and gruesome visage. Without me, he is lost."

"As long as he keeps his feet on the rafts and out of the water, he will be difficult to lose.

"Xva!"

Xva rose. "As surrogate sco-lo-ti, I accept Spako into the Crane."

Atamoda looked on as Kus-ge and Virag exchanged quick glances. She wondered what the slaver and patesi-le of the Minnow could possibly be conspiring about.

Atamoda looked back at her husband, wondering why he decided to split Virag and his henchmen up at the last minute. She saw the wisdom of such a move, but did he see something deeper, something she did not?

Eyes darting nervously, Spako remained in the center of the Köy-lo-hely, uncertain what to do now that his master had been taken from him. Atamoda didn't know why, but a pang of pity struck her for the Sammujad warrior.

"Spako, the Crane Clan is your family now."

Spako looked at his hands, wringing them incessantly. "Spako have family?

Su-gar emerged from the crowd. All eyes followed her as she stepped forward and took the giant's hand.

"We are family now," she said.

Atamoda saw an instant change. Spako's gaze never left Su-gar. His breathing slowed, his shoulder's relaxed, as he stepped over the Spine and followed Su-gar onto the Crane side of the Köy-lo-hely.

Amazing.

And then it dawned on Atamoda; the thick, frizzy beard, the meaty lips, the deep brow.

He reminds me of Ood-i.

She wondered if Su-gar even recognized Spako's resemblance to her dead father.

Aizarg pointed to the Master of Boats. "Okta...your turn."

The Master of Boats entered the Köy-lo-hely. "Ezra, get out here!" he bellowed.

Beaming, Ezra took his place alongside Okta.

"I, Sco-lo-ti of the Carp, bring Ezra into my clan." A cheer went up. Aizarg held up his hand to quiet them.

Okta continued, "Ezra not only enters my clan, I take him as my adopted son."

A hush fell over the Lo.

"Should my other sons...should they," Okta hesitated, voice trembling. "My wife would..." Unable to finish, the sco-lo-ti held trembling fingers tightly against clenched eyes, fighting for control.

Ezra placed a hand on his new father's shoulder.

In Okta's spirit, the ashes finally fell.

Atamoda, too, began to cry. "Out of darkness, mercy."

"Out of darkness, mercy," the assembly repeated.

Ghalen came forward and embraced his friend, followed by Levidi and Aizarg. Soon, both clans surrounded Okta, sharing his joy and his grief.

***

The Lo resumed their places on either side of the Spine, Okta and Ezra among them. As the hum of conversation died down, Atamoda looked to the Crane's surrogate sco-lo-ti, whose turn in the ceremony had arrived. Xva nodded, ready to fulfill his role.

Atamoda turned to Aizarg, who had returned to his stool. He stared at the staff, as if in a trance.

"Aizarg," she said. "Xva is ready."

He didn't answer.

"Aizarg?" she repeated.

He finally dragged his gaze off the staff and onto her.

"Xva is ready," she said.

"For what?" he asked, looking as if he didn't know where he was.

"Sana...it's time for the Crane to accept Sana. Are you well?"

"Hmmm. Sana." He rubbed his beard and considered Xva. "Sit, my friend."

Unsure, Xva sat back down next to Sahti.

"Aizarg, what are you doing?"

"Things have changed. Ba-lok, rise."

Ba-lok stood, frowning and looking about. "Yes, my Uros."

"Sana, come forward," the Uros commanded.

Excited whispers danced through the crowd as the Scythian girl timidly emerged from behind Ghalen and stepped into the center.

"Sana, Setenay placed you with Ghalen until other arrangements could be made. I do not want any to walk away from this council without a clan they can call their own. We

339

were going to place you with the Crane, but I have decided your needs, and the needs of the Lo nation, will be better served among the Minnow Clan."

"Aizarg!" Atamoda leaned forward.

Aizarg held her gaze. "The Uros has spoken," he said resolutely.

The thought of the Scythian girl in Kus-ge's clutches, helpless to her abuses, frightened Atamoda.

Impassive, Aizarg returned his attention to the council.

"Ba-lok, does the Minnow Clan accept this a'gan as one of their own?"

Ba-lok looked down at Kus-ge. Kus-ge raised an eyebrow and pursed her lips, before nodding once.

Sana looked to Atamoda with pleading eyes, trying not to look frightened as others decided her fate.

Poor child, I cannot help you.

"Sana, you are now of the Minnow Clan. Go sit among your people."

Except for the rain, the stunned Lo sat in complete silence as Sana took her place.

Atamoda caught Kus-ge staring at her, smiling. She fought her anger and sense of betrayal, wanting to get Aizarg alone to demand answers. Only her sense of duty, as strong and true as the Spine itself, kept her from fleeing the Köy-lo-hely.

"Atamoda, let us begin the adoptions," Aizarg said.

"As you wish, *Uros*." She could not look at him.

Atamoda entered the circle. "Let the orphans come forward."

Eleven children, boys and girls from three to ten, meekly stepped from the both sides of the crowd, faces downcast with the terrible burdens thrust upon souls too tender to support them. The two little Minnow children, E'laa and Toma, held hands.

"Gather around me," she beckoned them. "Minnow and Crane, our children." Atamoda held her arms out over the children, presenting them to the Lo nation. "We must find new parents, loving and nurturing hearths so that we may honor their mothers and fathers who have gone before."

One by one, couples came forward to claim the children. Some were childless, while others suffered the raw wounds of their own children lost to the sea. With each, guilt and relief stabbed both sides of Atamoda's heart as she thought of her own family. Husbands and wives led the children back into the crowd until only the twins remained.

Alaya stepped forward, tearfully looking over to her husband. Levidi gazed upon his wife with tenderness and a hint of a nod.

"Levidi and I accept E'laa and Toma."

Atamoda ushered the two children into Alaya's arms, who knelt and embraced them. Levidi left his place next to the Uros and joined Alaya.

Atamoda knew these moments of joy where also moments of healing. Making such moments were the burden of the patesi-le.

"Are not these Minnow children?" Kus-ge's voice rose above the rain.

A knot formed in Atamoda's stomach. Slowly, she looked up and matched Kus-ge's stare. "These children are Lo. What are you implying?"

"I imply nothing, other than these two belong with their clan."

"Alaya and Levidi claimed these children and will be good parents. They've cared for them all these weeks. If someone from Minnow desired that role, they should have said so."

Kus-ge stood with a relaxed expression narrowed on Atamoda.

"I'm sure the Staff Bearer and his woman would be good parents, but they are Crane. These children are Minnow."

Atamoda looked to Ba-lok, who tugged on Kus-ge's hem like a little boy, obviously uncomfortable with the confrontation and trying to get her attention. She swatted him away, eyes never leaving Atamoda.

"They are Lo. We are Lo. No one among the Minnow claimed these two. The children will go with Alaya and Levidi," Atamoda straightened and crossed her arms.

"I claim them," Kus-ge said.

Ba-lok bolted up and grabbed her arm. "Kus-ge!"

Kus-ge shrugged him off. "The disposition of children is the realm of the patesi-li, isn't it *my sco-lo-ti?*" Her voice dripped with contempt.

Ba-lok sat back down again, leaving Kus-ge in full command.

"The children are mine by right."

"No, they are not." Atamoda looked at Alaya. "The Isp has spoken."

"Isp? So you are the Isp?" Kus-ge's eyes suddenly gleamed, as if she'd been expecting this moment. Her boldness, her eagerness, took Atamoda aback.

"Of course I am the Isp," Atamoda shot back. "I am the oldest and most experienced patesi-li. That is the way of our people."

"Setenay was the Isp. Is your name Setenay?"

"Setenay is dead."

"Yes, and you are patesi-le of the Crane, wife of the Uros and the One Who Chose. The Isp cannot be the wife of the Uros, nor the One Who Chose. I am patesi-le of the Minnow, successor to Setenay. If there is an Isp, it is I."

Atamoda felt like a fish, the hook firmly set in its mouth. She'd never considered anything, but that she would fulfill her mentor's role. Obviously, Kus-ge had her sights set on taking Atamoda's place beside the Uros for some time.

Atamoda did what any fish would do; she committed her will to fight regardless of the odds

"I am Isp. The children stay with Alaya."

Kus-ge turned to the Minnow and held her arms wide. "Do I ask for anything not in accordance with our ways? Was not Setenay one of us? Are not E'laa and Toma *our* children?"

"Minnow with Minnow!" Ro-xandra shouted from the crowd, quickly joined by others.

"Kus-ge is rightfully the Isp!" bellowed another Minnow woman.

Alaya began to cry. "I've cared for them since the rains came. I love them. If they are your children, why did you not claim them?"

"Atamoda has cared for us all!" Su-gar stood and shook her fist at the line of Minnow.

Kus-ge spun around to face Su-gar. "I cared for our people, too. Did I not bring the Minnow in search of the other clans? We found the Crane, not the other way around. It was my magic that saved us from the demons."

"Lie!" Su-gar shouted. "You collapsed and Atamoda fought on alone."

Both clans were on their feet, shouting at one another across the Spine with only the brazier and the staff separating them. Kus-ge turned away from the Crane, shouting at her own people, stirring them with both her words and gestures. Now the numerical superiority of the Minnow became painfully apparent to Atamoda.

It also soon became apparent the shouting match primarily involved the clan women. Atamoda looked on dumbfounded as the men on both sides did nothing. Ba-lok sat at Kus-ge's feet, as if studying the grains in the logs. Okta and Ghalen seemed as if they would bolt into the center at any second to reassert order, but kept their tongues in deference to Aizarg. The Uros merely sat on his stool, leaning forward with his chin resting on his fist. Occasionally, he glanced back and forth at both sides, as if studying the situation.

Behind the line of Minnow, slouching in the shadows, she caught the glint in Virag's eye. The slaver grinned as if taking great pleasure in the confrontation.

Only when the two clans' women began to step forward did the Uros rise and lift his staff from its hole. The clans fell silent, ebbing away from him. His presence filled the gap between the clans, white hair reflecting the firelight.

"Setenay's wisdom is still with us. She foresaw what was to come. She knew the Narim held the key to our salvation. Where our gods fell silent, she heard the call of the Nameless One. She saved our people, and her council is still present even now, in our hearts. I will listen to her voice, will you?"

Aizarg strolled around the inside of the circle, casually examining the staff and occasionally directing his attention to those in the crowd. He stopped and let the full weight of his gaze rest upon the people.

"Will you honor Setenay's will?" he asked.

A few people murmured, "Yes."

"Atamoda, Patesi-le of the Crane, will you honor Setenay's will?"

Heart still stinging, Atamoda didn't know where Aizarg intended to carry this, but she only had one reply to give. "Yes."

"Kus-ge, Patesi-le of the Minnow, will you honor Setenay's will?"

"Of course," she huffed.

"Sco-lo-ti and men of the Lo, will you honor Setenay's will?" he asked, staring straight at Ba-lok.

Ba-lok looked up, joining the men. "Yes."

Aizarg stepped across and knelt directly in front of Ghalen. Atamoda could not fathom what thoughts were running though her husband's mind, but something else unexpected loomed over the Lo.

"Ghalen, will you honor Setenay's will and the will of your Uros?"

Ghalen looked about uncertainly, but nodded. "Of course I will."

Aizarg clasped his shoulder and smiled before returning to the center of the circle.

"On our journey to Hur-po, Setenay spoke to me of many things, knowledge reserved for the patesi-li. She told me of seeds planted long ago, though I didn't know why she shared these mysteries...until this moment."

Aizarg resumed his place on the stool, but kept the staff.

"Kus-ge is correct regarding the children. The Minnow have first claim to their own. The twins will now become the children of Ba-lok and Kus-ge. The Uros has spoken."

Without hesitation, Kus-ge snatched the children from Alaya and then handed them off to Ro-xandra before resuming her place next to Ba-lok. Alaya released a long moan and fled the Köy-lo-hely.

Levidi's shoulders sagged as his gaze lingered on his retreating wife.

Aizarg turned to Levidi. "I am sorry, my friend. Go to Alaya and comfort her."

Levidi slipped into the shadows.

Atamoda's anger and sense of betrayal turned to fury as she watched Levidi and Alaya depart.

"A Uros needs an Isp," Aizarg continued. "Kus-ge is correct in this matter. Atamoda, my eternal love, you will advise me as wife, but you cannot advise me as Isp."

Atamoda sank back to the deck. She felt as if the wave loomed over her once again, about to crush her world. Except she feared there would be no reprieve. She looked up to see Kus-ge leering at her.

Why has she chosen to be my enemy? I've done nothing to her.

With a haughty smirk, Kus-ge stood. "I am ready to serve, my Uros."

"Sit," Aizarg said coldly. The confidence washed away from Kus-ge's face as she sat back down

"One among us holds a secret. She must come out of the shadows and stand among us." Aizarg lowered his staff until it pointed into the center of the circle. "Sana, come forward once again."

Excited whispers danced through the crowd as the Scythian girl stepped from behind the line of Minnow, the naked fear on her face.

"Aizarg?" Atamoda whispered.

Aizarg ignored her, eyes locked on Sana.

Atamoda considered the Scythian, trying to discern Aizarg's intentions. The girl tried to be brave under the eyes of the Lo nation. Several times her arms came up, to hug her own shoulders, but dropped. Finally, she set her trembling jaw high and clenched her fists.

"What does the Uros of the Lo wish of me?" Sana asked.

"Sana, are you the daughter of Sawseruquo, granddaughter of King Sosa, great lords of Scythia?"

She rubbed her arm, and frowned. "I am."

"Who is your grandmother?"

Sana's frown evaporated, replaced with dawning understanding. "Please, no..."

"Speak your grandmother's name!" Aizarg commanded.

Sana closed her eyes and took a deep breath, "Setenay."

The crowd erupted in gasps.

"No!" Kus-ge leapt to her feet. "You cannot do this, she is a'gan. She is an outsider."

Numb, Atamoda looked on, her mind reeling with the implications of Sana's statement.

"By my decree, she is now Lo," Aizarg shot back. "Not only is she Lo, she is by blood Minnow and a descendent of the Isp. And she will be *my* Isp."

Atamoda put her hand over her mouth, not knowing whether to laugh or gasp with the rest of the crowd.

"She is not a patesi-le, therefore she cannot be Isp!" Kus-ge crossed her arms, nose in the air.

"You're correct again, wise patesi-le," Aizarg said. "And all our sco-lo-ti are married, whether their wives are present or not." Aizarg nodded to Okta. "The bond of marriage is sacred, not even a Uros can sever it."

Aizarg tapped his cheek as his gaze fell upon Ghalen. "Stand, Ghalen, brother of Ma-sok."

Ghalen shook his head.

"Stand," Aizarg insisted.

Ghalen took his place next to Sana, both not looking at one another.

"Ghalen, I share your hope Ma-sok lives, along with your people, somewhere out there beyond the curtain of rain. Your Uros needs the sco-lo-ti of the Turtle now, not the promise of one later. While I cannot dissolve the bonds of marriage, I can dissolve the bonds of leadership. Therefore, let it be known, Ghalen is now Sco-lo-ti of the Turtle. Also let it be known, in seven days' time he will wed Sana, granddaughter of the great Setenay."

Ghalen flushed, teeth gritted.

"You said you would honor both Setenay's will and mine, Ghalen," Aizarg said.

"I did," Ghalen pleaded. "But..."

"I need you to do this, Ghalen," Aizarg repeated slowly, softly.

Atamoda saw the fight ebb from Ghalen's eyes at Aizarg's words. Ghalen closed his eyes and nodded. "I have pledged my spear. As you command, my Uros."

The new sco-lo-ti looked down at Sana, but she would not meet his eye. Atamoda saw sadness and resignation in Ghalen's eyes, and blind hatred in Sana's.

This will be interesting.

Aizarg turned his attention back to Atamoda.

"You planned this all along?" she asked.

"As the oldest patesi-le, you will train her."

"A man has no say in these affairs, even a Uros! They are the realm of the spirit, of women!" Kus-ge screamed.

Aizarg turned and slowly raised the staff until its crimson end pointed directly at Kus-ge's chest.

"I have trod the realm of flesh and spirit and have seen the will of the Nameless God. I have a say in *all* affairs."

Ba-lok snatched Kus-ge arm and pulled her down. "Shut up!"

"She is Minnow by blood. That is why I placed her with you, Ba-lok. As her cousin, you will stand instead of her father at the wedding. Her dowry will be one cake of dried fish."

36. The Fight

"The Uros looked to The Staff for answers, but the Nameless God didn't dwell there. He lived in the hearts of our people." – Sana, Isp of the Lo.

The Chronicle of Fu Xi

***

"It could be worse. She *is* beautiful."

"Levidi, I don't want to talk about it."

Ghalen leaned over the bow and pushed his weight against the adjacent boat. All morning Ghalen and Levidi inspected the vessels along the arun-ki's rim. Boat by boat, they neared the storm wall on the Minnow flank.

The young Minnow widow they called Fleyla and her toddler stood on the adjacent raft, awaiting Ghalen's verdict.

The boat rested low in the flat water. Ghalen lifted the tarp and peered in at its contents, but recoiled at the smell of rotting grass.

"How bad?" Levidi asked.

"As bad as I've smelled this morning."

Ghalen had noticed the faint rotting smell wafting more often across all quarters of the arun-ki as the hulls began to succumb to the Black Sea.

"I know it's starting to soak, but it still rides well," she huffed defensively. "We only use it to sleep."

"With that smell?" Ghalen considered the woman. "Where are your belongings?"

"With Kus-ge."

"It's waterlogged and rotting. You'll have to move to the rafts."

"Perhaps Ba-lok will say different."

"If you desire to sleep in a rotting log on the verge of sinking, then you are a fool. I say let fools find their own way, but The Master of Boats has commanded all waterlogged vessels be cut away." Ghalen tore off the canopy and tossed it at her feet. He pulled out a few meager blankets, and then froze.

Ghalen reached in and withdrew several bundles of leaf-wrapped fish. "Hording?"

"I am not hording! My boy is hungry. He cries at night, not only for his father, but for the fire burning in his stomach. What are we to do?" She defiantly held Ghalen's stare.

Ghalen sniffed the bundles and turned up his nose. "Dammit, woman! The fire in his belly is likely more than hunger. If you store fish in a wet, rotting boat, you'll end up with rancid food." He tossed the cakes into the water.

"That was mine! Ba-lok will hear of this."

"Fine, would you also like me to inform the Uros of your hording?"

Fleyla snatched the child by the arm and disappeared amongst the rafts.

"You're welcome," Levidi called after her.

Ghalen leaned over the boat and cut lose the mooring lines.

"This tub isn't even fit for the storm wall." He pushed down on the bow, and it quickly disappeared into the deep.

Ghalen settled into the back of their boat, thinking about Virag's boat, and how it looked too clean. He didn't like the way the slaver smiled at him as he inspected the hull.

The fox is hiding something, and I'll find out what it is.

Levidi paddled on, glancing back at the four empty boats strung behind them. "Seven boats sunk, four salvaged for the wall. Our little arun-ki grows smaller."

"If we don't get these hulls covered and on the wall, they'll sink, too." Ghalen raised his face to the rain, squinting against the fat raindrops. "How much rope do we have?"

"Twenty paces, enough to secure these boats, but not much more."

Ghalen looked out over the listless sea as it passively received the downpour. Several boats floated a stone's throw from the arun-ki, men casting and recasting nets in vain.

Beyond the fishermen, the mists retreated somewhat, affording Ghalen an unusually distant view where the clouds met the horizon. The surface didn't look right to Ghalen, but he didn't know why.

"The sea goes on forever. How small our little arun-ki is in comparison."

Another Day of Rains had settled in. The Days of Waves were getting fewer and fewer. They slowly made their way toward the bow rafts as the people watched them from beneath the canopies.

Levidi followed Ghalen's gaze over the water expanse. "Yes, the sea is big."

"It's as if the sea toys with us. It could swallow us at any time, yet here we are."

"I don't want to think about it, and you're trying to change the subject. So..." Levidi continued. "Are you going to refuse her hand?"

"I told you, I don't want to talk about it."

Ghalen would have preferred talk about the sea, hunger, or death instead of marrying the Scythian woman. He kept his gaze out to sea, where the rain melted into infinite gray.

If I struck out on my own, if I just kept paddling, could I find land...or perhaps fish?

Levidi angled the boat around the corner. "Atamoda likes her, and Alaya doesn't dislike her."

"Then Atamoda can marry her."

"That's funny," Levidi chuckled.

Ghalen shot him a foul look over his shoulder. "It wasn't supposed to be."

"She's good with the children. That's always a good sign in a fiancé."

"Shut-up."

"The fact that she is Setenay's granddaughter, doesn't that change anything?"

"You marry her, then."

Levidi stopped paddling. Ghalen turned to see him tapping his chin with his finger, as if considering the idea. "Once we make landfall, we'll have to get busy making babies."

Ghalen rolled his eyes. "You always think about sex."

Levidi laid the paddle across his lap and offered his hands palm up with an exasperated shrug. "What else is there to think about? Come on, Ghalen, it's not the end of the world..." He frowned. "That happened already.

"Anyway, Aizarg wouldn't have decreed the marriage if it weren't important."

Ghalen snapped around. "And that is why I obey! Isn't that good enough, or do I have to like it, too? If it keeps Balok and that witch of his in check, I am willing to marry the Scythian. But I don't have to like it. I *won't* like it. The Scythians killed Ood-i and Sarah. Did you also forget Sana tried to kill me, Levidi?"

Levidi shrugged and resumed paddling, dragging the oar and turning the boat hard to the left in front of the storm wall. "I've seen good relationships start off worse.

"Anyway, I heard Atamoda plans to marry you off to Doinna if you won't take Sana's hand."

Ghalen couldn't help but smile. "I see no reason for the patesi-le to threaten me."

Ghalen's smile died as the storm wall came into view.

"By the goddess!" Levidi exhaled. "We inspected this only a few days ago. How could this have degraded so quickly?"

Most of the barrier logs had sunk, their lashing either rotted off or pulled tightly underwater. Enormous ledges of fungus grew from the stacked timbers along the wall. The boats dipped to the waterline, some even partially submerged.

Ghalen leaned out and tugged some of the timber. The sticks collapsed with wet, sickening snaps. He pulled gently at the underlying boat, but the moldy reeds tore away as easily as warm bread.

"Ghalen," Levidi whispered. "Check the anchor rope."

Ghalen leaned even farther forward and tugged at the cable.

"It holds, but it's blackened. We'll need more rope and reeds to repair the damage."

A thought, sharp and cold, poked at Ghalen's mind. He turned his gaze back to the sea. Now he understood why the water disturbed him so.

"Levidi, look at the water. Do you see it?"

Levidi turned and scanned across the sea. "What? I see nothing."

"I see nothing, too. The flotsam is gone. The sea is clean."

Levidi's eyes grew wide in understanding. "No more wood, no more reeds...

"No more rope."

***

Canopies shook as if about to fly off and decks bucked wildly. She'd seen Okta crisscross the Supply Barge countless times tonight, fretting over ropes and cautiously eyeing the Spine. The results of Ghalen and Levidi's inspection weighed heavily on everyone's mind. Atamoda pushed his worried expression aside as she sat down to eat with her family.

As she relished a few moments with Aizarg and the children, Atamoda also tried not to notice how low the decks rested, or the dwindling pile of leaf-wrapped fish on the Supply Barge. Whispers circulated they would soon cut rations to every other day. Instead, her thoughts drifted to the upcoming wedding.

Atamoda welcomed the wedding's blessed diversion from the hunger and ever present rain. She'd spent the day pacing the Köy-lo-hely, trying to picture how it needed to be arranged, what supplies she would have to glean from the rest of the flotilla. She could not convince Sana, who sulked alone on Levidi's raft, to help. Neither did she feel comfortable asking Kus-ge, whom she'd come to accept as an enemy.

The thought of an enemy among her own people tied a cold knot in her belly.

Another wave slammed into the bow, spraying the arun-ki with fine mist. They calmly grabbed the deck line and braced. Atamoda held Ba-tor as the Supply Barge lurched up and then dropped.

The deck settled, and the family resumed their meal.

A loud crashing, followed by shouts, emerged from the Crane rafts. Aizarg and Kol-ok jumped to their feet as Ezra erupted through the rain curtain to her left, pursued by Spako brandishing a broken deck log.

Spako smashed the log against the mast, just missing Ezra's ducking head.

"Stop this at once!" Aizarg commanded.

353

Su-gar burst onto the Supply Raft, burning with anger. "You heard the Uros, both of you. Stop it!"

Ezra ducked as Spako swung again, denting the mast. The entire raft shuddered under the blow.

If he doesn't kill Ezra, he'll sink the raft.

Atamoda snatched Ba-tor away and hid his eyes.

"Momma, I want to see!" Ba-tor protested.

Ghalen, Xva, and several Crane men leapt through the rain curtain from her right. Ba-lok, Okta and a few Minnow men appeared from the left. Some brandished spears as they ringed the combatants.

Raging like an angry bear, the Sammujad giant swung again and again, each time missing Ezra by inches.

"I said *stop*!" Aizarg shouted, but madness shut out everything except Spako's quarry.

Levidi appeared between Atamoda and Aizarg, calmly chewing on a piece of fish. "I'm surprised Ezra's lasted this long. He's quick, I'll give him that."

"Where did the giant get the log?" Aizarg asked.

"He ripped it out of my raft. I hope he doesn't beat it up too much. I don't know where I'll find another."

"You didn't try to stop this?" she asked.

Levidi shrugged.

"You're enjoying this, aren't you?" Atamoda chastised.

Levidi smiled. "I don't think he'll hurt him much, he just wants to send the boy a message."

"What message?"

"Spako's been taking his rations with Su-gar. I don't mind, he's docile enough. He weighs down the raft, too; great ballast, you know. Tonight, Ezra joined us. He sat down next to Su-gar. They talked, they laughed, he touched her shoulder, and then the giant roared. Before I could react, he ripped out the deck log and tried to bash Ezra's brains in."

"He ripped it out?" Atamoda couldn't believe it.

"Yep. With his bare hands."

Ezra scurried up the mast, Spako swatting at him. Some of the men, including Ghalen, began to laugh.

Spako dropped the log and with both hands began to shake the mast.

"Now it's getting serious," Levidi stuffed the rest of the fish in his mouth

Aizarg signaled Ba-lok and Ghalen. "Take him down."

Head pressed up against the canopy, Ezra hugged the mast. He grabbed a long rope used to secure part of the canopy, snatched the knife from his loincloth, and cut it free. Swinging around the mast in a wide arc, he circled Spako as he descended. Before Spako could react, the rope tightened over his neck. Ezra landed lightly behind the mast and yanked with all his strength, just as another wave slammed against the flotilla. Spako stumbled backwards against the mast, and Ezra wasted no time tightening the slack. Ba-lok and Ghalen joined him, while Xva and Kol-ok threw another rope around Spako's feet.

Soon, a dozen men strained to bind the giant. Spako's face turned red and then purple as the rope dug into his neck.

Atamoda spotted Virag's furious face in the crowd.

She tugged Aizarg's arm. "Tell them to stop."

"Spako must be rendered harmless."

Su-gar pushed her way through the men. "You're hurting him! Let him go."

"Get away, Su-gar," Levidi warned, but Su-gar shoved him aside.

She knelt in front of Spako, rubbing his cheek. "You have to stop. Do you understand?"

Spako visibly relaxed, the rage ebbing from his eyes.

"Promise me you won't hurt Ezra."

"He...touched...you," Spako rasped.

Su-gar peeked behind the mast and nodded at Ezra. "That's okay. Ezra is my friend."

"Release him," Su-gar commanded the men.

They looked to Aizarg, who nodded. The ropes went limp and the giant slumped coughing to the deck.

Always touching his arm, Su-gar spoke softly, as if addressing a child, "Promise me you won't get angry like that again."

He wouldn't look at her.

She lifted his chin. "Promise me."

Atamoda marveled at how Su-gar controlled him, absorbed his rage like a poultice draws venom from a wound.

"He touched you."

"Promise me!"

"Spako promise."

She removed the ropes and he stood, towering over the Lo.

Aizarg approached. "Spako, we can't have any more of that, do you understand?"

"Spako promise Su-gar. Spako promise Uros."

Ezra meekly walked around the mast. "Spako...? Are we friends now?"

A low growl rumbled in Spako's throat. "Ezra is quick."

Ezra grinned. "Spako is strong."

Spako looked at Su-gar. "Friends?"

Su-gar beamed. "Friends!"

Spako turned to Ezra with childish glee and nodded enthusiastically. "Friends!"

Spako lifted the log in one hand and handed it to Levidi who, with both arms, *humffed* under its weight.

"Sorry, Levidi," Spako shrugged sheepishly.

Okta laughed and slapped Levidi on the back. "Come on, let's see if we can fix it.

Ezra and Su-gar took Spako's hands and led him away.

"Spako is strong. Spako is hungry," Atamoda heard the giant say as they vanished through the rain curtain.

The waves roared, the wind blew, and the rain pounded as Atamoda's family sat down to finish their meal.

A few minutes later a sharp cry, followed by a moan, rang out from beyond the rain curtain. Atamoda and Aizarg rushed to Levidi's raft to find Sahti lying on the deck, her head in Alaya's lap. Xva knelt over his pregnant wife as blood gushed from between her legs.

"Atamoda, help her!" Xva pleaded.

37. Boats and Blankets

Gods and mortals share an equal disposition for self-delusion.

The Chronicle of Fu Xi

***

A Day of Rains.

Atamoda knew a calm sea would make the task easier.

"The boat is small, but it will do." She tried to ignore the faint rotting smell drifting up from the boat as she lined the bottom with handfuls of salvaged reeds.

"I need more reeds," she remarked to herself, hands frantically flattening fronds across the slimy bottom.

"Levidi says there are no more." Sana passed her a small handful of yellowed stalks.

Atamoda looked up, trying to focus across the empty Supply Barge where they knelt around the little boat Okta pulled off the storm wall. Kol-ok tried to donate his boat, but Atamoda would not hear it.

"Where is Alaya?" Atamoda asked.

"In her boat. She won't talk to anyone, even Levidi," Sana whispered.

Alaya had helped Atamoda as she tried to deliver the baby. She last saw her standing over Sahti, arms and torso covered in blood.

"Su-gar?"

"Washing and preparing the bodies."

"Kus-ge?"

"I don't know."

Emptiness invaded Atamoda's spirit. "Mother delivered Sahti; it was the first birth she let me assist."

Sweat dripped from her brow as she stuffed more reeds into the boat, slapping them down and trying to make the yellowing strands lie flat.

But she couldn't cover the rot.

"I couldn't move her to the water. It happened so fast." Atamoda snatched another handful of reeds. "I couldn't turn his head. I've never delivered a child out of water before." She shivered and wiped the sweat from her eyes. "I need more reeds. Sana, find me more reeds."

"There are no more."

Atamoda ignored her, scraping the deck with her fingertips for bits and pieces.

"I should have had Aizarg carry her to the Lagoon. In the water, I could have turned the baby's head. I could have stopped the bleeding."

"The baby was dead, Atamoda. There was nothing you could have done for either of them."

"What do you know about birthing, girl?" Atamoda snapped.

Sana lowered her head.

Atamoda looked about, searching the decks. "Where are my people? I need reeds. More reeds. We can't put them in here."

Sana placed her hand on Atamoda's shoulder.

Atamoda stared at her trembling arms, still covered in Sahti's blood and then into the boat. She'd unknowingly smeared blood in the bottom.

Atamoda turned her gaze to Sana. "Where are my people?"

"They are here. You are not alone."

"I can't put her in there. It's rotting. We need more reeds."

"I will find more reeds."

***

Sana knew nothing could have saved Sahti or the baby. In her young life she'd known several famines, when hunts and raids did not yield enough food for expectant mothers during the long winters. The following spring always brought a plague of stillborns.

"I will find reeds and finish the boat. Go lie down. If I need you, I will call you."

Atamoda didn't answer.

"Please, Atamoda."

"You don't know how."

"I will find Su-gar. She will help."

"It is my duty."

"Let others share the burden."

"So much blood. We must wash the deck."

"The deck can wait."

A scraping sound rose from the Minnow side of the Spine. Okta emerged from the rain curtain, closely followed by Spako dragging a boat. Kirabol limped behind.

Spako rested the good boat next to the rotting hull.

"Kirabol donated her boat for the funeral," Okta said. "She'll take up residence on Levidi's raft. This one is longer and in better condition."

Okta pointed to the old hull. "Spako, grab that boat and help me secure it to the storm wall.

Spako scooped up the little boat and lifted it over his shoulder.

"Su-gar has prepared the bodies. Summon us once it is ready, and Spako and I will carry it to the water. Aizarg is assembling the people around my raft for the funeral."

Atamoda stared at the boat, not acknowledging The Master of Boats.

Sana looked up. "She will be alright. I won't leave her. We will summon you when we are ready."

Okta nodded and led Spako back through the rain curtain.

Kirabol stepped around the hull and picked up the bloody blanket used to birth the child. "Don't wrap the baby or the mother in that." She handed it to Sana. "Toss it overboard. Find a blanket, maybe two, to wrap the dead. I will stay with the patesi-le."

Sana took the blanket. "All the other blankets are used by the living."

"Go to Levidi's raft and look next to the place where you sleep. You'll find my blanket. Bring it here."

Sana opened her mouth, but the hag's expression deflected all argument.

***

Sana stepped lightly over others' sleeping places until she came to hers. Other than Alaya, sobbing a few feet away under her boat's canopy, Sana found herself alone. She briefly thought about consoling Alaya, but knew she must complete her task.

Sana found Kirabol's blanket rolled tightly, Lo style, with both ends neatly tucked to keep water from penetrating and soaking the inside.

She imagined the old woman shivering at night without her blanket. It baffled her why Kirabol insisted on surrendering her blanket to the dead.

Sana sighed and reached for her own blanket, folded square and proper as if ready to be thrown over a horse's back.

I am young, and Scythians are used to cold nights.

"It wasn't mine anyway," she whispered, remembering when Atamoda gave her the blanket shortly after she saved Ba-tor.

A hand grabbed her wrist. Sana whirled about, ready to strike, and came within a breath of Ghalen's red rimmed eyes.

Ghalen placed a tightly rolled blanket in her arms. "Use this."

He vanished through the rainwater curtain.

Sana examined the blanket, wondering where he found a spare. She pulled the cord and unrolled a small portion. For some unknown reason, she sniffed it.

It smelled like a man.

It's his.

Sana made sure no one watched before completely unrolling it. She wrapped the blanket around her shoulders, buried her face in the warm, roughhewn flaxen, and deeply inhaled Ghalen's scent.

She rerolled the blanket in Lo fashion as best as she could before sacrificing it to the dead.

***

Arms folded, heads bowed, Okta and Spako waited patiently as Atamoda prepared Sahti and her baby for their final journey. A fold here, a tuck there; Atamoda doted over little details as she molded the blanket over the mother embracing her child.

"I helped do this for her mother," Atamoda said to no one in particular.

"We must take Sahti to the water." Okta touched her shoulder. "Everyone is waiting."

"She must be completely covered." Atamoda would not be hurried.

"Others grieve, too. Xva stands in the cold rain. Kol-ok won't leave his side," Su-gar said. "Xva needs to see his wife and baby off to Heli-dar. Let Okta and Spako take the boat."

"So much death," Atamoda whispered. Su-gar embraced her from behind and helped Atamoda stand.

Atamoda gestured for them to take the boat. Spako shuffled to one end, Okta to the other.

"Careful, whatever you do, don't tip it. Lift on three," Okta said.

"What is this?" Kus-ge's voice emerged behind them. She stepped forward and inspected the funeral boat.

"Go to my raft, Kus-ge," Okta said in a low voice. "We'll honor our dead there."

"Yes, of course. But why, I ask, are we wasting a perfectly good blanket on the dead? Isn't that a Minnow boat, too?"

"Go away!" Su-gar hissed.

"It's a legitimate question." Kus-ge ignored her. "I mean, there are so few to go around as it is." Kus-ge reached into the hull as if to take the blanket.

Atamoda next found herself standing over Kus-ge, breathing heavily with balled fist. "Don't...touch...her!"

The Minnow Patesi-le rubbed a red cheek, staring up in shock.

Like a cat, Kus-ge sprang so quickly Atamoda didn't have time to bring up her hands. Kus-ge slammed Atamoda's head against the deck until bright lights flashed in her vision. The Minnow woman fell upon her, pinning Atamoda's arms down with her knees, and raining blows across her face and chest.

"Kus-ge!" Okta shouted.

Through blinding pain Atamoda saw hands reach for Kus-ge. Spako fell into a ball, holding his groin.

Atamoda tasted blood as the beating resumed.

A shadow darted to her right. Kus-ge's leg snapped out again, and Okta landed flat on his back.

Kus-ge clenched Atamoda's neck with crushing force, dark fire dancing in her eyes. "Never strike what you're not prepared to kill, stupid bitch!"

The world faded, and then the pressure around her neck vanished. Air, sweet and cool, filled her lungs as light returned to the world.

Atamoda blinked, wondering why Kus-ge looked so surprised. Then she saw a thin black dagger drawing a crimson bead at Kus-ge's jugular. Sana clenched a wad of Kus-ge's hair, pulling her head back as far as it would bend. Kus-ge's eyes bulged in shock.

"Touch her again, I beg you," Sana whispered into Kus-ge's ear like a lover. The wicked edge sank almost imperceptibly deeper as Kus-ge held her breath.

A drop of Kus-ge's blood fell on Atamoda's abdomen.

"Sana," Okta held out his hand. "Let her go."

"Yield or die."

"I yield," Kus-ge sputtered.

Sana's next words were so faint Atamoda could barely hear. "Raise a hand against her again, and I will finish this."

Sana threw Kus-ge to the deck and stood, licking the blade before sheathing it against her thigh.

Kus-ge staggered up, rubbing the bloody streak. "Atamoda struck first! I only wanted to teach her a lesson." She pointed accusingly at Sana. "The Scythian is dangerous. You saw what she did to me!"

Okta pointed to the Minnow side. "Go to your boat, Kus-ge. We'll deal with this later."

Su-gar helped Atamoda up and examined her. "A few cuts and scrapes. Are you hurt anywhere else?" She looked up at Spako. "Go fetch Aizarg."

"No." Atamoda waved her off. "We must commit our dead."

Atamoda turned to thank Sana, but the Scythian had vanished.

Okta and Spako picked up the boat. Supported by Su-gar, Atamoda led the pallbearers through the rain curtain toward the waiting mourners.

38. The Last Daughter of Scythia

The final dagger given a Scythian Maiden is Death, with which she will defend her last breath and deny her body to her enemies. Vengeance and Death are the Black Blades, common to all daughters of Scythia.

The other three daggers, known as the Silver Blades, the maiden names herself. Forged to protect what she loves, in these she instills her secrets.

The Chronicle of Fu Xi

***

As the Lo mourned Sahti, Aizarg held council deep into the night with Kus-ge and Ba-lok. Dawn brought another Day of Rains and vows of reconciliation from the Minnow leaders. Atamoda had her doubts, but survival demanded she concentrate on the needs of the moment. This morning began Sana's training as patesi-le of the Turtle and Isp of the Lo people.

Atamoda's throat still ached; yellow and black bruises testified to Kus-ge's rage. She tried not to think about Sahti or the fight as she attempted to focus her thoughts on Sana's training.

"This presents a difficult situation," Atamoda scanned the jumble of odds and ends scattered in front of her; strands of frayed rope, a few bits of reed, leaves, and a handful of dried herbs from her healing pouch. "I'm not sure where to begin in your training."

Sana stood with her back to her, arms folded and leaning against the mast. "Where did yours begin?" she asked absently, staring across the Arun-ki.

Atamoda sensed rage still smoldering behind the Scythian's glare.

"I am not the daughter of a sco-lo-ti, so I started late. Setenay formally took over my training as a patesi-le when I was about your age, after my father arranged my marriage to Aizarg." Then a thought occurred to Atamoda.

"What do you know of healing lore? Perhaps that is a good place to start."

Sana turned around, eyebrow raised as if Atamoda had asked perhaps the most ridiculous question possible. "Unlike our men, most Scythian women learn to both kill *and* heal. I've stanched enough blood and fought enough infections to know the uses of weed and root, both of the steppe and *Limita*. I've seen your bag of herbs, most of them are known to me."

I see it now, so clearly. The way she folds her arms, the arch of her brow, the fire in her eyes. She is undoubtedly Setenay's blood.

"Of course. Well..." Atamoda struggled to find a place to begin. "We can't very well take a stroll along the shore, can we?"

"No. We can't do that."

Her easy manner with Sana evaporated in the wake of the Adoption Ceremony. Everything had changed, and now Sana had built a wall around herself, one Atamoda didn't know how to penetrate. The confrontation with Kus-ge only aggravated matters.

"Healing and midwifing is at the heart of being patesi-le."

"As it is for a Scythian *kotiama*."

"I...I didn't know." Atamoda had heard many terrible stories of the *kotiama*, the Scythian witches.

Sana's expression turned icy. "The steppe is a hard life, our lore and craft acknowledge this fact. Food does not swim up under our tents, begging to be caught. The grasslands deliver death to our yurt, not fresh water and cool breezes. The weak die, the strong thrive. Still, there is a place for mercy..." Sana paused. "...or *was*."

She paced back and forth like a caged animal, nervously fiddling with a hem of her thigh length loin cloth. "Unlike the Lo, who throw about their mercies without thought or consequence, the Scythia believe mercy must be *earned*."

Atamoda lowered her head, knowing her words unwittingly struck a raw place in Sana's spirit, a place that hadn't begun to heal.

"Why didn't you tell anyone you were Setenay's granddaughter?"

Sana frowned, as if the answer obvious. "I am a captive, a slave taken in conquest. My name has no honor."

"But you are Setenay's granddaughter! That alone gives you great honor for both Lo and Scythia. The Uros himself chose you to marry a sco-lo-ti, and be his Isp. There is no greater honor."

Sana spun around, throwing her hands up in the air. "*Honor?*" She clenched her teeth and tugged at her hair. "I do not understand you Lo! I never will. What do you know of me other than The Lady of the Water gave birth to my father?

"I am not Setenay. I am not Lo."

"You *can* be."

"You cannot change the scales of a snake by calling it a worm, nor a fox by calling it a dog. You can call me an Isp, and marry me off to a man who likes himself more than most, but it won't change who I am."

"By the Lo right of mercy, you are one of us now."

"Mercy will be your undoing."

"Mercy is part of who we are, as much as the sea."

"Atamoda!" Sana shouted, making her jump as if she'd been lashed. "Wake up! Open your eyes. Even the sea is trying to kill you. Your sultry lagoons are gone, the isolation among the tall reeds vanished. The sea is the new g'an. It is wholly unmerciful."

"I don't..." Atamoda stammered.

Sana knelt. Heads turned to watch them from the edges of the Supply Barge.

"Do you not see the poison festering in your Arun-ki? Aizarg brought perhaps the vilest man on the steppe among you. Virag is wholly unmerciful."

Atamoda didn't like the Scythian questioning her husband. "He did what he thought best."

"He is a fool!" Sana turned her back to Atamoda.

Drawn by raised voices, people began to rise and approach the two women, including Aizarg and Ghalen.

"My husband is not a fool."

"If your husband had been thinking, he would have let Ghalen slit Virag's throat the minute we found him."

"It is not our way."

"Make it your way if you want to live."

After a long pause, Atamoda finally said, "He spared you, didn't he?"

The Lo encircled them, spectators to an unexpected drama. Ghalen looked on, grim faced. Aizarg stood impassively, hands resting on his staff.

Sana stood, stepped back a few paces, and turned to the patesi-le. "What do you know of me, Atamoda?"

It occurred to Atamoda she knew very little about Sana. She had been an empty vessel, quietly accepting whatever expectations Atamoda poured into her.

"You are Setenay's granddaughter and the woman who saved my child. You have shown mercy." Atamoda tried to sound confident, trying to convince Sana and herself her expectations were reality. "You protected me."

Sana's arms dropped to her side, shoulders suddenly relaxed. She became like stone, flesh without so much as movement or quiver. Her breathing seemed to stop entirely. Sana transformed into something alien. The girl had made a decision, though what decision Atamoda could only guess.

"Do I frighten you?" Sana whispered.

"Yes."

Atamoda shuddered as Sana glanced at Ba-lok and gave a wicked little grin.

Aizarg brought a she-wolf among us.

Sana whirled about. Blades flashed like the lightning.

Thunk! Thunk! Thunk!

Two daggers sank into the deck a hair's breadth to either side of Atamoda's thighs, the third between her legs so close to her groin she felt the air flee from the blade.

Sana's cold eyes provided a terrifying backdrop for the fourth blade as it hovered inches from Atamoda's face.

"Ba-lok has seen me like this, haven't you...*cousin?*"

Atamoda glanced at the Minnow's sco-lo-ti, who sneered back at Sana. Sana's mirror image, Kus-ge breathed heavily, lustfully.

"Sana," Ghalen held out his hand pleadingly. "Don't do it."

From behind Aizarg, Levidi and Kol-ok appeared, spears in hand; but the Uros pressed their spear tips down.

"Is this how you repay our kindness, Sana?" Aizarg said. Atamoda didn't hear fear in his voice, nor urgency, only a strange calmness.

Sana ignored him, eyes locked on Ba-lok. "Do you know what we were doing when we found Ba-lok on the steppe?"

Atamoda barely shook her head, each shallow breath bringing her flesh in contact with the icy blade. All vestiges of Setenay had vanished. Before Atamoda crouched a killer, a she-wolf ready to tear her throat out.

A Scythian.

"I accompanied my brother, Prince Tuma, on a raiding party. Scythian women accompany men on raiding parties for only one reason."

"You were to be married!" Kus-ge exclaimed in breathless epiphany.

"Before I could feel a man inside me, I had to slay an enemy of my tribe.

"While searching for my brother and our horses, we found this fool sleeping exposed under a tree on the highest ground for miles. We were taking him to my village, where I would sacrifice him with *this* dagger on my wedding night." She waved the tip terrifyingly close to Atamoda's eyes. "With *Vengeance* I would cut his throat, spilling his blood under a full moon."

"Sana," Aizarg spoke slowly, softly. "Come away from Atamoda."

"Do you still want to grant me mercy, Atamoda? Am I still worthy?" She looked around at the surrounding crowd. "Will you accept me as your Isp now that you know who I am?"

"I know who you are," Atamoda whispered. "You are Sana, the woman who saved my son's life and granddaughter of Setenay. You said you trusted her wisdom."

"See, she is dangerous." Kus-ge pushed her way forward. "Someone kill her!"

"There will be no killing," Aizarg said.

The heat ebbed from Sana's glare as an almost imperceptible tremble shook her knife hand.

"I am *Vengeance*, a burning fate thwarted by a Nameless God." She withdrew the blade from before Atamoda's eyes and returned it to the thong.

Atamoda began to breathe again as Sana yanked a knife from the deck.

"I am *Hatred*, relentless in the pursuit of my people's enemies." The blade slid into its appointed place.

The blade between Atamoda's legs, buried deep in the wood, would not pull free so easily. Sana twisted it, gritting her teeth and spitting out her words as if they were sour bile. "I am *Honor*, for which I am now bound to a strange god, a strange people, and a strange man."

The blade came free, leaving a splintered gouge in the deck. She glared up at Ghalen. "For Honor, *Death* is denied me. For Honor, I am a captive and slave."

The blade joined its companions.

Sana reached for the blade to Atamoda's right, but it was gone.

"Sana," Ba-tor whispered, holding the dagger in both hands. "You dropped your knife."

She took the knife and placed it in her thong. Tenderly, she caressed Ba-tor's cheek and kissed him on the forehead. "I am *Love*. It is for love that I will lay down my life for my tribe, and for my family."

Desolate, she turned to Atamoda. "Who am I? I am the last daughter of Scythia, and I mourn my family and people whom I love, every bit as much as you love yours. There are not enough ashes in the Arun-ki to ease my pain."

The Lo silently stepped aside as Sana walked away.

Aizarg knelt beside Atamoda. "Do I need to intervene?"

Atamoda couldn't quit shaking. "No. If she wanted to kill me I'd be dead."

"Mommy, is Sana sad?"

Atamoda embraced Ba-tor. "Yes, baby."

***

Mesmerized, Ghalen watched the woman he would soon call his wife pass by towards the Lagoon.

Levidi nudged him. "Is Doinna looking better now?"

39. Swimming Lessons

It is by the sea the Lo mark the transitions of their life, including birth. The mother floats on her back in waist high water, supported by the village women and tended to by the patesi-le. The men wait with the expecting father on the Köy-lo-hely.

While the baby is still underwater, the cord is quickly cut and tied. The patesi-le raises the child to the sky for its first breath and declares, "From water you emerge, by water you will be sustained, and through water you will pass."

The Chronicle of Fu Xi

***

Since the Adoption Ceremony, Levidi's raft bustled with activity. He busied himself inventorying salvaged rope, watching events transpire around him.

Su-gar rarely left Alaya's side since the Adoption Ceremony. Levidi tried to console his wife, but she kept driving him away, spending the days alone in their boat. Both Sahti's death and losing the twins had devastated her. Only

Su-gar had any luck coaxing her out. For this, Levidi was thankful. Since Su-gar spent so much time on the edge of the Lagoon, so did Spako and Ezra.

Ezra, Su-gar, and Spako had become almost inseparable. Strangely, Spako seemed to grow fond of Ezra as the days progressed, following the young man around as much as he followed Su-gar. The giant granted fealty to Ezra, as if in tribute for defeating him in combat.

Levidi figured every man had a code by which he lived, even a simpleton like Spako. Levidi liked having them around. Everywhere the giant went, the children followed, and children always made Alaya feel better, even though Kus-ge forbade E'laa and Toma from visiting.

Perhaps that was best, Levidi thought. Having them present would only drive Alaya back into her seclusion.

When Alaya felt better, the crowded raft felt like family. Levidi liked it that way, a blessed bright spot in a gloomy world.

For Levidi the night would only get gloomier. Soon, he would relieve Ghalen by Xva's side. Atamoda decreed the man should not be alone during his mourning. But for now, Levidi enjoyed the delicate light and laughter the moment afforded him.

And at the moment there was ample supply of both. Spako wallowed around Levidi's raft; giggling children crawled all over him, tugging his beard and climbing his shoulders as if he were a tree. Sometimes the children tried to tickle the giant's belly, sending Spako rolling on the deck in huge gouts of infectious laughter. In a chorus of giggles, the children piled on.

"Spako!" a cold voice commanded from the edge of the raft. "Come, we have work to do."

Virag emerged from the rain curtain and marched up to Spako. The children shrank away from the slaver, scurrying towards where Alaya and Levidi sat next to the brazier.

Levidi stood. "What do you want?" He almost called Virag 'slaver'.

"I am only paying a visit, and come to fetch my old friend." He grinned and tugged Spako's sleeve.

"Get up, fool!"

Spako shambled to his feet. Eyes downcast and face slack, he dutifully followed Virag. Then, right before stepping through the rain curtain, Spako stopped and looked mournfully over his shoulder.

Virag reemerged from the rain curtain. "Come on, you oaf!"

Spako's eyed narrowed on the slaver. "Virag not Crane. Spako, Crane." He looked at Su-gar, who stood next to the Lagoon. "Su-gar, Crane, so is Levidi."

"What are you talking about? Come!"

Spako returned to his place next to the brazier. "Spako, Crane." The children screamed with joy and mobbed Spako once again.

Virag burst forth, brushing the children aside. "You will not ignore me. You'd be dead without me!"

It happened so fast Levidi didn't have time to react. Su-gar screamed as Spako seized Virag around the throat, lifting him off the deck. As casually as a fisherman tosses a net, Spako hurled Virag back through the rain curtain and onto the adjoining raft.

Everyone stared at the sheet of rain water, behind which there rose a great cacophony of crashes and snaps and shouts. Then, they heard Virag utter such a string of Sammujad curses, Alaya told several of the children to cover their ears. But the former slaver did not return.

Spako plumped back down and crossed his arms. "Spako, Crane." He looked quizzically at Levidi. "Crane Spako's family."

Levidi threw his head back with deep, joyous laughter. He slapped Spako on the back. "Oh, yes, my friend. We are your family!"

***

375

The raft settled down following Virag's exciting departure. Soon, the children returned to their own rafts and boats, and everyone began to quiet down for the evening.

Su-gar watched as Ezra splashed from one end of the Lagoon to another. Back and forth he went, swimming against the current to the upstream rafts, and then letting the current drag him back to the downstream boats.

She wanted to giggle, but knew better. He only came here after the children went to sleep. Sometimes Okta or Ghalen came and gave him pointers, but mostly he swam alone, trying to learn in a few days what the Lo knew how to do from birth.

More than once over last two nights she considered jumping in to save him. But following a big swell which swamped him or slammed him against the downstream boats, he always came back up.

Alaya appeared next to her. "He's getting better."

Su-gar nodded. "I suppose." She crinkled her nose and turned her head sideways. "I think all that splashing frightens the water into submission."

Alaya smiled, highlighting the dark circles under her sunken eyes. Su-gar hadn't seen her smile since the Adoption Ceremony. Sahti's death had sent her even deeper into mourning. Seeing her come out of the boat tonight gave Su-gar hope.

"Maybe you could give him some tips instead of standing here all night watching him suffer..." She poked Su-gar in the ribs. "...*and* admiring him!"

Su-gar smirked and batted her hand away. "I guess I could give him a few good tips."

She stepped to the edge of the raft and sat down, feet dangling in the water, waiting for Ezra to make his way back to the upstream edge.

Gasping and grasping, Ezra finally reached the edge beside her legs. He wiped the water from his eyes and looked up as if surprised to see her.

"Why are you watching me?" he said defensively.

"I'm not. I'm listening to the rain."

Ezra looked around at the raindrops dancing off the water. "I don't notice it anymore."

"I do. Sometimes it sounds like voices, especially when it splashes."

Ezra frowned and looked about. "What do the voices say?"

Su-gar wondered if she'd said too much, if the a-g'an boy would think her mad. She looked down at her toes sticking out of the water. "It's nothing."

"Back home, when I was a boy, my sister and I used to climb the mountains. She swore she heard spirits in the wind echoing down the canyons, though I could never hear them.

"What does the rain say?"

Su-gar relaxed. "It tinkles, like a bronze leaf tied on a string outside the smithy's bellow. It laughs when the breeze blows. I think the spirits are happy tonight."

"Happy? I don't know if the spirits will ever be happy again."

Suddenly uncomfortable, she wanted to change the subject.

"You should really have someone watch you," she said. "One good wave and you're going under. Your legs and arms don't seem to talk to one another."

Ezra turned red. "Okta says I'm making good progress.

Su-gar shrugged, trying not to let Ezra catch her admiring his shoulders. "If he says so, but I bet he's never taught anyone to swim."

"He taught his boys how to swim."

Su-gar bit the inside of her lip, trying her best to suppress a smile. She crossed her arms and put on the most serious of looks. "Fathers and mothers don't teach their children how to swim."

"Okta says he taught lots of children how to swim."

"That's what he wants you to believe, but it's children who teach each other how to swim. I mean *really* swim, like a fish."

Ezra considered her quizzically. "How do children teach each other how to swim?"

Su-gar's eyes danced with mischief. "Like this!" She jumped on top of Ezra, dunking him underwater.

He came up, sputtering and furious.

"You can dunk me back, but you have to catch me first!" She laughed, and kicked gracefully toward the downstream edge.

Half screaming, half laughing, Ezra lunged after her.

***

The water is warmer. Before, Sana couldn't bear to put her feet in the icy sea. She sat alone on one of the downstream boats, letting the rain caress her body and kicking at the swells as they passed below her. Behind her, light and laughter drifted across the arun-ki. Excitement at the prospect of the wedding breathed new life into the Lo, helping them forget their hunger and Sahti's death, at least for a little while. She looked over her shoulder at Ezra and Su-gar laughing and swimming together.

Perhaps Ezra and Su-gar's laughter warms the sea. She knew the makings of a blooming romance. She liked Su-gar, though Sana often caught her looking at the Uros with a lover's longing.

Atamoda sees it, too. The patesi-le's patience amazed Sana. If a Scythian maiden looked at another's man in such a manner, she'd have found her throat cut before the next sunrise.

The Lo were brimming with patience, but whether that was wisdom or folly she did not know.

Su-gar feel's a girl's love, strong but harmless. Perhaps with Ezra, Su-gar would learn to love like a woman.

Sana giggled. *How would I know what it is to love like a woman?*

She turned and stared across the infinite blackness as her smile faded.

I am so lost.

Atamoda told her the Lo gods were driven away by the Nameless God. She said their ways would have to change, just as the world had changed. Perhaps the grim Scythian gods, Be'laam and Molok and a dozen blood-drenched others, were gone, too. Perhaps it didn't matter if she no longer possessed *Death*.

Sana leaned over and peered into the water, wondering if she fell in, would her soul be condemned to a coward's death. She didn't know if her gods still reigned, but she knew the demons were real, even if they were banished.

"You take chances for someone who can't swim," Ghalen called from the end of the line of boats.

Sana pulled up her legs and held them against her chest. She slid into the bottom of the boat.

"You weren't in the line," he held up a small ball of fish. "I drew your ration. May I join you?"

"No."

"Good." Light as a cat he stepped through the boats, the little hulls barely dipping as he passed.

Ghalen settled cross-legged beside her. She drew away, looking around to see if Ezra and Su-gar still swam. Now only waves frolicked in the empty lagoon, reflecting the dimming braziers on the Crane side of the Spine. They were as close to alone as anyone could be in the arun-ki.

"I want to be alone."

He held out the fish. "Eat, and I'll leave you alone."

Her stomach growled fiercely. As tired of dried, stale fish as she was, Sana's mouth watered. She took the fish and stuffed it in her mouth.

"I've eaten," she said with muffled voice around the dry wad. "Now go."

Only wearing his loin cloth, he looked so at ease, arms resting on his knees. She didn't want to look at him, and stared away instead.

"What was his name?" Ghalen asked.

"Who?"

"The prince to whom you were betrothed."

"What makes you think it was a prince?"

"You are a princess...or were. You're of age, and not disagreeable to look at. I assume your father would have arranged your marriage to a prince."

Not disagreeable?

"His name was Warzameg, a prince and powerful warrior from the northern steppe. We were to be wed in late winter before the elk returned to the Adyghe Mountains."

"War...zah...meg," Ghalen slowly intoned. "You a'gan have some very strange names, difficult to pronounce."

"*Our* names are difficult to pronounce?" Sana shot back. "Every mark on the mast is a day my tongue has tripped over itself trying to spit out your impossible Lo words."

Ghalen looked hurt, but she knew better. "What are you talking about? Our words are easy, once you know what they mean."

"They are gibberish!"

"What does your name mean?"

Sana paused.

"Is it a secret?"

"Among my people, the source of one's name is power. There are words one speaks every day, and there is the language of names, spoken only by the witches and the dead."

"Hmm," Ghalen grunted and shrugged. "Well, my name comes from old words, before the time when your people invaded the g'an, when Aryan, Sammujad and Lo spoke very different tongues. It means *iron spirit.*"

"That is a powerful name."

A warrior's name. "Why?"

"I don't know." He hurried past the subject. "Or take Aizarg's name, for example. He has a strange one. It could mean *Good Father* or *Father of the East,* depending how you say it.

"Are you going to tell me what Sana means?" he pressed.

"It is from my grandmother's name," she relented. "I was the first daughter born in her line."

"Ahh!" Ghalen smiled.

Sana kept looking out of the corner of her eye at him, drawn to his smile and laughing eyes; unsure of the new man who sat beside her, speaking so free and easy. Tall and blond and fair, he struck her so differently than compact and dark Scythian men.

"Then you have a blessed name, a holy name."

"Tell me, what does it mean?" She asked too eagerly, letting her guard down. But she needed to know. Ghalen offered her a window into her own past, he held a precious mystery hostage, one she'd only guessed at since she could remember. Even the tribal witches did not know the origins of Setenay's name; hence, they held no enchantment over her.

"Are you sure you want to know?" He winked.

"Tell me!" She wanted to hit him.

"Oh, alright. Setenay means *Life Giving Mother.*"

"So Sana means...?"

"Life..." Ghalen shrugged. "I think. Maybe *Sena* would be a better, more 'Lo', way of saying it. I suppose it doesn't matter. During the council celebrations, my mother used to complain the old words were so corrupted with Sammujad mish-mouth, it was hard to speak in proper Lo anymore."

Life. My name means 'life.'

Great power had just been handed to her, and she knew this man had no idea what he'd just done. He gave it to her freely, without price, as if were a common thing like a wildflower plucked from the steppe.

She looked up to catch him staring at her. His eyes were too deep, so clear she could see his soul. It lay there, unguarded and innocent, open to the daggers of a cruel world.

He was like Atamoda, trusting and good and a fool.

Ghalen leaned in close, brushing aside the invisible shield she'd erected around her body and heart since the Scythian maiden learned that blood and cruelty were the ways of the world.

"Sana," he whispered, casting the man's spell with his deep, silky voice.

She nodded, his warm breath caressing her cheek.

"If you are to be Isp, you have to learn to swim." Ghalen leaned backwards, rolling head over heels into the Lagoon.

Spell broken, a wave of disappointment and relief passed over her. She stood up quickly, almost losing her balance in the rocking boat.

He emerged, hair slicked back with that infuriating smile of his, gripping the side of the boat. He held up his hand. "Come on, I'll teach you."

"No!" she said, arms tightly wrapped around her shoulders. She glanced at the line of boats, wondering if she could make it all the way across to the rafts while standing. She'd crawled out here before on all fours while no one was watching.

Her eyes darted about, looking for an escape.

"Sana, you must learn to swim. It's dangerous if you don't. If Ezra can do you it, you can, too."

"Atamoda can teach me," she protested.

"She isn't here. I am." He extended his hand again.

If I enter the water, I am fully in his power, defenseless at the mercy of...an enemy.

He seemed to sense her fear. "Sana, this is my horse, this is my steppe. Water is my people's blood. You've only seen the water offer death, but for us, it offers life."

Life.

Memories of demons, and heads and hands vanishing below the silt-choked water filled her thoughts.

"I will protect you."

Cautiously, she knelt down, grasping the sides of the boat. Sana took his hand and lowered one foot into the lagoon.

"If you don't want to lose those, I'd leave them in the boat," Ghalen nodded to the daggers around her thigh.

The thought of removing them gave her one more reason to hesitate, but she found herself untying the thin leather thong and placing the knives in the bottom of the boat. Each slender blade rested inside a double-slit cut in the thong's widest portion, which firmly held the blades.

She tried to stop shaking, but couldn't. The daughter of Scythia closed her eyes and committed to her fate.

It happened so quickly she didn't have time to register the transition between the air and water. She inhaled, shocked by its frigid embrace.

"It did not feel this cold on my feet!"

"It never does," he laughed.

His arm, warm as a river stone under the summer sun, locked around her waist. Sana drew her arms in close to her chest, fists under her chin. She stretched out her toes, instinctively feeling for a bottom she knew wasn't there. Sana clenched her eyes, ashamed of her fear, ashamed of her urge to draw closer to him.

"Don't let go!" she whispered.

The sensation of his warm body, locked warmly, intimately with hers, made her stomach flutter with each wave.

Sana knew at that moment, her fate no longer belonged to her.

Maybe I never truly had control.

Ghalen's legs began slowly pumping in a steady rhythm.

"Open your eyes." His breath tickled her nose, his voice reverberated through her body.

She shook her head violently.

He lifted her chin. "Look."

If he is holding me with one hand, and lifting my chin with the other, then...!

She opened her eyes to find them floating in the middle of the Lagoon.

"Take me back to the edge. *Now!*"

"I will, but we'll do it together. First, we must learn to hold our breath. Do this."

Ghalen pinched his nose, made big puffy cheeks, and put his face underwater.

"That looks silly. It is beneath me."

"Drowning is sillier. Do it."

Resigned, she puffed out her cheeks and pinched her nose.

He frowned.

"What?" she exhaled.

"It does look silly."

She kicked him.

"Ouch! Don't do that if you don't want me to let go."

"A Scythian princess does not look silly."

"I'm only joking. Please, let's try it together."

Ghalen didn't seem to struggle the least bit, swimming and supporting her. She felt herself relaxing slightly as the passing moments found her still alive.

He held his breath again. Reluctantly, she copied him.

"Good. Now, do it again, and this time we're going under water."

The thought of descending into to the black abyss terrified her. "I changed my mind. I am not a fish. Take me back to the edge."

"Sana, have you ever watched a bird and dreamt of flying?"

She nodded.

"This is as close as you will ever come. You can fly like an eagle beneath the waves. One day the water will turn from black to dappled blue again, warm under a summer sun. Fish will dance around you like flocks of sparrows, and you will know such joy, joy you never thought possible. We have a saying: From water we emerge, by water we are sustained, and through water we will pass."

For a moment, Sana saw those blue, sunlit waters in his eyes.

"I am ready." She held her breath and prepared for whatever fate had in store.

The first few dives were terrifying. The water invaded her ears, making them feel stuffy. But, like many new experiences, the fear melted away, replaced by the exhilaration of new frontiers. Time passed, and soon she held her breath without pinching her nose.

Grasping her waist, Ghalen began to swim around the Lagoon, showing her how to kick, move her arms, and float.

She didn't feel as if flying, but welcomed the sense of lightness with each swell. Together, they swam against the waves to the upstream rafts.

Ghalen's arm slowly relaxed, his hand finding hers.

Her fear reemerged. "What are you doing?"

"Teaching you to fly." He held up his finger. "Listen."

In the distance she heard the familiar boom of a large wave striking the bow rafts, then the Spine creaking, and the rapid, successive splashes along the ribs.

"Get ready, it's a big one!" He smiled like a little boy.

"What are you doing? No, stop..."

With a mighty kick, Ghalen pushed off the rafts edge, just as the wave passed under them, rushing by as if it were air. Sana kicked away and, arms outstretched like wings, she rose above the boats ahead of her.

For a fleeting moment, she became a little girl again, chasing a feather drifting beyond camp's edge where the pickets stood vigil.

I am a feather!

She glanced to her left to see Ghalen smiling back at her, both arms extended outward. He wasn't holding her hand, and a boat loomed ominously ahead of her. She grabbed its side, but the wave dragged her underneath the hull. Sana struggled against the current, but it yanked her with unbelievable force, trying to pry her fingers from the boat.

Ghalen snatched her to the surface, pressing her hard against his chest.

She spit out a mouthful of water. "Let go of me!"

Sana wiped the water from her eyes and looked up, irritated by his silence.

Ghalen wasn't smiling anymore. As if in a trance, he stared down at her. Sana realized how close he pressed her against him. Blood pumping, she found her arms firmly wrapped around his waist. Skin to skin, they slid achingly against one another in harmony with the sea.

Only a moment separated her from a choice; surrender to the overpowering instincts building within, or leave the water's embrace. Perhaps he would not afford her a choice. She'd seen it before, when a man's passion becomes so inflamed he's taken by madness. The water did nothing to quench this fire, only feeding its flames.

She wanted to wrap her thighs around his waist, to pull him in tight, to seize him and take him. But if she surrendered now, she surrendered everything.

I am still a captive. I am still Scythian.

"No," she grabbed the side of the boat and squirmed from his grip.

Sana turned her back to him and closed her eyes, prepared for what may come next. Would he take her? Would it hurt? Being the daughter of a great king, she never imagined her first sexual experience would be rape, or that it would occur in the sea.

She could see the lightning flashes through her eyelids, feel its energy coursing through her body as she waited for the thunder.

Cold water filled the void between. He seized her between the legs. Sana gasped.

And then he hurled her upward in the chilly air and into the boat. She flopped into the hull like a wet fish.

Gracefully, he slid in after her, grabbed her knives, and stood up. "Don't forget these." He tossed them in front of her.

Dizzy from the emotions fighting for control of her heart, she hastily retied the thong. The knives felt different against her wet thigh, chaffing in a way they never had before.

She could not read his impassive expression, just as relaxed as he was when he sat down beside her. He turned to make his way across the boat, as if the moment never happened.

Before he reached the rafts he hesitated. Ghalen paused for several moments before turning around. He withdrew something from a hidden fold in his loincloth.

How can they hide so much in their loincloths?

Her heart almost stopped when she saw him holding *Death*. She hadn't seen that black dagger since Setenay took it.

"A woman taken in war is, by right of combat, a slave to the victor. Her life is completely his, correct?" He toyed with the razor edge.

She nodded, staring at him defiantly, a cold sense of betrayal settling into the pit of her stomach.

I was weak to let my guard down, to trust him. The hope she'd felt only moments ago vanished.

"So, if I command you to marry me, you must by your own custom. Is that true?"

"Yes."

Ghalen approached to within inches, turning the dagger over in his hands. To the Scythian maiden, *Death* served as a symbol of liberation from one's oppressor. In his hands, it became a symbol of her slavery.

She tried to forget the way his arms felt. Staring hard at him, her last act of defiance only served to stir the conflicting feelings tearing down her defenses.

He's no different, Sana. Learn to hate him, and accept your fate.

Ghalen's expression softened. "Setenay told me many things before she died, about her days among the Scythia. We revere her as a holy woman. She is legend, but she was also a woman. In you, I see her spirit.

"An Isp cannot be a slave to anyone's will but her own. She told me never to return this to you. I didn't know why then, but I do now." Ghalen held out *Death* to Sana, hilt first.

"If Aizarg is to have an Isp, she will be a free woman, in both body and spirit. If I am to marry, I will marry a woman who chooses me, in both body and spirit. My bride must be whole.

"I release you from the bond of conquest."

With that, Ghalen vanished into the arun-ki.

Sana stared at the dark blade in her palm, the edge forged to drink her blood. The Scythian slowly fell to her knees in the bottom of the boat.

Sana lightly grazed the tip against her abdomen, not sure if she feared life or death more at this moment.

***

Ghalen couldn't breathe, wondering what insanity had come over him. He paced back and forth on the bow raft, fighting the urge to run back and wrest the knife from her hands.

Setenay told you not to give it back.

He crouched against the storm wall, running his hands through his soaking hair, and praying for a speedy dawn.

40. Betrothed

The newly wedded couple poled to the upstream edge of the arun-ki, all their earthly belongings secured to the wedding barge. There, they anchored and erected a small thatch tent on the deck in which to spend their first night as man and wife. After sealing their marriage, they woke the next morning, eager to begin their life together.

The Chronicle of Fu Xi

***

Sometimes he paced. Sometimes he squatted against the storm wall, letting the rain pour off him, hoping the bucking and rolling deck might shake some sense into him.

Ghalen couldn't get over the way she felt in his arms, the way their bodies blended in the water.

The wind picked up from the north when Atamoda found him.

"Come," she said.

Ghalen followed her between sleeping forms and dim braziers until the reemerged into the rain on the farthest downstream raft.

Relief and joy flooded his spirit when he saw her standing where Virag's raft used to be moored.

Atamoda held Ghalen's hand and patted his forearm as she led him to Sana. "She woke me and asked me to find you."

"I don't understand."

"Understanding is not important. Being here is all that matters."

Ghalen looked down at Sana, but she wouldn't meet his gaze. She held a small pouch.

"Are you ready?" Atamoda asked.

Sana nodded and slowly raised the bag.

"Do you remember the words?"

Sana nodded and stepped to the edge. She extended the pouch into the downpour as the sky lightened in the east.

"The only power left to us is our choices. The choice I make this day is I remember my lost. Today, I speak for my dead, the Scythia."

She slowly tipped the bag and, at that moment, a gust of wind snatched the ashes.

To Ghalen, the north wind smelled like dry grass, orange sunsets, and upturned earth. The ashes swirled across the waves, for a moment almost taking the form of a galloping horse. With a peel of thunder they vanished in the downpour.

She reached down and untied the thong around her thigh, five blades secured in their slots. Sana rolled up the thong, tied the ends into a bow, and tossed them over the edge. With a plunk, they vanished beneath the waves.

Ghalen could not believe his eyes.

"The Five Daggers have no place in a patesi-le's hut."

She embraced Ghalen without reservation. He lifted her chin, savoring the anticipation of their first kiss.

Sana shoved him backwards. "No."

"No?"

"No, I said. Not until I am your wife. Is it not Lo tradition? Now, go away. You may kiss me after the wedding, and not a moment before." Sana turned up her nose, crossed her arms and marched away, Atamoda in tow.

"Atamoda!" Ghalen pleaded.

Atamoda winked at him. "She's learning our ways quickly, isn't she? You heard her, go away. I'm going to be busy begging and borrowing to prepare your bride, so stay out of our way."

The two women vanished among the Minnow, who were beginning to stir.

Ghalen grinned, thinking of what his wedding night might bring. A song bubbled in his throat, a low thrum rising and falling with the waves. The Minnow men rose from their slumber and watched Ghalen stroll through their rafts, a spring in his step.

***

Aizarg and Kol-ok listened from the Köy-lo-hely as Ghalen's low bass rhythm spread to several other throats. Aizarg rose from his stool and placed his hands on the staff. Men's voices rose and fell from bow to stern with each wave, saturating each log, beam and rope.

The arun-ki vibrated with life, yet no women joined the song.

"Why do they sing, Father?" Kol-ok asked.

"Because they are tired of being afraid."

The song grew with each crashing wave, not in harmony with the sea, but in defiance of it. Aizarg felt its power course through his body, drawing him in.

"The ai doesn't join the halah," Kol-ok said.

A pang of sadness penetrated Aizarg's happiness. "The women cannot find their song."

Then, a long, high note floated above the men. It waivered up, up, up; riding the men's voices like a wave.

Powerful and strong, an exotic note never before heard among the Lo.

Then, it plunged downward in perfect harmony with the men's, yet uniquely apart.

"Who is *that*?" Kol-ok peered through the rain curtain toward the Supply Barge.

"*That* is our future," Aizarg grinned and slapped his son on the back. "In this terrible forge, our chain grows stronger."

He knew Sana had joined the ai-halah, and in the process forever changed his people's spirit. On this thirty-eighth day of rain, a song gave birth to something new on the Black Sea.

Atamoda's voice joined Sana's, struggling at first to match, but then blending with the harmony. Then, in rapid succession, Crane and Minnow women joined the wondrous chorus.

***

Spako woke and lifted his nose like a dog sniffing the air, peering into the distance as if trying to seeing the music as it floated through the air.

"What is it?" Spako whispered.

"They're singing," Ezra replied.

"Spako never hear singing before."

Side by side, they listened as the song gained strength as it rolled along. Ezra looked over to see large tear drops rolling downs the giant's cheeks.

"What's wrong?"

"Singing make Spako happy and sad."

Ezra patted Spako's shoulder. "Me, too."

He gazed out over the endless ocean. "I wish my sister could have heard this. She deserved it, not me."

***

Virag crouched alone in his boat and cursed. He cursed Aizarg for taking Spako from him, and that damn Hur thief for robbing Spako of any terror he could induce among the Lo. He cursed his hunger and the rain and the sea and the damnable noise pulsing through the arun-ki.

Virag pressed his hands against the sides of his head.

"Shut *UP!*" he screamed and kicked his feet.

His heel went through the bottom with a wet crunch. A foul, fetid reek exploded in the boat as the sea flooded into what had been his home.

Virag sat dumbfounded as water surrounded him and covered his horded fish. The water brought him to his senses, and he scrambled onto the adjacent raft just in time. The mooring line pulled tight as the hull slipped beneath the waves with a sucking sound.

Virag grabbed the line and pulled, hoping to save as much as he could. The rope snapped and the boat vanished into the deep.

41. Night Watch

At winter's end, when a Lo boy is deemed ready, his father released him to an elder for the Marsh Journey. The elder blindfolded the boy and took him deep into the marsh, far away from their people or neighboring Lo villages.

The next morning, the elder would depart, leaving the boy with only a knife with which to survive until his return. The boy would exist in isolation until the first north wind. In that time he must not only survive, but construct his own shelter, nets, spear, and boat.

In the Marsh Journey, the boy endured both a physical and spiritual test. Here, for good or ill, the boy met the man he would become.

The elder returned to find either a thriving Lo man or a dead boy. It wasn't uncommon for boys to simply vanish forever. If the boy died, the elder would commit his remains to the sea and gather what objects he could salvage. The elder would present the objects to the father and recite the terrible words, "I return your boy's spirit to his family."

If the boy survived, the elder would present him to his father with words of joy.

"Your boy is dead. Before you stands a man."

The Chronicle of Fu Xi

***

The air always felt cooler after a big storm. Exhausted, everyone slept deeply after a day battling wind and waves. Only Okta and Aizarg remained awake, exchanging whispered council on the Köy-lo-hely.

Okta's beard had grown long, his cheeks sunken. Holes had begun to form in the sco-lo-ti's winter tunic. Aizarg wondered if he appeared as feral.

We are lean and hungry, like wolves.

"No more rope. No more wood. No land in sight and no end to the rain." In the dark of night, Okta knelt close to Aizarg's stool, voice low. "What we have now may be all we ever have. If something doesn't change soon, the arun-ki *will* sink."

"The Nameless God will not forsake us."

"You faith strengthens me, Uros, but it doesn't strengthen the ropes binding this flotilla."

"How much longer?"

"The outer rafts rest two hands lower in the water today than seven days ago. Half the barrier boats are gone, the remainder are practically worthless. The storm wall is a blackened, stinking heap. Another good storm and its gone." He wrinkled his nose. "The family boats are almost as bad. This infernal water eats everything. If we didn't have rainwater to drink, we'd be dealing with sickness now, too."

Aizarg gazed up at the leaking canopy. The reeds had turned from pale green, to yellow. Streaks of brown and black mold infected the roof, with ghastly fingers of white fungus poking through.

"There is one raft showing no signs of rot, or waterlogging for that matter."

Aizarg raised an eyebrow.

"My raft floats high, the wood is firm and without a single soft spot."

"We made that out of unpitched scrap wood. It should be completely waterlogged by now. The deerskin strips alone should have been eaten through weeks ago."

Okta shrugged. "The bindings are still strong. How that can be, I don't know, but I am resigned to merely accept it and be thankful."

Okta pressed on. "We must move everyone to the Spine rafts. Cannibalize what material we can from the boats and rafts to keep our central vessels seaworthy as long as possible."

"How much time will that buy?"

"Two weeks, maybe a month. I've dived under the rafts a few times, but there isn't enough light down there for me to get a feel for the rot on our underside."

Aizarg's shoulders sagged as he placed his head in his hands. Long moments passed until he spoke.

"Let the people enjoy the wedding. The morning after, gather the men, break down as much good material as you can from the outlining vessels, and pile it on the Supply Barge. We'll move those still living in boats to the Köy-lo-hely."

"We must do this without delay." Okta leaned closer. "One more storm, that's all it may take."

"The people need good news, something to take their minds off their suffering. Packing everyone around the Spine will only serve to deepen their misery. Tomorrow, tell Ghalen, Ba-lok and Levidi the plan, but no one else. The morning after the wedding, make it so."

Okta opened his mouth to protest, but Aizarg shook his head. "This is my decision."

Okta nodded.

Aizarg took a deep breath and looked about, visualizing the arun-ki as a long, narrow strip of rafts packed with his people.

"The arun-ki will be more streamlined," he said. "It will put less strain on the sea anchor and Spine."

Okta stared hard at Aizarg.

"You have more to say, I can see it in your eyes."

"You've been a good leader, Aizarg. The only reason we're alive is due to you. But we need purpose. Floating aimlessly on the tide, waiting for a miracle while we waste away is not a plan. We need to take action. We must retrieve the sea anchor, convert the extra canopies into sails, and catch the wind."

"Catch the wind to where?"

"The Southern Land."

"You'd have us chase myths."

"Weren't the Narim a myth, too? And yet we chased them and found a new chance for life. No other clan sailed as far to sea as the Carp. Our legends of the Southern Lands are the strongest. My grandfather spied far off hills on the southern horizon after being lost in an ice fog for days."

Aizarg shook his head. "With no idea of where we are, we'd be striking out blindly."

"I am Carp. At sea, I am never lost.

Aizarg looked up at his friend and said a silent prayer of thanks for one such as Okta.

"The current is slowing, sometimes even ceasing all together. On Days of Rain, the anchor line floats limp, but sea still flows from the north. The wind has died down, but predominantly from the north, too. Even if our homes are no longer submerged, we are far from them. If the Southern Lands truly exist, and above water, I wager my life we are close."

"If we are destined to make landfall in the Southern Lands, it will happen only if the Nameless God wills it."

"Aizarg, please..."

"Reinforce the arun-ki, move everyone to the center rafts. But our fate is not our own, the Nameless God sets our course."

Okta lowered his head. "As you wish."

The Master of Boats stood to go, but turned around. "She would have killed Atamoda had it not been for Sana. Kus-ge fought like a..." Okta frowned, as if choosing his words carefully. "…like a Scythian. I've never seen anything like it."

Aizarg's mood darkened. "We will have no further trouble from Kus-ge. We had a long talk."

"You weren't there; you didn't see her savagery. She's bad, Aizarg. No amount of talking will change that."

"She is patesi-le."

"She is dangerous. Ba-lok is weak. Our people are rotting, too. They also need reinforcing. Ghalen, Ba-lok, myself…we are like the outlying rafts and you are the core. The old ways and the old gods are dead, washed away. Dissolve the clans. You have your Isp. That is all you need."

Okta's words struck Aizarg numb.

"Do you realize the weight of what you say?" Aizarg stammered. "You renounce your clan leadership so easily?"

"Not easily, friend. Somewhere over the waves I pray my people have a new sco-lo-ti, leading them to us. They need him, and you need a Master of Boats, not a sco-lo-ti."

Aizarg's sighed. "Things are different now."

"Yes, things are different now."

***

In the flickering lightning Kol-ok stared up at the canopy, watching raindrops drip onto the deck. Embers from the dying brazier gave the darkness a crimson edge. Sleep eluded him, his mind drifting between hunger and his nearly completed boat only a few paces away.

No pitch, but Father and Okta say we can get it a little wet.

He hoped tomorrow brought a Day of Rain so they could test the hull.

Bat-or rolled over, slapping Kol-ok in the face. He shrugged off his brother's hand and rolled onto his side, staring through the rain curtain dividing the Supply Barge and the Köy-lo-hely.

Okta is gone, but Father is still awake. Maybe he will help me make a spear tomorrow.

A cold draft tickled his toes, and he suddenly realized Bator was completely rolled up in their blanket. Kol-ok entertained the thought of snatching it from his little brother, but changed his mind.

He doubted he could sleep, even with a blanket.

If the Master of Boats cannot figure a way to pitch our boats, how can I?

Every few minutes he heard the pops and creaks from a rolling wave lifting the bow rafts. The Spine, only an arm's reach away, stretched against the sea's power. The wave splashed along the ribs as the wave marched toward him. A moment later, the barge gently lifted and then settled back down. After a few more splashes, the wave exited from under the arun-ki with a *whoosh.* Only the occasional rumble of thunder interrupted the cycle.

Kol-ok let the sea's ballad rock him, and tried to push thoughts of his beloved boat from his mind. But other, equally obsessive thoughts took its place.

He'd thought of Su-gar more often than not. Several years older than he, Kol-ok knew she thought of him like a little brother.

I am a man now.

Kol-ok knew if he had a proper boat and a proper spear she might see him differently. Maybe she would see him and not Ezra.

He liked Ezra, but the a'gan boy could barely swim. He didn't know how to properly use a spear, and still walked like an ox across the deck. Ezra didn't have any of the qualities of Lo man, yet Okta spent hours teaching him.

Father has no time, he is Uros.

Slowly, the waves' cadence began to work its magic upon Kol-ok's eyelids.

Clack.

An odd noise, one which did not belong, interrupted the beat. Kol-ok's eyes flew open. There it came again, this time accompanied by a soft shuffle.

Wide awake, Kol-ok waited for the noise again, wondering if his father had finally decided to come to bed. He craned his head, looking about the barge. His mother slept a few paces away, curled up on a stack of unfinished mats. A Minnow elder, an ill-tempered man named Ameck, slept sitting up against Kol-ok's upturned boat, facing the neatly organized food pile. Men from both clans took shifts guarding the fish, and tonight was Ameck's turn.

His father's motionless figure still sat on the Köy-lo-hely, though judging by his lowered head, Aizarg might have nodded off.

From the other side of the food pile the shuffle came again, like a mouse. Kol-ok knew someone else lurked on the barge. Then he heard the faint tearing of a leaf.

Kol-ok briefly thought about waking Ameck, but refrained.

Letting the next wave mask the noise, he rose into a crouch and grasped his spear. Staying low, he crept around the pile, now barely high enough to conceal him, even in a crouch.

Whoever it was, they snuck in from the Minnow side of the Spine.

It's that nasty Virag, I know it.

Kol-ok would handle this himself, save their food, and prove his manhood. Pulse pounding, trying to control his breathing, he tensed.

The shuffle came again.

Catch him before he flees.

Kol-ok rose like an avenging spirit, spear cocked over his head, ready to strike.

Alaya crawled on the deck like an animal. Startled, she looked up at him, a stack of fishcakes cradled in her arm.

Lips trembling, she scrambled up and snatched his arm. Stunned, Kol-ok stumbled behind her as she dragged him between sleeping forms to the storm wall.

Once there, where no one could see, she placed his hand upon her belly.

Kol-ok tried to pull his hand away, but she held his palm against her warm flesh.

"I have a baby in me, but Levidi doesn't know. I'm hungry, Kol-ok. If I starve, the baby dies. Do you understand? We've tried so long to have a child. I can't lose it like Sahti. Please, *please*, don't tell anyone!"

Kol-ok didn't feel like a man anymore. He didn't want to see Alaya this way, eyes swollen with tears.

"Wha-why don't you tell Levidi?"

"He'll try to get more food for me and the baby. He'll steal it if he has too. He's the Staff Bearer; he'll have to choose between the baby and the Uros. I can't make him choose."

"Tell Mother. Tell Father. They will help." Kol-ok grabbed her hand and began to drag her back across the rafts.

"No!" She snatched him back. "You can tell no one. Levidi mustn't know."

She pressed his hand harder against her abdomen, drawing closer to him. "If I lose the baby, and Levidi knows..." her words came in between heaving, racking sobs, "I could not bear it, if he knew he had a son and lost him."

She pulled him close, closer than he'd ever been to a woman, and whispered in his ear. "I beg you!"

Kol-ok nodded dumbly, mesmerized by her softness and smell.

"Thank you!" she repeated over and over, kissing his cheeks. Kol-ok flushed, a strange feeling fluttering in his stomach.

Alaya knelt down and snatched up the fish cakes she'd dropped like a greedy gull pecks mudfish from the surf.

Alaya backed away, muttering "I'm sorry" until she disappeared under the dark canopy, leaving Kol-ok alone in the rain.

The son of the Uros lingered on the bow raft for a little while longer. Somewhere before dawn, he threw the crooked stick he once called a spear, into the sea and laid down under the nearest canopy to sleep.

42. Two Shadows

Evil casts two shadows, goodness only one. – Lo Proverb.

Chronicle of Fu Xi

***

Ba-lok flopped into his boat, smugly satisfied with how events were proceeding. Twice Aizarg had done what he asked - decreed anyone stealing food would face exile and allowing Virag to enter the Minnow Clan. Aizarg sought his advice more often. Ba-lok sensed himself gaining standing in the inner council. He crossed his legs and nibbled on his daily ration of stale fish.

Across the Minnow rafts, his people made their way to the Supply Barge and their evening rations, chattering excitedly about tomorrow's wedding. He spotted Virag and Ro-xandra in the shadows, close to one another and engaged in whispers.

Virag began to spend a great deal of time with Ro-xandra. This struck him as odd, but the nights were long, and Virag no longer had a boat. Ro-xandra, being a widow, could bed any she chose.

Maybe we'll make a Lo man out of the old fox, yet.

He scowled at the dried cake's strong sour odor. *It's getting ready to turn.*

Ba-lok thought of the shrinking pile of fish cakes on the Supply Barge. The stack now only stood knee high.

We must find fish in this great big sea.

Kus-ge emerged from the crowd and squatted next to the brazier, tossing in a few sticks. Ba-lok noticed how drawn she looked. Perhaps the hunger sapped her vitality, or maybe it was more.

Leanness.

"Are you going to eat?" he asked.

"When my work is complete."

"And what work is that?"

"I have to retrieve a rabbit from a snare."

"What do you mean?"

Kus-ge considered him with her usual coldness as the corner of her mouth lifted. He couldn't remember when he last saw warmth in those eyes.

Maybe I've mistaken passion, or lust, for warmth all this time.

She didn't answer his question; instead, she just broke twigs and threw them into the brazier. "Tell me, husband, what are you doing to ensure our people continue to eat?"

"You know what I am doing. I don't need to answer that question." Ba-lok put his hands behind his head, pushing the negative thoughts aside, trying to recapture his previous confidence. "Aizarg listens to me. He values my council."

Kus-ge snorted. Her snort transformed to a sneer. "Are you blind or just stupid?"

"I am sco-lo-ti and your husband. You will not address me that way."

"No, you are Second. *Second!* That means you are Aizarg's little boy, scurrying about the decks doing the jobs unfit for Okta and Ghalen."

"I've had enough of your foul words."

"My words are what you carry to the Uros, not your own."

Ba-lok flinched and visibly shrank back into the boat. "I don't need your council."

"Of course you need my council. Without me, you'd be lost, just like you were on the steppe. If I had been with you on the g'an, you wouldn't have gotten lost...and captured." Kus-ge's voice turned smooth, like polished bronze. "I wonder what the Scythians planned to do to you before Sana would have cut your throat."

Shame bubbled up in his gut at memories the rain could not wash away. "They did n-nothing."

"Your face bears scars from a great deal of nothing. Do you have other scars I cannot see?" She shrugged, warming her palms by the fire. "I would not know. You haven't taken me since your return."

"I've heard stories about what Scythian raiding parties do to captives, especially those they capture without a fight. My grandmother told me they don't consider captive men *as* men, more like women to be used as they see fit," she laughed.

"Shut up."

Kus-ge crouched towards him like a panther. Ba-lok found himself scooting backward in the boat.

"You are weak and I'm tired of pretending otherwise. I saved the Minnow, not you. While you played on the g'an, I led our people to safety. Our children's bellies growl while you sit on the Köy-lo-hely, listening to Aizarg and his lackeys.

"We outnumber them, yet they dictate to us. They dictate because you are weak." She leaned in close, lips pouting, breath caressing his face. "You...are...*worthless*."

He slapped her.

It felt good.

Kus-ge smiled and licked her lips. "I'll forget about that for now." She spread her legs and lifted her loincloth, revealing knives like Sana's, weapons he'd never seen before.

Ba-lok's eyes widened in shock.

"Next time, I'll kill you. But before that time, all will know of the humiliation you suffered at the Scythians' hands.

"If you want me to continue playing the dutiful patesi-le before our people and the council, you will listen and obey."

Virag emerged from behind Ba-lok's wife, grinning like a living skull. "Good evening, Sco-lo-ti." He frowned. "I've always thought that such a clumsy word. I think the smaller words carry more power, like king or *Uros*."

Ba-lok's head swam. "What is going on?"

Kus-ge slid into the boat, resting her thigh seductively over Ba-lok's leg. He felt the daggers slide threateningly over his skin, gliding their way toward his groin.

"While our people receive rations, Virag and I thought we'd have a private talk with you."

***

Like caged tigers in heat, the two seas raged to reach one another. Hurricane-whipped waves pounded the rocky barrier from both directions, but the tide favored the greater southern sea. Breakers lifted warm water over the thin granite damn, giving the icy Black Sea a salty taste of its eager lover.

Nuwa sensed cracks rapidly multiplying along the miles-long bridge separating the two continents. Already, the southern sea blasted holes along the cliff's base far below in the abyssal deep.

Nuwa's spirit waned, exhausted from her toils. Across the four corners of creation, she'd witnessed a world die and gathered the dead unto the Emperor of Heaven. Here, along the narrow bridge between continents, would begin the last great act of the Deluge, the Cataclysm's death rattle.

The flotilla drifted out there, far over the horizon, their souls twinkling like campfires on a distant shore.

So delicate, so easily snuffed out like a candle's flame between the fingers.

The Emperor of Heaven had sealed a covenant with these people. Now her duty wasn't gathering the dead, but protecting the living.

Wails drifted on the western wind, as the last divine spirit cried out in his struggle to cling to flesh.

Nine times she heard such a cry rise from the mighty city in the west, now buried under the ocean, never to rise again. The race of demigods and the age of the Nephilim had all but passed.

So far, Fu Xi had escaped their fate. She prayed to the Emperor of Heaven this would be the last time she heard such a cry.

His voice thundered in her spirit. *Keep your promise and I will keep mine.*

She considered the narrow rock dam again. "They still have time, just a little."

She transformed into a pillar of golden fire and raced away into the clouds. A fresh shock wave rumbled through the land bridge as another tidal wave rolled over naked rock.

He waited until he no longer sensed her presence before emerging from the whirlwind. A shadow born from a shaft of rain, a wisp of sea spray, he solidified and strolled across the land bridge, watching the clouds seal over the hole Nuwa punched open as she fled east.

"Most likely flying east to hover over that brat of hers," he murmured.

The Black Dragon thought it ironic that time had become so important to immortals. Nuwa fled east to watch over a son she'd been forbidden to help, and he raced to destroy those aboard the flotilla before her return.

He could not touch the Ark, but that didn't matter. Time would serve as his faithful ally in that war. A push here, a nudge here, and, over thousands of years, bloodlines would corrupt, patriarchs would fall, and nations would be led astray. The Ark bore promised hope for mankind. The flotilla carried something far more important to the Black Dragon; the seed of his doom.

"No, my love, they *are* out of time." He knelt on one knee and placed his palm flat against the rock. "From the shadows beneath Creation, my kingdom rises. This world is mine."

The Black Dragon stood and strolled away, body melting into the sea spray.

A shock waved ripped outward from the heart of the land bridge where his palm rested only a few moments earlier. The center collapsed inward. Millions of tons of rock tumbled into the Black Sea, chased by an enormous waterfall. The waterfall rapidly widened, eating away at the brittle granite on either side, until the waterfall stretched several miles from end to end. The warm, salty sea invaded the cold, fresh water. A gush of mist lifted high, feeding the storms above.

The Black Dragon rose into the storms, his rage energizing the tempest. Lightning danced across midnight wings, which whipped the heavens into a maelstrom with but one purpose.

The Lo must perish.

43. Kirabol

"Love is creation. In the young, love is born from innocence. As we grow, it is born from sacrifice. In the old, it is born from pain." – Sana, Isp of the Lo.

The Chronicle of Fu Xi

***

Alone where no one could see her, Sana indulged in a guilty moment of girlish delight. Eyes closed, she waited for the dawn next to what remained of the storm wall. Tonight, the rain felt comforting. Water reminded her of Ghalen, and she wanted to share his love for it the way she once loved the wind and the open grasslands.

Sana held up her hands toward the lightning as if to embrace it, and laughed.

"You are foolish, girl," a voice like grating bone cackled from behind. Sana turned and found Kirabol glaring at her, each lightning flash revealing a face of stone.

Her euphoria ebbed away, leaving ill will toward the hag. Kirabol reminded her too much of the old Scythian witches who despised her for being the great Setenay's granddaughter.

"Leave me in peace."

She stepped around Sana, tugging at the tattered fox fur shawl wrapped around her bony shoulders. She approached the storm wall until water sloshed around her feet.

"What does a Scythian know of peace?" Kirabol cackled. "But what does a girl know of peace, either? The young know only restlessness."

"I don't want to spend my last night as a girl, suffering a tongue lashing from a bitter old woman. I'm leaving; you and the storm can torment one other." Sana turned to slip back below the canopies.

"I tried to hate you from the moment you came aboard," Kirabol called after her.

Sana turned around. The old woman tugged a stick off the storm wall. "Perhaps more than anyone, I understand what's happening to this flotilla. The Uros calls it an arun-ki, but he is wrong. Aizarg and Atamoda see this flotilla as they want to see it."

"And how do you see it?"

"Exile."

"From what?"

"From the sun, and all else that is good. I've lived my whole life in an exile. There are many things I do not understand, but I understand exile. Perhaps we've even crossed into the underworld and do not yet realize it. The Nameless God has banished us to a watery wilderness until we are ready."

Kirabol clenched the thick limb and easily snapped it. "The flotilla is rotting beneath our feet. The people grumble about their bellies, but we will sink before we starve. Okta knows this, as does Aizarg. Your time is running out."

No longer comforting, the rain now chilled Sana.

"You're a hateful woman. If you're trying to frighten me, it won't work."

"No. I could never hope to frighten the granddaughter of the great King Sosa. Did you know I met your grandfather once?"

Kirabol's eyes narrowed and foreboding wrapped its black arms around Sana's once joyous heart. She wished she had kept walking.

"I was there that day, when Sosa took your grandmother. There are songs about it among your people, yes? Romantic ones, I'm sure. Do any of them mention me?"

Sana shook her head.

"Not surprising."

Kirabol's eyes glazed over as she stared north, as if she could see a distant shore. "The creeks ran deep and cold from the north that summer. It was hot, as hot as I've ever remembered before or since.

"My first blood had just come, and I was frightened. My mother had recently died and my father fell into a deep mourning. Setenay's mother, our patesi-le, took ill with the same fever that had claimed my mother. Setenay had just entered her fourteenth summer and wanted to take care of me."

She smiled in a way Sana didn't think possible for such a twisted face. "She always took care of me; my mother, my sister, and best friend all in one."

Sana tried to erase the hard lines on Kirabol's face, to transform it around that warm smile and imagine her as a young girl on the precipice of womanhood.

"I didn't mind the blood as long as Setenay was with me. We went into the marshes looking for moss, talking about boys.

"Boys!" The hag actually giggled and covered her mouth. Sana no longer strained to imagine the young girl. She revealed herself like a ray of sunshine.

"We ended up swimming in a sandy bottomed creek around the bend from the arun-ki. The reeds were so thick and lush around us we felt safe, like a cage. I always felt safe around her. And I remember how cold the water felt on my naked skin! The Lo say water on your skin is the next best thing to a lover's touch. When you're young, cold can feel good, because you always know the sun is waiting for you."

The girl vanished and old Kirabol returned, her gaze falling squarely on Sana. "The sun wasn't waiting for us that day. Setenay told me later that they'd been watching us for a while, though we didn't know it at the time.

"Do the songs speak of how they fought over her? Do the chants celebrate how Sosa gutted one of his own men to claim Setenay as his own?"

"No." Sana wanted to put her hands over her ears, to flee before Kirabol uttered another word.

"I think Sosa took Setenay because she fought back to protect me. She was so beautiful, so brave.

"He laughed as he stepped into the reeds, Setenay's unconscious body slung over his shoulder like a freshly slain doe. He left me to his men. I don't think they mentioned that in the songs, either."

"My people can be wolves," Sana whispered, regretting the words immediately.

"Ha!" Kirabol howled.

Sana flinched and found Kirabol suddenly in her face.

"Wolves eat what they bite. I am not dead, but let me show you where their knives gnawed on me."

She lifted her doeskin dress, revealing a nightmare recorded in scars.

Sana turned away and squeezed her eyes shut, unable to unsee the horror.

"Your people have a word for what they did to me, though I've never heard it from a Scythian's lips."

"The Eviscare," Sana whispered.

Kirabol stood holding her dress up, rain pelting her nakedness, speaking to Sana as if showing her a mole or boil. "Setenay told me it means 'The Hollowing.' They do it to render women of the conquered barren and unable to nurse;

horrid to look upon and unfit for a man's love. Though I think they did it to vent their anger. They didn't even rape me before they carved me up.

"My people exiled me to an abandoned hut downstream. Setenay's mother cared for me at first, though she died of grief before Setenay returned."

She dropped the hem.

"After she died, they left fish on my stoop like I was an animal. No one came to see if I were alive or dead until Setenay herself returned almost two years later."

"I am sorry...so sorry for what my people did to you."

Kirabol's eyes brimmed, and her stone face softened into a raw wound. "Pity doesn't suit you, Scythian."

Kirabol sat down on the storm wall. It crackled and popped under her meager weight.

"My life has been spent hating. I hated the Scythians for what they did. I hated my people for ostracizing me. And I hated Setenay."

Sana knelt down in front of Kirabol, water sloshing around her knees. "Why did you hate her?"

"Because she came back stronger, even more beautiful than when Sosa took her. Fate made her something powerful and wild, while it broke me."

Kirabol sighed. "Later, I hated her because she always left my hut. It reminded me no one else would visit until I saw her again. Every time she left, she took the sun with her." She looked up to the blackness, rain pelting her face. "Now she's gone, this time for good. Maybe the sun is gone forever, too."

Kirabol caressed Sana's cheek. "When you stepped onto the flotilla, I foolishly thought that the Narim had transformed Setenay back into a girl, and that perhaps they could do the same for me. I tried to hate you, but I couldn't. The worst part of spending a lifetime hating, is eventually you only hate yourself."

"Let me take care of you! When we find land, Ghalen and I will take you into the Turtle Clan."

Kirabol beamed and patted Sana's cheek. "So ready to dole out mercy, aren't you? My, how you have picked up our ways!"

Kirabol slapped her.

Sana bolted upright, rubbing her cheek.

"Stop this foolishness!" Kirabol commanded. "As Setenay was not truly Scythian, you are not truly Lo. She adopted their ways only to survive. Do not adopt those Lo customs which will get you killed."

She glared at Sana, all softness vanished. "I overheard Atamoda say you threw your daggers into the sea."

"I am now Lo," Sana said defiantly. "I will be a patesi-le, an Isp."

"Did you not hear anything I just said? Tossing away your daggers was stupid, the act of an emotional child."

"That was my choice, and none of your business."

"Is living your business? Do not let my people fool you. The Lo can be as vicious and cruel as any. Take it from one who has suffered a lifetime under their torments. Aizarg doesn't need a Lo girl spouting mercy; he needs a woman with an edge as hard and sharp as a Scythian blade." She poked Sana's belly. "He needs Setenay's granddaughter!"

Kirabol removed her shawl and unrolled something from a bulge in its middle.

"When you've spent as many years alone as I have, you think. I've prayed to the gods not to think so much. I've often wondered why some lead a life full of blessings and others are cursed through no fault of their own. Sometimes these thoughts make me angry, but I think them anyway. And sometimes I wonder why the gods give fools so many second chances."

She withdrew a rolled leather strap with four daggers protruding from the ends.

Sana inhaled.

"These were your grandmother's. She gave them to me the night before she departed for the Council of Boats. She never said it, but Setenay knew she wouldn't return. I asked what she wanted me to do with them. She said I would know."

Kirabol held them out and removed the Black Blades first, each with a slender, unadorned hilt. "You know their names, their purpose is well known."

Then she pulled forth two Silver Blades, their thin shafts and bone handles indicative of Scythian craftsmanship. "Setenay called these..."

"*Hope* and *Mercy*," Sana gasped. "Setenay was a Scythian queen. She carried a fifth blade. Tell me you have it!"

Kirabol grinned and withdrew a cloth-wrapped dagger from somewhere in her dress, and held it up. She slowly revealed a weapon unlike the others.

"Here." She handed the large dagger to Sana hilt first. "If you know of it, then you know it has tasted blood."

"Scythian blood." Sana took the unexpectedly light weapon. "It's called *Sacrifice*." She turned it over, studying the holy blade; a weapon clearly not crafted by Scythian hands. A golden, serpent-like creature formed the hilt, which wrapped partway down the blade. The blood red metal blade, neither iron nor bronze, gleamed even in the darkness.

Kirabol returned the four other blades to the thong and rolled them up. She thrust the bundle at Sana. "They are rightfully yours. You will need them, perhaps sooner than you expect."

Sana took them.

"Of all the people in the Minnow Arun-ki, Kus-ge was the cruelest to me. Setenay wouldn't say her name if she didn't have to, preferring to call her the Snake. She tried desperately to prevent her marriage to Ba-lok." She snorted. "He's endured the Eviscare, though not in the way I did. I think Setenay still held hope for him. And don't forget, Scythian, Ba-lok is the only blood relative you still possess."

Sana wrapped the thong around her thigh, not even attempting to conceal the blades under her loin flap. For a brief moment, she worried the thong may be too long or too short, but it tied perfectly, as if tailored just for her.

Too large and ungainly for the thong, she briefly wondered how Setenay carried *Sacrifice*.

"Thank you," she said.

Kirabol cackled. "I give her a burden greater than she can imagine, and she thanks me!"

"These..." Sana held up the red blade. "...are sacred. You've honored me."

"If you say so. If you want to thank me, make me a promise."

"Anything."

"Don't go throwing them in the water."

Sana smiled.

"And be a good Isp. Protect Aizarg. Protect the children. Don't let Kus-ge hurt them."

"I will, I promise."

Kirabol's shoulders sagged, and her head dipped, as if an enormous burden had been lifted.

Sana whirled about and took a few steps toward the canopy and the dim brazier light. "I want to see it in the light to see if it glows like fire as the legends say!"

"Dawn is coming, and your wedding," Kirabol's depleted voice whispered behind her. "Perhaps the rain will end today."

Lighting flashed, and the dagger answered with a ruddy glow.

"I hope the children see the sun again." Kirabol sounded weaker.

Sana briefly thought she should get the old woman out of the rain, but the blade captured her attention. "There is something familiar about the knife," Sana called over her shoulder. "Something I've seen before."

The glowing blade teased her, its truth hovering only a few inches from Sana's grasp.

"It's cold. So cold," Kirabol croaked. Sticks on the storm wall snapped as Kirabol stood up. "I don't think the sun will be waiting for me this time."

Sana held it closer to the firelight, but needed more light. "Come, Kirabol..." She turned, but the Minnow woman had vanished.

Sana rushed to the storm wall in time to see a fox shawl slip beneath the waves.

44. The Wedding Barge

A chorus of cheers greeted the newlyweds as they emerged from the tent at dawn, their marriage consummated. A flotilla of boats and rafts laden with food, ropes, and heavy stones surrounded the wedding barge. Over the course of several days the clan prepared the wedding barge for the newlyweds' journey.

First, they converted its heavy beams into the couple's hut. The stones were used to sink and set the hut and dock pylons, the rest of the deck beams formed the floor and support posts. Family and friends brought more wood to finish the dock and ladder, as well as reeds for the walls and roof.

The wedding barge would always be with them, supporting them as they began a new family. They need only look under their feet or touch the walls to know they would forever be surrounded by their people's love as they traveled together on the Longest Journey.

The Chronicle of Fu Xi

***

The sky still lingered gray as Atamoda supervised rearranging the Köy-lo-hely, reverting it to its original purpose. Today, it became a wedding barge once again. Aizarg's stool now rested on the Supply Barge, and that is where she hoped it would stay. Atamoda wanted the canopies raised as high as possible to give the feeling of open air, but it only resulted in rips opening in the rotted portions and more rain leaking through. The patesi-le relented and instructed Okta and Ezra to restore the original pitch, which gave the barge a claustrophobic feel, but kept everyone dry.

Sana leaned against the mast with arms crossed, carefully watching the preparations. Atamoda eyed the four new daggers tied around Sana's thigh. The mysterious red blade, larger than the rest, was secured tightly against Sana's other thigh with a deerskin scrap. Another scrap, tightly bound, concealed the hilt. Sana would only say that they were once Setenay's, but promised to tell Atamoda about her encounter with Kirabol after the wedding.

Okta stood beside her, arms crossed and tapping his foot impatiently. "There are only so many times we can rearrange an empty deck, patesi-le. It's almost sunset."

"It's not ready. Something is wrong, but I can't put my finger on it," Atamoda replied.

Kus-ge strolled about, arms crossed, examining the deck. "I don't think anything is missing. I think something is added." She pointed to the Spine.

"That's it!" Atamoda snapped her fingers.

Kus-ge smiled warmly. "And I have another observation, patesi-le. We should disperse the wedding party evenly across the barge, irrespective of clan."

She stepped over the Spine to the Crane side and embraced Atamoda. "We've been divided for too long. Let this joyous event unite us."

Atamoda didn't know how to handle this new Kus-ge, the one who came to her in tears, apologizing for how she'd acted and begging for forgiveness. They talked on the Supply Barge until dawn. Kus-ge opened up to her about her own grief, the trials of being married to a man she didn't love, and her fears about their survival.

Atamoda desperately wanted to believe Kus-ge's intentions were genuine, but still harbored doubts. Those doubts were severely tested when Kus-ge showed up on Levidi's raft with E'laa and Toma in hand.

She put their little hands in Alaya's and departed without another word.

Kus-ge's change of heart wasn't as good as seeing the sun again, or the children's bellies full, but it lifted the spirits of both clans nevertheless.

"Well then," Atamoda exhaled with finality. "I suppose we're ready." She turned to Kus-ge. "Are you sure Ba-lok is comfortable proceeding with the wedding in the wake of Kirabol's death?"

"Setenay cared for and loved Kirabol. I think both of them would want Setenay's granddaughter to proceed with the wedding. We've all suffered so much; it's time to make room for a little joy."

Atamoda rubbed her neck and nodded. "As you wish."

Sana snorted an icy laugh.

There will never be reconciliation between those two. That thought both gave Atamoda chills and left her frustrated. The hope of landfall, and if it were truly the Nameless God's will, a promised land, sustained her people. Two patesi-le, two clans, at odds could destroy everything.

Atamoda took Sana's arm. "Come. The wedding is almost upon us, time to prepare the bride."

Kus-ge approached Sana, eyeing the blades around her thighs. "Let us not feud, sister. Forgiveness is Mercy's silent sister, let us begin a new life without open wounds."

Sana's eyes narrowed as she turned away.

***

"I want to move everyone from my raft to the Supply Barge a day early," Levidi whispered into Atamoda's ears as they waited for the wedding ceremony to begin. "Do you and Aizarg mind the company?"

Atamoda shrugged. "Of course not, but why?"

Levidi grinned and nodded to Ghalen and Sana, who stood nervously side by side near the front of the Wedding Barge.

"Ah!" Atamoda laughed. "That is very kind of you. Yes, some privacy tonight might be nice."

"Look at him. He's terrified. I've never seen Ghalen afraid, even when the wave struck."

Ghalen and Sana held hands and stared at one another as the crowd gathered. Ghalen looked pale, but Atamoda saw unmistakable tenderness in his eyes.

"If he passes out, I'll never let him live it down."

Alaya mockingly punched Levidi in the arm. "If he passes out, it's because you've teased him unmercifully."

"I didn't tease him too badly."

Alaya looked drawn and tired, but having E'laa and Toma, along with the wedding, clearly buoyed her spirits. Atamoda glanced at how well Alaya's dress fitted.

She hasn't lost as much weight as most of the women.

"Everyone else will move to the center rafts tomorrow night," Levidi continued. "I'll give Ghalen a day with his new bride before I drag him out of my boat and put him to work."

"Shhh." Atamoda held a finger to her lips. "Talk of work can wait. Let's enjoy the wedding."

A sense of peace and acceptance filled Atamoda's soul, and she didn't want anything to spoil it. They were alive and well enough to celebrate. That would have to be enough.

Even the rain seemed to cooperate. The downpour slackened to its lightest since the beginning of the Deluge. Aizarg said it was a good omen. Atamoda agreed.

Okta fretted about the deck like an old woman, shuffling people from the edges toward the raft's center, contrary to the customary wedding party arrangement. Proper etiquette placed the couple and the patesi-le at one end, and the people at the other.

"We're riding lower, the raft will be better balanced," he had told Atamoda.

This ceremony lacks so many proper customs, one more change won't matter.

As the presiding patesi-le, Atamoda had made many concessions regarding the wedding. Sana would have no beautiful wedding dress adorned with colorful shells and wildflower garlands. There would be no feast, or hut-raising tomorrow at dawn. After the wedding, there would be a night of bliss and then only survival awaiting the newlyweds.

It will have to be enough.

There were some areas, however, where Atamoda would not compromise.

Warmth, almost to the point of being uncomfortable, filled the spaces below the canopy. Atamoda demanded all the braziers be moved to the Wedding Barge for the ceremony, but Aizarg balked. Since the driftwood had vanished from the sea, the Lo had begun to burn the rotted hulls, and even those were beginning to run out.

"I want *light!*" she begged. "Please, for one night let us drive back the darkness and rejoice."

Aizarg relented, and now the Wedding Barge blazed in the smoky glory of seven braziers. She knew they would have to hurry, as Aizarg only allowed enough reed bundles to complete the ceremony.

It isn't home, but it will do.

Aizarg caught Atamoda's eye. The time had come.

She took her place next to Xva, who hadn't emerged from his boat in the days since Sahti's death. Atamoda arranged for someone to always be with Xva, day and night, fearful he would throw himself into the sea out of grief.

Atamoda locked arms with him and rested her head on his shoulder. "You don't have to be here, but I'm glad you are," she whispered.

Xva looked down on her and managed a bittersweet smile. "I am Aizarg's surrogate and Sahti loved weddings."

Atamoda hugged his neck and pecked his cheek. "We love you."

Aizarg clapped Xva's back and stepped into the open area to address the people.

Okta took his place as Ghalen's surrogate father. Kus-ge took her place next to Sana as her patesi-le. If Kus-ge's role in the ceremony bothered her, Sana didn't show it.

Ba-lok and Xva stood at the head of the raft, representing their Clans, while Atamoda would preside over the ceremony. Oddly, no official role existed for the Uros, as no one could remember a time when a wedding transpired in time of war. Aizarg thought it best they shouldn't invent any new traditions. He would only say a few words before Atamoda officiated what should be a short ceremony.

Excited murmurs drifted through the crowd as Aizarg took his place before Ghalen and Sana. He kissed her on the cheek and hugged Ghalen around the neck.

Atamoda raised her hands and, except for a crying child and shushing adult, the crowd fell silent.

Aizarg rubbed the red orb on the staff, brow furrowed in thought as the rain drizzled on. As he often did before speaking, he paced in front of his people, everyone waiting for the Uros's pronouncement.

In the bright light Atamoda finally got a good look at the Lo. Haggard and pale, their clothes sagged over gaunt frames. They were starving, but hope still flickered in their eyes. They still love Aizarg. They want to follow him.

They want to believe.

Aizarg cleared his throat. "Let us not say a prayer for tomorrow, it will only carry our fears to heaven. Those prayers are always answered with worry. Let us say a prayer for today, for those are lifted on wings of gratitude and will always be met with hope." He stared as his hands. "My daughter said that. I thought it appropriate for today's occasion."

He paused and, for a moment, looked back at Atamoda. "Few of you met her, but by now most of you all know her story. Sarah's spirit dwells among us in her brother, but it also lives in all who walked the g'an with me. It dwells in all the Lo, because she was one of us." He turned to Sana. "She never gave up, and she never lost hope, even in the darkest moments.

"Her last moments were spent in joy." He paused and raised a finger. "Let that be a lesson to us. Do not let joy die in your hearts. Keep it like a seed; nourish it beneath the cold soil of our suffering until the sun kisses it again.

"We've endured so much pain, lost so many loved ones. Yet, in this moment we defy death. We defy pain. We defy the sea, and rain, and this damnable hunger gnawing at our bellies!"

He stood before the betrothed and rested his hands on the staff. "Through this wedding, we find new hope and lift up our gratitude on wings of joy."

Aizarg returned to his place beside Ba-lok and Xva, but not before turning once more to his people. "The Nameless God decreed the sun will return. Whether joy returns, that is our choice."

His last words reverberated more like warning than inspiration.

He nodded to Atamoda.

She looked at the braziers. A few had begun to wane. Atamoda took a deep breath and began to step forward, but Xva pulled her back, his smile kindled with genuine warmth.

"I will find my joy again, Atamoda. One day. Thank you for all you did for Sahti...and for me."

She felt another burden lift from her spirit as she slipped from Xva's arm and took her place before Sana and Ghalen.

Words. I only have to speak words, and they are married.

She had no sacrificial fish to burn, and they're would be no prayers to Psatina. The brazier light would have to be enough.

Two of the seven were reduced to flickers.

424

What can I say that Aizarg has not already said?

A sudden impulse to hurry seized her, to pronounce them husband and wife and be done with it. Ultimately, the formation of a new family merely rested with her pronouncement. In the realm of the heart, the patesi-le ruled supreme.

Atamoda knew the marriage chant by heart, yet now felt the words were somehow insufficient.

Sana's eyes were closed, mouth moving in some mysterious silent prayer.

"Please, Atamoda," Ghalen pleaded. "I'd be joyful if we got this over with."

Okta smiled warmly. "You better hurry," he whispered. "Before the poor boy loses his nerve."

Atamoda opened her mouth to begin the wedding chant when she caught Kus-ge staring at her.

Her blood froze. The wicked grin she'd come to associate with Kus-ge had returned, her mask of kindness evaporated. Behind that grin Atamoda saw cool savagery.

"Uros!" A voice called from the crowd. "Uros, I demand to be heard!"

The crowd parted to reveal Ro-xandra.

"What is the meaning of this?" Atamoda challenged.

"My words are for the Uros, not you, patesi-le." Ro-xandra entered the inner circle.

"Ro-xandra!" Kus-ge shouted. "Whatever you want to say it can wait until after the wedding."

"As I said, my words are for the Uros. I demand to be heard."

All the good feelings in Atamoda's heart dissipated.

Aizarg stepped around Ghalen and Sana, who joined the others in staring incredulously at Ro-xandra. He pointed the staff at her as if a weapon, his voice full of menace."

"Ro-xandra, whatever you have to say will wait until this ceremony is over."

"A hidden wound festers among us. It threatens all of us, and will bring a curse to this union if not brought into the open."

"It will wait!" Aizarg commanded.

Ro-xandra's eyes darted from Uros to Kus-ge.

"Listen to the Uros," Kus-ge's voice fell flat. "It will wait."

All eyes rested on Ro-xandra as she hesitated, shrinking back into the crowd, courage suddenly gone.

Atamoda didn't look at Ro-xandra, instead focusing on Kus-ge, who glared at Ba-lok. Husband and wife locked eyes in a battle of wills until he surrendered and lowered his head.

"I demand Ro-xandra be heard," Ba-lok said stiffly, spitting out the words as if they tasted like poison. "A marriage cannot be joined under threat of curse."

Atamoda's heart raced as a brazier died in a puff of smoke.

The rain began to pour harder.

"Uros," Ghalen spoke in a low, grumbling tone, not even attempting to mask his contempt. "Whatever games the Minnow want to play, play them after my wedding."

Ro-xandra stood tall, her sco-lo-ti's authority giving her freedom to speak. "One among us has stolen food."

The crowd fell silent under Ro-xandra's revelation.

Another brazier ebbed into smoky death.

"Well," Kus-ge smirked. "That changes things."

"Aizarg, put a stop to this." Atamoda shouted and pointed accusingly at Kus-ge. "This stinks of Minnow lies!"

Kus-ge folded her arms. "Lies? Why do you accuse us of lies, Atamoda? We have nothing to do with this."

"Let Ro-xandra speak!" someone shouted.

"I will speak to Ro-xandra in private," Aizarg took her by the arm and began to pull her away.

"Who stole food?" shouted another voice from the back.

"Yes! Tell us." The call began with the Minnow, but spread to the Crane, all united in their hunger.

Another brazier died. And then another. Ro-xandra did not wait to be led away. With a sharp peel of unexpected thunder, she pointed a bony finger at Kol-ok. "There is the thief who stole food from the Supply Barge."

45. Lightning and Fire, Part One

Clad in the Traitor's Armor, I stormed through the palace toward the foyer, only to find Quexil barring the doors.

"Lord Fu Xi, you are forbidden to leave..."

I back handed him, sending Quexil sprawling against Poseidon's statue, where he crumpled unconscious to the floor.

"The God of Names is not yours to command."

In the distance, the pounding hammers echoed the thunder from the approaching storm. Seeking truth, I followed their ring across the palace grounds toward the harbor.

I kept to the shadows, behind tall hedges and trees shielding the great Olmec houses from the city. The air turned sticky as the wind blew stronger from the sea. To my left, the city fell away toward the harbor lights as I crested the hill away from the city and beheld all which had been hidden from my sight.

Thousands of campfires, arranged in orderly rows, blanketed the hill. A grand army camped only a stroll from the palace, and I had no idea. The campfire banter of thousands of Olmec warriors, laughing and enjoying a meal, floated up the hill and burned my ears. The orderly rows led to the harbor's western shore, where a fleet of carracks anchored. Processions of torches snaked in neat lines toward piers and the black ships.

Leviathan's army prepared to sail.

My failure crushed down on me. No mortal kingdom could stand against this army. My beloved land would fall into slavery.

I darted from tree to tree along the hill top, circumventing the camp's pickets and made my way toward the quarry where in the lightning, I spotted a line of trees leading to the water's edge. Using the trees as cover, I would slip unnoticed for a closer look at the ships. But I didn't make it to the harbor, waylaid by the moans floating like ghosts from the quarry's bowels.

Amiran's scrolls describing the Empire's engineering feats did not adequately prepare me. Standing on its rim, thousands of dingy torches flickered across the scaffolding covering the quarry's sheer cliffs. The quarry formed a deep, box-like pit with a narrow opening to the sea. In its center, a giant wooden and iron tower rose almost equal to the rim. A dozen elephants, hitched with thick ropes to a forest of pulleys and gears, circled the tower. A massive crossbeam rested atop the tower and reached over the scaffolding.

Mesmerized, I watched as hundreds of men secured chains to enormous slabs freshly cut from living rock. Once secured, whips cracked and the elephants lumbered around the tower. The arm lifted the block and slowly swung it around to the opposite end of the quarry, where a long series of rollers led to the pier and a waiting ship.

Fat rain drops began to fall as I knelt down and examined some rock chips. They mined marble and granite, the building blocks of empires.

Shouts echoed up from the highest scaffold, perhaps only twenty feet below where I knelt on the rim. In the torchlight, three naked slaves cowered under an Olmec's whip.

"You know what happens to those who drop their chisels!" the taskmaster laughed. "You have to go get it." He picked up one of the slaves, perhaps only a child, and hurled him to his death far below.

I dropped to the platform, landing in a crouch. The taskmaster barely had time to register astonishment before I sliced him in half, his pieces tumbling to join the slave's body below.

An emaciated old woman and young boy, naked except for their iron collars and shackles, cowered before me.

"Mercy, Lord!" the old woman begged in my tongue. The boy merely crouched and hugged his knees.

The Red Blade severed their chains. The old woman gazed up at me, a spark of recognition flaring in her dull eyes.

Shouts rose from the pit as torches gathered below.

I knelt down and cradled her, fury rising with every scar my fingers discovered on her back. "Be at peace, dear mother. I will not hurt you."

A bulky bronze hammer and a rusty chisel lay next to her. How the old woman or the child managed to pick up either I cannot imagine.

She stroked my cheek. "Blessed be the Goddess and her beloved son, Lord Fu Xi. He has come to deliver us."

Blazing torches and angry shouts snaked their way up the gantries. I turned to the boy. "Do you understand me?" I said in Wu.

He nodded.

"Comfort her."

Water poured from the quarry rim above as I trod down the spiraling gantry toward the oncoming Olmecs. Two slaves, both young men, flattened themselves against the rock as I passed.

"Is there another way out of the quarry other than the pier?"

One pointed to the far wall, where I spied a narrow ramp leading out of the pit. I cut their chains.

"Pick up your hammers and chisels. Follow me. Free any prisoners you pass. Slay any guards who survive. When we reach that ramp, tear it down."

At first, they came with only whips and curses, thinking they would be dealing with rebellious slaves. Making short work of them, I stepped over their bodies as the ranks of the liberated swelled behind me.

Below, the elephants began to trumpet, whether in fear of me or the growing storm, I did not know. The tempest fueled my rage as the Red Sword sliced through iron and flesh again and again. With a thousand hammers, the slave army at my back assaulted the ramp leading to the surface. It came tumbling down not a moment too soon. Torches appeared along the cliff's rim, along with a hail of arrows.

"Hide under the scaffolding!" I commanded the slaves.

I pressed on alone, arrows bouncing harmlessly off the Red Armor. Olmecs swarmed me one level before I reached the quarry floor. Orichalcum clashed with steel, god pitted against men. The Red Sword, the Traitor's Sword, melted through their weapons as Leviathan's blade had once sliced through mine.

The rainwater pooling in the quarry bottom turned crimson. Arrows and rain pinged against my helmet as a horn sounded in the distance. The warriors retreated toward the pier, ceding me the quarry. The elephant handlers abandoned their beasts and fled. I stepped around the tower's base as the elephants strained against their harnesses.

A line of several hundred warriors blocked the narrow quarry entrance. Lances bristling behind a shield wall, they advanced forward into the pit. From somewhere behind them, a voice commanded they not wound the elephants.

Glancing up, I saw a marble block suspended high above on the tower's crane arm.

I snatched a whip from a dead guard and ran behind the tower. Cracking the whip, I drove the elephants toward the pier. The beasts reared and heaved against their harnesses, but the ropes and chains held. I sliced the nearest elephant's hind quarter. Trumpeting in pain, it hurtled toward the enemy formation. The harness chain snapped tight, and the elephant crumpled to the ground. The marble slab swung back and forth as the tower popped and groaned, but stood.

The warriors briefly hesitated, and then resumed their slow advance. With my enemy only yards from where the narrow entrance widened, I whipped the elephants with greater fury, but still, the tower held.

Then, with a deafening boom amplified by the quarry walls, a lightning bolt blasted the crane arm. The elephants stampeded and snapped the tower's four thick base timbers at once. The elephants dragged flailing chains and timbers through the armored line, as tons of wood and iron collapsed over man and beast. The marble block shattered squarely on top of the warriors.

I scrambled over the jumble of dead beasts, splintered timbers, and broken stone toward the pier. A forest of masts waited for me. The ships could not be allowed to reach my homeland.

A dozen sailors fell to my blade on the first ship before someone rang the alarm. By then, I'd already lit several fires. In retrospect, I believe Leviathan ordered the ships packed tightly in the western harbor to keep them from being seen from the palace. This, combined with the gale, enabled the fire to spread quickly from ship to ship. Sails, rigging, and tar-pitched planks exploded into flames so hot they defied the pelting rain. I jumped from deck to deck, slaying all who battled the fire. Like paper lanterns consumed by their own flame, burning men leapt into sea.

Sizzling heat caressed my skin, but could not rival my wrath. My sword and armor glowed, as if drinking in the hell storm I'd created. I buried pity. I buried mercy. In this moment, these mortals would shoulder the price of Leviathan's ambitions and deceit. In this moment, they would bear the cost of my failure and shame. In this moment, I become the Dragon, Cin's guardian and avenger.

Flames at my back, I perched on one caravel's prow and surveyed the long line of burning hulks. A shadow emerged from the firestorm. Under a single triangle sail, a lone ship drifted from the line, untouched by fire.

I leapt across the burning decks until I arrived just in time to see the escaping vessel's stern drift by. Terrified sailors pointed and screamed, warning their captain that a demon hunted them. I snatched a flaming rope, swung out over the water, and dropped onto the stern.

Shrieking sailors scattered before me until I faced one who did not flee. Whip in hand, the steely eyed Olmec captain bravely stood his ground.

"I don't know what hell spit you out, but this is my ship. You'll have to kill me before you burn it."

I glanced over the captain's shoulder at the city side of the harbor and its great pier directly ahead.

"As you wish."

The crew leapt into the harbor to join their dead captain. With oil lanterns, I transformed the ship into a torch moments before it reached the great pier.

Lightning and fire danced from one end of the harbor to the next as I staggered from the water. To my right, Leviathan's fleet blazed like

432

islands of fire. To my left, a conflagration raced throughout the city and climbed the hill, already halfway to the palace.

Thoughts of Amiran's safety suddenly cooled my wrath. I turned, and faced a wall of torches. Olmec warriors in full battle armor stretched across the hill in ranks hundreds deep.

A god stood against an army.

If I fought my way through, the palace would burn before I could reach Amiran. But every Olmec I slew was one who could not set foot on my beloved soil. This night had already purchased time for my homeland, but if I destroyed Leviathan's army, I could buy enough to build such an army in Cin.

A warrior stepped from the ranks and called to me.

"I knew you were trouble from the beginning," Quexil shouted. The only god we fear is our master, Paqua. How I relish the thought of killing you!"

Fire blazed across the villas just below the grand palace.

"I am Fu Xi, Son of the Goddess Nuwa, Queen of the West!" I shouted so all could hear. "In me dwells the divine spirit of the Emperor of Heaven. I am the God of Names, but tonight you will call me Death."

I sensed doubt and fear creeping through their ranks

Quexil raised his sword and tried to gird his warriors' courage. "Not even a god can fight an army. Prepare to charge!"

I pointed my sword at Quexil. "I will slay every man on this field except you, Quexil. You shall escape unharmed."

Quexil's arm wavered.

"Leviathan trusted you to mind me in his absence. Weren't you supposed to keep me pacified and under control until his return?"

I grinned and pointed my sword left. "I've burned his invasion fleet and demolished his prized quarry." I pointed right. "And laid waste to his city. Now you, his trusted dog, graciously offer up his army so I can destroy that, too. I will be sure to leave you alive so you can greet your beloved master when he returns, and bask in his gratitude."

Quexil grew pale.

Again, I pointed my sword at him. "Or you can let me pass."

Conflict raged in the Olmec for what seemed an eternity as flames licked the palace grounds.

"Bah!" He screamed. "Let the god through!"
I strode through the open ranks.
"The Traitor's Armor suits you, Fu Xi," Quexil called after me.
"He will find you, but not before Cin suffers a thousand fold. Their blood shall be payment for your betrayal."

46. Lightning and Fire, Part Two

"Evil calculates what is probable, while goodness dreams of what is possible." – Conversations with the Uros

Chronicle of Fu Xi

***

"Lying bitch!" Atamoda lunged at Kus-ge, but Sana held her back.

"She laid a trap," Sana whispered urgently. "Do not fall into it."

"Ro-xandra is your son's accuser, not I," Kus-ge countered coolly. "Tell us, woman, what proof you have against the son of the Uros."

"Father, I..." Kol-ok entered the circle.

"My son is no thief! Ro-xandra lies. This is Kus-ge's deceit."

"Quiet!" Aizarg shouted. "Son, approach. Did you steal food? Yes or no."

"I did not."

"Ro-xandra, what proof do you have?"

"I saw him with my own eyes, several nights ago."

"Are there any other witnesses?"

"No," Ro-xandra turned up her nose. "I was alone, everyone else slept deeply after battling the storm."

"What were you doing on the Supply Barge late at night?" Atamoda said.

"I heard voices, perhaps in distress. I followed them. I saw Kol-ok rummaging through the fish."

"I slept on the barge, yet I heard nothing," Atamoda glared at Ro-xandra.

"We should search his mat," Ba-lok said.

His words are rehearsed.

Okta stepped toward the Supply Barge. "I will search his mat, with the Uros's permission of course."

Aizarg nodded.

"And I'm sure I'll find nothing!" he sneered at Ro-xandra.

It didn't take long for Okta to return, empty handed. "As I suspected, only his belongings. Aizarg, let's stop this foolishness and get on with the wedding."

A chorus of cheers answered him.

"Yes, of course. I knew he was innocent the whole time," Kus-ge said and turned her attention to Ro-xandra. "We will discuss this after the wedding."

Ro-xandra shrank back, and Atamoda's heart began to slow again.

"Oh," Kus-ge said, as if just remembering something. "One more thing, Ro-xandra; you said you heard voices. Was Kol-ok alone?"

Atamoda looked at her son, who had turned pale as ice.

"I think I might have seen someone with him," Ro-xandra let the words come out slowly, as if twisting a knife.

"Tell us, Kol-ok; were you alone by the fish pile?" Kus-ge asked too innocently, too smoothly.

Kol-ok turned to his father. "Ro-xandra speaks truthfully. I stole the food."

"No!" Atamoda screamed.

"Kol-ok," Aizarg held him close. "Why did you say that?"

Kol-ok didn't answer, looking apprehensively over his shoulder at the crowd, as if looking for someone.

Alaya fainted.

Sana pointed to Su-gar. "Take her and the children to Levidi's raft."

"He confessed!" Virag pushed his way to the front, wagging his finger. "He should share the same punishment as Alad."

"The same punishment as Alad!" several of the Minnow shouted.

The cry of "Exile!" rippled across the Minnow.

"There will be no judgment until I decree it!" Aizarg shouted.

"Is the son of the Uros above the law?" Virag cried out again.

The clans began to separate, stepping over the Spine to their respective sides. Kus-ge and Ba-lok joined their people, flanked by Virag and Ro-xandra.

"He confessed," Ba-lok said.

"He didn't steal!" Atamoda teetered on hysteria.

"As I said, there will be no judgment until I decree it!" Aizarg shouted again, but Atamoda sensed his control slipping.

Kus-ge further stoked the fires. "Ba-lok surrendered Alad immediately. If I remember, that judgment came swiftly. Is there one set of laws for Crane and another for Minnow?"

"My child starves, and the son of the Uros steals?" A Minnow woman raised her fist.

"Atamoda has always given more rations to the Crane than the Minnow!" another cried.

Okta slapped Ghalen on the back and whispered something. They grabbed Levidi's arm, and all three vanished from the barge.

Virag smugly tucked his thumbs into the rope securing the tunic around his waist. "Perhaps we cannot trust the Uros to deal fairly in these matters. The Second has already demonstrated his impartiality. Alad met justice. Alad is dead."

Virag turned to the crowd and raised his arms. "Perhaps it is time for a new Uros!"

The Minnow cheered, and to Atamoda's horror, sticks and clubs began to circulate behind Ba-lok and Kus-ge.

Sana stepped between where Aizarg stood with his son and the restless Minnow.

"Stop this!" Aizarg raised his staff. "We are one people. Justice will be served, but only after all the facts are heard."

But the Minnow weren't listening, and the Crane were unarmed. Aizarg and the Crane slowly began to back away.

"Take the flotilla!" Virag shouted. "Take the food!"

Brandishing fishing spears, Okta and the men reappeared and stood side by side with Sana.

Behind them, Spako loomed, log in hand.

"We will not let you take Kol-ok or the food. Aizarg is Uros. You pledged your spears," Okta shouted.

"Treachery," Ghalen extended his spear toward the Minnow.

"I see. It is all clear now," Kus-ge hissed. "Conspiracies, alliances...this wedding was nothing more than a plot to neutralize the Minnow and take our food." She reached between her legs and withdrew a black dagger.

Sana drew *Vengeance*.

Aizarg pushed his way between the clans. "Enough!" He lowered Ghalen's spear tip. "This is madness. Lower your weapons and let sanity prevail."

"Liar!" Virag brandished a club.

"No!" shouted another voice, a man's voice. She turned to see Kol-ok step into the center beside his father, dragging the boat he and Aizarg had crafted together.

"I am guilty. I accept exile."

Atamoda pushed Sana and Okta aside and embraced her son. "Tell them you didn't do it! You're not a thief."

Kol-ok gently pushed aside her hands, Aizarg's determination in his eyes.

"No. Mother, you must let me go."

She turned to Aizarg. "Husband?"

Aizarg lowered his head.

"Aizarg?"

Gently but firmly, Sana came between Atamoda and Kol-ok. "Atamoda," she whispered where none could hear. "You son is saving his people. You must put aside the mother and become patesi-le."

"I cannot," she sobbed.

"You must."

Sana's heart ached for Atamoda and the Lo as she witnessed them changing, becoming like those she left behind. Yet, Kol-ok's sacrifice gave her hope. One day, Atamoda would rejoice in her son's courage, but that day lingered far away.

Atamoda sagged to the deck, sobbing into her hands. Sana knelt over her, glancing back at the Minnow.

Clubs and spears began to lower, as disappointment painted Kus-ge and Virag's faces.

I should have killed her.

"Ghalen." Sana tried to get her betrothed's attention. She would be strong for Atamoda, but he needed to be strong for Aizarg.

Ghalen nodded and then lowered his weapon. "The Uros has spoken. Justice is served. Everyone put down your weapons, go back to your rafts while we do what is necessary to prepare for Kol-ok's exile."

Ghalen snatched Ba-lok by the tunic and slammed him against the mast. "I'm watching you and that snake you call a wife."

"Get your hands off...!"

Ghalen lifted him off the deck, shoving him hard into the mast again. "You are now my enemy."

Ghalen threw him to the deck. Ba-lok slunk away, rubbing his shoulder.

"Okta, look over Kol-ok's vessel, make sure he has what he needs." Ghalen turned to Sana. "We will stay with Aizarg and Atamoda."

Kol-ok faced his father, but Aizarg would not look at him. The Uros leaned heavily on his staff, looking suddenly old. For a while, they said nothing while Okta and Ezra solemnly prepared the boat.

Okta stood close to Kol-ok and whispered, but Sana heard every word. "There are six fish cakes in there, Ezra and I donated our rations in addition to the three allocated. A sail and a paddle are hidden under the blanket. I've placed a net in the boat, too. Cast whenever you can. Once you are out of sight, catch the full wind and let it carry you. If you can see the stars, then sail south, Kol-ok. Always south."

Kol-ok nodded. "Thank you."

Ezra held out his metal knife. "I always liked your flint knife. Want to trade?"

Kol-ok swapped knives. "Thanks, Ezra."

"If you don't like it, we'll swap back when I see you again."

Okta and Ezra stepped away, leaving Kol-ok with his mother and father.

"Ba-tor..." Kol-ok choked. "He won't understand. Just tell him I went looking for the fish."

Aizarg nodded. Sana feared this could break the Uros. If he broke, they would all break. Sana grew up among warriors desperate to prove their bravery. She'd witnessed great feats of courage the way others watch the sun rise and set. Scythian bravery was born in blood, but she'd never witnessed courage such as this.

Silent tears rolled down Sana's cheeks as she leaned over and brushed Atamoda's hair and kissed her head. Words came out of her mouth, though they seemed like someone else's. "Go to him. Give him love and strength, the way you once suckled him to your breast. Gird him. When your grief ebbs, and the desolation that rends your heart is no more, remember this: The greatest courage is that born in love, and the greatest love is that which lays down its life for another."

Atmoda rose and approached her firstborn.

"Why?"

"Because I must."

"But..."

"I need you to accept this. Trust me, Mother. Please, I beg you."

Heart breaking, Sana watched Atamoda embrace her son for the last time. Atamoda sniffled and wrapped her arms around his neck.

"When did you get taller than me?" she laughed through her tears. "I don't understand, but I will trust. I will serve. I will wait until we see one another again. And I will always love you."

The canopy fluttered as warm, moist wind swept unexpectedly over the arun-ki. The decks groaned and popped, and the Spine went limp.

"The wind and tide have shifted!" Okta raced for the flotilla's edge.

Confused, Sana looked at Ghalen. His worried expression told her everything.

"I'll be right back," she told Atamoda and followed Ghalen after Okta. The decks began to buck before they even reached Okta's raft, where Okta and Ghalen peered south.

Warm rainwater pelted them as the horizon pulsated with lightning. Thunder began to boom like war drums.

In the thunder Sana though she heard something else, though her mind told her it could not be.

Upon the gale, a beast roared.

"Uros!" Okta shouted as he leapt onto the Wedding Barge, followed by Ghalen and Sana. "A storm bears down from the south, and I don't like the looks of it. The wind, the current, everything has changed. We don't have much time."

"Everyone to the center barges," Aizarg commanded.

Atamoda leapt to her feet, grief pushed aside as lightning began to strobe around them. "Sana, help me move the children to the Supply Barge."

"We must complete the exile!" Kus-ge screamed.

"One more word out of you and I will place *you* in exile," Aizarg said. "Get the Minnow to the barges, now!"

The rafts began to bump and bang into one another as the flotilla lurched sideways, slowly rotating about its axis to face the wind and current.

The Lo streamed onto the Supply and Wedding Barges, as Okta arranged them to best balance the rafts.

The decks started bucking and pitching as Ghalen ran ropes across the decks for the woman and children to cling to.

"We've endured many storms," Atamoda tried to comfort the crying children. "We'll be fine."

Sana knelt next to her, helping Alaya secure Ba-tor and the twins to the line. "Do you hear it, Atamoda?"

"What?"

"In the thunder, do you hear it?" Sana's eyes darted about.

"I don't understand."

A violent wave swept over the deck, almost washing Atamoda away. Hanging onto the line with one arm, she sputtered and tried to clear her stinging eyes. The warm water tasted like sweat.

Where only minutes ago, the Minnow and Crane prepared to fight, they now united in battle against the maelstrom. She heard Aizarg's voice above the rattling canopies, "We're riding too low!"

"The storm wall is gone!" Okta shouted back. "The bow rafts are breaching."

One moment, the overhead canopy protected them. The next second, it simply vanished. In quick order, the gale stripped away every canopy from the arun-ki. The Lo huddled against the decks, as naked against the Deluge as they were the first day.

Sana grabbed Atamoda's arm and pointed up, shouting above the gale. "Look! Do you see it?"

Atamoda wiped the rain from her eyes and peered straight up into the stormy vault. Pillars of glowing clouds towered into the heavens, trading lightning as if they battled one another for the little flotilla at their feet. And then Atamoda saw it, or *thought* she saw it. Each lightning bolt silhouetted black wings stretching across the sky. Two glowing red orbs floated at their center.

Before Atamoda could scream, the Wedding Barge pitched down and buried itself into an oncoming wave.

The raft shot from under the waves. Atamoda fought for breath as she searched the rope for the children. They were all there, the women gripping them tightly.

Except for Ba-tor.

She looked back and, to her relief, saw her terrified little boy clinging to the mast. She released the line, seized him and hugged the mast.

A moment later, Sana joined them.

She felt the raft lurch broadside to the wind, followed by sickening splintering sounds which competed with the thunder. Around them, the flotilla they called home for the past 40 days began to disintegrate.

"The sea anchor is gone, I can feel it." She squeezed Sana's hand. "Here we are again!"

"At least I can swim a little now," Sana smiled nervously.

Whitewater shot over them like raking claws, smashing raft chunks and boats against those clinging to the decks. Something slithered next to the mast, making Atamoda jump in fright. Then, to her horror, she realized it was the Spine, that mighty cable they'd spent so much time weaving. It ran out from beneath its guide loops and fled over the side.

Horrified, Atamoda stared at what remained of her nation, clinging to the life lines and masts. Every snapping rope and breaking log signaled the end of their world.

We're not going to make it.

The sea felt too warm, like shallow lagoon water under a summer sun.

Another wave hammered them, accompanied by loud grinding and crackling. When Atamoda looked up, most of the flotilla had vanished. Only the two barges and one bow raft remained intact and lashed together. The men ran across the decks with salvaged rope, trying to bind what remained together. Aizarg stood in defiance only a few feet away, tightly gripping the staff resting in its hole. Hair matted to his face, he grimaced against the howling wind.

She heard the roar again, mingling with the thunder. Above, a black, whip-like shadow writhed from the sky. Glowing sickly blackish-green, it snaked from the clouds and emitted a pulsing, whirling sound. Sana followed her gaze and screamed, but no one else seemed to notice the sinister apparition bearing down on them. As if possessed with a malignant will, the twisting sky demon kissed the raging sea in an explosion of water and snaked toward them. Atamoda had no chants against this evil.

The wind strengthened with such force, Atamoda thought it would strip them away. Then a beam, bright as the sun, poured from above. Atamoda stared into the heavens filled with lightning and fire. As if they could not see, no one else save Sana and Atamoda paid attention to the brilliant light or the demon zigzagging toward them.

A ruddy light from her left caught Atamoda's eye. Glowing tendrils emitted from Sana's largest dagger. Then, in a peel of thunder, a serpent of golden fire with eyes of blue lightning, bolted from the clouds and plunged toward the whirling demon. Atamoda heard another roar, and then the red orbs vanished. The blackish funnel evaporated before reaching the rafts.

The heavenly apparitions disappeared, but the storm remained.

Another wave assaulted the barges. A log slammed into Atamoda's arm and knocked her from the mast. Sana reached for her, but Atamoda didn't take her hand, fearful the girl would lose her grip on her son.

"Hold on to Ba-tor!"

She clawed frantically at the deck and ropes as the torrent dragged her toward the edge. Hands reached for her, but none could catch Atamoda before she slipped over the side.

At the last moment, her li-ge snagged a ragged log. The thin leather necklace sliced into her neck, but prevented Atamoda from falling into the sea. Each trough plunged her underwater. Each crest yanked her from the sea by her neck. With one hand, she desperately reached for a protruding log. Her other hand clawed underneath the strap, fighting strangulation.

Fingers emerged from the edge and gathered up the leather strap, pulling Atamoda up slightly.

She tried to call out, but the necklace choked her.

Kus-ge's grinning visage leered over the side. Atamoda extended her hand, but Kus-ge didn't take it.

A dagger flashed.

Leather surrendered, and Atamoda plunged into the sea.

47. Chase the Sunset

Smoke and fog clung heavily to the forest at dawn. Outside the stables Elda and Ercole tended to Amiran, who sported minor burns on both hands.

"You were foolish to linger so long," I chastised Amiran.

"I had to get my pipe," he said.

"He stumbled out of the gray tower with an armful of scrolls, trying to drag those heavy boxes," Elda chastised her teacher as she wrapped his blistered fingers in torn linen. "If you had not been there to drag him the rest of the way, Lord Fu Xi, he would have died."

"They are important, child! More important than you can imagine; more important than my life."

"What is in there?" I asked, kneeling next to the iron-bound chest Amiran sat on.

He tapped the box. "This box holds hope for mankind's freedom." Amiran nodded to the other nearly identical chest, perhaps knee high and partially blackened. "And what's in there will hopefully keep me alive long enough to set those events in motion. But we must dwell on this moment if hope is to survive.

"Listen carefully, friend. It wouldn't surprise me if Leviathan is close enough to see the smoke rising from his ruined city. You must flee."

"Flee? No, I will face Leviathan."

"No!" Amiran grabbed my arm. "You are powerful, but you've made an enemy of eleven gods. Each can summon great fleets and armies in the hundreds of thousands.

"The world shall descend on Cin."

The Chronicle of Fu Xi

***

Fu Xi twisted a stalk of grass between his teeth and considered his watery reflection, thinking of the ghastly image that once stared back at him. He rubbed his chin, noticing how his face had taken on an edge, how his eyes had hardened. His strength had returned, but even on a steady diet of deer and antelope, he hadn't fully regained his weight. Fu Xi knew something inside had changed, though his transformation's true nature had yet to reveal itself.

"I'm not quite so terrifying anymore, eh Heise?"

The horse flicked his tail noncommittally. Heise waited in the middle of what had been Fu Xi's camp, bulging bags hanging off both flanks. The lean-to appeared as if ready to host another night's sleep, the fire pit need only be rekindled.

But he could not stay. The thunderheads, ever present guardians of the southern and western horizons since his arrival, vanished a week ago. Clear blue skies stretched in all directions, beckoning Fu Xi to resume his quest for the man with white hair.

The curse is lifted.

He twisted the golden stalk in his hand, running his thumb over the full head of grain. Wild grains, like this wheat, flourished around the enormous lake.

He knelt down and picked up a twig. Fu Xi idly scratched a crude drawing in the dirt. He had spent several weeks exploring this land and discovered the lake rested in the center of an enormous oval basin. Protected from the Deluge on all sides by a ring of mountains, the basin stretched three hundred miles east and over a hundred miles north from his camp on the western border.

He considered the map, wondering if Amiran would be proud.

It looks like an eye.

"The Navel of the World, that's what Mother called this land, Heise. I like the name."

A place of healing.

***

I didn't know if I had saved my people, or condemned them to generations of war. "I must go home."

"Exactly. There is a small ship waiting for you on the western coast, about a day's ride across the coastal range. Sunnah will guide you. Thankfully, this ship wasn't in the harbor last night, and the captain owes an old friend of mine a favor. He will take you across to Cin. You must prepare your people for Leviathan's coming."

"Come with me."

"I cannot."

"He will kill you."

Amiran dismissed my question with a shrug. "Of course, but only when I'm no longer useful."

"Surely Quexil will try to blame my rebellion on you."

"He will, especially to save his own skin. Someone must pay for your little fit."

"I still don't understand."

He chuckled. "When Prince Gadeirus slew his dragon thirty years ago, it was a young expedition scholar with a taste for tobacco who removed the beast's bile sacs." He nodded slightly in a mock bow. "You're looking at the last living Royal Butcher. Leviathan wants a dragon as badly as he wants to conquer Cin, and your tales made him believe dragons might still exist. He can't bring home fire bile without me."

448

A cloud passed over Amiran's face as he considered Elda and Ercole.

"He won't kill me, but there are other ways to exact revenge."

He reached into his soot stained toga and, with some pain, removed his pipe and tobacco. "Elda, be a dear and light my pipe."

Amiran smiled. "Lord Fu Xi, will you care to take a smoke with me one more time before you go?"

"I would be honored."

"I am sorry I have no tea," Amiran passed the pipe.

"I am glad you don't have any coffee," I laughed.

The Chronicle of Fu Xi

***

Fu Xi spent the first few weeks snaring small game. Once he summoned enough strength, he ventured east into the wetlands to hunt bigger game. Now he had enough smoked meat to last months, as well as a deerskin tunic, trousers, and wolf skin shoulder cape. He even fashioned crude repairs to the saddle and bags. He'd repaired most of his gear, but he couldn't replace the Red Sword.

Fu Xi would have gladly lost everything except his horse and the Red Sword. Even the Red Armor felt unnecessary, as Fu Xi trusted his own speed and agility against all possible threats...

...except Leviathan.

He's out there. Maybe Amiran is with him.

Fu Xi stood and considered the map once more.

A map keeps the wandering heart from losing its way home.

Fu Xi strode back to the horse, shrugging to shift a chaffing spot under the armor. Now that he'd lost weight, it sagged slightly.

He looked west, wondering if the Gray Eyed Queen, or any of the Eleven Princes, survived the Cataclysm.

"I would have liked to have met her, Heise. I find the thought of a female immortal intriguing."

Nuwa's warning echoed in his thoughts as he mounted Heise.

"If you survive to see the end of the scourge, depart the Navel of the World to the west. As you pass into unknown lands, keep the Red Sword close and always wear your armor."

"Why?" Fu Xi asked.

"In case your brother finds you first."

He'd often thought about this long lost half-brother.

In case your brother finds your first...

***

In the dew covered grass I sat at my friend's feet, giving the place of honor to a mortal like none I'd met before or since. I tried not to contemplate that we may never meet again, or the torments he would endure under Leviathan.

I will not tell you, Dear Reader, whether we smoked the sweet or bitter weed, only that Amiran and I stitched together our last moments with short words and long silences.

"Do what you must in Nushen," he said between puffs. "If you can, journey west and find The Gray Eyed Queen, Leviathan's twin sister. She leads a rebellion against the Eleven Princes on the far side of the world, in the land called Attica.

"There are many in the Kingdom secretly loyal to her. The resistance grows stronger every day, but should Cin fall into Leviathan's hands, there will be no hope for victory."

He put his hand on my shoulder. "Should Cin and Attica join together, hope lives. She is like you, Fu Xi. She remembers why the gods came to earth."

Baffled, I pictured the world map Amiran showed me in the Library.

"Two oceans and two continents stand between Wu and Ereb, which is east, not west."

Amiran grinned in that infuriating way of his. "I have weighed and measured the entire world, Fu Xi. If you chase the sunset long enough, you will find the dawn. Keep the North Star on your right shoulder until the natives eyes turn blue and round. Keep going until you encounter a warm sea. Follow the shore north, and keep going until you hear the sounds of war. I cannot tell you what you will encounter between Nushen and Attica, but barring an unknown ocean, you will find her."

The brush rustled behind us. Elda and Ercole darted behind me as I rose and turned, sword extended. Sunnah emerged from the trees riding his chestnut mare and leading my horses.

"The Draco and two other ships sail from east. Riders gallop from north. He is coming," Sunnah said.

Amiran stood and tapped out the pipe. "Go."

I embraced my friend. "I left my land a teacher, and return a student."

Amiran's eyes misted over. "They were once like you, Fu Xi. We were once Poseidon's beloved children, the Princes, our patient shepherds. Immortality drove them mad."

He clasped both my hands. "You will see days without number and wonders unceasing. I beg you, do not let eternity poison your heart. Immortality is a curse when it serves its own selfish desires.

"Flesh isn't meant to live forever."

The Chronicle of Fu Xi

***

Heise pranced as if ready to continue their adventure.

"Excited?" A spark kindled in Fu Xi's heart, and a mischievous grin lit his face. He wheeled the horse toward the distant mountains and nudged Heise with his heels. "Well, what are we waiting for? Let us chase the sunset until we find the dawn!"

The steed broke into a full gallop as he let loose a joyous cry. Together, they pursued the wind westward.

48. Tears of the Dead

"Do not dwell on your love's final breath; instead remember those words last spoken in love. In these, you will find courage and shall fear death no more." - Scythian Proverb

The Chronicle of Fu Xi

***

A flat sea reflected a lifeless mist. The very air seemed to absorb the moans and wails rising from the shattered rafts.

"We drift between worlds," Aizarg mumbled into a fog so thick they couldn't see the flotilla's opposite side.

Ghalen supported Aizarg by one arm, Sana held the other as Ba-tor clung to her leg.

Sana spoke to Aizarg softly, "Ghalen and Okta swam around the rafts. They are nowhere to be found."

"Have them take out a boat and search the surrounding water."

"The storm destroyed the boats."

Ba-tor looked up at Sana with an expression as blank as the fog. "Is Mommy gone now, too?"

If Ba-tor had been a Scythian child, she would have told him the truth. Now, she found the truth too heavy to bear.

"I'll take him." Su-gar scooped up Ba-tor and returned to the mast, where the Lo huddled, stripped by the storm of everything except their clothes and lives.

Aizarg peered into the grayness. "The rain stopped. Tell me, Sana, how many marks are etched upon the mast?"

"Forty, my Uros."

"Forty days and forty nights...The silence, it hurts my ears." He patted her hand. "You will have to make the marks from now on, my Isp."

"Aizarg..."

"Say nothing."

She lowered her head.

"Aizarg," Ghalen said. "We grieve with you."

Aizarg wouldn't take his eyes off the fog, as if it would surrender his wife and firstborn any moment. "Does my grief hold any greater value than any of our people who have lost so much?"

"Sana, Ghalen, come here for a moment." Okta motioned them a few paces away from Aizarg.

"How is he?" Okta asked in a hushed voice.

Sana looked back at Aizarg. "I don't know."

"No one saw either of them wash overboard?" Ghalen asked.

"A wave hit, I opened my eyes, and she was gone. I spent the rest of the night holding Ba-tor and the mast, afraid to let go of either. No one else saw her or Kol-ok after that."

Okta put his hands on his hips. "We're lucky we only lost two." Sana followed his gaze across the broken flotilla.

How are we even still afloat?

The Master of Boats rubbed his beard, expression as dark as Sana had ever seen. "The food is gone, our shelters destroyed. The storm took everything. The two barges are beaten up, but they'll float in a calm sea. The bow raft's bindings are rotted, she's coming apart. We'll have to cut her loose." He glanced over his shoulder as Aizarg. "We're going to have to make some tough decisions, with or without the Uros."

"We still have plenty of water," Sana said.

"Maybe not," Ghalen blew out between puffed cheeks.

"You haven't told her yet?" Okta frowned.

Ghalen shook his head. He pointed to the water. "Taste it."

Sana knelt down, cupped some water and took a sip. She grimaced and spat it out. "It tastes like salt!" Horrified, she looked up at Ghalen.

Ghalen shook his head. "We've never seen water like this."

Sana shook her head. "We can't drink it. Watering holes that smell of brine kill, but only after it drives you mad."

Okta looked out over the Lo spread across two barges. "We better tell everyone before people try to take a drink."

Sana spied something slither just below the surface. Ghalen snatched her from the edge as demons drifted from below the rafts. Panic ensued as others spotted the demons.

"I thought we'd seen the last of them," Okta growled.

"Get Levidi," Aizarg commanded from behind them.

In a few minutes the Lo lined the edge of the Supply Barge, staring at demons swimming around their flanks. They merged into a black stream flowing away from the flotilla.

Levidi held out the staff nervously, ready to banish the monsters. "This fog reminds me of the ice mist. I don't like it a bit, not a bit."

"Just banish them, Levidi," Kus-ge said.

"I follow the Uros's command, not yours."

"They don't seem interested in us," Ezra said. "Where are they going?"

"Wherever they are going, so are we," Okta said. "The current draws us that way." He pointed to where the demons swam.

"Something floats up ahead," Ba-lok squinted.

Okta shrugged. "It's a piece of flotsam or debris."

"It's a body." Sana immediately recognized a bloated human abdomen.

"No!" Aizarg pushed his way forward.

"It's not one of them!" Sana grabbed Aizarg's arm, trying to quell his fear. "It's been floating for a long time."

The nude, grossly distended male corpse drifted a few yards to their right. A claw encircled its neck and dragged it down.

Su-gar walked up. "The children are asking for..." She glanced over the water and screamed.

Hundreds of bodies floated ahead, suspended in the glass-like sea.

"Su-gar, go back with the children!" Okta demanded, but she kept screaming. Ezra hid her face. Spako braved the raft's edge and put a protective arm around both Ezra and Su-gar.

"Ezra," Okta said. "Take her back. Spako, tell the women to hide the children's eyes.

The fog lifted slightly, revealing clumps of bodies. Sana couldn't look away from the blackened, bloated faces staring vacantly into the sky. Along with beasts of every sort, they formed grisly floes stretching as far as they could see. Demons circled the ghastly islands, pulling one body after another into the depths.

"What are they doing?" Levidi asked.

"Feeding," Aizarg said grimly.

Ghalen turned to Okta. "We're being drawn into it. Do we have anything to steer with?"

"Nothing." Okta gritted his teeth in frustration. "Not even a damn pole to push away the corpses."

"We can't go in there," Kus-ge's voice teetered on panic's edge.

Virag peered around her. "It looks like we don't have a choice. I think I'm going back to the mast."

"There are thousands," Ezra whispered.

"Tens of thousands," Aizarg said as if in a trance. "The demons feast on the dead. They will leave no trace of the time before the flood."

"Do something!" Kus-ge grabbed Ba-lok's tunic.

"I don't...I can't..." he stuttered impotently.

"This is Heli-dar! Don't you understand, fool? We are dead!" Kus-ge shrieked again and again until Sana struck her squarely on the jaw.

Sana stepped over Kus-ge's unconscious body and glared at Ba-lok. "Drag your woman to the mast before I throw her in."

Ba-lok obeyed.

Soon, an overpowering reek blanketed them.

"Are we truly dead?" Ezra gagged.

"No," Aizarg said.

Sana peered over the edge as the demons danced beneath her reflection. As if falling into a trance, calmness spread through her limbs.

"The water..." she whispered. "The salt...something Atamoda once said." Words slowly congealed in her mind. *"Woe to those who forget the lost, for at the end of all things I will disgorge them upon you, and the waters will be filled with the tears of the dead."*

A high-pitched scream jolted her from the trance, as the demons shrieked and parted before them like autumn leaves in the wind.

Everyone stared at Aizarg's staff, which shone with a brilliant blue light.

Levidi stared at the staff. "Aizarg?"

"I asked nothing from the Nameless God. Its power is summoned by another."

The fog darkened behind the flotilla. Sana blinked, and then frowned, trying to comprehend what she witnessed. She looked up, and then kept looking up, as a dark shape peeled back the mists and loomed over the flotilla.

Trembling, Sana covered her mouth and sank to her knees.

"Sana?" Ghalen knelt beside her.

Speechless, she could only point.

Aizarg took the glowing staff from Levidi, raised it high, and shouted to his people. "Behold, the Black Fortress!"

"A mountain upon the waters. What a mighty vessel!" Okta gasped.

"What a mighty God," Aizarg replied.

The Uros and his people fell to their knees and bowed their heads as the Ark drifted by only a few feet away; a black wall vaulting high above into the mist. It slid by without sound or ripple, propelled by an unseen force. It repelled the dead; they parted before it to create a wide, clear channel. The flotilla drifted into its wake and followed the Ark through the watery passage.

Soon, the flotilla began to lag behind the Ark. The dead floated away to either side, slowly vanishing into the thinning mist.

"It protects us," Sana whispered, and the people rose and watched in wonder as it drifted farther away.

Ghalen wrapped his arms around her shoulders. "The dead are gone. We are not forsaken."

She rested her head against his chest. "We are not forsaken."

At that moment a blinding light erupted from behind the Ark. They turned away and shielded their eyes.

"What is it?" Okta squinted. "Is it some new magic?"

Sana held her hands toward the warmth and laughed. "It is the most wonderful magic of all. The sun!"

The Ark pierced the horizon and vanished into the sunrise of the new age.

Ghalen squinted. "Where are they going?"

Aizarg turned away. "They sail to their destiny. We sail to ours."

The Lo cheered and danced, raising their hands to the sun and a new chance of life.

A grudging smile momentarily graced Virag's face. "Remind me never to curse the sun again."

After a few moments, Sana looked around for Aizarg among the rejoicing people. She found him standing on the flotilla's opposite side, staring at the retreating fog bank and the land of the dead. Sana wrapped her arm around his waist.

"Tell me what you told Su-gar, the day we found the flotilla," he rasped.

She paused for a moment before speaking. "Those words were for a grieving maiden. They hold no magic for your heart."

"Then does my Isp have words of comfort for her Uros? Tell me, I beg you, so I can find the courage to face the sun again."

She opened her mouth to utter an old Scythian proverb, but stopped. Sana looked about at the vast, endless expanse of water and thought of her grandmother, the legendary woman she met only once.

She's the one who truly spared me. What would she say?

"The sea comes first." Sana didn't know why she spoke those words, only that she must.

As the Lo danced and praised the Nameless God, Aizarg's tears fell into the salty sea.

Epilogue

"You were forbidden from aiding him." The Black Dragon stood apart from Nuwa, watching Fu Xi's retreating figure in disgust. "How easily you disobey the Emperor of Heaven, but I'm sure he'll forgive you...*again*. You were always one of his favorites."

Perched on a rocky pinnacle overlooking the fertile grasslands, Nuwa gazed upon Fu Xi and Heise, soaking in the joy radiating from her child.

"I didn't help him." She crossed her arms and smiled wryly. "I helped his horse."

He threw his head back and laughed. "And I thought I hadn't taught you anything about deception!" He raised an accusing eyebrow. "And the apple that saved his life?"

She turned to him, eyes narrowing with blue fire. "*That* gift came from another."

She'd never known him to display fear, even if he could experience fear. But her enemy suddenly appeared uncomfortable, looking about suspiciously.

"Is something wrong?" she mocked.

"There are many ways to win a war. Hold no hope Fu Xi will reach them. The Lo will perish."

"I stopped you from killing them once. I can stop you again."

"You didn't stop me on the mountainside."

"Fu Xi still lives, doesn't he?"

"As you said, *that* wasn't your doing," he said dryly.

He transformed into mist and blew away, chased by the morning sunshine.

The goddess returned her attention to Fu Xi as the Red Sword materialized in her hand. Caressing the muddy orichalcum blade, she thought of her first born.

Totaresh will try to slay him the instant they meet. Fu Xi is powerless without this sword by his side, but I am forbidden from returning it to him.

She examined the blade forged to slay gods, smiling the way women often do when they possess a secret.

And Nuwa had many secrets.

But I am not forbidden from giving it to another.

"Your trials have just begun, my beloved sons."

***

"Mother."

She groaned as sleep lifted its veil.

"Mother, wake up."

Someone gently shook her.

"Mother!"

Disoriented, Atamoda shot upright.

Kus-ge!

She found a world shrouded in fog and Kol-ok staring at her.

She fell forward in the boat, hugging and peppering kisses on her son. "I thought I'd lost you!"

"I thought I lost everyone. The storm washed me overboard. Not long after I found my boat, I saw you treading water."

"I don't remember anything after..." Atamoda cupped her hand over her mouth, remembering Kus-ge cutting her loose.

She tried to kill me. Again. The betrayal felt like bile in her throat.

"You've been asleep for a long time. A day has come and gone. It's dawn again."

"Something is different..."

"It stopped raining."

She closed her eyes and leaned her head back, "Oh, thank the Nameless God!"

"The water is foul."

Atamoda reached into the water to palm a sip, but quickly spit it out.

Salt.

"I tried to drink some after the storm, but it made me vomit.

"Don't worry. We will find good water."

"We are alone."

"We will find our people," she nodded vigorously, trying to convince herself. "Or your father will find us."

Kol-ok lifted the blanket between them. "We have food, even if there isn't any water." He handed her a fish cake, and then craned his head left and squinted. "Do you hear that?"

Atamoda lifted an ear. "No."

He turned around and peered into the fog.

Then Atamoda heard the distinct lapping of waves against a shore. "I hear it."

"I smell fish, too. Land!" Kol-ok snatched the paddle and began to row.

"Can it really be?" Atamoda started to cry as the boat plowed through sheets of dead fish. She scooped up a dead trout and sniffed it.

"It's fresh, dead only a day or so."

"We'll eat well tonight. Oh, think of it, fresh fish for supper!"

She sniffed it again. "Perhaps the salty water killed it."

Jagged boulders stood like ghostly giants along the shore as they beached on a steep, rocky bank.

Kol-ok tested the ground with one foot before fully committing to the earth.

"It's real!" He held out his hand to Atamoda.

She wobbled from the boat, her balance not yet trusting solid ground. Atamoda sank to the earth, grabbing fistfuls of pebbles and breathing in the muddy scent. Touching her forehead to the ground, she uttered a silent prayer to the Nameless God.

Atamoda pulled Kol-ok down beside her and hugged him hard, realizing how close she'd come to losing him.

Kol-ok looked out over the foggy water. "Father cannot be far away. The current which brought us here will do the same for them. We'll make camp here. If you will gather up fish, I'll look around for some wood and good water. If we can light a fire, maybe they will see it."

Kol-ok stood and turned around.

"Mother." He nudged her.

A few feet away, an old man, tall and bony, gawked at them. He carried a strange metal pot in both hands, his long gray beard fell over a heavy wool vest. Combined with a conical wool cap and furry leggings, he looked half sheep.

Atamoda staggered up. "Hello," was all she could think to say.

Her voice seemed to shake him out of his trance. He dropped the pot with a *thunk,* and fish spilled onto the bank. Atamoda realized the pot was actually a metal helmet.

Her stomach tightened. *Sammujad warriors sometimes wear metal helmets.* But this man didn't dress, or look, like a Sammujad.

He knelt down and stuffed the fish back into the helmet, apprehensively looking over his shoulder. That's when Atamoda noticed horrible scarring, as if the right side of his face had once been scorched.

He stood and tucked the helmet under his arm, astonishment transforming to hostility.

"Pahak chay yel!" He pointed to their boat. "Pahak chay yel!"

Kol-ok slid between Atamoda and the old man. "We're not welcome here."

She stepped backwards.

He shooed them toward the boat. "P'akhch'yel ! Veradarrnal depi tsov. Miayn mahy spasum e dzez aystegh!"

He's afraid.

"Zeljko!" A whip-like voice barked from her right.

The old man dropped to one knee and bowed his head.

Before Atamoda could turn to look, she heard a loud crack. Kol-ok spun about, blood shooting from his mouth, and fell motionless to the ground. Atamoda didn't remember the blow, only an explosion across her cheek, and then darkness.

She awoke to excruciating pain in her scalp and across her back. Coming to her senses, she kicked and screamed, but couldn't see who dragged her by the hair. A moment later, he released her. Before she could get up, a sandaled foot pinned her neck.

Strange male voices laughed jovially with guttural, alien words, drawing pleasure from her torment.

Terrified, she struggled vainly to push away the foot, but they only laughed louder.

A gaunt face with high cheekbones and grotesquely pointed teeth leered down at her. Black hair cut like a bowl dropped over a face red as an autumn sunset. Strange, rust-streaked metal mesh covered his chest.

Then a black-skinned giant clad in gleaming crimson metal filled her vision. He towered above the red man, and considered her dispassionately, like a fisherman wondering if a minnow was worth keeping.

Demons!

Atamoda squirmed, wanting to scream, struggling to breathe.

"Rantaian," the giant said and turned from her sight.

A look of disappointment briefly passed over the red man's face. Rusty iron chains appeared in his hand. He gleefully rattled them over Atamoda's face before once again snatching her by the hair. She shrieked in agony as he dragged her toward the echoes of screams, and the reek of burning flesh.

To Be Continued in the Chronicles of Fu Xi, Book III, *Totaresh*

ABOUT THE AUTHOR

Brian L. Braden is the author of the *Black Sea Gods* and the novelette *Carson's Love*. He is a founder and assistant editor at Underground Book Reviews.

Please support indie literature. If you enjoyed this novel, please rate and review this book on Amazon, Goodreads, or Shelfari.

Glossary of Terms and Characters

ai-halah: (eye-HAL-ah) "The reed and the wood", traditional Lo music. Ai is female vocals, halah is male vocals.

Adyghe (ad-YAH-gay) Mountains: Eastern edge of the known world, home of the Hur-po and the Narim

a-g`an: (AYE-ghahn) Lo word meaning 'of the steppe' or 'enemy'.

Aizarg: (AYE-zarg) Lo phrase meaning *I give him the east*, or *He leads the east*. Sco-lo-ti of the Crane Clan and Uros of the Lo Nation, husband of Atamoda, father to Bat-tor and Kol-ok.

E'laa: (Aye-LAH) Orphaned Minnow child, twin sister to Toma

Alaya: (ah-LAH-ya) Wife to Levidi.

Amiran: (ah-MEER-ahn) Scholar in the service of Lord Leviathan or Wu.

arun-ki: (ah-ROON-ki) Lo word meaning "village upon the womb," a stilted village built off-shore in shallow lagoons.

Aryans: (air-EE-ans) One of the three nomadic tribes of the g'an.

Ashtoreth (ASH-tore-ehth) Called "The Snake of Hur Ar", a ruthless member of Hur-ar's nobility bent on placing her son, Baal-eeb, on the throne at any price.

Atamoda: (At-uh-MOWH-dah) Patesi-li of the Crane Clan, wife of Aizarg, mother to Ba-tor and Kol-ok.

Atta: (AT-uh) Levidi's grandfather, oldest man in the Crane Clan.

Ba'al: (BAH-awl) A sinister deity called The Black Dragon, worshipped by cult in Hur-ar.

Bal-eeb: (BAHL-eeb) Second Prince of Hur-ar, Captain of the City Gate. Son of Ashtoreth.

Ba-lok: (BAY-lok) Sco-lo-ti of the Minnow Clan, Second to Aizarg, husband to Kus-ge, son of Aie-lok, grandson of Setenay.

Bat-or: (BAHT-or) Toddler and youngest son of Aizarg and Atamoda, brother to Kol-ok.

Bla-la-te: (blah-LAH-tay) Xva's uncle and sco-lo-ti of the Gar Clan.

Carp Clan: Lo village of which Okta rules as the sco-lo-ti, the chieftain.

Crane Clan: Lo village of which Aizarg rules as the sco-lo-ti, the chieftain.

Council of Boats: A gathering of the more than one Lo village or perhaps the entire Lo nation, usually a festive event.

Doinna: (DOH-ee-nah) Young Minnow Clan woman

Ezra: (ezz-RAH) Sarah's brother. Thief and gang leader of pack of feral children in the slums of Hur-ar.

Fu Xi: (foo-HI or foo-ZI) Immortal demi-god, son of Goddess Nuwa, often called the God of Names, or the Wanderer.

Gar Clan: Also known as the Lost Arun-ki. Kus-ge, wife of Ba-lok, hailed from arun-ki, once the farthest east of all Lo villages. Shortly after Kus-ge departed as Ba-lok's new bride, the villagers vanished without a trace, the arun-ki burned to the water line.

g`an: (gh-AHN) Lo word for the open steppe bordering the marshes north of the Great Sea.

Ghalen: (GAY-lehn) Lo phrase for *iron spirit*. Younger brother of Masok, sco-lo-ti of the Turtle Clan.

Great Sea: Immense body of fresh water and home to the Lo people. Its northern shore is lined with vast expanses of reed beds, marshes and narrow coastal forests which give way to open steppe.

heli-dar: (hell-EYE-dar) Lo word for the afterlife. The Lo believe it is far out to sea beyond the reach of any boat.

Heise: (HAY-suh) Fu Xi's black stallion, his name simply means "black".

Huise: (Hhway-suh) Fu Xi's gray mare, her name simply means "gray".

Hur-ar: (her-AR) "City of the Yellow Metal," located at the base of the Adyghe Mountains in a deep canyon overlooking the Hur River; also called *Ghund-Ghund*, The Place of Mazes, by the Scythians.

Hur-Po: (her-POE) "People of the Yellow Metal, those who inhabit Hur-Ar.

Hur River: River running north to south separating the Adyghe Mountains from the open g'an; spanned by the Kupar Bridge.

Ice Men: Savage race living in the far north lands.

Isp: Patesi-le selected to serve the Uros.

Kol-ok: (kall-AWK) Aizarg's and Atamoda's oldest boy, brother to Bat-or.

köy-lo-hely: (coy-ee-LOW-hell-eye) Lo word meaning "the sacred place where the people gather"; a large wooden platform without a hut at the heart of the Lo community, usually a in the middle of a lagoon encircled by huts.

Kus-ge: (kuss-GEE) Ba-lok's wife, hails from the mysterious Lost Arun-ki, the farthest Lo settlement to the east that vanished years earlier.

Ood-i: (OO-die) Member of the Crane Clan, husband of Ula, father to Su-gár.

Levidi: (lev-EE-dee) Aizarg's best friend, husband of Alaya.

li-ge: (lie-GHEE) Lo symbol meaning "balance" or "joining of flesh and spirit."

Lo: (LOW) "The people" or "the family." Nation of fishing tribes divided into different clans. They live along the Great Sea's northern shore in stilted villages over the water.

Masok: (MAY-sock) Sco-lo-ti of the Turtle Clan and Ghalen's older brother.

Narim: (nah-RHEEM) Race of demi-gods who live in the Black Fortress in the mountains above Hur-ar.

Nushen: (NEW-shen) Village of Goddess, an ancient village that has served the goddess Nuwa for ages.

Nuwa:(NEW-ah) She is also called the Queen of the West and the Celestial Queen. A goddess who sired Fu Xi with a human man. She dwells in seclusion in her temple on Tortoise Mountain above the village of Nushen.

Minnow Clan: Lo village ruled by Ba-lok as sco-lo-ti.

Oeto-sy: (oy-TOW-see) the sky god or "father above" of the Lo pantheon. Husband of Psatina, father of Sethagasi.

Okta: (AWK-tah) Leader of the Carp Arun-ki. An older sco-lo-ti, but not yet an elder. Tall, lean and light complexioned like Aizarg, but older, nearing the age of an elder.

patesi-le: (pah-TEH-see-lee) A lo shaman, always a woman and the wife of the sco-lo-ti.

Psatina: (sat-EEN-a) The Earth Mother, prime goddess of the Lo pantheon.

Quexil: (Kek-zil) Captain of the Obsidian Guard, warrior and Lord Leviathan's closest servant.

Ro-xandra: (Row-ZAN-drah) Old Minnow Clan woman.

sco-lo-ti: (skoh-LOW-tee) "leader of the people", village chieftain

sagar: (SAY-garr) Sammujad spears, heavier and longer, made to defend against Scythian horse warriors.

Sahti: (sah-TEE) Wife of Xva.

Sammujad: (sam-MOO-jahd) one of the three nomadic tribes inhabiting the g'an. They occupy the fringes of the steppe and rely mostly on trading to survive. They have been pushed back in recent years by the Scythians.

Sana: (SAH-nah) Scythian princess, sister of Prince Tuma, daughter of King Sawseruquo, granddaughter of King Sosa and his captive bride, Setenay.

Sarah: Former pleasure slave in bondage in Virag's camp. She is originally of the Hur-ar and vows to lead Aizarg's party to the Narim.

Scythians: (sith-EE-ans) Horse warriors who've come to dominate the g'an over the course of several generations, they are the most savage and feared of the three steppe tribes.

Setenay: (set-EN-aye) Patesi-li of the Minnow Clan, grandmother to Ba-lok, oldest living member of the Lo people. Called "The Grandmother of the Lo."

Sethagasi: (seth-ah-GOS-ee) The sea goddess of the Lo pantheon, daughter of Psatina and Oeto-sy. Synonymous with Great Sea. Also means "womb."

Spako: (SPAY-koh) Sammujad mercenary in the employ of Virag. Enormous and imposing, but dimwitted and, if left to his own devices, gentle.

Summoning of Spears: Ceremony where the Lo choose an Uros to lead them in time of war.

Silt Flats: Place near Crane Clan village with the shallows meet the deep sea and large waves form and the village boys wave ride atop their small reed boats.

Sunalei Ostu: (Sue-NAH-lay OH-stooh) Called "Sunnah," he is Lord Leviathan's master of horses.

Su-gar: (sue-GARR) daughter of Ood-i and Ula.

Tiejiang: (Teh-ZHANG) Blacksmith of Nushen, raised by Fu Xi.

Time of the Spear: Lo term for a time of war when an Uros leads all the Lo nation, superseding the power of individual sco-lo-ti.

Toma: (Tow-MAH) Orphaned Minnow child, twin brother to E'laa

Tortoise Mountain: Home of the Goddess Nuwa.

Turtle Clan: Lo village ruled by Masok as sco-lo-ti, also home to his younger brother, Ghalen.

Ula: (OOW-lah) Wife of Leedi, mother of Su-gár.

Uros: (UR-ouws) War Chieftain of the Lo.

Valley of the Beasts: A valley discovered by Aizarg and Levidi filled with a milling multitude of animals of every sort.

Virag: (veye-RAG) Sammujad Slaver, former owner of Sarah.

Wu:(WOO) A mysterious land far to the east of Cin. Fu Xi thought of this land as the end of the earth.

Xva: (ZEE-vah) Aizarg's cousin and youngest man in the Crane Clan Nation. Husband of Sahti.